Praise for *A Place of Her Own*

"Janet Fisher is such a good writer and brings Martha, her family, and her times so vividly to life!"
—Riane Eisler,
New York Times best-selling author of *The Chalice and the Blade*

"Janet Fisher has a compelling story to tell about her land and its history . . . a riveting tale . . . going back to her great-great-grandmother Martha Ann Poindexter Maupin. . . . The two women share an almost mythical bond forged not only by the land, but also by Martha's remarkable life . . ."
—Kathy Westra, *Woodland* magazine

"The two women had more in common than Fisher realized until she embarked on a quest to learn who her ancestor really was. The search introduced her to a rich family history she never knew existed . . ."
—Randi Bjornstad, *The Register-Guard*, Eugene, Oregon

"It is a story of strength and courage, as Martha overcomes the many hardships inherent to the times in which she lived and the roads she chose. . . . A very readable tale . . ."
—Amanda Bird, The Book Nest, Springfield, Oregon

"When Janet Fisher writes a scene, you are there. Whether she takes you across a raging river or through the majestic fir trees on Martha's land, you live the moment."
—P.E.O. Chapter CU, Oregon Book Club

The Shifting Winds

A Novel

JANET FISHER

TWODOT®

GUILFORD, CONNECTICUT
HELENA, MONTANA

A · TWODOT® · BOOK

An imprint and registered trademark of Rowman & Littlefield

Distributed by NATIONAL BOOK NETWORK

Copyright © 2016 by Janet Fisher

All rights reserved. No part of this book may be reproduced in any form or by any electronic or mechanical means, including information storage and retrieval systems, without written permission from the publisher, except by a reviewer who may quote passages in a review.

British Library Cataloguing-in-Publication Information Available

Library of Congress Cataloging-in-Publication Data

Fisher, Janet, (Novelist)
  The shifting winds : a novel / Janet Fisher.
    pages ; cm
  ISBN 978-1-4930-1884-0 (softcover) — ISBN 978-1-4930-1885-7 (ebook) 1. Women pioneers—Oregon—Fiction. 2. Frontier and pioneer life—Oregon—Fiction. I. Title.
  PS3606.I7753S55 2016
  813'.6—dc23
                        2015027752

∞™ The paper used in this publication meets the minimum requirements of American National Standard for Information Sciences—Permanence of Paper for Printed Library Materials, ANSI/NISO Z39.48-1992.

To

Judy Emmett

Legendary mountain man Joe Meek played a critical role in the 1843 meeting at Champoeg when he called for a divide of a close vote to decide if Americans in the Oregon wilderness would have the protection of law. This large mural in the Oregon State Capitol building portrays Meek's historic moment when that vote appeared ready to fail and he strode forth with his immortal words, "Who's fer a divide?" Supporters followed his lead, hoping to turn the winds toward Oregon's future as a part of the United States.
PHOTO COURTESY OF OREGON STATE ARCHIVES

Acknowledgments

These pages of thanks carry me back to the most wonderful memories of generous people sharing their time and talents with me to make this book a reality.

First, I must mention the late George Abdill, longtime director of my local Douglas County Museum of History and Natural History. When I decided to write some novels about Oregon's early pioneers, I contacted George with many questions. George was one of those people you could ask a question, and he would give you a chapter. He truly loved the era portrayed in this story and happily shared his depth of knowledge with me, even kindly reading segments to be sure I had it right. I wish he were here to thank.

And I want to thank George's wife, Joyce Abdill, a former sales rep in the book industry, for her encouragement along the way.

A special thanks to Judy Emmett, who read this book at its earliest stages and read it again in its revised form, offering editing suggestions and patiently listening as I struggled with the nuances of wording. Thanks also to my new reader, Carol Beckley, who added her own expertise, not only with the writing but also with area history. Carol serves with me on the writing team for our local Elkton history pageant, and she helped implement reconstruction of Fort Umpqua, the southernmost fort of the Hudson's Bay Company in the Oregon Territory, located near what is now Elkton, Oregon.

Other readers who influenced this book include my daughter Carisa Cegavske and friend Patricia Kellam. Thanks to Judy Ammerman, a former Oregon City resident, who traipsed with me over the back roads around Oregon City to see the lay of the land, then later commented on the story. Thanks also to Heidi M. Thomas for reading and assessing the first few pages, and to Stéphane Morel, my friend in France who helps me with my French.

I wish I could thank my late cousins, Larry and Lorena Fisher, who hosted me in Portland during the early research phase. Larry even helped facilitate a canoe trip down the Willamette River so I could absorb the

Acknowledgments

haunting beauty of this historic waterway. I'd also like to thank Chris Peterson for an exciting boat ride on the busy Columbia River.

And thanks to David Hansen, former curator of the Fort Vancouver National Historic Site, and the staff at this reconstructed Hudson's Bay Company fort in Vancouver, Washington. They gave me the grand tour of the fort, and offered me copies of the historic structure reports that had provided data for the reconstruction. The tremendous details in these reports were invaluable to me in showing scenes and details of life at Fort Vancouver.

Thanks also to Stella Shannon, Karin Morey, Roxandra Pennington, and other staff and volunteers of the Clackamas County Historical Society in Oregon City, particularly for their hard work ferreting out information on the early Oregon Lyceum meetings. And thanks to the wonderful staffs at the Oregon Historical Society Research Library in Portland, the Douglas County Library in Roseburg, the Multnomah County Central Library in Portland, and to the friendly people at the Green River Rendezvous in Sublette County, Wyoming, who depicted the historic gatherings of fur trading days.

A special thanks to my wonderful agent, Rita Rosenkranz of New York, for making one more book a reality and for being so great to work with, and thank you to my fine editor at Globe Pequot, Erin Turner, who acquired my first book and who was happy to acquire this second one as well. She has made the whole publishing experience a pleasure. Thanks to production editor Meredith Dias too for all her fine work in ushering the story through the detailed process of becoming a book.

And of course thanks to my wonderful family for their continuing encouragement. Carisa I already mentioned. Thanks also to my daughter Christiane Cegavske, my grandchildren, Alex and Calliope, my son-in-law Robin Loznak with his fine photography, and all the extended family of cousins and shirttail kin who have celebrated these books with me—from relatives I've known for years to all those Maupins and Poindexters I found after publication of my first book about my great-great-grandmother, Martha Poindexter Maupin.

Many others helped on this project, whose names I don't have. But I well remember the kindness of people so ready and willing to assist me in any way they could. Whether named or not, please know how much I appreciate you all.

Lithographer J. H. Richardson traveled west to Oregon City in the 1840s during the city's earliest days, one of several artists who were sent out to record images of the West during the joint occupancy of the United States and Great Britain. This lithograph was published in *Holden's Dollar Magazine*, Volume III, Number 11, February, 1849, in New York.
CLACKAMAS COUNTY HISTORICAL SOCIETY PHOTO, ALL RIGHTS RESERVED

Chapter One

Oregon Territory, October 5, 1842. The forest looked like a place only giants should enter. Jennie grasped the soft little arms locked about her waist, seeking comfort in her smallest brother's familiar presence, while the gentle mare carried them along the dark trail. Jennie peered up into the monstrous firs for a glimmer of light, but only scattered pinpricks penetrated the thick boughs.

So different from the woods back home. This forest enclosed her, the pungent scent of evergreens filling her nose until she could scarcely breathe. She nudged the mare Rosy to go faster. Two more little brothers rode ahead on Pa's horse Ranger, with Ma leading them. And Eddie, eldest of the brothers, marched in front of Ma, probably thinking he was leading the family, but Ma just wanted him where she could keep an eye on him.

Two Indian guides on horseback led the way. One had a face like aged leather that had sat out too long in a spring rain before shrinking into cracked ridges under a summer sun. He hunched into the heavy blanket wrapped around his shoulders as if suffering a chill. The second man looked no older than Jennie with his baby-smooth skin. A buckskin shirt, fringed and beaded, covered his torso but left his legs bare to the world. Like most Indians she'd seen, neither wore beards. Whether they shaved or lacked face hair, she didn't know.

At a turn in the trail they all disappeared, swallowed in the tangle of greenery.

Jennie gripped the reins tighter and swerved in the sidesaddle to look back, expecting to see Pa following with the oxen. But she couldn't see Pa either. Her heart raced. She felt alone with little Robbie. Adrift in this strange land.

As she watched the trail behind, anxious to see her father reappear, a tree bough slapped the back of her head. She swung forward again, and the prickly needles scraped her face. A burst of anger flared, but she swallowed it for Robbie's sake.

He tapped her shoulder. "Most there, Jennie?"

She managed to keep her voice light, only a subtle huskiness betraying her distress. "It shouldn't be too long, Robbie."

He bounced behind her, as if that could somehow hurry them up.

Ahead, Ma and the boys appeared again. The faint semblance of a trail had straightened once more. She could only see a depression in the layers of woody debris. What if they were lost? Did those guides really know where they were? Was Pa right to trust them? The older one seldom spoke, but the young one seemed to defer to him.

Glancing back, she saw Pa and took a fuller breath. His expression softened with a quick lift of his lips on one side. She tried to smile in return before looking away. But she didn't know if she could ever forgive him for this. They had spanned a continent, the last two thousand miles without a sign of civilization except for a few crude forts and a couple of mission stations. They had crossed grassy plains, barren deserts, and rugged mountains to reach this Promised Land of Oregon. And what promise did she see now? Why had he brought them to this wild place?

She had never wanted to come. She'd hoped to stay at the academy, the Utica Female Academy, where she had begun her studies. She longed to do something interesting. Women had so few opportunities. Talk was buzzing among students at the academy about women demanding more rights after Mrs. Stanton and Mrs. Mott were barred from being seated at an antislavery convention in London—just because they were women. Jennie wanted to know what might come of those demands. Why couldn't she have stayed in New York to find out? What would she ever do all the way out here in Oregon?

She bit her lips together. Maybe the town would be nice. Willamette Falls. Pa had said they would find a community there. Friends. Others who shared his vision of making this Oregon Territory a part of the United States.

She came alongside the trunk of a fir so massive, the trail had to curve around it. Pa said some of these firs grew as much as three hundred feet high, and that two or three men could lie head-to-foot across the diameter of a cut stump. She'd never imagined trees so monstrous. From the few meadows in these woods she'd been able to see the pointy tops of this remarkable species, and the layered ranks of their drapey boughs. The proper trees back home would be dropping their leaves soon to let a little light in, as these never would. How could she bear a winter in this place? She needed light.

But once Pa set his mind on something, the family knew he wouldn't veer from his purpose. As the man of the house, he had that choice. Besides, he thought the American settlers in Oregon would need his talents as an attorney.

Shivering, Jennie drew her cloak tighter about her shoulders. With the canopy of firs blocking the feeble October sun, the air felt cold and damp. She patted the pudgy arms of her small charge. "Are you warm enough, Robbie?"

"Yeah."

Only three, Robbie was the youngest of the Haviland children. Jennie was the oldest, a young woman already at seventeen. Eddie came next. He strode ahead now, studying everything with open enthusiasm. At thirteen Eddie loved anything that smacked of adventure. And what Eddie liked, Charlie, just three years younger, liked too. Five-year-old Davie didn't say much. He just remained his agreeable little self, as if it was perfectly normal for a family to leave their pleasant home and wander into the wilderness.

"Jennie." Robbie's small voice quivered a little. "Wanna go home, Jennie."

She tried to sound cheerful. "We'll be there soon."

Home? Utica, New York, was home. But Willamette Falls would have to be now. Somehow she had to believe she'd find something there to make it feel like home. Just being back in the company of other people would help. Those they'd traveled west with had scattered into small parties after breaking down their covered wagons at Fort Hall. At the Columbia River, a few had taken a Hudson's Bay Company boat with Dr. White, who'd organized this group of more than a hundred westbound settlers, but most had come over the treacherous Cascade Mountains in small family parties like the Havilands.

The trail turned again, heading downward this time, and following the others, Rosy stepped along the narrow path where it dropped sharply along a steep sidehill. A few gaps between the trees let Jennie see out a little now. The terrain formed what looked like a giant stairstep, the trail coming out on flat land again to wind its way around great boulders and past deep gullies and creeks in its meandering course through the thick woods.

Movement ahead caught Jennie's attention. One of the guides, the younger one, rode back toward her. His black eyes homed in on her as he rode closer, and she pressed her elbows tight against her body. Narrow as the trail was, he had to squeeze by, and Jennie moved Rosy as far to one side as possible. The man's face revealed no hint of expression. Jennie stared back, as if that might block his invasive scrutiny.

Like the older guide, and like many of the Indians in the Columbia River country, he had a strangely disfigured head, flattened from the nose to a point atop the back of the head, so the head was no longer rounded but from profile appeared almost triangular—a result of their practice of placing the heads of their infants between boards.

As the young man passed by, he almost touched her skirts with his bare leg, and her attention focused on the nakedness of those legs. He wore nothing below the fringed buckskin shirt for decency except a skimpy breechclout. The old man at least wore leggings.

Managing to escape the touch of the young guide, Jennie watched him as he rode back to talk with her father. After a brief interchange, Pa called the oxen to speed up and left the guide behind. Pa gave Jennie a quick smile as he passed by, their two faithful oxen lumbering after him in single file. When he reached Ma's side, he spoke loud enough for Jennie's benefit. "Our guide tells me we'll be able to see the falls right through a line of trees over there." He pointed ahead. "Thought you'd like to know."

Ma beamed. "Oh yes!"

"Most there," Robbie said, a lilt of excitement in his young voice. "Most there, Jennie."

"Yes, honey, we're almost there."

They all hurried forward, and when Jennie pulled Rosy alongside the others, she saw why the trees formed a line. They stood on top of a sheer rock bluff above a grand river. Like a broad, deep-green silken ribbon, the watercourse made its way between thick, tree-covered slopes. Upriver the smoothness of silk abruptly gave way to a half circle of white froth. The falls. Then it turned to silk again, winding off to the right to join another ribbon in the distance.

Pa's words resonated with awe. "The Willamette Falls."

Jennie could only stare at the calm silken water with the majesty of the falls breaking it in two, the low ridge on the opposite shore showing a hint of gold amid the dark evergreens, promising autumn while not quite yielding summer.

She supposed the town must be nearby, since it was obviously named for the falls. A couple of shacks and the makings of a larger building perched on an island in the river to this side of the falls. On a flat strip of land between the bluff and the river, like another of those giant stairsteps, Jennie could see a couple of log cabins with a few outbuildings, no doubt the homes of isolated settlers. And on the opposite shore among the trees, she could just make out something that looked like high-pitched roofs on long wooden buildings. She could see people over there and others— right in the falls. "Pa, what are they doing in the falls?"

"Fishing. It's a prime fishing spot for the Indians. See the salmon jumping? I understand they sometimes have so many fish here a man can almost walk across the water on them. Can you imagine?"

Squinting, Jennie saw a huge fish leap in a herculean effort to reach the top of the falls. And another. Fishermen stood on scaffolds, using spears and dip nets to catch the struggling salmon. Fascinated, she watched for a while, then pointed toward the structures across the river. "What are those?"

Pa spoke with the young guide beside him, their voices low. Then Pa turned to Jennie. "It's an Indian village."

She frowned. "But where is the town? Where's Willamette Falls?" She wanted to find the town of proper houses.

The young guide mumbled to Pa again, and Pa nodded. "So that's it," Pa said. "That's our settlement."

Jennie scanned the tree-cloaked hills. "Where?"

"Those cabins are it." He pointed toward the flat bench of land. "And that's a mill they're building over on the island."

Jennie darted a quick look at the cabins on the flat, then jerked her head back to stare at Pa. "What do you mean?"

"That's Willamette Falls. The larger cabin with the square logs must be the Waller place. They're with the Methodist Mission and have a store there, I understand."

Jennie shook her head. Pa must have misunderstood the guide, given his accent and limited English. "It—it must be farther upstream or down or—" Jennie looked toward Ma, whose round face tightened into soft wrinkles. Jennie tried again. "Pa, the town must be beyond our sight now. It—"

Pa gave her a gentle smile. "It's not much, is it, sweetheart? But you wait. It'll grow fast. You'll see."

"Let's go." Robbie squirmed behind Jennie. "Most there, Jennie. Let's go."

Jennie squeezed the boy's tiny hands at her waist, and tears made the view swim before her. Rosy moved again, following the others along the top of the rocky bluff, which sloped downward as they rode in the direction of the falls that appeared now and then into their view. The trail emerged from the tree line and descended right down the cliff face on a ledge cut into the bluff's rock wall, dropping onto the flat below.

Through a blur of tears Jennie saw people. She wanted to cry out. They were Indians like their guides, all with those strange sloped heads, some wrapped in blankets like the old man, some in buckskin like the young one, others in cloth shirts and coats—some scarcely dressed at all. Like a welcoming committee, they surrounded the approaching riders, chattering to the guides, to each other, and to the Havilands, for all the good that did. None of the Havilands could understand a word of their language.

Pa shook the hands of several Indian men, talking to them through the help of the young guide. Then, looking unduly cheerful, Pa moved to Ma's side to help Charlie and Davie off their horse.

Jennie sat securely on Rosy's back, pressing herself hard upon the saddle as if she might truly become a part of it. She didn't want to get off. She wanted to stay on and turn around and ride back, all the way to Utica. Indians clustered about her now, and when Pa came to help her and Robbie down, she clung tightly to the mare. "I . . . I think I'll—"

Once he'd put Robbie on the ground, he reached for her. "Come on, honey. Better get off. We'll go over to the Wallers' house. It'll be good to be in the company of others after such a long time. Come now."

She eyed the Indians encircling her, making her feel more absolutely a stranger in a strange land.

"Most of the men are over working on the mill—on the island," Pa said, "but Mrs. Waller should be at the cabin. Come on, honey."

Still Jennie clung to the mare.

Pa's brow tightened. "Jennie, please get down and help Ma with the boys. I want to go talk to the men at the mill." His hands were on her waist, and there was no use resisting anymore. Pa didn't just support her to help her off. He took her off and set her firmly on the ground, but his voice softened. "Jennie, it'll be all right." Love shone in the face that puckered into ridges when he smiled, and Jennie wanted to return the love at the same time that she wanted to despise him for doing this to her. "Don't hate me too much," he said. "I do love you. Surely you know that."

Her eyes teared again, and she felt a lump in her throat that wouldn't let her speak. Nodding, she looked away from him. Ma stood beside Ranger, watching them, holding onto the two small boys, one in each hand. Eddie and Charlie casually wandered about, peering here and there.

Ma beckoned with a tilt of her head. "Come along, Jennie."

When Pa dropped his hands from Jennie's waist, she began to move in Ma's direction. The cluster of Indians moved with her, following close behind, and she couldn't help looking back at them. Nor could she help noticing an odd smell. She sniffed deeper, trying to identify the scent.

Fish. Of course. They were fishermen, and the rank smell of stale fish clutched her nose.

Still moving away from the Indians, but with her head turned to watch them, Jennie stopped short when she smacked into something. Someone. She looked ahead and saw buckskin. She had run into one of the Indians. Shuddering, she drew her arms forward to push herself away, and felt herself caught. She couldn't push away because he was holding her by the shoulders.

"Please," she said, "let me—"

She looked up into the man's face. Not an Indian. Her mouth dropped open. He was dressed for all the world like an Indian. His dark-brown hair came halfway to his shoulders, the brown eyes almost black, but clearly he was no Indian.

"Beggin' your pardon, ma'am," he said, his voice deep, mellow, the dark eyes glittering with a smile.

She managed to push back to arm's length and quickly surveyed him from the smiling face down over the buckskin-covered length of him to the moccasins on his feet. He wore a buckskin shirt, much like their young Indian guide's—fringed, embroidered, belted at the waist—but unlike the guide he wore long, trim-fitting buckskin breeches with fringes running down the outer seams. He was armed—a knife in a sheath on his belt, a pistol stuck into the belt, and powder horn and bullet pouch slung over his shoulder. With determination, she pushed back harder and he released his grip on her.

He spoke with a drawl, still smiling. "Ma'am, may I have the utmost pleasure and privilege of welcoming you to the fair Willamette Valley? My name is Jacob Obadiah Johnston." He backed up a step, sweeping one hand before himself as he gave her a deep bow, the long fringes on his buckskin sleeve swishing with the motion. Standing straight again, he grinned wider. "My friends call me Jake. And you would be . . . ?"

She could only stand and stare, until another man approached, dressed almost the same, his dirty buckskins showing more wear, the fringes more ragged, his dark straggly hair longer, and this one had a brushy tangle of beard covering his chin. He stepped up beside the other and stood before her with a broad smile, and she felt herself surrounded by the two of them.

The first man spoke again, his tone deepening. "May I present my friend and comrade from the mountains, the rather famous—or infamous—Joseph Lafayette Meek. His friends call him Joe."

The other man bowed. "Pleased to make yer acquaintance, Miss . . ."

A bold young voice rose beside her. "This is my sister, Jennie Haviland, and I'm Eddie—er—Edward Stephen Haviland, that is, but my friends call me Eddie."

Jennie glanced at her younger brother, standing so tall he almost measured up to her height. The one called Jake nodded, unsmiling, and reached out to shake Eddie's hand, only the brightness of the man's brown eyes showing amusement. "Pleased to meet you, Eddie."

Eddie turned to the other man, no longer containing his excitement. "Are you Joe Meek, *the* Joe Meek? The famous mountain man in the wax museum in St. Louis fighting the bear?"

Mr. Meek grinned. "One and the same, but don't ye let that statue fool ye none, boy. Old Joe didn't lose nary a finger from that ol' bar, do ye hear, now?" The man held up both hands, fingers stretched to show he still had all ten.

"But did you really fight a bear?" Eddie asked.

Mr. Meek began to laugh and slapped the other man on the shoulder. "Do ye hear that, Old Jake?" He was so caught up in laughter he didn't attempt to speak further.

Jake Johnston smiled at Eddie. "This man has fought more bears than any man I know."

Mr. Meek lifted a hand. "Why, bar fightin'—that's what this old coon is famous fer."

Jennie heard a heavy throat clearing to the other side of Eddie. Charlie, Eddie's chubby little shadow. Charlie stood tall too, as tall as he could with the way he had of raising his shoulders to make himself appear taller than he was. Plump and fair-haired like Ma, he had her same chubby cheeks and sweet disposition. But in everything he did he stretched to catch up with Eddie. Now was no exception. Eddie smiled, lifted his chin, and peered down at him. "This is Charlie, my little brother."

Mr. Johnston reached out to shake Charlie's hand like a man. "Charles Something-or-other Haviland, no doubt."

"Charles Donald," Charlie answered, extending his pudgy hand to Mr. Meek as well.

A deafening blast rent the air, shaking the ground under Jennie Alarmed, she looked around. People scattered like wild animals taking flight. She became aware of a strong hand gripping her arm. Mr. Johnston had taken hold of her as if to protect her. She started to draw away, not wanting the protection of one like him, but a sudden silence pressed in on her following the loud explosion.

Mr. Meek spoke up, his words relieving the agonizing stillness. "Well now. Blastin' over on the island, and it don't look jist right somehow, I'm thinkin'." A waft of smoke rose near the falls, looking like more of the froth that tossed about the mighty cascade. Mr. Meek sounded worried. "Hope there ain't nobody got hurt—or thrown cold. Reckon we oughta go see, Jake?"

Ma moved closer to the children, her anxiety unhidden. "Your pa just went over there."

A thought struck Jennie. She imagined Pa hurt—or worse—and them in this godforsaken country without him. Robbie and Davie began crying, and her own tears started up. But wanting to be strong for them, she blinked away the tears and stood tall. Even so, a thickness moved into her throat, like the beginning of a sob, and when she tried to swallow, a terrible sound came out.

She heard a low voice next to her. "Ma'am, it'll be all right." Mr. Johnston.

She wanted to believe him, but she didn't. Who was he, after all? What did men like these know?

She looked down at his hand, still on her arm, then up into his face, her eyes flashing fire at him, and he lifted the hand, palm up, to let her go.

Chapter Two

Willamette River, October 1842. The river swept beneath the long canoe, an unbroken line of hardwoods on either side leaning over the glossy sheath as if looking into their new gilded reflections. The reedy smell of river foliage permeated the air. Alan Radford watched his men move the craft over the water with deft strokes in perfect rhythm. They were making good time with the low water. Fall rains hadn't set in yet, and the lack of current made for fast traveling, even upstream. He smiled, hoping to make quick work of this assignment.

Throwing back his wool cloak, he smoothed his frock coat and trousers, dipping his tall, gray beaver hat to study a shore so alike from one place to another that a man had to observe carefully to know where he was. His *voyageurs* always knew, of course, these French Canadians who spent their lives following the watery pathways of North America.

He leaned toward the man in front. "How much longer, Lévêque?"

Lévêque made an obvious point of surveying the area about them, his movements quick, catlike, the bright, black eyes missing nothing. He answered in his thick French accent. "I think, *M'sieu* Alan, a half hour, maybe less." He gave a firm nod, rubbing his wiry fingers over the dark point of his chin, shadowed by remnants of the heavy beard he could never quite eradicate. "*Oui,* I think so."

"Good. I should rather like to be done with this and get back to the fort."

Alan glanced at Marceau in the rear. Short and stocky, the man was as reliable as Lévêque was devious. But Lévêque's connections could be useful. He possessed all the stealth of an Indian, moving easily from his culture to theirs. He claimed to have a wife in Canada and one in every tribe in Oregon, which he declared good diplomacy.

Lévêque swung around to frown at Alan. "Is bad business, *n'est-ce pas?*"

"What's that?"

The man's lips twisted as he ran a hand over his long, stringy black hair. "Helping these Bostons. *Américains.*" The word sounded like an oath.

Alan had to agree with Lévêque, but the man's animosity made him uneasy. Alan had no fondness for the kinds of people who comprised the American population in this country, the shiftless mountaineers escaping a dying beaver trade in the Rocky Mountains, the missionaries more interested in colonizing the country than Christianizing the Indians.

Lévêque drew his heavy black brows together over his thin, hooked nose. "These Bostons—they are the enemy, *n'est-ce pas?*"

"Perhaps."

"So, why the good *docteur* want to help these Bostons?"

Alan shrugged. It didn't make sense to him either, but Dr. John McLoughlin, Chief Factor in command of Fort Vancouver, had insisted. Despite the caliber of the Americans who'd just straggled into the country, Alan was to go to Willamette Falls and offer valuable Hudson's Bay Company supplies to help them. Not only was Alan to offer these supplies, but he was to give them on credit if the Americans were unable to pay. "Not good business at all," he said under his breath.

Marceau cleared his throat and spoke in a French accent thick as Lévêque's. "This helps the Bostons stay. *Oui?* Maybe we don't help. Maybe they go."

Alan lifted the tall beaver hat and rubbed his forehead. "I do rather wish they'd just go back to the United States where they belong and leave this land to us. I should think our efforts here have given us every right to it."

"The Company is here more than twenty years with no *Américains*," Marceau said. "Why this is not British land? Why these Bostons come now? You think they want to take it from us, *M'sieu* Alan?"

"A man has to wonder. We've had joint occupancy since 1818, but the Americans haven't seemed interested until lately. I don't know what they have in mind."

Marceau raised a brow. "But you are not trusting them."

Alan had to be careful what he said, especially given Lévêque's volatility. Turning to face ahead again, he found Lévêque staring at him, a gleam in the man's eyes sending a chill across the back of Alan's neck.

"I think we should not help these Bostons," Lévêque said. "Maybe we should sic the Indians on them, scare them off." He let out a sharp laugh. "Or I could kill a few myself."

Alan sat straighter. "You can't kill innocent people."

"Ha! So, I just slice a few." Lévêque patted the knife on his belt and showed his scanty supply of teeth.

Alan closed his fists. "We won't make trouble, Lévêque."

Shrugging, Lévêque turned his face away and dipped the paddle with new vigor. Alan marveled at the man's strength. His wiry frame looked as if it would snap apart like a brittle twig, but those scrawny limbs, with scarcely enough flesh to disguise the skeletal image, were like bars of iron, especially the arms that had worked canoes throughout this vast continent.

The *voyageur* swung back toward Alan. "Why not sic the Indians on them? We could do it. The Company could. The Indians do what British King George men say."

Alan corrected his attendant. "We're the queen's men now, Queen Victoria's. And we won't bring the Indians into this."

Marceau spoke up. "Will there be war, *M'sieu*?"

Alan paused before answering. "London will decide on that."

"But you talk to London." Concern edged Marceau's voice.

"I send reports, yes, but they don't go quickly." Alan wondered if London had received his reports about last year's influx of Americans, almost a hundred people. And more coming this year, from what he'd heard.

Lévêque's gaze darted from Alan to Marceau and back. With a scowl, he faced the front again, shoulders slumped. Alan settled deeper into the canoe, jaw tight, listening to the steady wash of the river.

The Hudson's Bay Company did have some measure of control over the Indians. The respect they had for the fatherly McLoughlin seemed to filter down to his men. And to some extent the local tribes were influenced by those who'd been fathered by Hudson's Bay Company men. If it came to war, Alan surmised the British could rally several thousand Indians and men of Indian descent, given the natural tendency for the tribal leaders to distrust Americans. Still, he couldn't condone the idea of siccing Indians on American settlers.

Marceau grunted softly. "Dr. McLoughlin is not wanting the Indians to make trouble for these Bostons, I think."

"No," Alan said, turning to give Marceau a quick smile. "He won't even let the Americans suffer want as long as he has means of helping them."

Marceau's round face twisted, eyes alight. "We do not argue with the good *docteur*. What he say, we do, *mais oui?*"

"Ah yes. I should say. Nobody argues with Dr. McLoughlin."

Looking ahead again, Alan recognized a bend in the river and took a long breath. They would soon reach their destination. He glanced at the sky. How soon could they get back to Fort Vancouver?

The sound of roaring water rose before they had sight of it. When the canoe rounded the bend the bordering trees seemed to draw back like a curtain, and the roar struck with force as the curved white wall of the mighty Willamette Falls swept into view. Alan straightened his hat and sat taller. Below the falls a surprising number of buildings stood in various stages of completion on the bench of land between the river and the sheer rock bluff, where trees along the top rose like bristles of a brush. And construction of the mill on the island showed progress.

"See the tents?" Marceau said. "Must be many newcomers."

Tents were scattered among piles of logs and partially built log walls. Alan stroked his chin. "If they raise a cabin for every tent, Willamette Falls will be quite the little town."

The canoe thumped against shore, and the two *voyageurs* sat watching Alan. He lifted a hand. "You're on your own for a while, but be back by dusk."

A weight pressed on his shoulders, but he climbed out of the canoe and marched toward the nearest group of working men to offer the assistance his job as Hudson's Bay Company clerk demanded of him.

The pile of logs near the closest group reflected much effort already, hours of cutting and trimming and hauling, the logs unfinished, not squared, the bark still on. Most settlers used them rough like that, only a few cleaning the bark or squaring the timbers. Alan turned to the Waller house with its trim square logs. Waller had gotten those logs from Dr. McLoughlin, who'd planned to use them himself. Alan couldn't help wondering if the American had ever paid McLoughlin for them.

Heaving a sigh, he approached a middle-aged man bent over a log, carefully notching it so it could be interlocked at a corner of the cabin walls. Alan removed his beaver hat and tipped his head toward the man.

Not stopping in his work, the fellow nodded back. A gash on his cheek appeared recent, and a fresh bandage covered one arm below the rolled sleeve of his blue-striped hickory shirt.

"Rough business this," Alan said, "what with all the work needed to get settled."

The man lost his grip on the log in his hands and let it drop. "Blessed arm." He rubbed his palms on the black jeans cloth of his pants, streaking more dirt and sawdust onto the grime that already coated the fabric.

A younger man, a tall, dark-haired fellow dressed like a mountaineer, hurried to his side and picked up the log. "Here, let me help you, Mr. Haviland. That's why you hired me." The mountaineer turned toward a couple of boys he thought were probably not yet in their teens. "Give us a hand here, now. Your pa's hurt and needs help."

Alan brushed a little dust off his frock coat and faced the father. "Sir—Mr. Haviland, is it?—I'd like to introduce myself. I'm Alan Radford, clerk for the Hudson's Bay Company, and I've come to offer assistance as needed. Dr. John McLoughlin, Chief Factor at Fort Vancouver, asked that I come to offer supplies to newcomers who may have need." His speech done, Alan observed the man's reaction and detected no warmth. Supposing the man was anti-British like so many Americans, Alan still retained his amiable air. "I've been asked to offer credit, sir, if you feel you're unable to pay right now. In any case, we do have food, clothing, tools—"

"We'll pay for anything we buy."

Alan winced, but answered back with an attempt at sociability. "Did you hurt yourself getting your logs, sir?"

Mr. Haviland shook his head. "A little blasting accident. Somebody got explosives too close to the fire."

"Indeed! Anybody seriously hurt?"

"No, just me with this blamed arm that slows me down right when there's so much work to be done."

"Well, sir, I'll be around today and tomorrow. If you want supplies, I'll be at the Hudson's Bay Company storehouse over there." Alan indicated the small shack the Company used to store supplies.

The man noted the location and returned to his work. The boys were intent on their conversation with the mountaineer. A few words drifted Alan's way. "I sure wish . . . a dog . . . back home . . ."

Looking for friendlier company, Alan stepped nearer the boys. "You fellows have a dog?"

The older boy gave Alan a sharp look, but the younger one gulped a breath and spilled it out. "We had to leave our old dog back home, 'cause Pa said the trip would be too much for her and we might not have food enough and we almost did run out of food for just us, but now we don't have a dog and we need one."

Alan gave the boy a kindly smile. "You most surely do, but I suppose a good dog is hard to find in a place like this. I'm sorry you had to leave your good old dog behind, son. Too bad you had to do that."

The older boy yanked on the younger one's sleeve. "Better get to work, Charlie. Pa needs our help."

"All right, Eddie." Charlie gave Alan a flickering smile and turned away.

Eddie's frown broke into a sudden smile. For a moment Alan thought the boy was looking at him, but soon realized the boy's focus was directed behind him. "Hello, Joe," Eddie said, beaming.

Alan turned to see who had evoked the boy's delight and, recognizing the source, almost lost his poise. Joe Meek. Not Alan's favorite person. Even Dr. McLoughlin had refused Meek credit for farming supplies last year when the doctor gave credit to other mountaineers. Meek was a total good-for-nothing, as far as Alan could see, a tale-teller who wouldn't recognize truth if it smacked him in the face.

Meek spoke to Alan in an exaggerated drawl. "Well now, if'n it ain't that purty feller from the fort up yonder, Mr.—uh—Mr.—what was it?"

"Alan Radford."

Meek turned to the group working on the logs. "How's the work a-comin', m'friends?"

The responses, even of Mr. Haviland, sounded cordial, warm, unlike the responses they'd offered Alan.

Shaking his head, Alan was about to march off in disgust when he saw a young woman walking from the river toward the tent nearest the group beside him. Her long brown hair flowed about her shoulders, glistening in the sunlight with flashes of gold and red, her lovely face aglow. Something about the way she walked caught him, her step proud, determined, yet graceful. And she had a strong profile, yet sweet. He had a feeling she could turn and stun him with a gaze, and he wouldn't mind at all. But she didn't even look his way. She slipped inside the tent without a glance in his direction, and he let out a long breath.

He decided he must say something to Mr. Haviland. "Beg your pardon, sir. Would that be your tent?"

"Yes, it is. Why?"

Young Charlie spoke up. "Yeah, and that's my sister."

"Your sister?"

The boy nodded, then lowered his chin, eyes lifted beneath a pinched brow, as if he'd said something he shouldn't have.

Alan gave him an encouraging smile. "Indeed! And what's her name?"

Charlie looked at the ground. "Jennie."

Alan hesitated, not wanting to appear too interested. She might be married.

The boy went on. "Jennie Haviland."

"Ah! Very well, son." Alan's chest rose with a sudden light feeling. Not married. Perhaps this assignment wouldn't be so bad after all.

Movement at the tent doorway caught Alan's attention, and he watched, hoping to get another glimpse of the lovely young woman. But an older woman came out, a plump, pleasant-faced person he guessed to be the mother. The woman looked straight at him and smiled, her cheeks turning rosy.

Alan bowed. "How do you do, ma'am?"

She watched him as she stepped his way. "I'm well, thank you, and you, sir?"

"Very well, thank you. And you must be Mrs. Haviland."

"Why, yes, I am, and you're . . ." She turned toward Mr. Haviland, imposing on his duty to make introductions.

The man cleared his throat and managed a smile. "This is Mr. Radford of the Hudson's Bay Company. He's come to offer us supplies, assistance, such as that."

Mrs. Haviland's face brightened. "Why, Mr. Radford, how nice. I'm pleased to meet you, and that's a lovely gesture. Why, the stores here are so limited, and there are so many things we need. Neither the Methodist store nor Couch's store has half what a store might be expected to have. You can't imagine how little a family can carry on such a journey as we've had."

"Well, Mrs. Haviland, let me assure you I will do anything I can to help you. I'll be here for a day or two now, and I'll be back from time to time. Please call on me for whatever you have need of, won't you?"

"I will. I certainly will."

Alan smiled at the woman. He couldn't help responding to her open kindness. With some surprise he realized he'd meant every word he said to her. Briefly questioning his motives, he wondered if he only wanted to help this lady because she was the mother of a lovely daughter, but he didn't think so.

He smiled to himself. *Of course, it couldn't hurt my cause with the lovely daughter.*

The woman began to turn away, then stopped. "Mr. Radford, I haven't a great deal to offer, but I'd be most pleased if you'd join us for supper this evening."

Alan felt the woman's warmth surrounding him and warding off the earlier chill. Delighted, he spoke with sincere pleasure. "I'd like that very much indeed, ma'am."

"About dusk, then? Right here outside our tent."

"I'll be here, ma'am. You may be sure of it."

The Shifting Winds

Jake started to tie the rope around the last log and hitch it to the ox to drag it out of the woods. But as he bent down, rope in hand, he heard a scream and a whacking noise. He snatched his rifle that he'd propped against a nearby tree and headed toward the sound. Charging through the brush as quietly as he could, he stopped when he saw the source.

A man stood hovered over a woman, striking her with a stick, while she crouched on the ground trying to ward off the blows.

A chill gripped Jake, putting an icy edge in his low voice as he raised the rifle. "Hold it right there."

The man wheeled about, startled, and glared into the end of Jake's gun. Small and wiry with stringy black hair and black stubble on his chin, he looked like a *voyageur* with the wide red sash around his waist, red headband, faded blue shirt with buckskin trousers, and moccasins. Probably from Fort Vancouver. Recovering quickly, he snarled in a thick French accent. "Is none of your affair."

The woman stared at Jake, unmoving. She didn't appear to be from a local tribe, given her round head. An unusual scar like the curved wings of a bird marred her left cheek. Attractive despite the scar, she wore a bright-red tunic and cedar-bark skirt made from strips of cedar, a style common to Indian women in the area. Maybe she was a slave.

The *voyageur* continued speaking, spitting out each word. "She is my woman. She is bad. I punish. You go. Leave us alone, *Américain*."

Jake made a show of fingering the trigger and tipped his head toward the woman. "Go ahead. Go."

Her eyes flared like a frightened doe, and when she didn't respond he motioned with the gun, speaking again, but in the Chinook jargon known to most of the tribes in the area. "Go. Run to safety. This man has no right to hurt you. Go."

With a glance at the *voyageur* she burst into life, scrambled to her feet, and ran into the cover of the woods. The sound of her running footsteps soon dissolved in the green damper of the forest as if she had vanished. For her sake, Jake hoped she could do just that.

The man's voice rasped. "I'll get you for this."

Jake put all the menace he could in his own voice. "I don't ever want to see you hurting a woman again. And if I hear anything has happened to this woman, I will hunt you down. Do you understand me?"

The man didn't answer, but his hatred emanated with such ferocity, Jake could feel the impact. Jake motioned for him to go, and the man slipped away, melting into the forest as the woman had done. Taking a deep breath, Jake shook his head and turned back to his work.

"Is that the one I saw talking to Pa this afternoon?" Jennie asked her mother as the two prepared the evening meal. "The one all dressed up like someone from civilized society?"

Ma put on her scolding voice. "Civilized society indeed, Jennie. How you talk. As if we were all uncivilized here."

"I'm sorry, Ma."

Jennie hadn't made a secret of her feelings about coming to Oregon, but Ma held grumbling to be disrespectful. "Besides," she'd said to Jennie, "it doesn't help anything in a situation that can't be changed. You just make the best of it."

Jennie's mother hovered over the big black kettle of boiled wheat, stirring in chunks of venison from the deer Jake had brought them, softly humming a cheerful tune.

How could she be so lighthearted?

Ma lifted a brow at Jennie. "So you saw Mr. Radford, then?"

"From the back."

Ma's eyes came alight. "Then, you didn't see that face. Well, wait until you see. He's a fine-looking one, he is."

Jennie thought it would have been difficult not to notice a man dressed in frock coat and trousers with shiny black boots and holding a fine beaver hat. Even from the back she could see he wore his clothes well, having the broad shoulders and long trim frame upon which such clothes seemed to belong. She'd also noticed the crown of thick golden hair and supposed he was a young man. But she hadn't seen the face.

Ma nodded. "A real gentleman, that one. It surely will be a pleasure to have the company of such a gentleman for supper. I just wish we had something finer to offer, but the venison is nearly gone and—I suppose we'll be having Jake and his friend Joe too." She sighed.

Clearly Ma was not impressed with Jake and Joe, but they'd been a lot of help, especially Jake, hunting for them, working with Pa on the cabin. Joe had a wife and family several miles away on Tualatin Plains and couldn't be here all the time, but Jake evidently had no such ties. He'd stayed on at Willamette Falls, sleeping under the stars, ever since the Havilands arrived.

Pa didn't know what they'd do without him. The boys weren't quite big enough to give Pa all the help he needed, especially since Pa got hurt in the accident at the mill. When Jake offered to help, Pa had readily agreed.

Jennie looked toward the cabin site and saw Jake leading Rosy and Ranger to a spot near the oxen where they could be staked out for the night for grazing, not far from his own black horse.

Ma tapped Jennie's shoulder. "Honey, would you stir this, please?"

Jennie took the big spoon and slowly stirred the gruel of boiled wheat. It smelled more like paste than food. *Oh, for a taste of good raised bread.*

The nearest gristmill was miles away—one at Champoeg almost twenty miles away and those at Fort Vancouver and at the Willamette Mission Station at Chemeketa even farther. Flour was not only hard to come by, it was expensive too. Since boiled wheat offered good nutrition cheaper, that became regular fare for most everyone. Sometimes they had meat, sometimes not. Hunting was so poor in the area, even expert hunters like Jake and Joe had trouble bringing in game.

The local tribes retained fishing rights and sold fish. Five charges of ammunition bought one salmon, or a common shirt bought ten, but the Havilands didn't have ammunition or shirts or any other trade items to spare. Jennie hoped folks would soon need legal services so Pa could start to earn—provided those folks had means to pay.

She shook her head, wondering how they would ever survive here, and made a face at the gruel. "How long will we have to live on boiled wheat? It's ghastly."

Looking westward she could see the sky growing dim, and wondered what their guest would be like. Eddie came up behind her, making her jump. "What's for supper?"

"Don't startle me like that. What else?"

"Oh, yum! Boiled wheat!" Eddie leaned over the kettle, sniffed, and gave his sister an exaggerated grin while he rubbed his stomach.

"Get out of here, Eddie." Jennie tried to sound stern, but couldn't help laughing.

Charlie joined his brother, frown lines creasing his round face. "Do we have to eat boiled wheat again?"

Jennie raised her brows at him. "Are you hungry?"

"I'm so hungry I could eat a horse." Charlie took a sudden breath. "Well, not really a horse—I mean, not one I know—well, personally—but something big."

Joe swaggered over next to the boys and gave a definitive nod. "Painter—that thar's number one."

"Painter?" Charlie looked up at Joe.

"Shore." Joe's face pinched into a thoughtful frown. "'Course, meat's meat. In the mount'ins a man had to eat what a man could git."

Charlie's face pinched like Joe's, but his eyes were wide with a questioning look. "What's painter?"

Joe shrugged. "Ye know, *painter*—big cat."

Eddie moved closer. "I thought buffalo was best."

"Well now, it's hard to beat buffler hump rib cooked over an open fire, but ye won't be findin' no buffler in these parts. Thar's painter, though, if'n ye kin git one."

"Are they hard to kill?"

"Not hard. Not like a buffler that has to be hit jist right or he won't even know ye shot him. But painters—they's tricky and skittery-like."

"Ever fight one of them?" Charlie asked.

"Cain't say I have. Farmers in these parts are havin' a bad time with painter and wolves eatin' their livestock." Joe bent down to give Charlie a contemplative look. "Painter might as soon eat a young feller, though."

Charlie's eyes widened again on his round face, his voice scarcely above a whisper. "Would they?"

"So's I've heard tell. Mind ye, I wouldn't go wanderin' off alone if'n I were sich a tasty-lookin' morsel as you, Old Charlie. Ye won't, now, will ye?"

Charlie shook his head. Jennie wanted to smile but managed to keep a straight face. In a way Joe was teasing, but then again panthers—or *painters*—could be dangerous, especially to a small boy like Charlie—or Eddie, who was listening intently himself.

Jennie saw Pa and Jake coming, walking toward the tent, talking companionably. It surprised her they got along so well. Pa was always cordial with people who worked for him, but not sociable. And Jake wasn't the type of fellow Pa usually regarded as a friend. The man wasn't a bad-looking sort. Jennie supposed if he had decent clothes he might even be considered attractive, with his square jaw, the strong set of his mouth, full lips, the large dark eyes. Yet he had a roughness about him that made her want to keep her distance.

Pa smiled. "How's supper coming?"

She gave the brew another stir. "I think it's ready if Ma's ready to serve, but we have a guest coming."

Pa's smile faded, and Jennie glanced at Jake. He wasn't smiling, but a sparkle lit his eyes as he watched her.

Ma bustled out of the tent with Robbie and Davie in hand. "Mr. Radford isn't here yet?" Her face lit up. "Oh, here he comes."

Jennie turned to see two men approaching. She couldn't see them well in the dim evening light but recognized one as the well-dressed man she'd seen earlier. He had topped his fine suit with a flowing gray cloak and wore the tall beaver hat, but she couldn't mistake the golden blond hair and the brisk rhythmic step.

Glancing at the other man, she stared a moment. Not a gentleman, that one. A ragged black coat draped over his stooped shoulders, a dirty blue shirt and red cummerbund underneath, with sagging buckskin breeches and worn moccasins. A red bandanna circled his head to draw back his shoulder-length black hair, and when he came within a few paces of her, Jennie could clearly see his gaunt cheeks and crooked nose and the riveting black eyes.

He came to a halt and spoke to Mr. Radford and, with a hint of a nod in the direction of the Havilands, slipped away into the darkening shadows.

Released from an obsession to stare at him, Jennie turned her eyes to the other man and caught her breath. He was studying her, hat at his waist, and

Ma was right. Such a face. Like a sculptor's masterpiece. Jennie had never seen one carved to such perfection. Dark-golden brows arched over large eyes, cheekbones finely chiseled, white, even teeth showing with his smile.

He started toward her, but when their gazes locked, he stopped, still as one of the sculptures he looked chiseled to be. Then he gave his head a little shake and walked straight to her. And she looked up into eyes blue as a high mountain lake.

Ma's voice warmed with pleasure. "Jennie, I'd like you to meet Mr. Radford. Mr. Radford, this is my daughter, Jennie Haviland."

Bowing, he took Jennie's hand and kissed the back of it before he stood tall and smiled again. When he spoke, she was surprised to hear the clipped British accent. "I'm most happy to meet you, Miss Haviland. *Alan Radford*, it is. I should be spending a good deal of time at Willamette Falls, and I rather hope we can become friends, eh?"

Jennie gave him a quick smile. "Nice to meet you."

Ma touched her shoulder. "Jennie, perhaps we'd best be serving supper. Mr. Radford, you have met the others, have you not?"

"Indeed, ma'am, I believe I have." He nodded graciously in their general direction.

Ma quickly directed everyone to find places on various stumps and logs with apologies for the lack of chairs, and Alan Radford lifted a hand, voice warm. "Quite all right, Mrs. Haviland. I should say, it's my customary seating more often than not."

Silence settled over their small circle around the cloth spread on the ground for a table. While Jennie and her mother served the boiled wheat and venison, no one spoke, but Jennie remained aware of the handsome Britisher and the following gaze of those blue eyes. Once she and Ma joined the circle, she avoided Alan Radford's eyes to observe the others. Pa appeared unusually stern, as did Jake and Joe. Eddie and Charlie watched with open faces, waiting.

Ma smiled at their guest. "Do you live at the Hudson's Bay Company fort?"

"Fort Vancouver, yes."

"How nice. I wish we could have come by there on our way, but we came over the mountains."

His eyes warmed. "It's a fine place, ma'am. Remote, but fairly civilized, considering the location."

Ma nodded. "Where are you from?"

"London originally, but Montreal more recently."

Jennie stared at him. *London.* She'd read about that city, and she blurted out her thoughts. "They have a million people in London."

He flashed a smile at her. "A couple million actually."

"How do you like—? Well, this must seem very different to you after living in a place like London."

"Quite different, yes," he said. "And for you."

She sat back, shaking her head. "Utica has only—maybe twelve thousand people. New York City is big, but I never went there. Ever. It was too far."

Lights from their cook fire glinted in his eyes and reflected warmth straight to her. "And you have just traveled how far?" he asked.

She put a hand over her heart and laughed. "Oh, dear. About three thousand miles."

He lifted a brow. "I'd say that's pretty far."

"Not as far as London." She looked into the fire, trying to imagine. London. Montreal. Such intriguing places. No wonder he had such an air of sophistication. She took a long breath and inhaled a bouquet of smells—the smoke of many campfires, the tang of venison, fresh-washed clothes, the conifers, and something different tonight: leather, rich oiled leather. She glanced at Alan Radford's tall, black boots, glossy in the firelight.

Ma filled a lingering silence. "Have you been with the Hudson's Bay Company long, Mr. Radford?"

"Eight years, ma'am. I left England eight years ago."

Jennie bit her lower lip. Did he miss home? She'd been gone from Utica only months. But eight years? Her chest tightened. Would she ever see home again? Would he? A wave of compassion swept over her for this man, for all of them so isolated in this wild country.

Eddie's heavy sigh broke into her thoughts, and she glanced her brother's way. His shoulders lifted and fell as he turned to Jake. "You were gonna tell us more stories about life in the Rockies, Jake. You promised you would."

Jake pursed his lips. "So I did, but if you want stories, here's the best storyteller sitting beside me." He motioned toward Joe, who grinned with a thinly disguised show of modesty.

Jennie clutched the fabric of her dress skirt. She wanted their dinner conversation civilized for the benefit of Alan Radford.

Eddie smiled. "Would *you* tell us some stories, Joe?"

Charlie echoed his brother. "Yeah. Stories about the mountains and bears."

Ma frowned. "Boys, don't pester, now. And mind your manners. It's Mr. Meek and Mr. Johnston."

Charlie leaned closer to Joe. "Are you really old, Mr. Meek?"

Joe reared back and looked down his nose at Charlie. "Well, I guess compared to some young critters like yerself, but I ain't seen more'n thirty-two summers—or is it thirty-three? This coon left home at sich an early age, I have more trouble trackin' my years than keepin' after a grizzly on hard ground."

Jennie was surprised the man wasn't older. He had a few flecks of gray in his dark beard already, and a tracery of faint lines across his broad face. But he appeared fit certainly, with a proud bearing—if he weren't so rough around the edges. She let her gaze move over their circle, and for a moment she imagined a curtain between these mountaineers with her father and the older boys on one side, and Alan Radford with her mother and the little boys on the opposite. Why did she feel they were on two competing sides? Because Alan Radford was British, and being British made him the enemy? He wasn't acting like an enemy, and Ma seemed to like him better than the American mountaineers.

Jennie felt herself in the middle. Her imaginary curtain could rest at one side or the other. But she didn't want a curtain. She didn't want hostility between any part of her family and this fine British gentleman. She didn't understand why the two nations should be at odds. Folks on the trail west had talked of war. If war broke out, what would happen to the friendship this man offered?

Charlie's eager voice drew her attention. "Was it snowy in the mountains, Mr. Meek?"

Ma's tone sharpened. "Charlie."

Joe smiled at Ma. "Oh, ma'am, mind ye, it's no trouble." He tilted his head toward Charlie. "Yessir, boy, we had us'n a heap o' snow in the Rockies."

"And you just stayed up there in the snow?"

"Well now, we couldn't rightly leave on account of a little snow. That wouldn't shine. What d'ye do when the snow comes to yer town?"

"But we had a house."

"Well, mind ye, we had houses too, buffler skin lodges. Why, my woman could put together the snuggest, warmest house o' buffler skin ye ever hoped to see. Doggone if'n she couldn't."

Charlie's hazel eyes widened in his round, ruddy face. "Did you stay in there?"

"A heap o' the time. Couldn't trap beaver in the winter. They's all holed up, so we hole up too. But we passed the time—jawin' at each other, tellin' stories—" He looked down at his lap. "Some of us as couldn't read learned how to. Had us'n a college, *we* did."

Eddie wrinkled his face. "College?"

"Shore! The Rocky Mount'in College. Didn't we, Old Jake?"

Jake nodded, face sober. "Yep. Many a man learned to read in the Rocky Mountain College."

Eddie let out a huff. "I don't believe you had college up there. You didn't even have towns."

Jake smiled. "Well, Rocky Mountain College is just what we called it. We'd get together and talk about books, and a lot of us fellers learned to read up there."

"Yessir," Joe said, "in the winter we had us'n the college and in the summer we had rendezvous. My heavens! That was the time fer big doin's, mind ye, when the company sent out supplies, and after bein' temperate all year, we let loose a mite, *we* did. A man would spend mebbe a thousand dollars a day on—"

Joe broke off at the sound of Pa's throat clearing. Jennie had begun to lean toward Joe on the far side of the campfire, caught in her own love for a story. She wanted to hear about this rendezvous, and she wondered why Pa's interruption stopped the telling.

Eddie appeared oblivious to Pa's reaction. His eyes took on a gleam as he smiled at Joe. "Is it true you guys all kept Indian women? I heard that—"

"Eddie!" Pa said, and Jennie glared at her brother.

Joe shrugged. "Thar's a lot of us fellers as had Injun wives. This coon's had three hisself. One of 'em, Virginia, she's still my wife, *she is*."

Eddie continued despite Pa's stern look. "Three? All at once?"

Pa's hand came down on Eddie's shoulder, and the boy slunk lower, his head dipped.

Joe waved his hands in a dismissive gesture. "No, no. Not me. This child's only had one at a time."

Jennie stared at the man, wondering what had happened to his first two wives, and she glanced at Jake. He had no family ties now, but had he kept Indian women before? A shudder rippled through her.

Charlie also faced Jake, the boy's high voice filled with childish innocence. "How many Indian wives did you have, Mr. Johnston?"

Jennie almost choked on her boiled wheat. Jake just laughed, and Jennie took a quick drink of water to wash down the wheat, while she observed Jake Johnston with increasing skepticism.

"Charlie!" Pa's stern voice. "That'll be enough."

Joe raised his brows. "These fellers have questions aplenty, don't they?"

Pa scowled at each of the boys. "I think they need to learn when a question is appropriate and when it is not."

Charlie wrinkled his face, and Eddie ran a hand over his dark-brown hair that was growing overlong. It occurred to his sister that he would need a haircut soon or he'd look as unkempt as Joe Meek.

A sudden loud squeal startled them all—from the direction of the horses. The men leaped to their feet, guns materializing in their hands.

Jennie set down her tin plate and stood. "What is it?"

Alan Radford moved to her side and placed a hand on her arm. "Something bothering the horses, I presume, but if you stay here, Miss Haviland, I trust you'll be all right."

Pa hurried away with Jake and Joe, while Alan remained behind, keeping close to Jennie, as if he wanted to protect her.

A gun sounded. A wailing cry. Jennie put a hand to her throat. At the edge of the aura of light from their campfire, two green eyes shone. The huge face of a cat appeared. The beast let out a chilling scream and charged straight for Jennie, mouth wide, baring white jagged teeth. She froze. The beast stopped and stared, its luminous eyes catching the firelight, its long body sleek and golden. A big cat. A panther. It snarled and hissed, gaze fixed on her, mesmerizing her. A spot of blood oozed from the creature's neck and dripped onto the ground. The cat was hurt, but kept standing. Would it attack? Could it?

From the corner of her eye she saw the small black pistol in Alan's hand. Why didn't he shoot?

Someone yelled from the other side of the cat. "Don't shoot!" Jake's voice. Why was he telling the Britisher not to shoot? "You'll hit the camp," Jake said.

The camp. He was talking to the others out there with him. The cat was between them and the camp. They didn't dare shoot in this direction, and neither did Alan dare shoot in theirs.

As instantly as the animal had come, it faded into the darkness beyond the light of the campfire. Where it had stood, the men stepped into the flickering glow.

Ma ran toward Pa. His voice rasped. "It's all right now. Blessed panther. After the horses. He got to Rosy."

Jennie let out a soft cry. "Not Rosy."

Pa looked up at her. "She'll be all right. Just a scratch. Lucky we got there when we did—and the French Canadian. That was his shot."

Annoyance edged Jake's words. "But he missed the vitals. The cat's wounded, but it had no trouble getting away. And none of us could get a clear shot to finish him."

Ma looked up at Jake, hands clasped over her heart. "Why did he come at us that way?"

"Just confused," Jake said, "hurt and confused."

Pa heaved a sharp breath. "Yes, and he's more dangerous than ever, now that he's wounded. I don't want any of you going off into the woods alone—you boys especially. Understand?"

Eddie and Charlie nodded, lips clamped tight.

Peering back into the darkness where the cat had been, Jennie caught sight of the man she'd seen earlier with Alan. He stood at the edge of the light from their campfire, watching them, then disappeared, illusory as the cat.

Jennie shivered with a sudden chill and noticed Jake Johnston looking at her, forehead creased. Only then did she realize Alan Radford was still holding her arm. She slipped from his grasp and stared back into the darkness where she had seen—or thought she had seen—that man.

Chapter Three

Woods above Willamette Falls, October 1842. Dusk settled over the forest like a veil, graying every living green form, shadows blending with the foliage. Not quite ready to give up, Jake led Mr. Haviland to the edge of a small meadow where deer often grazed toward the end of the day. Screened by branches, they scanned the opening.

"See anything?" Haviland asked.

Jake shook his head, gripping the cold barrel of his sleek Hawken rifle. "Nope."

"Maybe there's something in the woods beyond."

Jake looked at the sky, then into the dimming woods. "Probably better head back. It'll be near dark by the time we get home. Hate to go back empty-handed when you folks are out of meat, but—"

"That's all right. We have plenty of wheat to boil." Haviland chuckled under his breath.

Jake laughed as they headed down the trail. "That's a poor excuse for food, but I guess it fills a man's stomach. Meat's what a man needs. We didn't eat much else in the mountains. Of course, I do recall a time or two when we went a long time between meals."

"You fellows pretty well lived off the land, didn't you?"

"Except for the few supplies we bought in the summer at rendezvous, which never lasted long. Can't survive off the land here, though. Not enough game."

Jake stopped to listen. A prickly feeling tickled the back of his neck. A sense beyond hearing made him believe something was behind him. He turned to peer into the deepening shadows and saw only the trees and lacy fronds of giant ferns amid twining low brush. A long breath filled his nose with the familiar scents of conifers, the decaying needles crushed underfoot, the ever-present blend of his buckskins and gun oil and metal, a whiff of smoke from the fall fires. Nothing out of the ordinary.

Haviland frowned. "What is it?"

Jake held up a hand for silence. A few leaves rustled with a slight breeze, but he couldn't pick out any sounds of a presence. Shrugging, he faced ahead and continued walking. "Thought I heard something, but I guess not."

Haviland picked up the conversation, apparently untroubled. "You fellows had quite a time at your rendezvous, didn't you?"

Jake tried to ignore his own uneasiness. "Sure did."

"I don't know what Joe was about to tell my boys about that—and in the company of the ladies—but it's my understanding that some of the purchases you men made in the mountains might have included both alcohol and women."

Jake twisted his lips in a wry smile. "Joe forgets his manners sometimes. It's true enough we had alcohol flowing freely up there, and it was wicked stuff. They'd send pure alcohol out from the States and we'd mix that with water. Men got pretty tight on it."

"I can imagine."

"As for women—" Jake wasn't sure what to say to this gentleman he didn't know all that well. "A—uh—an Indian woman's father would expect a bride price for his daughter, of course, maybe some horses or beaver pelts. And sometimes when a man ran out of gambling money he might gamble his woman away in a game of chance."

"Well, I don't think my boys want to learn about that."

Jake lifted a brow at Haviland. "Sir, I think they may be wanting to learn as much as they can get by with."

Haviland had to laugh. "Let's not rush that, shall we?"

"I won't be talking about it, sir."

"Call me George, why don't you? And you don't have to share your own history with me, but I assume you're not attached to a woman at this time."

"No, I'm quite single, sir."

Jake studied the man. He had a certain air of dignity about him, the way he walked with head high, shoulders back. Strong jaw, maybe a little stubborn. A gentle smile softened Haviland's features as he spoke. "Well, my wife and I have been married for eighteen years, and I am a lucky man."

"You are that, sir, and you have a fine—" Jake stopped short. That feeling prickled his neck again. Somebody, or something, was watching him. He pivoted to look behind again. With his rifle still capped for the hunt, ready for firing, he aimed back up the shadowy trail. Nothing. Shaking his head, he walked on. "Just checking," he told Haviland.

"For game?"

"Could be, but we'd better be moving along."

"Yes. I don't want to worry Mrs. Haviland. I'm kind of glad the boys stayed home. She won't have them to worry over."

Jake smiled. "They weren't too happy about that, were they?"

"No." Haviland let out a soft laugh. "They want to be men already, and I have taken the two older ones out. They know how to shoot, all right. But with that wounded panther in these woods, I didn't want them out here right now." He glanced at Jake. "Am I babying them too much?"

Jake smiled, not wanting to say.

"I suppose I should buy them a gun of their own," Haviland said. "I could get one from the Hudson's Bay Company fellow that keeps the storehouse. He's got a few—not good ones, but good enough for boys to start out with."

"Might be an idea."

A twig snapped. Not far behind. Swinging around, Jake raised his rifle again. Nothing in his sights. But that feeling on the back of his neck told him he was being followed. He wanted to shoot, but it could be a person. He called out. "Hello!"

A friendly person would answer. But no one responded.

"Do you think someone's there?" Haviland whispered.

Jake kept an even tone to ease the man's concern. "Probably some small animal." As he headed on, Jake tried to convince himself that he had only heard a harmless little critter.

Haviland went on talking, sounding chatty again. "So, what will you do when you're done helping us?"

Jake raised his brows. His reassurance must have been convincing. Jake wished he could feel as comfortable, but he couldn't shake the prickly feeling. Still, he answered offhandedly. "Don't know."

"How old are you?"

"Twenty-four."

"Ah! A young man with most of your life ahead of you. How long were you in the mountains?"

"Four years. I went in '36 when I was eighteen. Stayed till the fall of '40 when Joe and Doc and I came on to Oregon. That's Doc Newell, a friend we trapped with. He's been farming since we came, like Joe, but I understand he's going to move into town."

"Business got pretty bad in the mountains, did it?"

"Yeah. Prices low, beaver about gone. I don't think the American Fur Company even held rendezvous after the summer of '40." Jake felt a hint of regret at the mention of it.

"Did you ever get back home to the States?" Haviland smiled at him. "And by the way, where is home?"

"Kentucky, and no, I haven't been back. Most of us never went back to the settlements once we went into the mountains." He shrugged his shoulders. "A good many of them were out there a lot longer than I was—as much as fifteen years or so from the first rendezvous in '25."

"Oh, yeah?"

Jake grinned. "All that time away from civilization—hell, in four years I almost forgot how to behave in polite society. I'm afraid your wife and daughter pretty well see me as uncivilized yet."

Haviland laughed. "Well, I don't know about that, but I don't doubt you lived pretty close to nature for a while."

"You could say so."

"But now you've turned settler."

Jake glanced at the elder man walking beside him. His statement had the feel of a question. George Haviland had a way of poking around for information, no doubt from years of work as a lawyer, and Jake wasn't sure how much he wanted to reveal. "I guess it's time I changed direction some."

Haviland lifted a hand to punctuate his words. "I've changed direction considerably myself. I may still be a lawyer, but it sure won't be the same here as in New York."

Jake turned the questions back to him. "Why did you come to Oregon? Why would you leave a law practice there for the uncertainty of an unsettled place like this?"

Haviland rubbed a hand over his chin. "Sometimes I wonder myself, but I guess there are times a man just needs a change."

Jake pressed further. "You must think there's a future for a lawyer in Oregon."

"Absolutely. Of course, we need a local code of laws and a court structure in Oregon before a law practice can amount to much."

"Law and order."

"That's right. We do have probate officers, selected last year to probate the estate of Ewing Young. Beyond that, I can't see we have much. Our law and order is pretty tenuous. Lacking local law, the officers use New York law. And lacking a constitution, our order simply comes from the willingness of the people to cooperate. It's a volatile situation."

Jake turned to Haviland, intent on his reaction. "There's talk of setting up a government here, you know."

"Yes, I've heard."

"What do you think about it?"

"Well, the British already have a government in a sense with Hudson's Bay Company officers acting as justices of the peace, taking authority from the Crown of England. We Americans have nothing like that." Haviland stopped and faced Jake, his brow twisted. "What if we have legal conflicts? Where's our authority? Who's to act on our behalf?"

"Nobody, I guess."

Haviland's tone rippled with passion. "That's right. As it stands now, this is essentially a land without law and order for American citizens. We have no courts. No military to protect us. The Indians around here could do away with us easily if they chose to. Or we could be at the mercy of outlaws from the States or from California."

Jake reflected on that. "What do you think our chances are in the boundary dispute with the British?"

Haviland smiled, though the lines still creased his brow. "If I didn't think they were good, I wouldn't have taken the trouble to come."

"No, I suppose not. You aren't worried about war?"

The man heaved a sigh. "I don't know. I hope men in Washington and London have better sense than that, but history doesn't reassure me."

The two walked quietly awhile, and Jake dared another question. "What would it take for a man out here to become a lawyer?"

Haviland gave him a long look. "You'd have to read the law. It'd be best if you could go east, but I do have law books with me, New York law books. Why do you ask?"

A twig snapped on the hillside above, and Jake stopped, all his senses alert again. The sound was close. And distinct. Somebody or something was above the trail beside him. He pointed his rifle in the direction of the sound.

A dark form leaped out of the shadows and came down on Jake with such force it knocked the gun from his hands before he could draw back the hammer. A big cat. It let out a shrill cry, and Jake hit the ground, pinned by a furry mass of claws and teeth.

The great claws swiped at his clothes, slashed through the buckskin hunting shirt to his skin. Raw pain ripped down his chest. Jake tried to get his hands on the animal's neck, tried to hold off the great paws that tore at him. He stared into the dark, cavernous mouth, the white teeth shining in startling contrast in the dim light. A rush of rank hot breath enveloped Jake's face with the cat's hiss. The sharp teeth came for his throat.

Jake twisted, and the teeth clamped down on one shoulder instead. Jake cried out from the piercing pain. The cat let go with its teeth, as if startled.

Haviland's shrill voice resonated. "Jake! I can't shoot. I'll hit you."

"Stay back!"

Jake couldn't reach his own rifle. The pistol in his belt was useless. It was loaded, but not capped. He'd never be able to get a cap out of the leather container on his belt and get it in place. The sheathed knife was his only chance—if he could reach it. He gripped the cat's neck, tried to hold it off with his left hand while reaching for the knife with his right. But the cat moved that right hand aside with its head as if Jake were no stronger than a child.

A thump echoed, and the panther backed off a little. Jake didn't know what had happened, but he used the moment to reach for his knife. He had it. More thumping. Haviland was hitting the beast. The cat gave another scream and bared its teeth once more. Jake tried to push the animal aside to get a better angle with the knife but couldn't get the blade past the thrashing feet.

The beast's yelp told Jake he'd nicked it, but not hard enough, just enough to make it angry, more determined. A snarl sent a chill through Jake, as the cat landed one mighty paw on his knife arm. The wide grinning jaws came for his throat again, and he lurched aside. The teeth closed on buckskin, and the cat lifted its head with a piece dangling from its mouth. In that instant of the cat's confusion, Jake used all his force to pull his right arm free of the great paw.

The cat spit out the buckskin and turned its teeth back to Jake's throat. Another thump. The cat paused. Jake aimed the knife upward and thrust toward the furry neck. The blade went home. The great beast let out a gasp, shuddered, and crumpled on top of Jake.

Haviland's voice reverberated. "Are you all right?"

Jake could scarcely draw breath beneath the animal's smothering weight. Then he felt the beast sliding off him.

Haviland was dragging the cat away. "Are you all right, Jake?"

"I—I think so." Jake wasn't altogether sure. His heart pounded in the fresh raw wounds, a sticky warmth spreading from the pain.

Haviland reached out a hand. "Can you get up?"

Letting Haviland do the lifting, Jake stood. Though weak and winded, he could stand on his own. He looked down at the dead beast, its pale fur catching the last shimmer of daylight so it appeared oddly luminescent.

"Is it the one?" Haviland asked. "The one that was wounded?"

Jake peered more closely. "Looks like an old wound on the side of the neck there, but it's getting pretty dark to see."

Haviland took his arm. "We'd better get down the hill, Jake, if you can make it."

Jake kept staring at the panther. "Wound may have weakened it." He gave Haviland a quick smile. "Sure would hate to fight a strong one."

The man huffed. "Oh, he was strong enough, I'd say. I just wish I could have helped you more. I didn't dare shoot. I tried to hit him with a big stick, but I don't think I fazed him."

"Oh, you did. If you hadn't distracted him with that stick, I don't think he'd ever have backed off enough so I could knife him." Jake raised a brow. "Looks like we got game after all. Panther meat is good."

Haviland nudged the animal with his toe. "I can carry him if you can walk on your own. Are you sure you're all right? I'm not much of a doctor, but maybe we should wrap up your wounds."

"We'd better go on. I can manage."

Haviland picked up the giant of a cat and slung it over his shoulders to head down the hill. The walk felt long. Pain throbbed with Jake's every step, as blood dribbled down his chest. He stumbled over roots and stones in the growing darkness.

By the time they came in sight of the town's glittering campfires, he could barely lift his feet. His knees had turned to mush and his whole body trembled, as if beneath a terrible weight. He staggered across the flat, straight toward the Haviland campfire. He was surprised to see his friend Joe Meek outside the tent.

Joe looked up, eyes widening on sight of him. "My heavens! What happened to ye, old hoss?"

Others clustered around, gaping at Haviland with the cat around his shoulders, then at Jake, and back at Haviland as he dropped the animal at their feet. Their mouths hung open, eyes questioning, while they seemed to have lost the capacity for speech—except Joe.

Brows raised, Joe leaned toward Jake. "It ain't rightly clear which one o' you fellers looks the worst fer wear, you or this painter here." His voice lowered. "Are ye all right, son?"

Jake let out a long breath. "It was a close one, but I'm all right."

Eddie found his tongue. "What—well, what happened, Jake?" He glanced at his pa. "I mean, Mr. Johnston."

"Cat jumped me. Had to fight him off. Thanks to your pa here we got the best of him."

Haviland brushed a hand aside. "No thanks to me. Jake fought this one single-handed. I just hit the thing a couple of times with a stick. Don't think it even noticed me."

Mrs. Haviland stepped closer to Jake, urgency in her tone. "You'd better sit down, Mr. Johnston, and let us tend to you. It appears you're hurt. Jennie, run get some water and rags and some of that bear fat."

Jennie hesitated, her gaze fixed on him, then pivoted away to disappear into the tent. Jake realized Haviland and Joe had taken hold of him at either side, and feeling as if the starch had washed right out of him, he let them lead him nearer the campfire to sit on a log stump.

Eddie and Charlie plopped on the ground close by. "Is it the one?" Eddie asked. "The one that got Rosy last week?"

Jake looked at the cat. The old wound showed clearly in the light from the campfire. "Appears to be."

Charlie gazed up at Jake with beseeching eyes. "Tell us about it, will you, Jake? Please, Jake, will you?"

Jake smiled, but with waves of weakness rolling over him, he wished the boys had remained speechless.

Their mother scolded. "Don't bother Mr. Johnston about it now. Can't you see? He's hurt and doesn't feel like telling you stories, and please remember how to address your elders."

Joe cleared his throat in a meaningful way. "Critters. They shore kin be mighty pesky. I kin recollect a bar or two as got mighty pesky, *I* kin. Ain't never tangled with a painter, though."

Eddie and Charlie, responding to the compelling tone of a true storyteller about to launch into his specialty, turned their eyes to Joe. "Would you tell us some, Joe?" Charlie lowered his chin almost to his chest. "Mr. Meek, I mean."

Jake grinned, then became aware of Jennie kneeling next to her mother in front of him. Jennie handed her mother a bucket of water, a handful of rags, and a kettle of grease.

Mrs. Haviland reached toward Jake. "We'll have to take this shirt off."

He tugged at his shirt. "That's all right."

Together they peeled off the torn buckskin and the flannel shirt under it, every motion sending new stabs of pain into his flesh. When they exposed his bare chest, Jennie's eyes grew wide, her brow twisted. Looking down at himself, Jake winced at the sight. Gashes sliced across his chest, while puncture wounds from the cat's teeth created dark-red blots on his shoulder. Blood had dripped and smeared over much of his torso, and still oozed from the deepest cuts.

He gave Jennie a tenuous smile. "Afraid I'm not too pretty." He flinched when Mrs. Haviland touched the wet rag to an open wound. Clenching his teeth together, he tried to present a stoic front while she worked, and he sought solace in the expression of sympathy in Jennie's clear blue eyes.

She seemed to be a remarkable young woman. In the days since the Havilands had been here, he'd heard her visiting with her ma from time to time and got the idea she was like her pa in being a thinking person, not so given to the frilly notions he'd observed in most young ladies he'd known in the States. He admired that in her. But she kept her distance from him and turned quiet whenever he came near.

Now he scarcely noticed when the boys' attention left him as they pried a story out of Joe. At the sound of Joe's melodic drawl, Jake listened too, though still aware of Jennie so close by.

"Well, I do recollect one hard winter," Joe said, "and bein' near to starvin', me an' the fellers that's winterin' with me. Why, if'n ye think you're short o' meat here—my heavens, we hadn't found meat in a heap o' time, *we* hadn't, and no biled wheat to fill our stomachs at that."

Charlie let out a big groan at the mention of boiled wheat.

Joe continued, talking with his hands in his usual way. "Well now, we go up on the side o' this old mount'in, tryin' to make our way on frozen snow, and doggone if'n we ain't thinkin' all the game has jist left the face o' the earth. Some fix we're in, I kin tell ye, but we keep our eyes skinned, and then, right thar afore us, what d'ye know but we see tracks in the snow. Bar tracks. Grizzly bar tracks. And ye know, boys, thar ain't nothin' more fierce'n a grizzly. But he's got meat, mind ye, a heap of it."

Joe nodded his head in one firm nod, looking at the boys as if defying them to disagree. Neither said a word.

"Well," Joe said, "we figger that old bar must've come out'n his winter den, so we follow his tracks and afore long we find the den, shore as you're sittin' thar. Yessir, a mighty big cave at that, and we figger thar's meat inside. Well now, we fellers take a look at each other, thar bein' four of us, and each one a-hopin' somebody else will come up with a right smart idea fer gittin' that meat out'n that den. Old Doughty finally speaks up, says he'll go up on the rocks above the mouth o' the cave and shoot the bar when he comes out if'n somebody else will go in and shoo him out."

Charlie's eyes went saucer wide. "Go in?"

Joe nodded, and Charlie visibly shuddered.

"Well now," Joe said, "keepin' company with grizzlies jist don't shine, and I'm skeered as any man would be in his right mind. But them fellers, they's a-lookin' at me, so what kin I do?

"'I'm yer man,' says I.

"'And I too,' Claymore says, not to be outdone.

"'Well now, I'll be dogged if'n I'm not as brave as any of ye,' Hawkins says.

"So, mind ye, we jist march right inside, all three of us, and let me tell ye, that cave's plenty big so's we can stand straight up, and mebbe sixteen or twenty feet square. And what d'ye figger we find?"

He looked at Charlie, then Eddie. Neither had an answer, but their eager faces begged him to go on. Jennie was listening intently too, and Jake smiled to himself.

Joe continued. "You thinkin' we found us'n a bar?"

Charlie nodded, but Joe shook his head.

"Nossir, mind ye, we don't find *a* bar," Joe said. "We find *three* bars!"

Eddie's hands flew upward. "Three?"

"Three. Yessir. They's a-standin' thar, all three, jist lookin' at us and growlin' kinda low-like, three of 'em, one bar apiece. Well now, we fellers, we're a-keepin' to the edge o' the cave so's not to be in the light from the openin', and this old coon jist happens to be in front o' the pack. It ain't sich a comfortable place to be, I kin tell ye. But I pulls out my wipin' stick from this trusty old rifle, and I reaches it out and taps the biggest old bar on the head."

To stress his point, Joe pulled the ramrod from the rifle that lay beside him and tapped it gently on Eddie's head. Eddie didn't move a muscle.

Charlie grabbed Joe's arm. "What'd he do?"

"What's that?" Joe asked.

"What'd the bear do?"

"Why, he runs right out'n that cave like he's s'pose to, *he* does."

"And that man up on top shoots it?"

"Oh, he shoots it all right. He does at that. Hows'ever, that old bar, he jist turns 'round slick and comes right back in the den, madder'n ever fer bein' hit, jist snortin' and runnin' in circles. By gor, if'n that ain't some, now, I wouldn't say so. Well now, nobody asks, I kin tell ye. All three of us, we shoot, and all three of us kills that'un right thar on the spot."

Charlie sighed with relief, then looked worried again. "But the other bears."

"Yessir. That's right, boy. Thar'd be two more and our rifles empty. Old Hawkins, though, he's in sich high spirits fer killin' the first one, he begins to hallo and dance 'round, and he's jist laughin' like ever'thing whilst he goes up and strikes the next bar. And then, what d'ye know but the next bar runs on outside, and do ye hear, now, Old Doughty kills it. Well, we git our rifles loaded ag'in and jist one more bar.

"Old Hawkins, he's showin' his excitement plain as beaver sign, *he* is. 'We're all Daniels in the lions' den and no mistake,' he says.

"And we're all a-feelin' right smart when we drive out the third bar and three of us shoot him at once. Thrown cold, they are now, all three. And if'n them doin's don't shine, I'm dogged. Yessir!

"And Old Hawkins, he's a-goin' some now, *he* is. 'Daniel was a humbug,' says Hawkins. 'We're as good Daniels as he ever dared to be. Hurrah for these Daniels!'

"Yessir, them critters kin be mighty pesky, *they* kin, but ye don't have to let 'em git the best of ye, as ye kin see over yonder." He nodded toward the panther lying by the tent where Haviland had dropped it.

The boys' grinning faces gave Joe his desired response, and Jake caught sight of a fleeting smile on Jennie's face. Mrs. Haviland was wrapping Jake's wounds, after cleaning them with water and rubbing in bear grease for healing. The pain had subsided a little while Joe's story offered distraction.

Charlie scooted toward Jake. "Would you tell us about the panther now?"

Mrs. Haviland tapped her son's shoulder. "Later, Charlie." She motioned to Jennie. "Why don't you get one of Pa's shirts for Mr. Johnston. Get that new one. It's bigger than the others."

Jennie leaped to her feet and hurried into the tent, returning in a moment with a folded shirt made of sturdy blue hickory cloth. Jake thanked her and put the shirt on with a little help from her mother. It fit snug but covered him. He wanted to say more, but the two slipped away, back inside the tent. He let out a long, slow breath. The women seemed to maintain a barrier, like a heavy wall, between themselves and him. Just when he'd thought they might drop that wall, it rose again.

He was torn between a desire for truth and a desire to be accepted as he was now. He and the friends he'd chosen. Old memories pricked at him like a cat's angry claws.

Jake held the log in his lap while he worked the broadax to shape a notch at the log's end. The better the notching, the tighter the fit and the less chinking they would need. An occasional streak of pain shot through his shoulders from his bout with the panther the night before, but he could work. The Havilands were anxious to get their cabin built, and he wanted to do what he could to help. He and George Haviland were working alone, since Haviland had let the boys off early this evening to go hunting. With the wounded panther dead, the man had relented.

Jake observed the quiet strength in Haviland as the man notched another log. Graying hair had begun to thin on top, but a fierce intensity lit his blue eyes. Though Jake guessed him to be unaccustomed to hard labor, the man wasn't afraid of it. And given the set jaw, Jake had a feeling no one ever pushed George Haviland around.

A soft, clear voice interrupted Jake's thoughts. "Would you like some water?" Jennie.

Jake looked up into eyes blue like her father's, with that same fierce intensity, but framed with long eyelashes in a lovely feminine face. He smiled. She set her jaw more prettily, but the effect was the same. And those eyes could shoot fire right through a fellow.

When she handed him the tin cup of water, he thankfully took a drink before passing it on to Mr. Haviland.

She brushed a few stray hairs off her forehead. "Eddie and Charlie aren't back yet?"

"Not yet," her father answered.

"Ma's getting worried. It's a bit late, isn't it?"

Haviland pulled out his watch and frowned. "It is late. Wonder what's keeping them."

She looked toward the ridge above town. "Did they take the trail above the bluff?"

Jake set down his log. "Yes, they did. Maybe I—"

"I should go after them," Jennie said.

Her pa made a sound like a low growl. "You can't go up there alone."

Jake stood. "I could go." He picked up the dark-navy wool coat he'd gotten to replace his ruined buckskin and slipped it on.

She frowned at him. That wall again. "But I—"

He gestured toward the bluff. "You can go with me. You could—" Jake sought a way to make this acceptable, and brightened at a thought. "Why don't you bring Davie? He'd enjoy it, I'm sure. And your ma might appreciate one less to watch for a little while."

Haviland nodded, his voice decisive. "Yes, Jennie. That's a fine idea. Run get Davie and you go with Jake."

She hesitated, but didn't argue. Wheeling about, she dashed for the tent and soon came out with Davie in her arms. Jake slung his powder horn and bullet pouch over his shoulder, grabbed his rifle, and reached out to take the boy in the other arm, resting the child's small weight on his hip to avoid the injuries from the cat. He gave Jennie a slight bow and smiled. "Shall we go?"

With only the merest flicker at the corner of her lips, she pulled her shawl tight around her shoulders and fell in step beside him. Their footsteps almost sounded loud despite the soft ground. He tried to think of something to say to her, and had a sudden wish that he'd chosen a better coat at the Hudson's Bay Company store. Would she find that more presentable? But this one was practical, durable, and cheap, and he had no real use for anything fancier. He smiled at young Davie. Just five, wasn't he? The boy smiled back but remained as quiet as his sister.

A thick haze reddened the eastern sky from the Indian fires. They burned great swaths of prairie every fall to keep the brush down and improve the grass for game, also making it easier to find the camas and other root plants that provided a major source of food for them. The scent of smoke lay heavy on the air.

At the rocky bluff Jake let Jennie go ahead on the narrow trail. On the top where they stepped into the trees, the pathway turned moist and he could see tracks. A damp chill gripped him beneath the conifers, and he detected a shiver in Jennie as she clasped her shawl tight.

He moved up beside her. "Warm enough?"

"I'm all right."

"You could use my coat if—"

"I'll be fine."

He nodded and continued in silence, glancing from time to time at the upturned tilt of her chin. A flash of memory reminded him of the reception he and Joe had received from the missionary ladies in Oregon. They didn't hide their contempt for the trappers from the Rockies—as if the men were nothing but savages. He gave his head a little shake. Jennie wasn't like that, was she?

He decided to jump right into the fire. "Pardon me, Miss Jennie, but it occurs to me you aren't very friendly."

She stopped and stared at him. "Well, I—I—well—"

"Why not?"

"Well, I'm not—" Her cheeks flushed a brighter pink. "I don't know what you expect."

"Have I offended you?"

"Well, no, I—"

"You're not unfriendly to all men, I've noticed."

She reared her head back, brow knit. "What do you mean by that?"

He gave her a quick wry smile. "You seemed most friendly toward the Britisher the other night—that Radford fellow."

Her cheeks flushed even brighter, her words sharp. "What right have you to—Jake Johnston, you *are* offensive. And you wonder why I'm not friendly?"

He set the boy down on the trail and reached out to lay a gentle hand on her shoulder. She started to draw away, but he held her there. "Miss Jennie, I'm sorry. I wasn't meaning to be. I'd like to be your friend. You may need a friend sometime."

She looked down at Davie and stroked her fingers over the boy's silky crown of dark hair before looking back into Jake's eyes. "I don't need looking out for."

He released her shoulder and gestured with a broad sweep at the surrounding woods. "It's rugged country. Many dangers—panthers, as you know, and bears. Indians haven't given us any cause for alarm here, but there's trouble in the interior, and that could affect the local tribes." He raised a brow. "Even some white men may be dangerous."

The firmer set of her chin suggested she might be placing Jake in the latter category, and he tried to smile his chivalrous best.

A rifle shot startled them both. Then a discordant squawking noise.

Jennie turned to Jake, eyes round. "What is that?"

"Sounds like geese. Maybe the boys got something." He tried to keep his tone cheerful in spite of the uneasiness niggling at him. Scooping up Davie, he headed toward the ruckus with long strides. If the boys wounded something big, they could be in trouble. The squawking moved closer until several giant white birds swept overhead. "It's geese, all right, on their way south for the winter."

The birds weren't in vee formation and their loud squawks showed their distress. Jake broke into a run toward the source of the gunfire. In a small open meadow, he caught sight of the two young hunters. Something about the scene worried him, and when Jennie reached his side he handed Davie to her.

"I'll go ahead," he told her. "Wait here."

"What's wrong?"

"Probably nothing. Just wait."

"But—"

"Please?"

Jake stepped out of the trees toward the boys, rifle in one hand. Charlie was on his knees, bent over something, while Eddie stood nearby fidgeting, shifting from one foot to the other.

Jake called out to them. "Eddie? Charlie?"

Eddie turned to face him, but Charlie didn't turn around. Charlie's shoulders trembled, as if the boy were crying.

Jake strode closer. "Are you hurt, Charlie?"

The round blond head shook slightly to indicate the negative.

Eddie spoke up. "He—uh—shot a bird."

Jake stopped directly behind Charlie. A huge white bird lay in front of the child. Bright-crimson blood oozed in a row of drops, like a string of rubies at the back of the bird's neck. Jake went down on one knee and reached over Charlie to stroke his fingers across the fine white feathers. "Beautiful, isn't it?" Jake said.

Charlie nodded, shoulders still shaking, still not facing Jake. A telltale sniffle told Jake the boy was indeed crying, and Jake kept his voice soft but natural. "A snow goose. They're not easy to hit. Did you get him in the air?"

Charlie nodded again but didn't speak.

Eddie filled in the silence. "They were flying low."

Jake pursed his lips. "Probably going down to water. Ever kill one before, Charlie?"

The boy's head moved slowly from side to side, and Jake continued to stroke the silken feathers, being careful to stay behind Charlie so he couldn't see the boy's face. A nice bird, almost two feet in length, the span of the black-tipped wings probably five feet. The long slender neck, so graceful in flight, lay lifeless on the ground.

A tightness gripped Jake's throat. "I remember the first deer I ever killed. I'd never killed anything before, and was I ever excited. I'd hit him square and he fell right down. A good shot, I figured, a real good shot. Well, I ran up to him, so proud, and when I got to him I saw he wasn't dead yet, and he looked up at me with those big brown eyes, and all of a sudden it occurred to me this big beautiful critter would never run again. I'd put an end to that, and his eyes seemed to accuse me. You know what I did?"

Charlie shook his head again, and Jake's voice turned hoarse. "I got down on my knees beside him and I petted him and I told him I was sorry." Jake swallowed. "And I cried."

Charlie swung around to face Jake, tears streaming down his red, chubby cheeks, his words broken with sobs. "He won't ever . . . fly pretty again . . . will he . . . Jake?"

"No, but you see, we need the meat, and there's lots of good meat here. You're providing your family with food so your family can live."

Charlie looked down at the bird, and back into Jake's eyes. "Did you really cry?"

Jake nodded and cleared his throat.

The boy rested a hand on the bird, then reached his chubby fingers around the bird's legs and stood with it. Jake picked up the boys' rifle from the ground nearby and handed it to Eddie. Only then did he see Jennie standing right behind them, Davie clutched in one hand. She hadn't stayed put as he'd asked her to, and she was looking at him with furrowed brow, as if she didn't quite know what to make of him.

Jake stared back a moment, but he had no more words. He lifted young Davie and started toward the trail after Eddie and Charlie, the bird now clasped between the two, and Jennie kept pace beside him.

Chapter Four

Willamette River, October 1842. Alan sat low in the canoe, one hand gripping the pup's collar, the other stroking its silky ears. The dog huddled against the crook of Alan's leg, panting softly, watching the shore for any sign of excitement. A good little dog. Alan's friend Barnaby had gladly offered this one, last of the litter from Barnaby's fine bulldog bitch. She'd had an unplanned encounter with one of the Indian dogs that hung around outside the fort, so the pups had a look of their own. Longer noses, slimmer bodies than the mother. But this one had her fine red and white color.

The dog swiveled in the canoe, ears pricked. Alan held tighter. "What is it, boy?"

Alan finally caught the sound the dog must have heard. A slow crescendo of rushing water. The falls. Lévêque gave a quick look back at the dog, a faint sneer on his thin lips. Alan suppressed a smile. The catlike man didn't like dogs. If things went well, Lévêque wouldn't have to tolerate this one much longer.

Alan gave the animal a quick embrace. "Good boy. You're doing fine."

Almost a year old, the animal was well mannered. Barnaby had a way with dogs, and this pup had always been agreeable.

The roar heightened until it pulsed through Alan's body. A quick turn and the falls came in view, the little town snuggled close by on the flat below the bluff with its bristle of trees at the top. Many log walls had risen from the ground since Alan's last visit. More cabins nearing completion. His gaze riveted on the Haviland site. A peaked skeleton of pole rafters rose above their tidy rectangle of log walls.

He held the dog closer. "Very well indeed."

As soon as the canoe bumped ashore, Alan grabbed the leash and jumped out, the dog leaping after him. Pausing just long enough to give his men leave, Alan bounded up the bank, the dog at his side, and headed straight for the Haviland cabin. The new-cut wood gave off a pleasant aroma. George Haviland peered out the open doorway and tilted his head in greeting. Alan could hear the two older boys chatting inside and wondered if the whole family was there.

"Mr. Haviland," he said, "I hope you're well on this fine day. And the family."

"We are, yes, thank you." Mr. Haviland glanced at the dog.

Alan bent down to touch the animal's head. "I should ask you first, sir. I know your boys were missing their dog, and my colleague at the fort had this nice pup out of his fine bulldog."

Mr. Haviland lifted a brow and cast a closer look at the animal.

Alan smiled. "This one's a cross, I'm afraid, due to his mother's encounter with an Indian dog, but very gentle and well mannered. Almost a year old. With your permission, sir, I'd like to give him to the boys." Alan stopped and took a long breath.

Mr. Haviland said nothing for a considerable length of time, then nodded. "I'm sure they'll appreciate your generous offer." He turned and spoke into the room. "Eddie, Charlie, you'd better come outside."

The two came to the doorway and peered around their father. Both faces lit up on sight of the dog.

"Mr. Radford has something for you," their father said.

"For us?" The words spilled out in unison, and both plunged through the opening, straight to Alan and his little furry companion.

Alan bent down to hold the dog as still as possible while both boys dropped to their knees, hands out. The dog wagged its tail so hard, the whole body shook. It leaped into the open arms, and Alan let go, laughing to see a nugget of tumbling, giggling boys and a delighted pup licking faces and wagging and rolling in the mix.

Mr. Haviland walked over to look down at them, a smile softening the lines of his face. "I think you could say the meeting was agreeable."

Alan stood. "I think you could say so, sir." He peered into the cabin, but saw no one else.

Mr. Haviland, noticing the direction of Alan's gaze, set his jaw a little tighter. "The womenfolk have gone over to the Wallers' with the little boys. They'll be visiting for a while, I would imagine."

A nettling warmth scuttled across Alan, but he maintained a calm expression. "Well, sir, maybe that's a good thing. I was wanting to talk with you a moment in private, if I may."

A high-pitched voice interrupted. "Mr. Radford."

Alan turned to see Eddie looking up at him. "Yes?"

"Does he have a name?"

Alan smiled at the boy, glad to see a bit of the barrier dropped between them. "My friend Barnaby called him Muffin. But you can name him whatever you like. He belongs to you and your brothers now."

Charlie giggled. "Muffin. Hello, Muffin. I'm Charlie." The dog licked Charlie's nose, and the child laughed harder.

Their father grunted. "Did I hear a thank you, boys? Mind your manners, now."

They offered quick thanks and polite smiles, and Alan wasn't sure if the barrier had fallen entirely. Maybe he was oversensitive. Such social conventions were never quite comfortable for youngsters. He recalled that from his own youth. But never had a social convention gripped him more than the one he faced now.

His throat filled and he tried to clear it. "Mr. Haviland, about that matter I wanted to—"

"Yes, you had something to say to me."

"Sir, it's—" Alan smoothed his frock coat. "Well, I wanted to ask if I might court your daughter."

Mr. Haviland straightened and faced him, gaze direct. Time seemed reluctant to pass. The two men stood staring at each other. Alan couldn't move. The sound of the boys and their dog drifted in a far distance. A slow frown carved deeper lines in the man's brow. When finally Haviland spoke, his voice didn't sound as Alan remembered it. "Are you wanting to court her with the intention of marriage?"

The word sent a jolt through Alan. *Marriage.* Had he even thought that far? "I—I—of course we need to get to know each other, but if—if everything goes well, I guess that's ... the logical outcome." Alan clamped his teeth together. He hadn't put that quite the way he intended, and Mr. Haviland didn't appear impressed.

The man's frown hardened. "And do you intend to go back to London? That's a terrible distance to think of sending a daughter."

Alan lifted both hands, then brought them back to his coat when they began shaking. "I see opportunities here in Oregon—at least north of the Columbia River."

"You think your people are in Oregon to stay, then?"

"I should rather think so."

"And if the boundary settlement doesn't go to your liking?"

Alan took the edge of his lapel and began rubbing a thumb over the soft wool. "Sir, the British have been in this country for years. We're well established north of the Columbia." He tried to smile. "It shouldn't be a difficult journey to visit her across the river."

"And you'd consider staying in this far country, giving up London, your home, all for my daughter who you scarcely know?"

Alan lifted his hands again. "That would be the reason for the courting, I think, to know her better, and—sir, I am at home in this wilderness. Or can be."

Mr. Haviland's expression reflected a tangle of emotions that Alan tried to read. Concern? Surprise? Disbelief? Finally the man nodded. "I'll talk to my daughter. If she wants this, I'll allow it." His gruff voice had dropped so low, Alan struggled to make out the words. For a moment he stood deciphering them, unaware of their meaning.

Then realizing, he took a sudden breath. "Thank you, sir. I'll be kind to her, sir. I assure you."

Haviland started to turn away, but he spun around to face Alan again. "You hurt my daughter, I'll have your head on a platter."

Alan swallowed, unable to answer.

Jennie looked up from stirring mud for chinking the cabin walls. She had to smile. There Ma was, adding a touch of color, setting out plants around her cabin before it was even finished, as if they hadn't enough natural greenery around them, with all the trees and the profusion of brambles that threatened to take over their small settlement faster than they could build it.

Ma tamped dirt over the last of the starts Mrs. Waller had given her and stood back to survey her work. "Makes the cabin look kind of homey, doesn't it?"

Jennie rubbed a little mud off her wrist. "Looks nice, Ma. When can we move in?"

"Soon, I hope. Tent life is about to do me in."

Jennie studied the trim structure. Pa had done a fine job carving out the windows on either side, and the doorway at the end, Pa and Jake. A gable of logs rose at each end, rafters forming a triangle for the peaked roof and the floor of the loft where the boys would sleep. "Why can't we move in now? Even like this it's better than the tent."

"Oh, I think I'd rather have a roof first. Good thing the rains have held off, but that can't last."

Shocks of peeled cedar bark, tied with braided buckskin rope, lay beside the eastern wall. The bark would serve as a temporary roof until Pa could make shakes. "I wonder how long it'll take to put the roof on."

"Not long. Jake told your father he'd seen cedar-bark roofs laid in little more than an hour. I do hope they get it roofed soon. After all, if you're to be courted, we do need a proper house." A twinkle lit Ma's soft hazel eyes.

Trying to ignore the odd currents Ma's words ignited, Jennie added more water to the mixture she was stirring and reached in with both hands to knead it to the right consistency, the acrid smell of wet soil rising like steam. Her youngest brother reached in beside her to help. "Robbie make mud," he said, wiping a muddy hand across his brow and smiling up at her.

Jennie couldn't help laughing. "Oh, Robbie, you're such a mess."

He giggled and continued to attack the job with enthusiasm. Intent on Robbie, Jennie brushed stray wisps of hair out of her face, forgetting the mud on her own hands. She felt it smudge her cheek and attempted to wipe it off. The more she wiped, the more she smeared.

Robbie squealed. "Oh, Jennie has mud." He threw his hands upward as he spoke, and mud splattered from his hands to hit Jennie on the chin and down her neck.

"Robbie, be careful."

Eddie sauntered up, grinning. "What happened to you, Jen?"

"Go on, Eddie." She motioned with her hand, accidentally flinging mud into his face.

He put on a wicked grin. "If it's war you want—" Scooping up a big wad of the muck, he brought it straight down the front of her from her forehead to the middle of her dress.

Jennie reached out with her own muddy hands and grabbed her brother's throat while Robbie shrieked with delight.

Their mother scolded. "Eddie, Jennie. For goodness sakes, quit that."

Their father called out. "Let's have that mud over here."

"Right away, Pa," Eddie answered, swiping a sleeve across his face, for all the good it did. He scooped up a bucketful and gave his sister a triumphant grin as he headed back to the cabin.

Taking the rag her mother handed her, Jennie attempted to clean her own face, without much success, and when she looked up she clasped the rag against the bodice of her dress. Pa and Jake were observing her, their amusement not well hidden. Then all was business again. The boys went back to putting mud in the cracks between the logs, while Jake and Pa set three-cornered strips of wood over the mud in each crack, pegging the strips so the chinking would hold.

Ma joined Jennie to help stir mud, and Jennie dipped her hands again into the gooey mixture, kneading it like bread dough. At least it offered something to do to keep her mind off other things.

"I'm so happy for you," Ma said, jolting Jennie's thoughts back to those other things. "He's such a lovely man."

Jennie envisioned the handsome face, the crown of golden hair, the fine frame of the man who filled his clothes so well. He'd be here tonight to see her. What would she say to him? She'd never been courted before.

Ma went on. "Your father was a bit reluctant, but don't you worry. Fathers are always reluctant to think about their daughters being courted."

Recalling the coldness she had noted when Alan joined them for supper, Jennie supposed the hostility wasn't too serious or Pa wouldn't have consented to Alan's courtship of her.

As Ma talked she never missed a stroke in her steady kneading. "You know, Jennie, what really worried me about coming west was that you, my dear, so close to marriageable age, wouldn't have the chance to meet the right kind of man. But here in this wild country we find one like Alan Radford. So cultured and refined." She paused for a breath. "My dear, I don't think I've ever seen a more beautiful man in my life."

Jennie squeezed the mud through her fingers and watched the squishy ribbons slither back with the rest.

Ma leaned toward her. "Don't you think he is?"

Jennie kept her eyes on the mud. "Yes." When her father had spoken to her about the man's offer, he'd left it up to her. "I won't stop it if that's what you want," Pa had said, "but I won't require it of you either."

She wondered what the courtship would amount to and wasn't entirely sure why she had agreed to it. *There must be something more for a woman in this world than having a man.* But if she had to have one, he did seem rather fine, all right. She'd always supposed she would marry someday, but later—after she finished school and did something interesting.

Looking toward the unfinished cabin, Jennie tried to imagine it finished. Maybe it would turn into the sort of place where he might call upon her. Certainly it was going to be a humble dwelling compared to the frame house they'd left in New York.

Pa had assured them the family would have another frame house one day, a house every bit as fine as the one they'd left, the log cabin providing only temporary shelter until they had the time and money to build a proper house. Jennie looked at the bench of land upon which other cabins stood in various stages of construction. Everyone did it this way. In fact, she had yet to see a real house in this country and wondered if anyone would ever get around to building real houses. Would the country ever be truly civilized?

Her mother's decisive voice brought Jennie's attention back to the mundane business at hand. "This all looks about right now. Let's go help with the chinking." Piling mud on slabs of bark because they had no more buckets or kettles, Jennie and her mother scooted the slabs beside one cabin wall, and together they filled cracks.

Robbie, never far away, moved a little closer. "Robbie help?"

Jennie smiled at him. "Sure, Robbie can help. Just in the cracks, though. Don't get it all over the logs." The little hands were surprisingly careful, and Davie, not to be outdone by a younger brother, quietly began helping too.

Pa ambled around the corner and watched them. "Coming right along. This is the last wall." He paused to look at Ma's planting efforts. "Well! What's all this greenery, Catherine?"

"Something to make it homey." Her eyes brightened. "They should do well in your year-round paradise."

He let out a laugh.

Ma nodded toward the cabin. "So, you've finished the other walls, have you?"

"Yes, the boys are doing a good job—notwithstanding a little time out for war." He grinned at Jennie. "They had to have some help where they couldn't reach the top, but they've done good work. If it keeps going this well, I'd say we'll be moving in by tomorrow or the next day."

Tomorrow! Jennie smiled up at her father, but her smile faded as the fine form of Alan Radford appeared at her father's side.

Mr. Radford bowed graciously. "How do you do?"

When he looked closer at Jennie, his composure vanished, his eyes widening. Jennie was acutely aware of the mud smeared over her face and dress, hair straggling loose from the bun she'd pinned in the back. And here stood this refined gentleman, impeccable in a gray-blue cape, a smart-fitting navy frock coat beneath, pale-blue satin vest and cravat over a spotless white tucked-front shirt, and gray trousers without a wrinkle— let alone a speck.

Jennie wanted to sink right into the ground out of his sight. The look of shock on his face slowly softened, and she thought his mouth was about to turn up into a smile.

She clenched her teeth. *He'd better not laugh.*

"What happened?" he asked, maintaining a straight face.

Jennie took a deep breath and looked around for Eddie, the heat of anger rising in her cheeks.

"I believe we had a minor war," Pa said.

Alan Radford's dark-golden brows arched. "Indeed." After an awkward silence, he gave Jennie a quick smile. "I—uh—I was wondering, Miss Haviland, if you'd like to take a stroll, but—well, perhaps a little later, eh? It appears you're busy yet."

Her mother spoke up, tone light. "Jennie can go now if she likes. Jennie, why don't you wash up and—"

"But, Ma, my dress."

"You can go in the tent and change—that is, if Mr. Radford has time to wait."

"I—well, yes, ma'am, of course. I have plenty of time."

Jennie glanced from him to Pa, whose chin jutted forward. Then she noticed Jake. His expression defied description. She tried to read it and couldn't. She didn't know if he was amused or perturbed or what. Why it mattered, she didn't know, but for some reason she kept trying to guess what he must be thinking. Then she forced herself to look away from the three men who stood watching her and saw instead her mother's reassuring smile. "Run along, honey," Ma said. "Eddie can walk with you and Mr. Radford, can't you, Eddie?"

Jennie spun, mouth open, to stare at her troublesome brother.

His face twisted and he answered in a choked voice. "Me? Why me?"

Pa grunted. "Because your mother said so. They'll need the company, and you have the time." He turned to Ma. "I'll help you here, Mrs. Haviland."

Jennie recognized Pa's words as her dismissal. No doubt he'd have preferred she stay to help, and she'd have preferred it as well. But, excusing herself, she hurried to the river to wash.

Back in the tent she pinned her hair back up and donned her best linsey-woolsey dress, a lovely dark blue, but hopelessly wrinkled from being packed so long. Looking down at her ragged boots, she debated whether to change into her dainty black flat-heeled dress slippers. The slippers weren't good for walking, but the boots were so worn the leather had almost no color, and several holes let her stockings show through. She longed for Utica where she could have made herself presentable.

Hearing the sound of her mother humming outside, Jennie stepped back so she wouldn't be seen when the tent door flap opened.

Ma smiled at her daughter, voice cheery. "About ready?"

"About. But my dress and boots—"

"You look wonderful, my dear." Ma reached out to smooth the bun in her daughter's hair. "You're beautiful. And he's waiting outside."

Jennie's heart pounded, her throat tightening. But with chin held high, she opened the door flap and stepped out.

He smiled, tipping his tall beaver hat, and extended an elbow to her. "Miss Haviland, you do look lovely, to be sure."

She glanced down to see that her skirt was hiding her boots, and returned the smile. "Well, I guess I look better than I did a few minutes ago."

His warm laughter put her at ease, and she took his arm. Eddie, source of her troubles, stood a few paces behind Alan, one shoulder up, head tilted, the skew of his lips making it obvious he wasn't enjoying this. It gave her the slightest pleasure to know that.

As Alan led her away from the tent, he bent his head closer to her. "A fine day, isn't it? Perfect for a walk, wouldn't you say?" The words in his British accent sounded crisp and clear as the sweet fall air.

"Lovely, yes."

"I trust you don't mind me calling on you so early in the day, but I'd finished my work and didn't want to miss this sunny afternoon with you."

"Oh, I don't mind." Her response belied the distress his earliness had caused, but she hoped he didn't notice the false note.

He seemed oblivious—or polite about it—and continued. "Have you ever taken the trail above the bluff?"

"I have. We actually came into Willamette Falls that way. It's a pleasant walk."

"So it is. Capital views of the falls. And we might be able to see Mount Hood. It's clear enough today, I should think. Would you like to go that way?"

"I would, thank you. Yes." She recalled the day she walked up that trail with Jake and found the boys with the goose, how hazy it had been. "The Indians must be done with their burning."

Alan lifted a brow. "I'd say so."

He glanced over his shoulder, and she followed his gaze to see her brother lagging far behind. Alan bent closer, voice low. "Your brother seems a reluctant chaperon."

She laughed. "I think it's not his favorite way to pass time. And it looks like Pa didn't even let him bring the dog—a very nice gift, by the way."

"I was happy to do it. The dog needed a home, and the home needed a dog, eh?" He gave her a long look, his mouth showing the slightest tilt, but his eyes smiled with the warmth of a summer sun on this crisp day. "So, my dear, I don't quite know where I can escort you around here. Willamette Falls may be lacking in social events for a while."

Her heart fluttered at his expression of endearment, and he went on. "We will have parties at Fort Vancouver. Perhaps you can go to some of those."

"Isn't that pretty far away?"

He shrugged. "Only a day by canoe." Moving a hand to her back, he gently encouraged her ahead of him on the narrow bluff trail.

She turned her head slightly to speak to him as they climbed. "There aren't roads or trails?"

"Trails, yes, but water travel is faster. It's rather thickly forested between here and Fort Vancouver, and of course you still have the Columbia River to cross."

"Aren't there houses along the way? Or farms?" Willamette Falls was the only settlement in the territory that resembled a town, though she'd heard of clusters of farms west on Tualatin Plains and south at French Prairie, and there were a few Methodist Mission stations.

"There may well be a cabin or two, but it's not good farmland in that direction until you cross the Columbia. We have a fine prairie around the fort. I presume that's why Dr. McLoughlin chose the site."

Jennie glanced toward the flat below, where she could see a couple of canoes tied at the riverbank. A sudden sense of isolation clutched her. But when they reached the top where the trail meandered into the woods, Alan returned to her side, and she gladly took his arm again, comfortable in his company.

The clarity of the air enhanced every color today, sharpened every shadow, and she thrilled to a beauty she had scarcely noticed before. This dense forest, which had felt so forbidding on that first day, had somehow changed. Was it the way the light shone now? Perhaps some leaves had fallen, making the foliage less enclosing. The fragrance of evergreen seemed soft now, pleasant.

The trail wound past picturesque rocks, glittering rays of sunlight finding a way through the thick boughs to diffuse in tiny beams of light. Magical, but so untamed. Could she ever feel at home here?

The gentleman beside her seemed as out of place in this wilderness as she felt. It was something they shared. She held his arm a little tighter. He was easier to talk to than she'd ever imagined, and delightful, his charming accent falling over her ears like the twinkling strains of a bright melody.

When they neared the clearing where Charlie had shot the goose, Alan placed a hand on her back again and smiled. "We should be able to see Mount Hood through those trees ahead."

She turned to look for her brother and caught a brief glimpse. He appeared to be studying a branch, then stepped out of her sight. Alan's arm came around her shoulder, and she didn't object.

As they moved toward the meadow, she pondered how different courting might have been if she were at home and this same Alan Radford called upon her there. Back home he could have escorted her to some event like a formal ball. Or visited her in the pleasant parlor they had in their Utica home. As a young girl she used to imagine courting and the elegant dresses she would wear—perfectly pressed, of course. She laughed to herself. No, she hadn't ever considered whether her dress might be pressed. No dream would include such imperfection as a rumpled dress.

At the meadow's edge, her thoughts vanished with the wonder of the view. Rising above the meadow's tweed of green and gold, between a line of dark, pointy conifers and a vivid blue sky, the sharp cone stood poised, traces of white marking its gray stone crevices. Mount Hood.

She sighed and turned to express her appreciation to Alan. He was gazing not at the mountain, but at her. With his arm around her back, he drew her tighter against his side, his face close, little crinkles around his eyes and mouth. "There is fine beauty to be found in Oregon."

The exquisite lines of his face nearly took her breath, and she smiled. "Yes. There is."

A firm voice sounded behind. "Well, hello." She leaped aside, out of Alan's grasp. She knew that voice, that drawl. She spun around to face the source of the greeting. Jake Johnston stood watching them, with brows high. He continued in his slow, mellow way of speaking. "I thought I'd come along and keep Eddie company, maybe look for a little game at the same time. Seems Eddie's having a little trouble keeping up with you two."

Jennie frowned. "Game? I thought—" Wasn't Jake helping Pa with the cabin? Suspicion began to burn. He was following her and Alan.

Jake rubbed a hand over his chin. "I'm not meaning to barge in on you."

Doubting his sincerity, she turned to Alan. A glimmer of anger reddened Alan's face. "Quite all right," he told Jake. "We were simply enjoying the scenery."

Eddie leaned against a nearby tree to watch, his gaze flashing from one speaker to the next, a tiny smirk on his lips.

Jake's dark eyes glinted. "Don't suppose you've seen sign of game."

"No," Alan said, "but perhaps you'll find something if you keep looking, eh?"

Jake gave no indication he intended to leave. He propped his rifle on the ground and rested a hand on it to gaze in the direction of Mount Hood. "Pretty thing, isn't it?"

Alan nodded. "Yes. Well—"

"Nice day too."

An edge sounded in Alan's voice. "Indeed."

Jake lifted his face, brow furrowed. "Wind's shifting. We may get a little rain before dark."

Rain? Jennie couldn't imagine it raining on such a lovely day. Not a cloud in sight. She hadn't noticed any breeze at all, but she felt it now, coming out of the west, from the direction of the coastal waters of the great Pacific Ocean.

Jake grunted softly. "If you don't want to get wet, it might not hurt to think about heading back."

Alan held a hand out to her. "Perhaps we should leave, Miss Haviland."

She took his hand and let him tuck her fingers into the crook of his elbow. Giving her brother a frown, she motioned ahead. "Come along, Eddie. You need to keep up."

Jake picked up his rifle. "Guess I'd better be going back myself."

"You're going back without game?" Alan asked.

Gazing at the mountain again, Jake lifted one corner of his mouth, his drawl heavier than usual. "You might say that, and then again you might not."

Jennie looked away from the sudden brightness in his eyes and hurried with Alan into the trees. As they made their way down the trail, she could hear the low murmur of Jake and Eddie talking behind them.

Near the bluff where the trees thinned, a sudden gust whipped at their clothes. Alan grabbed his hat, and another gust lashed his hair. A chill wind. Jennie wished she had brought her cloak. The forest dimmed, as if someone had blown out the great candle that lit it.

Jake caught up with them. "Clouds moving in fast."

Jennie hugged her arms to herself and tried to stop shivering. Alan quickly removed his cape. "Miss Haviland, you're cold. Here. Allow me." He slipped the long wool garment around her shoulders and tucked it beneath her throat.

"Oh, but you—"

He shook his head, bending close to smile directly in her face. "I'll be quite all right."

The wool felt wonderfully warm. She looked over Alan's shoulder to see Jake watching them, brows high, an odd twist to his mouth. Not a smile. Nor a frown exactly.

The four reached the top of the bluff with a full view of the town as a heavy draft of wind tore at the many tents beside partially built cabins. The sun no longer shone, but on the western horizon beneath a billowing cloud bank, a golden glow infused a deep screen of mist. Tent cloth crackled like gunshots, and Jennie clapped a hand over her heart. The Haviland tent rose, as if a large invisible hand had snatched it up and dropped it flat on the ground.

She let out a cry. "Our tent!"

Atop the nearby cabin Pa crouched on the pitched rafters, struggling with strips of peeled cedar bark. She flashed a glare at Jake for leaving Pa, knowing rain was coming. And for what purpose? Hunting? Not likely. Anger laced her words. "Pa needs help."

Jake bolted ahead of the others and lunged down the narrow walkway, dark hair flying. Jennie clutched the cape with one hand and raced after him, Alan and Eddie right behind. By the time they reached the cabin, Pa was back on the ground trying to gather the jumble of duck cloth that had been their tent.

He yelled above the noise of the wind. "If we don't get some kind of cover up fast, we'll be left out in the rain. It's bound to start soon."

Moisture enveloped them as the golden glow spread across the flat bench of land, tiny water droplets suspended in light. Alan and Jake both reached for the duck cloth, and Alan called out to Pa. "You've got the corner on the far side done. Maybe you'd do as well to throw the tent cloth over the rafters on this side and get in there."

Pa frowned at Alan, glanced at Jake, and gave a curt nod. "Let's try it, and with luck maybe the wind will die down so we can get some more bark up." He turned to the others, calling orders like a commanding general. "Ladies, boys! You get everything inside the cabin, and we men will do what we can to get a roof over it."

The chinking remained unfinished on one wall, but Jennie supposed the threat of rain had encouraged Pa to move on to roofing first. Surely Jake could have foreseen the urgency and stayed to help. Her annoyance flared again, and she threw herself into the task of carrying family belongings into the cabin. Blankets that served both as beds and bedding had rolled with the wind, but she managed to get an armful to carry inside, wrapping Alan's cape with them when it slipped from her shoulders.

Her mother pointed toward the corner Pa had already roofed with cedar bark. "Throw everything in that corner."

Jennie dropped the blankets and cape on the packed-earth floor and went back outside. Her brothers scrambled to pick up soft-leather cases full of clothes, canvas sacks of foodstuffs, and utensils. Jennie had thought their possessions meager until they had to race a rainstorm to get it all inside. Even the little boys helped. Pa and Jake were on the roof, each holding one end of the long piece of tent cloth, while Alan worked alongside to bind it in place with a long pole and braided buckskin rope.

Pa grumbled. "Oh, for some nails. It'd go so much faster with nails."

Alan paused in his work. "Sir, I have nails in the storehouse. I can get some straightaway."

Pa sat silently a moment, then shook his head. "Can't really afford them, especially not for a temporary roof. We'll manage without."

He and Jake used strips of buckskin to tie the cloth to the rafters, making new holes in the canvas to add to the old. The poor old tent had seen hard service on the trail west and at Willamette Falls. They were bound to have leaks.

A drop fell on Jennie's hand. Not much time. She grabbed a couple of food sacks and ran toward the cabin doorway. "We don't even have a door," she said as she plunged inside, speaking to no one in particular. "The rain will come right in the doorway along with animals and everything else."

Their new pet, Muffin, ran into the cabin and out, back and forth, as if helping too. Ma brought in an armload of tin dishes, a satisfied lilt in her breathless voice. "I think that's it."

Pa called from overhead. "Eddie!"

Looking up, Jennie smiled. Pa was laying cedar bark. They must have gotten the tent cloth secured.

Eddie peered upward, face scrunched. "Yeah, Pa?"

"You come hand bark up—and, Charlie—"

The boy echoed his brother. "Yeah, Pa?"

"You'd better run get Jake's bedroll and put that inside. You know where he keeps it, don't you?"

"Sure." Charlie hurried out the doorway after Eddie.

Jennie fingered the sides of her dress skirt. Jake's things? Of course, he had no place of his own and was still sleeping under the stars. She glanced about the enclosed space. The cabin was bigger than their tent, but not large. Only fourteen feet by sixteen, Pa had said. Not a lot of space for a family of seven. Still, it wasn't the limited space that troubled her, but the prospect of Jake's presence in that small space where they'd have no privacy. If his things were in the cabin, did that mean he would sleep there too?

A louder patter of raindrops hit the packed earth beneath the uncovered corner. They wouldn't get the roof on in time.

Robbie squealed, running to the corner and holding out his tiny hands to catch the drops. "Look. Wet."

Still the men worked.

Ma propped her hands on her hips and craned her neck. "Mr. Haviland. Can't you come inside until it lets up?"

"And if it doesn't let up?"

"Of course it will. Please."

He finished fastening one more piece of bark and lifted his shoulders in a show of resignation before crawling off the roof. Charlie led the way inside with his short, chubby arms wrapped around Jake's wet bedroll. Eddie had the saddle. Soon the whole family, plus Jake and Alan, huddled in the driest corner.

Pa wiped a hand over his wet face and shook his head, making little droplets fly. "It is nasty out there."

Jake nodded. "That it is."

Ma handed them rags for drying, but they still looked drenched, hair stringing, clothes plastered against their bodies. Jennie had never imagined Alan so unkempt, but a warmth still put dancing lights in his blue eyes when he looked at her.

Muffin stood back, though not far enough, and shook himself, showering everyone again.

Jennie tried to shoo him back. "Oh, Muffin, get away when you do that."

The big boys giggled, and Alan took his rag to wipe the animal down. He turned his warm smile on the boys, but Eddie's laughter stopped. A tumult of emotions rippled across the boy's face—doubt, appreciation, something bordering on contempt, an effort at respect. Charlie watched his brother and mirrored every uncertain feeling. They wanted to dislike Alan, but he'd given them this wonderful gift. Jennie wished she could shake them, but her heart ached for them and for Alan, who was trying to win them over.

Eddie glanced at Jake, perhaps for some assistance in how he should behave, and Jennie lifted her gaze to Jake as well. His face looked set in stone, hiding whatever emotions he might be feeling. Or did he lack feeling? His eyes turned to meet hers and sent a thread of fire through her that made her shiver.

Davie's whine brought everybody's attention to him. "I'm cold," he said.

Pa set a hand on the boy's head. "We could use a fireplace, couldn't we, son? But I'm afraid it'll be awhile before we can get that done."

Jake motioned to the corner where rain splattered in. "We might put a stone ring there. Make a fire-pit. Smoke could go out where we don't have a roof yet."

Pa rubbed his jaw. "We'd have to leave that part of the roof off."

"You don't need a very big hole."

"Lots of weather coming in that doorway too." Pa looked at Ma. "Can you spare a blanket to cover that, Mrs. Haviland?"

She gave him a blanket, and he worked quickly to bore holes in the log above the opening. While Jake and Alan held the blanket, he pounded pegs through the cloth and into the bored holes. With a little bow to Ma he made a sweeping gesture toward the hanging blanket. "Your door, Mrs. Haviland."

She beamed. "Thank you, Mr. Haviland."

Hard rain kept pelting the uncovered corner, and Pa made a face at it. "If we'd just had a little more time." He turned to Jake. "Listen, you'd better plan to stay here with us. You can't be sleeping out in this."

Jennie bit her lips together. Her father had confirmed her fears. But maybe Jake would refuse.

Eddie piped up. "Sure, Jake. You'll have to stay here with us."

"Sure, Jake." Charlie's echo.

Jake scrunched his shoulders. "Well, I—uh—usually stay at Joe's place when the rains come. He can always use help on his farm, and—well—"

Eddie leaned toward Jake, the boy's whole posture imploring. "Oh, but, Jake—" Eddie gave Pa a quick look, then faced Jake again. "Mr. Johnston, we haven't finished the cabin, and we need you."

Jennie wanted to argue that point, but she said nothing.

Jake grinned at the boys, and glanced at Jennie and her mother. "It'd be a burden on the women."

Jennie felt an uplift of hope.

Charlie countered with a shining plea. "No, it wouldn't."

Pa made the grunting noise that showed he was putting his thoughts in order. "I do still need help."

Alan stepped close to Jennie's side, a hand extended toward Jake, palm up. "I could let you stay in the company storehouse—that is, if you need a roof over your head for sleeping while you finish your work here."

Jake faced Alan, fierce currents running between the two men. Jennie didn't think Alan's gesture was hospitable. More likely he was seeking a way to keep Jake from living under the Havilands' roof—such as it was. Jake, on the other hand, didn't seem friendly toward Alan, and she wondered if he would accept any gesture from the man.

Pa waved a dismissive hand. "That won't be necessary. He'll be no problem, will he, Mrs. Haviland?"

"Well . . . no."

Jennie stared at her mother. *How can you say that, Ma? He most certainly will be a problem. You know that.*

Jake tipped his head toward Ma with a slight smile, answering in his slow drawl. "I suppose, if you're sure it's all right, Mrs. Haviland."

"Why—uh—yes—yes, of course."

Jennie's gaze darted about the tiny cabin as she tried to imagine how they could all live together. With the rain beating down around them, the dark log walls seemed to close in. She wouldn't be able to move without his intrusive eyes watching her. Bad enough with all her brothers. A sudden, intense longing rose for her home in Utica where she'd had her own room.

Shuddering, she folded her arms and pressed back against one of those log walls. She breathed deep, trying to get enough air. Then she looked up to see Alan watching her, lips upturned only slightly, brow knit, a sympathetic warmth in his eyes. He seemed to be the only one who realized how she must feel, the only one who cared.

He tipped his head toward her and spoke softly. "Miss Haviland." He turned to her parents. "Mr. and Mrs. Haviland, I need to be going. I should see to the storehouse—what with all this rain. I don't know if the men will have got things inside."

Jennie felt she was being abandoned by the only person she could count on, but he gave her a bright smile. "Miss Haviland, I'll return a little later, and perhaps I'll have the pleasure of seeing you then, eh?"

With a gracious bow he left through their blanket-covered doorway. Jennie watched the drifting fabric, a warm feeling growing inside. Such a lovely man. For a moment she almost forgot she and her family were going to share their small cabin with Jake Johnston, but seeing him there in casual conversation with her father, she leaned against the log wall and dug her fingernails into the rough bark.

The fire in the newly dug pit provided light as well as warmth for the small enclosure of their home. Fortunately the rain hadn't lasted long, and the men had managed to dig the fire pit and get the rest of the roof covered with cedar bark, leaving a small hole above the fire for the smoke to escape. Smoke didn't always find the hole, letting hazy drifts waft about the room, but it was tolerable.

Supper was done, the dishes cleaned, and they could look forward to their first evening in their cabin home in this Oregon country. Pa's Promised Land. Jennie gripped her knees. A barely civilized place. Yet something about the fire in a space of their own made it feel homey. She sat on the pile of blankets she'd made into a chair and watched the dancing flames. The familiar whiff of lingering supper smells—wheat, venison, smoke—blended with newer smells of cut timbers, saddle oil, wet wool.

She let her gaze wander over the members of her family sitting in a half circle around the fire: Ma, Pa, the big boys, the little boys—and Jake. She wished Alan had joined them for supper, but he hadn't returned yet. Jake showed no sign of leaving. His presence at supper wasn't unusual. He'd been eating with them since he started helping Pa and had often stayed at their campfire afterward. But they had always eaten outdoors by an outdoor fire. Never had Jake set foot inside the tent. Now he was inside their cabin, and was going to sleep there too.

She had almost gotten used to the man, as long as he kept a respectful distance. But how could he maintain a respectful distance in a cabin as small as this?

The Shifting Winds

A knock sounded, like a knock on a door, though it must have been on one of the logs that framed the doorway, since they had no door. Still, the sound was familiar and brought back memories of home and polite society. Muffin gave a low bark, and Jennie straightened her back, knowing it must be Alan. When Pa got up and drew the blanket aside, she felt a glow of pleasure seeing it was.

Pa's voice showed no emotion. "Come in."

Alan stepped inside to let the blanket fall back over the doorway, and stopped. Muffin rushed to greet him, and he tousled the dog's ears before looking up at Pa. "Thank you, sir, but I wonder if Miss Haviland might like to take a short walk. The clouds have passed, so I think our rain is over for a while. We have a little light left before dark." He lifted a hand, palm up. "If it's all right with you—and the ladies. Maybe Eddie would like to join us again."

Eddie groaned, but cut off the sound at Pa's stern look.

Alan stroked Muffin's head. "Maybe he could bring the dog this time—since we won't go far."

The parents looked at each other. Ma smiled. "Why, of course."

Jennie leaped up, heart racing. Smoothing her skirts, she started toward Alan. Even before she reached him, Ma was there with Jennie's cloak and gloves. Eddie twisted his lips to one side, showing little enthusiasm, but he put the leash on Muffin and turned his usual agreeable nature toward the dog.

At the doorway, Jennie paused to look back into the room. Everyone was watching her, but Jake's dark eyes drew her focus. His brows rose, but otherwise his face was a mask.

Alan's warm hand touched her arm. "Ready?"

She swerved to face Alan, and taking a sudden sharp breath, she gave a small nod. "Yes, of course."

He drew the blanket aside and let her through the doorway ahead of him. The evening was as clear as the day had been before the storm swept through. A reddish glow still lit the western sky, casting a blush on the air around them.

He extended his elbow from the soft gray cape slung over his shoulders. "The ground's still wet. It may be a bit slippery, but if you hold on, I fancy you'll be fine."

She took his arm, and as they walked, his cape fell softly against her, adding to the warmth of his presence.

He smiled. "Would you like to walk over near the falls? They're quite remarkable in this light. We should be able to get there and back well before dark, I should think."

"That'll be lovely." Jennie took a deep breath of the air, so recently washed clean, the wet greenery and soil adding a piquant flavor. This courting business was actually quite pleasant, even if it only meant the occasional stroll. She hadn't made any real friends in Willamette Falls. Many acquaintances, but nobody with whom she felt a special bond. It was nice having a friend like Alan.

His soft voice rang clear against the growing rush of the great falls ahead. "I'm sorry to say I must be getting back to Fort Vancouver. We'll be leaving first thing in the morning, and I didn't want to go without talking to you. I do wish I could stay awhile."

Her shoulders slumped. "Oh, do you have to go?"

"I'll return as soon as I can."

"Will I . . . see you in the morning?"

He patted her fingers that held tight to his arm. "I think not. We have to leave early." He looked over his shoulder, and she turned to see Eddie lagging as usual. At least the boy appeared happy this time, laughing as the dog pulled the leash one way and another to sniff every exciting new thing.

Alan leaned closer to Jennie, his tone becoming brittle. "My dear, I'm not comfortable leaving you with a man like Jake Johnston in your home."

She looked away and heaved a sigh. "I don't like it either, but I don't know what I can do about it."

"Well, do be careful. These American mountaineers are ruthless men, and their attitudes toward women are—" He looked over her head as if seeking words. "Men like Joe Meek—they don't bind with their women in proper wedlock, you know." His eyes met hers. "Do be careful, won't you?"

Jennie wanted to touch his brow and smooth the creases away, but she didn't dare. His concern warmed her heart, while his words confirmed vague fears she didn't fully understand. What kind of marriages did these mountaineers have? And what would they do to women? Nobody had ever told her about these matters between women and men. There was more than kissing. She was sure of that, but the rest was pretty much a mystery. Even young Eddie seemed to know things she didn't.

Alan brushed a thumb over her earlobe, and tingles wisped across her neck. "I beg you," he said, "don't ever be alone in the house with him, will you?"

Her breath caught, and he smiled, the clench of his forehead softening. "Perhaps I'm being unduly cautious," he said, "but I do want you to be aware the man could be dangerous. I suppose you know that."

"I'll be careful. I . . . appreciate your concern."

Eddie and Muffin had caught up with them, and they turned to continue their walk, proceeding along a portage trail for boats passing the falls. The roar of water grew. They stopped in a wide spot with a fine view of the horseshoe cascade, the scene framed between two small trees. Jennie laid a hand over her heart. The rosy air had tinged the falls pink.

The thunder of crashing water rolled right through her, and she stood still to embrace the feeling. Such power in the unceasing explosion. No wonder men sought control of that power. The Americans. The British. Both wanted the land here. And the Indians as well.

Men and women from the local tribe clustered near the scaffolds across the river, while several men balanced on the upper decks of the high wooden frameworks, dipping their nets into the froth to scoop the great leaping salmon, tossing their catches to those below.

Alan pressed closer to Jennie, his warm hand covering hers. "Quite a sight, eh?"

"Truly lovely."

He gave her a bright smile. "Truly." He didn't seem to be talking about the falls anymore. The pounding of her heart matched the pounding cascade. His focus turned intense as he faced her. "Miss Haviland, I—"

A familiar voice boomed out over the sound of water. "Well now, isn't that nice."

Jennie took a sudden step away from Alan and swung around to see Jake watching the falls, his arms folded across his raised chest. She gave him an accusing look. Did he always have to follow her? Eddie stood near his side, about a pace behind, one hand on the dog that sat looking toward the mighty cascade as if enjoying the view with the rest of them.

Jake lifted his gaze to the sky. "Wind's shifting again. Another storm coming. I suppose you'll be heading back to get under a roof before long."

A bank of dark clouds loomed on the western horizon. If those moved in fast they would bring on an early dusk, and she didn't relish being on this precarious trail in the dark. She drew closer to Alan and spoke directly to him. "Maybe we should go in."

"Good idea," Jake said. "Shall we?" With a slight bow he gestured toward the trail home.

Jennie frowned at the mountaineer. He seemed to imply she should go home with *him*. She was about to protest when she realized she *would* be home with Jake, while Alan would be returning to Fort Vancouver. Glancing at Alan, she saw a flash of anger in his eyes that gave her a sudden chill. Jake, still pointing toward home, wore a cocky, self-assured grin, obviously pleased with his successful intervention. At that moment Jennie simply wanted to be back in the cabin with her family—away from both men.

As they started down the trail, Jake and Eddie in the lead, a gaunt figure loomed in the shadows below, then vanished. Jennie wasn't sure if she'd seen or imagined him. "Was that—? I thought I saw someone there." She pointed toward the spot. "It looked like the man who always comes to Willamette Falls with you. The thinner one."

Alan squinted. "Lévêque? I don't see him."

Jennie drew Alan a little faster along the path. Maybe she had only experienced the haunting memory of that other night when the cat appeared at their campfire and disappeared in the darkness—and that man had appeared and disappeared like the cat.

She shook her head to cast off the illusion. She was ready to go home.

Chapter Five

Fort Vancouver, November 1842. Alan hurried across the lawn of the fort courtyard toward the Big House, his boots sinking into the spongy carpet of grass, saturated from the fall rains. He bounded up the half-circle stairs to the wide veranda and charged inside, lunging to the open door of McLoughlin's office to the left of the entry. It wasn't wise to leave the good doctor waiting.

The giant of a man sat fidgeting at his desk, looking out the window. He showed no sign he'd even noticed Alan come in. Alan gripped the back of a mahogany chair just inside the door and waited, slowly rubbing his thumbs over the glossy wood. For a moment the doctor's unruly shock of long white hair gave Alan the impression of a madman. But of course Dr. John McLoughlin was no madman. While his temper might be as unruly as his hair, he was the most competent commander Alan had ever worked under. And most exacting.

McLoughlin continued to stare out the curtained window toward the east courtyard. Had he watched Alan's approach across the lawn? Probably. Alan waited. It would do no good to rush the doctor. It never did. No doubt McLoughlin in his own good time would come out with his reasons for calling Alan in.

With a sudden grunt McLoughlin pivoted to face him. The man's bushy white brows drew together over piercing gray-blue eyes that had a way of holding another man's gaze. The florid complexion appeared redder than usual.

Alan's shoulders tightened. *Have I done something? Something to invoke his rage?*

Perspiration prickled across Alan's flesh, and he fought back the sense of inadequacy he so often felt in McLoughlin's presence, wanting always to be in command of himself. But what man didn't feel this way before McLoughlin when the old Chief Factor was in such a mood?

McLoughlin blurted in his normal booming voice. "I think I'll go to Willamette Falls. I'm worried about my claim there, and it might be a good idea to have it surveyed. You've been there recently. What do you think?"

Relieved not to be the source of the man's agitation, Alan shrugged and tried to appear composed. His last visit to the Falls had been a month ago, which didn't seem recent to him.

"Well?" The man's impatience resonated.

"Sir! I believe that would be a good idea."

McLoughlin gave a curt nod, the large face twisted with thought. "I think I'll call it Oregon City." He repeated himself as he often did. "Oregon City. Yes. What do you think?"

"Sounds good. It has a—"

"I'll be wanting to leave tomorrow, and I want you to go with me. You know some of the people there already."

"Of course." The assignment pleased Alan. He would see Jennie Haviland.

McLoughlin turned away and stared out the window again, the folds of skin on his face drooping, as he riffled his fingers across the papers on the desktop. Certainly the man had cause for distress lately, given the conflict over his claim and young John's death.

The doctor's voice turned uncharacteristically soft, as if he were talking more to himself than Alan. "I scarce know what the world is coming to. A man can't lay claim to a piece of property in this country without another coming along to help himself to it. There's no law. And what's more, there's no law when the chief officer of a Company post can be murdered by his men and the Governor won't lift a finger to bring the guilty ones to prosecution—as if John had invited his own murder."

The Chief Factor flashed a look at Alan, eyes glittering, and faced the window again, voice turning raspy. "I'll find them. I'll see justice done if I have to do it myself. No law. No law."

A thickness moved into Alan's throat as the man's pain washed over him. Such a cruel blow for McLoughlin to lose his son John Jr. when the young fellow was just beginning to come around to some sense of responsibility. A troublemaker in his youth, John had finally settled down enough to be a fairly able worker. He'd been assigned to command the remote Fort Stikine—a dangerous place, not only from the Indians but from the lawless Company men themselves. The murder didn't surprise Alan. What did surprise him—and Dr. McLoughlin—was that the Company Governor was doing nothing to resolve the case.

McLoughlin continued to mutter. "No law. No law."

Alan leaned forward and put an encouraging lift in his voice. "There's talk of establishing laws in the country, sir."

McLoughlin pinched his face, reflective, and as if he'd just remembered his manners, he pointed at the chair Alan was gripping. "Sit, sit. Please."

Nodding, Alan stepped around the mahogany chair and sat on the edge. "But it's mostly among the Americans, I think."

"What's that?"

"The talk of government, sir. It's mostly among the Americans."

"Yes, yes. Well, some of them have been agitating for government since last year when Ewing Young died, but it's never amounted to anything."

"That was primarily for expedience, though, was it not, sir? To probate Young's estate?"

"True enough. True enough. But they did try to take it further." A gleam brightened the old man's eyes, and his lips almost made a smile. "They might have succeeded if Father Blanchet and some of our people on the constitution committee hadn't deliberately let the thing die by failing to act."

McLoughlin stood, as if he could no longer bear to sit still and, grabbing his gold-headed cane, marched out the door without the slightest acknowledgment of Alan's presence. Unsure what was expected of him, Alan rose and followed the man down the long entryway of the Big House to the front door and across the veranda to the grand curved staircase. He had to hurry to catch up when the old gentleman headed across the lawn toward the western courtyard surrounded by the principal storehouses.

The ever-present noise of the fort—the blacksmith's anvil, the carpenter's plane, the cooper's adze, the tinsmith's hammer—all the busy hum of productive activity nearly obliterated the sound of their brisk footsteps. The usual cluster of Indians, their Hudson's Bay Company blankets wrapped about their shoulders, waited near the long one-story, gable-roofed Indian Trade Store for a turn to trade. For safety, only one was allowed inside at a time.

Seeing McLoughlin, the Indians nodded with deference to this man they called the "White Headed Eagle." Their reverence for him did much to keep the peace. There'd been very little Indian trouble in the area since McLoughlin came in 1824. Alan had observed how the man treated them with kindness when he was pleased and with prompt and certain punishment when he wasn't.

McLoughlin stopped to speak to a few in their own tongue, then moved on to a couple of young men beating furs outside the fur store, sons of Company fathers and Indian mothers. He shook his cane. "Beat them with vigor, boys. Those furs are our livelihood. Keep at it. Keep them clean and free of vermin." He turned to Alan, as if he'd just noticed Alan was still with him. "Good job for a young man. Work keeps a young man out of trouble, wouldn't you say?"

Walking on, they passed a couple of *voyageurs* chatting together in French. Alan picked up on some of the conversation—something about the Indians—but could never quite follow their language when they spoke so fast. His French had certainly improved during his time in Montreal. He'd worked hard on it when he learned the lovely Marcella spoke nothing else. Beautiful, icy Marcella. His stomach twitched, and he stood a little taller. That chapter in his life was over, and he didn't want to think about it. He was ready for a new chapter.

McLoughlin's gruff voice startled him. "What do you think about the talk of establishing laws?"

Surprised at the abrupt return to their previous discussion, Alan took a moment to redirect his thoughts. "Well, sir, I'm rather concerned that the government these Americans are talking about would be a government for Americans only. I'm not sure where that leaves us, sir."

McLoughlin nodded. "I've given some thought to an independent government. I have trouble imagining either Great Britain or the United States ever extending jurisdiction over this land so far from either of them. But we are getting a larger population every year. The more people, the more need for government. What would be wrong with an independent government?"

"That might be quite all right, sir, as long as we're in the majority, but the way the Americans talk of immigrating here, I doubt we'll be in the majority much longer. Our government could simply become an American government."

McLoughlin shook his head. "Perhaps not, perhaps not."

"Beg your pardon, sir, but how long do you suppose we can hold our position here if the Americans put together some kind of government in Oregon?"

"We're certainly well established."

"Yes, we are that, sir, and we have a right to keep what we've gained. But do you actually expect the Americans to honor our rights? I'm afraid it could take a war to show them."

McLoughlin turned a deep frown on him. "I hope it doesn't come to that."

"I hope not too." Alan had little fondness for many of those Americans, but he had a great deal of fondness for one of them. What would happen to his relationship with Jennie if hostilities erupted?

McLoughlin cleared his throat to speak again, gazing distant-eyed about the tidy fort under his command. "Of course, if the inland Indians don't settle down, we may have to get together for the safety of British *and* Americans."

"You're not worried about the Indians bothering *us*, are you, sir?"

"There's a bit of unrest among the Cayuses at Waiilatpu. Mrs. Whitman had to leave the mission there to find safe refuge at the Dalles, you know, and then the Indians burned the mill there."

"No, sir, I hadn't heard. I knew there was some unrest in the interior. But Waiilatpu?"

"Yes, after Dr. Whitman left for the States in October, his lovely wife was attacked right in her own home by some of their own Indians."

Alan stopped and stared at the doctor. "Was she hurt?"

"No, just frightened, just frightened, but it has me worried. There's a lot of discontent among those tribes. And my biggest concern is that unrest among the tribes of the interior will spread to the tribes around here. They're upset about all these white men coming from the States, I think—afraid the Americans will take their land away from them."

"Well, sir, it's not an idle fear."

"Perhaps not entirely, but hopefully Dr. White can convince them otherwise."

Alan let out a huff. "Dr. White? The United States sub-Indian Agent?"

"Yes, he's gone to the interior to talk with them and to try convincing them of the goodwill of the white man. Tom McKay went with him, and I'm sure Tom will have some good effect."

Alan respected McLoughlin's stepson Tom McKay as one of the best men in the country for dealing with Indians. But White was a different matter. "I don't see what good a man like White can do with the Indians, sir. The man has no sense. And I don't see what right the American government had to send him into the country with such a title. Rather presumptuous when the country's jointly occupied, wouldn't you say, sir?"

"Perhaps that's one more reason we need to form a government for ourselves."

Alan bit his lips. He didn't think so, but he saw little use in arguing with Dr. McLoughlin. Maybe when they got to Willamette Falls, McLoughlin would see what he was up against.

The skies had nearly darkened by the time the long canoe touched the bank at Willamette Falls, and Alan jumped out quickly to offer McLoughlin a hand. The older man ignored his outstretched palm. Though nearly sixty, McLoughlin stepped out of the canoe with the vigor of a young man and marched with brisk steps up the bank. He gripped his usual cane, but never touched the ground with it.

Alan observed the growing settlement. Almost a real town. Most of the cabins looked to be near completion, tents gone, leaving a tidy little settlement of log homes. A clamor of voices came from the direction of the Sidney Moss cabin, and McLoughlin gravitated toward it while Alan followed close behind. The open cabin door let a shaft of light fall on the ground outside, sounds of oratory drifting out.

Alan stepped nearer the doctor. "Must be a meeting, sir."

"Yes, perhaps we should see what it's about."

Lévêque came up behind Alan, startling him. Alan thought he should be used to the man's ways, but when Lévêque appeared unannounced that way, it always gave Alan a start. He hoped it didn't show. It wasn't a good idea to let a man like Lévêque have the upper hand in any way. "Will you be needing us, *M'sieu* Alan?" the *voyageur* asked.

"Not tonight. Be at the shack in the morning, though."

"*Oui.*" The man stepped backward, turned, and melted into the deepening gray.

Alan pushed past the knot of men at the open doorway, struggling to keep up with McLoughlin, and managed to find a spot in the crowded room next to his superior. Lansford Hastings stood on a box at one end of the room speaking. Like George Haviland, the man was a lawyer who had immigrated this fall.

"I would like to offer a resolution," Hastings said.

Alan pursed his lips, hand on his chin. He'd caught only a few words so far, but it sounded like talk of government.

As the audience hushed, Hastings spoke with keen clarity. "Resolved, that it is expedient for the settlers on the coast to establish an independent government."

A murmur rose. Alan leaned close to McLoughlin so as not to be overheard. "Is he aware of your thinking on this, sir?"

"We discussed it when he stopped by the fort this fall."

A man in the audience bellowed. "An independent government will never have enough strength. We need the aid of a true government, the government of the United States of America!"

Another answered. "She'll never extend her jurisdiction over us. They've sent requests to Congress now for years. When was the first?

Back in '38, wasn't it? Four years ago. And what response have we had? Not a word. If we want a government, we'll have to create it ourselves."

George Abernethy, keeper of the Methodist store, stood up. "If we create our own government we'll have nothing. We need the power of the United States for adequate protection against the dangers here."

"That's right," another said. "Indians in the interior are rising up against their white benefactors. Poor Mrs. Whitman—though she's spent six years of her life trying to help the ungrateful savages, they turn on her, and when will those around us here turn on us? And if they do, can we defend ourselves against their numbers? We need military help, United States military help."

"Tell that to the United States Congress and see how far you get," his neighbor said, reaching out to touch the man's arm as if to ensure his attention.

The first man reacted, jerking his arm away and shoving his neighbor. Anger erupted into violence as the men grabbed each other, each trying to wrestle the other down.

"Gentlemen! Gentlemen!" Mr. Le Breton was shouting, having taken Hastings's place on the box. "Please be calm." A small man, George Le Breton could scarcely be seen above the crowd, most of the people having gotten to their feet, and his voice was as small as his stature. He tried again, pushing the spectacles up on his nose and gesturing with animation. "Please sit down, and let us go on with the meeting."

An energetic, bustling little man, Le Breton had been in Oregon almost as long as Alan—since 1840 when the man came as a passenger on the *Maryland*, the first ship Captain John Couch of Massachusetts brought to the country. Now Le Breton was working with another fellow trying to operate a store for Couch with goods Couch had brought on the brig *Chenamus* last summer.

At the moment, Le Breton appeared considerably distressed at the disruption of the meeting. "Gentlemen, please."

Abernethy tried to pull a couple of the men apart, but they ignored his efforts, and he made the mistake of bumping into someone else. A man near Alan grumbled. "Fools. It won't be long and the United States government will take over and drive the damned British out."

The Shifting Winds

Alan wanted to strike him, to join the tussle in the room—because he felt like it, and because he thought it might be good for his own cause if this American meeting dissolved into hopeless chaos. He touched the man's arm with the back of his hand, and the man turned, his eyes widening when he saw Alan. Clearly he'd been unaware of the presence of a Britisher. The man raised his fists, and Alan readied himself, then with disappointment saw the man back away, his gaze no longer on Alan but to one side of him.

Dr. McLoughlin. Seeing the scowl on McLoughlin's face, Alan knew why the man had decided not to fight. Who would dare antagonize such a face? And the cane. McLoughlin was fingering the gold tip of his cane, and Alan wanted to laugh. The old doctor's temper was well known—as was his inclination to use that cane on any man who seriously displeased him.

Le Breton called out once more. "Gentlemen, gentlemen. Let's not fight. Let us bring it to a vote. Do I hear a call for the question?"

"Question!" The word cut through the buzz of talk and the rustle of poking and shoving.

"Mr. Hastings has offered a resolution." Le Breton adjusted his glasses to peer at a piece of paper in his hand. "'Resolved, that it is expedient for the settlers on the coast to establish an independent government.' All in favor—I say, gentlemen, all in favor—" The confusion gradually subsided. "—all in favor, say *aye*."

A brief silence. Then Hastings's bold voice sounded. "Aye." And many others.

"Opposed, *nay*," Le Breton said. Only a low rumbling murmur followed.

Glancing at McLoughlin, Alan thought the man looked well satisfied. This was, after all, the position McLoughlin was taking, and Alan supposed it was better than a resolution to form an American government. Still, Alan was skeptical about any government, so long as these Americans were involved. Better to have them without a government, dependent on the Hudson's Bay Company for their needs.

George Abernethy stood again. "Mr. Chairman." At Le Breton's acknowledgment, Abernethy proceeded. "Mr. Chairman, may I offer a resolution?"

"Well, sir, we have several matters on the agenda. Could it wait until our meeting next week?" Le Breton's voice trembled. The man was probably worried about another eruption in his meeting.

Abernethy lifted a hand and smiled. "Mr. Chairman, maybe I could offer the resolution, and then we could hold the vote for next week. That would give people time to think about it."

Le Breton nodded. "I suppose that would be all right. Give us your resolution, and we'll vote on it next week, Mr. Abernethy."

The man made his way through the crowd to the box in front, and Le Breton yielded his place on the crude stand. Silence filled the tiny, crowded room when Abernethy cleared his throat to speak. "Resolved, that if the United States extends its jurisdiction over this country within the next four years, it will not be expedient to form an independent government."

The hush continued.

Alan frowned. That would completely neutralize Hastings's resolution. Exactly what the British didn't want.

Abernethy stepped down, letting Le Breton back on the box to break the silence with his high, thin voice. "Now then, ladies and gentlemen, we have a literary presentation."

As Le Breton introduced the next person to speak, Alan scanned faces in the audience. The Havilands were there—Mr. and Mrs. Haviland, and the older boys. And Jake Johnston, Alan noticed without pleasure, and Robert Newell, one of Johnston's mountain buddies. But Alan couldn't find Jennie.

Johnston turned and caught Alan's eye. Johnston's face hardened before he looked away, and Alan clenched his fists. He continued to look for Jennie and finally decided she must not have come. Perhaps she had stayed home with the younger boys.

With sudden decision, he touched McLoughlin's sleeve. "Sir," he whispered, "I have someone I'd rather like to see. I wonder if I might leave you for a while?"

"Oh, certainly, certainly," McLoughlin answered, even his whisper booming out.

Trying not to notice the heads turning their way, Alan slipped out of the close little room. Outside, he paused to draw a refreshing breath of the chill air, and turned his mind to more pleasant thoughts.

When he approached the Haviland door, he smiled to see they actually had a door. Heavy, hand-hewn boards had replaced the blanket. And a substantial roof of shakes. A month of work had made quite a difference.

At his knock, the dog barked. And Jennie's lilting voice sounded from inside. "Who is it?"

"Alan Radford. May I come in, please?"

He delighted in the surprised pleasure in her voice, and the sound of the door bar being raised. The rough planks swung inward to show her smiling face, a golden aura edging her silken brown hair that tumbled over her shoulders this evening, backlit from the lights in the room. The soft scent of hearth fire and freshly washed clothes drifted out through the opening.

He didn't move for a moment, caught in the embrace of his senses. Then little Muffin scrambled past her and leaped in welcome. Alan bent down to ruffle the dog's ears and allow a few licks. When he stood again and spoke to Jennie, his low voice sounded thick, unnatural. "How are you?"

"Fine." She showed no more inclination to move than he did. "It's good to see you."

The melodic sound of her voice rippled over him like warm water. "May I come in?" he asked.

She glanced back into the room and lifted her eyes to him again. "Well, my father and mother aren't home. But—well, Davie and Robbie are here. I guess it'll be all right."

Alan smiled. "I'm sure it will be."

Backing inside, she let him in and barred the door again. The little boys were nowhere in sight, and Alan felt a cozy intimacy being alone in the room with her, the door securely barred, only the dog to keep them company. After dancing around the room in excitement awhile, Muffin trotted to a blanket in the corner and curled up, still watchful.

A small blaze crackled in the clay-and-stick fireplace, which had been added to one end of the building since his last visit. A few pieces of furniture graced the room—crude, but at least they had furniture. A bed stood against one side, attached into the logs of the wall, probably for her parents, though it scarcely looked big enough for two.

A long table filled the center of the room, with benches on either side. A few cut stumps no doubt served as chairs, while a wall shelf opposite the bed held dishes and utensils. Various tools and harnesses and clothes hung on the many pegs driven into the walls. The packed earth still served for a floor.

Beside him, near the door, a ladder led up to a loft, no doubt where the boys were now.

She watched him in his observations. "Well, what do you think?"

"It appears to be coming along quite well. Are you comfortable here?"

A sudden shadow crossed her face, and she turned away to step near the fireplace.

Wishing he hadn't asked the question, he moved close to her. "Not what you're used to, I'd guess." She looked up at him and shook her head, light from the fire dancing over her hair. He reached out to feel the softness of it. "I fancy you didn't actually want to come to Oregon."

"Not really."

"I'm sorry." He gave her a sympathetic smile, then brightened. "For myself, I can't be too sorry you're here."

Her light laughter stirred the glow rising through him. She looked succulent as a summer rose with her pink petal cheeks, her full dewy lips. And the most delightful thing was, he didn't think she had any idea how seductive she was. He could almost taste the sweet nectar of her lips, so close. The glow flared, melting his will, and he stepped back. Maybe it was too cozy here. He'd better leave. The boys weren't adequate chaperons.

"I'd best go," he said. His voice didn't sound like his own.

She bent toward him, clutching her hands beneath her chin. "No, please don't. You've only just got here." She motioned toward the raw-cut table. "Why don't you sit awhile?"

Leading the way, she plopped onto the nearest bench with delightful abandonment of her usual grace and patted the space next to her. He hesitated, then slowly meandered to the other side, and when he lifted his boot-clad feet over the opposite bench to sit, she swung around so they faced each other across the protective table. With elbows forward she leaned toward him and smiled with apparent satisfaction.

What could he say to her? His mind jumped from subject to subject, and he latched onto an innocuous one. "Quite a bit of excitement at the meeting tonight. Some of the men got so stirred up, they almost got a fight going."

Her eyes grew round. "Really? What was it about?"

"It was talk of government. Someone offered a resolution of some sort." Alan frowned as he pondered the meaning of the resolution the Americans had passed. "By what authority I'm sure I don't know."

"Authority?"

He shook his head. "Beg your pardon, my dear. I was thinking aloud. It's not a matter to concern a lady, I suppose."

Her eyes flashed so he felt the impact. Then she looked away for a moment. When she met his gaze again, the flare had passed and she spoke in an even tone. "Pa says they're not official meetings. They're just lyceum meetings for the new debating society—the Pioneer Lyceum and Literary Club—and folks only present those resolutions at the meetings for discussion."

"I see." Her answer was more than he'd expected, but he was glad to hear it.

"Was the meeting over? My folks—"

"Oh, they had plenty of business left to last awhile, I'd say, but the interesting part was over when I left."

She nodded, and sighed softly. "I wish I could have gone, but Davie's not feeling well and somebody had to stay with him. I like to hear all the talk, and I enjoy the stories too."

"Stories? Oh, the literary presentation. Yes, some chap was giving a presentation. I didn't stay for that. I did see your parents there, and the two older boys—and Jake Johnston." He watched her for any reaction to Johnston's name. But he didn't detect any change in her expression. "Is Johnston still living here with you folks?"

She shook her head. "He moved in with the Newells a couple of weeks ago. Mr. Newell is a friend of his from the mountains. They call him Doc Newell. He's not really a doctor, but I guess he had some talent at healing. I think his real name is Robert. Maybe you know him?"

Relief washed over Alan at the news that Johnston was out of the house. "I know who the man is." He looked at her more intently. "Johnston didn't ever give you trouble, did he?"

"No."

Alan reached out to lay a hand on her arm. "I do wish I could always be here with you to look out for you."

Her brows rose at his words, and she leaned forward. "I wish you could too, but not because—well, I don't really need looking after." She tilted her head. "You have a queen in England, don't you? Queen Victoria. Does she need someone to look after her?"

Reeling a little at Jennie's response, he traced his fingertips over her long fingers spread flat on the table. "I...suppose she has many attendants."

"That's not quite what I meant. Doesn't she rule the country?"

He wanted to smile but wasn't sure he should. "She has certain powers, I guess, influence anyway, but Parliament holds the political power. It was the same with the king."

Jennie moved her hands a little, as if affected by his touch, then flattened them firmly against the rough tabletop. "As a woman she should use her influence to improve the lives of other women."

He lifted his brows. "I—uh—I would mention that to her, but I don't actually have the queen's ear."

Jennie pressed her lips together, only the corners tilting upward, a glint in her eyes. Then she let out a sharp breath. "At least women get to go to the lyceum meetings here. It's the best thing in Willamette Falls since I had to leave my academy back home. Did you know? A woman from New York went to a convention in your London a couple of years ago and they wouldn't seat her, just because she's a woman. Her and another lady. That's not right, and my friends at school think she's going to do something to fight injustices like that. One of my friends knows her. She lives only sixty miles from Utica. Elizabeth Cady Stanton. You may have heard about that business in London."

He grasped Jennie's delicate hands, and the strength of her return grasp surprised him. "I can't say I have, but I'm sorry you had to leave your school."

She looked down at their hands, then gave him a subtle smile. "How long will you stay this time?"

"Only a day or so, I'm afraid. I brought Dr. McLoughlin with me. He intends to stay until Christmas, I think, but I'll have to go back to the fort directly."

"Will you be here at Christmastime?"

"I'm not sure." He brightened at a sudden thought. "I rather wish you could go to the fort with me then. We have such capital parties there during the holidays." He imagined this lovely girl dressed in the finery of the ladies at Fort Vancouver at that festive time. What a delight she'd be. Could he arrange that?

They sat gazing at each other, and the soft, high-pitched voice of a child startled them. "Jennie?"

Alan reared back and dropped her hands.

"What is it, Robbie?" A subtle huskiness edged her voice, and she brushed a hand back and forth over one sleeve.

The child looked down through the opening in the loft floor, watching them with wide eyes. "I need a drink."

She got up from the table and headed for a water barrel set against the wall. "Well, come get a drink and then get back to bed."

The dog leaped up, as if to be helpful, but the little boy waited, still as a stone. Muffin yipped softly, and the child turned and climbed backward down the ladder, careful to hold up the skirt of his long white nightshirt so as not to trip, eyeing Alan as he came.

Alan attempted a smile. "Hello, Robbie."

The boy stared at him with big blue eyes. A beautiful child.

Jennie lifted the wooden lid off the water barrel and dipped a tin cup into the vessel. "Here, Robbie. Here's your water."

Robbie took the cup and drank so slowly Alan wasn't sure any water was going down. He was torn between amusement at the boy and a desire to get back to Jennie without the boy's presence. Robbie stopped to stare at Alan again.

Jennie placed a hand on his wee shoulder. "Are you finished, Robbie?"

He shook his head, eyes still watching Alan.

"Then, finish," she said.

Giving a long sigh, Robbie began to drink once more, blue eyes peering over the top of the cup. Finally the boy stopped drinking and held the cup down to look inside it, as if he was perturbed to see it empty but couldn't decide whether he ought to ask for more.

Jennie reached for the cup. "Enough?"

Robbie sighed again.

Taking the cup from his hands, she placed it on the table. "I think it had better be. Come on back to bed." She took him by the hand and led him to the ladder.

When she started to lift him onto the rungs, Alan jumped up from the bench and hurried to her side, putting both his hands on the boy's waist to do the lifting. Together they hoisted him up, and Jennie called after him. "Now, you go back to bed and don't get up again."

Alan smiled at her. "Will he?"

"I don't think so."

With the boy out of their hands, Alan and Jennie were left with their arms loosely intertwined. Gravity drew them closer, and Alan didn't want to fight it. Her warmth, the cozy room, the aching loneliness of days past and days yet to come—all ignited the waiting fires inside him.

A resounding knock shattered the moment. The dog barked.

Jennie jumped backward, away from his outstretched hands. "Who ... is it?"

"Jake Johnston."

Alan bristled.

Her voice carried a hint of irritation. "What do you want?"

She looked at Alan, and he shrugged. What could he say? She went to the door and lifted the bar that rested in the two notched pieces of wood, one on either side of the doorway, letting the door swing inward on its hazel-withe hinges. The man filling the doorway was not a welcome sight to Alan, but the dog leaped in greeting as it had for Alan.

"What do you want?" Jennie asked again.

Johnston peered into the room as he leaned down to pet the dog. "Is your father at home?" Clearly Mr. Haviland wasn't there, unless Johnston thought the man was up in the loft. But just as clear to Alan was the implication of Johnston's question. If Mr. Haviland wasn't there, Jennie was alone in the cabin with Alan—except for two small sleeping boys.

"He's not home yet," Jennie responded needlessly.

Johnston's raised brows punctuated his implication. "It appears your mother isn't here either."

Alan's anger rose. *The oaf is trying to embarrass her.*

Johnston barged into the room without waiting to be invited. "Well then, I guess I'll have to wait for them."

"But—" Jennie put out a hand as if to stop him, but let it drop.

Heedless, Johnston perched his long, humbly clad frame on a cut log in front of the fire. Leaning forward, he picked up the iron rod alongside the baked-clay fireplace and began stirring the coals with it. "Fire's going down a little."

Alan smiled wryly. *Indeed.*

He returned to his former seat at the table, and Jennie took her place on the other side. He wished he could leave, not wanting to stay in Johnston's presence and certain Johnston wouldn't go. But, of course, he couldn't leave Jennie alone with such a man as Johnston either. So he sat, elbows propped on the tabletop, simmering, as they waited for Mr. and Mrs. Haviland.

Chapter Six

December 1842. Jake knitted his brow as he read the open book laid across the saddle horn, barely aware of the gentle rocking motion of Old Blue's slow-walking gait. The big black horse knew the way, so Jake let the animal have its head on the homebound trail. Jake's focus riveted on the words and the ideas, the possibilities, expressed in them.

He'd thought to do some hunting today, the rains having let up for the first time in many days, but he'd found nothing more exciting than a coon. At least it would make a nice cap for one of the Haviland boys, and there was a little edible meat on the thing. The boys were off hunting too, Mrs. Haviland had said, but Jake hadn't come across them. He hoped their luck was better than his.

The crisp December air held a pleasant warmth. A good time to do a little reading. He wanted to get through this book and return it.

Jennie leaned back against the soft new buckskin pillow on her parents' bed, which served as a sofa in the daytime, and she glanced at the wide-open cabin door. Such a nice day for December. The skies sure knew how to rain in this Oregon country, but it could be surprisingly pleasant for so late in the season. Sunlight filtered through feathery green firs to cast a shimmering gilded light in the doorway. She studied the strange coloration before returning to her work of mending holes in Charlie's pants. They did have a window made of deerskin, which had been stretched tight into place while wet so it became translucent. But it never let in enough light, and on this rare warm day she enjoyed having the door open.

She twisted her shoulders one way and another to settle more deeply into the pillow. She'd made the pillow herself, stuffing the buckskin with native goose down, and found it surprisingly comfortable. The bed wasn't so soft, having no feather mattress. Only blankets covered the slats that ran crosswise, bound together and connected to the bedstead with rawhide. She could feel every slat.

But the bed was sturdy, resting on stakes on one side and anchored into the wall on the other. Sturdy and simple. Everything had to be made in the simplest way possible, given what little they had. They'd started west with feather mattresses, but those had to be thrown out with many other items too bulky or heavy to carry farther. Jennie's bed wasn't much either, only a trundle under her parents' bed, made like theirs but with a short-legged lightweight frame that could be pulled out easily at bedtime. Still, it was more than the boys had. They just slept on blankets on the loft floor.

Despite the lack of niceties in Oregon, they were getting along, and Jennie was enjoying this rare moment of quiet. Ma had taken the younger boys for a walk, and the older boys were out hunting. Jennie was glad her mother had taken a little time to go out. She worked too hard, with so few conveniences here, and Jennie tried to help as she could. Mending wasn't her favorite task, but it needed doing. Maybe if Pa brought flour back from Chemeketa they could do some baking. She could almost taste the baked bread, thinking about it. Wouldn't that be heavenly after all this time of eating boiled wheat?

Pa had chosen this nice day to ride down to Chemeketa, forty, maybe fifty miles south of them. He wouldn't be home for a day or two. This was his first overnight trip away, the first night for the family to be alone. Heaving a long breath, she tried to concentrate on mending the worn fabric. She and the family would be fine. They had good neighbors.

Pa was going to talk to Reverend Lee down at Chemeketa. About government. Pa was so passionate about organizing a government here in Oregon, she couldn't imagine anyone being against it. But the reverend was. Maybe Pa could persuade him. She smiled. Pa was good at that.

Would government make things better here? They needed better markets, Pa had said, more supplies, better protection. She rubbed a finger over the thinning jeans fabric of Charlie's pants. Clothes were so scarce, even thread and needles to sew them with. She didn't know about the need for protection. They hadn't really had trouble with the Indians, but folks kept talking about trouble in the interior, east of the Cascade Mountains, and they were worried about the local tribes getting stirred up by that. She wondered what Alan thought. She hadn't talked to him about it. Should she? Would her people ever get past thinking of the British as somehow the enemy? She kneaded the back of her neck. She'd sat too long, bent over the tiny stitches.

A sound startled her. Outside the door. She swerved her head to look, then chided herself. *It's just Ma and the boys back from their walk.*

She watched the doorway, expecting to see them appear in the shimmering haze. A shadowy figure filled the open frame. Her heart lunged. Not Ma. An Indian.

He seemed more illusion than reality, screened behind the strange filtered light. For a moment Jennie couldn't move. She sat and stared, unable to take in the reality of his presence.

He took one step forward, his huge form blocking out sun and light. Jennie tossed the pants aside and gripped the edge of the bed. She told herself to be calm. There were always Indians around the settlement, though she couldn't remember seeing this one before. She focused on his face, trying to remember him, wanting to recognize him, to know he was somehow familiar. Safe.

He wore only the breechclout and moccasins, with a necklace of animal teeth about his neck, his black hair hanging loose over his shoulders. He looked like the others with the usual sloped head, but she still didn't recognize him. What was he doing here? What did he want? She expected him to say something, but he just stared back at her.

She lifted her chin, spine straight, and rose from the bed. As she walked toward the door, she started to speak, but only a raspy sound came out. Trying to clear her throat, she spoke in a voice she didn't recognize as her own. "How may I . . . help you?"

He said something, but her mind wouldn't make any sense of it. A ringing in her head almost obliterated the sound. "Wh—what?" she asked.

He spoke again, a jumble of sounds. She thought her brain had taken leave of her so she was no longer able to decipher words. But of course he was speaking in his own language.

She reached a hand toward him. "Do you speak English? At all? I don't understand what you're saying."

He answered her, louder this time, and took another step forward, waving his arms.

She reached for the door, ready to slam it if he didn't stop. But he was already too far into the doorway. Her heart pounded so hard she felt the pulse through her whole body. "Please . . . I don't know what you want."

Old Blue snorted and picked up speed. Jake wrapped his fingers around the edge of the book to hold it steady and gripped the rifle wedged across the saddle seat in front of him. "What's your hurry, boy?"

Scanning the area, Jake saw nothing unusual through the thick curtain of brush and trees. The trail was narrowing, the trees thicker, making it harder to read. "Maybe we ought to hurry on home, Blue. Want to run?"

Blue snorted again, and Jake stuffed the book into his saddlebag so he could move the horse out. When Jake leaned forward and gave the horse's sides the slightest squeeze, the animal leaped ahead on the trail like a racer released onto the track, all that compressed energy exploding with power. Jake kept a firm grip on the gun. His own blood stirred as with the thrill of the race. Hooves pounding the soft earth reminded him of hooves on a racetrack, making his heart beat in time.

"You haven't lost it, have you, boy? I'll bet you could still take the race today."

Brush closed in on either side, like horses closing in on a track, and Blue charged through, as if he wanted to show he could still live up to his name, Kentucky Blue. Jake had won beaver more than once racing this one in the mountains at rendezvous, collecting piles of extra pelts for his winnings.

When the trail turned steep, Jake reined Blue in, and gradually the animal slowed until he moved with short mincing steps, tossing his head, blowing tremorous air out his wide nostrils. As they made their way down to the bench of land where the burgeoning little town of Willamette Falls lay, Jake's focus riveted on the Haviland cabin. He wondered if the family might need something now that George Haviland was on that trip down to French Prairie. "Let's go see, boy."

Approaching the cabin, Jake heard a strange voice coming from the far side where the door was. A strident tone. His hand tightened on the rifle. It wasn't a familiar voice. And the words—the man was speaking in an Indian tongue, but Jake couldn't make out which one. He nudged Blue faster. His mind spun with thoughts. Indian trouble spreading to the locals. Narcissa Whitman forced to flee Indians she was trying to help. Jennie's father not here to watch out for his family.

When he came around the corner, his throat went dry. He raised the rifle, still capped from his hunt, and drew back the hammer. A large Indian man, a Chinookan Jake didn't know, was waving both hands, whether in rage or frustration or simple emphasis, Jake couldn't tell. But the harsh voice implied threat. And Jennie stood alone in the doorway, eyes wide.

The Chinookan reacted to Jake's presence, wheeling about and drawing a knife from his belt. Jake aimed straight at the man's chest and spoke in the Chinook jargon long used for trade in the area. "What do you want?"

The man motioned toward Jake's rifle and stood in front of Jennie so Jake didn't dare shoot. "You put the gun down," he said in the jargon.

"Answer first."

"I want food. I am hungry. I want this Boston to give me food."

"Food?" Jake lowered the gun a little, ready to raise it in an instant. He was a marksman and could probably hit the man without endangering Jennie. But *probably* wasn't good enough.

The man's brow furrowed. "The white woman is dumb. She won't give me food."

Jake heaved a sigh. "The white woman doesn't understand you."

Glancing in the doorway at Jennie, the man gestured toward Jake. "I speak the jargon."

"She doesn't understand the jargon."

The Chinookan let out a huff. "The white woman is dumb."

Taking a deep breath, Jake let it out slowly. "I can give you food."

"What food?"

Jake reached behind his saddle and patted the fat coon he'd killed. "I'll give you this coon."

The man stood quietly, his knife still raised, then shook his head. "I want bread."

"I do not know if she has bread, but I will ask her."

"Ask."

Jake looked at Jennie and, wanting to ask her everything at once, quickly spilled out his questions in English. "Miss Jennie, he wants some bread. Do you have any? And are you all right? Has he hurt you?"

She gulped visibly. "I . . . I don't have any bread. Just boiled wheat."

"Are you all right?" Jake asked again, watching the man's face for any suspicion at the length of conversation over a simple question of bread.

"I . . ."

Why didn't she answer? Her response didn't do much toward helping Jake keep a stoic front for the Indian's benefit.

The man spoke up in the jargon to remind him. "I want bread."

"She has no bread." When the Chinookan raised the knife again, Jake went on quickly. "She has boiled wheat."

The man's face wrinkled in disgust, and he grumbled. "No boiled wheat."

Jake tried to think of something else—anything to get him away from Jennie's door.

But the man finally spoke with resignation. "I will take the coon if you put down the gun."

Lowering the hammer of his rifle, Jake laid the weapon across the saddle again and swung to the ground, pulling down both rifle and coon. With the rifle vertical at his side, he strode toward the man, holding the coon in his outstretched hand. "Here. Take it and go."

The Chinookan stared at the coon, not responding. Jake wondered if he'd changed his mind. Then the man slipped the knife back into his belt and grabbed the coon out of Jake's hand. With one last huff at Jennie, he turned and walked away.

Jake went straight to Jennie in two long strides, propped his rifle against the doorframe, and grasped her by the shoulders. He wanted to take her in his arms and hold her close, but didn't think she'd welcome the gesture. "Miss Jennie, are you all right now?"

"I—yes, of course. I—well, I didn't know what he might do. He—he never came in. He just stood there talking to me in this angry-sounding voice, and I couldn't understand a thing he was saying."

She put her hands on Jake's chest, as if to push him away, he thought. Then he realized her hands weren't pushing, but were clutching the wool of his black coat. He let out a long breath. "You scared me when you didn't answer."

"I'm sorry. I—Mr. Johnston, I—well, I want to thank you for—well, for coming by and sorting things out. I guess I should learn their language."

Jake smiled. It was the friendliest thing she'd ever said to him.

As if she felt suddenly embarrassed standing in the doorway with their hands on each other, she backed up a step, away from him, and glanced over her shoulder into the empty room.

"I take it you're alone," he said. She nodded, and he went on in a gentle tone. "You shouldn't be, you know. Where's your mother?"

"Out for a walk with Davie and Robbie."

"Eddie and Charlie still out hunting?"

"Yes."

Jake nodded. "I don't want to leave you alone, Miss Jennie. I think—well, until somebody comes, maybe—maybe I'd better stay—if you don't mind, that is."

"I don't mind," she answered quickly, and he felt pretty sure she meant it.

He motioned outside toward the circle of logs they used for seating around their campfire, which they still used sometimes, even with the fireplace in the cabin. "Maybe you'd like to sit down, enjoy a little sunshine on this nice day."

Jennie seemed a little flustered. "Oh! I should have asked you. Would you like to sit for a spell?"

He laughed. "Don't bother about formalities now."

She followed him to the circle and sat a small distance away. He didn't know what to say to her. He wanted to take away her fear and still be sure she'd keep safe. Maybe it was better not to talk about the episode at all. He glanced at her, and she gave him a slight smile, seeming as uncertain as he was.

She spoke first. "I thought he was going to barge right in when he stepped into the doorway."

"Why didn't you shut the door?"

She shrugged. "I don't think I could have. He was too far in."

"Was he threatening you?"

"I don't know." She rubbed her hands across her cheeks. "I've never really been afraid here, except about the panther and—" She looked away from him. "We know everybody in town. I thought I should recognize him, but I didn't."

"You still need to be careful."

They both looked into the cold remains of the long-dead campfire, and an uneasy silence lingered. Jake had plenty of things he wanted to talk to her about, like what she had in mind for the future—whether she shared his views on Oregon, or Radford's—and what plans she had concerning Radford. Of course, he couldn't come straight out and ask that.

He tried something else. "I guess you were at the lyceum meeting when we passed Abernethy's resolution not to form an independent government." It wasn't the best opening, but it broke the silence.

"Yes." Her simple response didn't help much to keep the conversation going.

"What do you think?"

"What do I think?"

"Yes. Do you support the idea of having an independent government or a provisional government until the United States comes in and takes over? Or do you think we should just stay with the status quo?"

She turned to face him, but he couldn't read anything in her blank expression. He wondered if she'd given any thought to these things. "Maybe you don't like politics," he said.

Her brow tightened. "I have thought about it—quite a lot. Pa talks about it so much."

"And?"

"Of course, Pa's for government, but I—" She looked into her lap, and back at him.

When she didn't continue, he scooted forward on the log, gesturing with his hands, the fervor resonating in his voice. "You know the British have been having their way with this country for a good long while, and now we're coming in for our share. Don't you think we ought to have a government to protect our own rights?"

She pursed her lips, then spoke softly. "I'm *for* the United States, of course, but I don't want to be *against* the British . . . really."

"On account of Radford." The words were out before Jake could call them back.

She shot a defiant look at him. "You don't like Alan Radford, do you?"

"But you do," Jake said, avoiding a direct answer.

"Of course."

"How much?"

"I—I don't—" She sat straighter. "It's really none of your business, Jake Johnston."

"No, of course not. Sorry." Jake let his gaze rest on her awhile, and he felt a weight in his chest. He hadn't meant to trouble her after her encounter with the Indian. Still, he wished he could keep all dangers away from her—even Alan Radford. He inclined his head toward his rifle still resting against the cabin wall by the door, and tried to turn the conversation back to less personal matters. "Right now we've got no law but the gun. I think we need something a little better than that, don't you?"

She spoke in monotone, as if to the cold fire rather than Jake. "I never wanted to come out here. I wanted to stay in Utica and keep going to the Female Academy there."

Jake leaned closer. "Did you want to be a teacher? You could do that here. There are ways to study and get credentialed for positions like that, even this far from the States."

"I don't know. I just wanted to read and learn and talk about important things. But I am helping Ma teach the boys. With no school here they need that."

"Did you tell your pa about wanting to stay at the academy?"

She frowned at Jake, then at the cold fire again. "It wouldn't have done any good. When he decides he wants to take us somewhere, he does it. We have no choice. At all." She gave him a quick glance. "A woman should have more say in things like this that affect her life. We were talking at the academy about women needing more rights. I wanted to be there and do something about that. But what can I do out here?"

"Well, maybe you could work to see that government in Oregon is more to your liking than it was back home."

She stared at him a long moment without a word. Her eyes seemed to speak to him, but it was like hearing a foreign language when he didn't quite know enough of it. When she looked away, he got up and went over to where Blue stood nibbling on tufts of green grass, rein-tied to the ground. Jake drew the big book out of his saddlebag and carried it back to where Jennie sat, her slender hands clasping her knees through the billowy fabric of her skirts. Maybe he could help her understand the possibilities, even in this remote place. But before he could say anything, her gaze riveted on the book in his hands. She jumped to her feet and reached for it.

"Is that Pa's book? Why do you have Pa's book? Does he know?"

"Well, I wouldn't just—why don't you take it, and you can give it back to him for me." He handed it over and she hugged it to her chest, giving him a dubious look.

A sudden loud yelp on the far side of the cabin drew their attention. A barking dog. Running feet. Jake rushed to the corner of the cabin and saw the boys' dog scampering after something—a small black streak that disappeared in a pile of logs near the neighboring cabin. Eddie and Charlie raced after the dog, Eddie in the lead, waving a rifle over his head as he ran, Charlie struggling to keep up.

Eddie yelled. "Get him, Muffin."

"Yeah, Muffin . . . get him," Charlie said, panting.

When Muffin reached the logs, he stood and barked, dug a little, trying to get at the critter, barked again, and dug some more. Eddie lunged to the dog's side and, still clutching the rifle, began moving logs with his one free hand. Charlie caught up and reached toward his brother. "Lemme have the gun."

Jake smiled, and Jennie stepped up next to him. "What's going on?" she asked.

"I think the boys and their dog have treed themselves a critter—or maybe I should say they've *logged* themselves one." He chuckled. "It's in that pile of logs there."

Eddie shouted at Charlie. "Help me move these logs." He didn't give up the gun.

Charlie scrunched his face. "Whyn't you let me have the gun?"

"'Cause I can shoot better."

"Can't neither."

"Can too. Now, help move these logs so's I can see him to shoot. He's right in there, right—"

Eddie raised the gun, but just before he shot, Muffin put up such a fuss, yelping and jumping, that the low-throated harrumph of the rifle sounded insignificant by comparison. No sooner had the gun sounded than Eddie dropped it and let out a groan, and Charlie echoed. The little black form scooted out of the log pile and disappeared behind the next cabin.

Jennie edged closer to Jake. "What's wrong?"

Jake wasn't sure, but he had a suspicion, and a smell wafted their direction to confirm it. "That critter was a skunk."

Eddie and Charlie wiped their faces and rubbed their clothes, then staggered toward Jennie and Jake, Charlie uttering loud moans.

Jennie raised a hand, palm out. "Don't come near us."

Eddie answered in a mournful whine. "But what'll we do?"

Jake hid a grin. "I expect you'll head for the river—and find different clothes."

Charlie kept rubbing at his face. "Oh-h. Gotta get this off."

"Well, don't count on losing all your perfume." Jake worked to keep from laughing. "But maybe you can tone it down a little."

Eddie bent toward his sister. "Do you have some clean clothes for us, Jennie?"

She backed away one step. "Yes, but I don't want you to touch anything clean."

"Maybe Jake could bring them to us."

Jake looked at Jennie, and she nodded. "I'll get some if you want to take them." Her words were matter-of-fact, but the brightness in her clear blue eyes suggested she was as amused as he was.

He tipped his head toward her. "I'll be happy to." Then he turned to Eddie. "I believe your target got away, and you boys just lost another hat."

Eddie shuddered. "Hat?"

"Well, I got a coon for you earlier today. Thought he'd make you a nice coonskin cap, but I had to trade him to an Indian for your sister here, so there went that cap." Jake gave Jennie a quick look and enjoyed her confused expression.

Charlie whined. "And I been wantin' a coonskin cap."

"I didn't have a lot of choice."

Eddie frowned at Jake. "What do you mean, you traded him to an Indian for our sister?"

"I'll tell you about that later, but you almost had yourself a fancier cap than any coon ever made—one with black and white stripes. You might have been the only boys in the country with a skunkskin cap."

Eddie's face looked as if he'd chewed a bitter seed. "Oh, no!"

A hearty burst of laughter sounded beside Jake. Jennie. He was so glad to hear it and so tickled by the whole thing himself, he let his own bottled amusement erupt, and together they leaned against the cabin and laughed until they had to hold their sides to keep from hurting.

Chapter Seven

December 15, 1842. Jennie stroked her fingers across the luxuriant green velvet laid across the rough counter in Couch's store. Her heart fluttered. When had she ever seen a more beautiful piece of fabric? And so perfect for the holiday. Christmas green—the color of holly and pine and fir. She imagined the dress she and Ma could make of it.

The storekeeper, Mr. Le Breton, moved the fat candle a little closer, and the glimmer of the flickering light rippled across the velvet, giving it life. The scent of candle wax rose to mingle with the bouquet of smells around her. Fabric, leather, new-cut wood, the slightest hint of mustiness.

The man's smile put warmth into his high-pitched, quavering voice. "I was holding this for the Christmas season. I think it might be just what you're looking for."

Jennie looked up into his round face as he peered at her over his spectacles, his eyes glittering. She wanted to tell him they would take it, but it wasn't her place to answer. Ma had to decide. Pa had agreed they could get something. He had some credit with the store for legal work, but the price was dear. She glanced at Ma, leaning over the fabric beside her.

Ma stood straighter, brows high, and began surveying the shelves that lined the log walls of the store. "Do you have anything a little less expensive?"

Jennie's shoulders slumped. *Oh, Ma.*

The man bustled over to a shelf at the end of the small room and pulled another flat, paper-wrapped package down. Setting it next to the green velvet, he opened the brown paper to reveal a drab gray linsey-woolsey piece. "This is good fabric, sturdy. You could make a nice dress of it."

Jennie looked around the room. There had to be something better. A few more wrapped packages lay on the shelves. Maybe they held fabric. Mr. Le Breton had every kind of merchandise, from farm tools to leather goods to these finer items—all from the last shipment of goods brought by Captain Couch all the way around the Horn on his ship, the *Chenamus*. The store was just another log cabin, but with the counter in the middle—which was simply a tall, slender table with rough-hewn boards for a top. Shelves lined three sides of the one-room building, while pegs held a wide array of tools and leather goods covering the fourth wall, barely leaving room for the door and one window opposite. Barrels of many sizes covered much of the floor, smaller ones stacked on larger ones.

A lantern hanging from the ceiling didn't add much light to the glimmer coming through the deerskin window. The door was closed to keep in what heat the iron stove in the corner provided.

Jennie drew her cloak tighter around her shoulders and looked back at the green velvet. How could anything compare with that? Mr. Le Breton watched her as Ma fingered the gray cloth that lay like a shadow beside the green. He rubbed a hand over the balding crown of his head. Did he see Jennie's disappointment? Probably. She'd never been good at hiding her feelings.

He made a soft sound, low in his throat. "Maybe—well, maybe we could do a little better on the price for this green."

Jennie could feel the lines soften in her face. Despite Mr. Le Breton's better price, Ma still hesitated. The price dropped again. Ma still refused. Finally she suggested a lower price. "And," she said, "I'll bake you a Christmas pie. I have a little flour and bear fat and honey and some nice dried berries. I think I can remember how to make one. My daughter has to have a nice dress for the Christmas parties at the fort."

Mr. Le Breton chuckled. "I think we have a deal."

Jennie couldn't contain her feelings any longer. She grasped her mother's arm as tears of gladness brimmed. "Oh, Ma, thank you. It'll be the most beautiful dress ever."

December 20, 1842. A flutter of excitement stirred through Jennie when she placed the treasured garment atop the other things she'd packed for her trip to Fort Vancouver. Ma had outdone herself on the sewing, with Jennie's help. A bit of lace at the collar and cuffs. Pearly buttons down the front. A bit of puffiness at the tops of the long sleeves. Long gathered skirt to float around her so candlelight could dance across the velvet and reveal the life within.

As Jennie closed the leather satchel over the dress, Ma patted her shoulder. "I wish I could be there to see you. But you'll be fine."

Jennie took a long breath and sat on the edge of Ma and Pa's bed to wait. "I wish my French was better. I believe Mrs. McLoughlin only speaks French—and of course the language of her Cree mother, which is no help to me."

Ma began to pace back and forth across the new puncheon floor that graced their snug little cabin, no doubt to combat her own excitement, and Jennie smiled, watching her. Ma so wanted Jennie to be happy and have good times, as she might have had if they'd stayed in Utica. There were no social events at Willamette Falls, except for the weekly lyceum meetings.

Alan had come into town with Mrs. McLoughlin a few days ago, Dr. McLoughlin having been at the Falls since the latter part of November when Alan was here last. Alan had invited Jennie to the Christmas Ball, and the McLoughlins had asked her to stay at their home. The short notice didn't give Ma and her much time for the dress, but it was done. Ma had thought about going along, but during Dr. McLoughlin's time here, Pa had become quite friendly with the man, and felt confident he could trust him and his wife to watch out for Jennie.

Excited as she was about the trip, Jennie still wasn't sure what she felt about Alan. She certainly enjoyed his company, and had warm feelings for him. She rubbed her hands over the twilled blue hickory cloth of the daytime coverlet that turned her parents' bed into a sofa. "Ma, how do you know when you're in love?"

Ma stopped bustling and stared at her daughter, brows high. Then she smiled, placing a hand over her heart. "There's a feeling right here when you're with someone—or thinking about him."

"But how do you know what you feel is love?"

Ma looked away from Jennie, then smiled at her again. "You just know—maybe not right away. You can be in love for a while, I think, and not realize it, and then all at once it hits you. And you know."

Jennie nodded. Maybe she was in love, but it hadn't hit her yet.

"Don't worry, my dear," her mother said. "Just have a good time. I do hope the boat trip won't be too dreary, but I'm sure it will be worth it. And you'll enjoy the company of Mr. Radford and the McLoughlins." She frowned. "I don't quite know why Jake Johnston is going, but—"

Jennie bolted to her feet. "Jake? Jake is going?"

Ma shrugged. "Yes, something about visiting the fort for supplies and to check their library. I don't know."

"Library? What would Jake—Mr. Johnston—want with a library?"

"Well, he's been reading the law, you know. Your father has loaned him books."

"*Jake?*" Jennie had trouble seeing Jake Johnston as an avid reader, much less one who'd care to read the law. "So that's why he had Pa's book." A more believable idea struck Jennie. "Of course. My protector. He's going along to protect me. Can't he ever just leave me alone?"

"What, dear?"

"Oh, nothing." Jennie had to admit there were times—like when the Indian came to their cabin—that she really was glad for Jake's presence. Not when Alan was courting her, though. Jake's intrusions then were most unwelcome. And now on this trip? Why did he think she needed his protection now? The McLoughlins would be there. And she was going to be attending all those lovely dances and parties at Fort Vancouver. She hoped he wouldn't embarrass her.

Ice scraped the side of the boat, sending shudders through the craft. Jennie hunched into the warmth of her cloak, hugging her arms to herself. Alan slid his chair closer and held his cape around her, his voice soft in her ear. "Don't you worry. Lévêque and Marceau are the best boatmen in the country. They've had plenty of experience rowing through ice."

Jennie nodded. "I'm just a little cold. I'm fine really."

"It is turning colder, eh? Getting late. But we'll be quite all right. Don't you fear."

Altogether six men were rowing, the two French-Canadian *voyageurs* and four Indians. It was a fair-sized boat—a bateau, they called it—a broad, flat-bottomed craft that appeared more stable than the narrow canoes she'd seen Alan traveling in. The deck was roomy enough for chairs so the five of them—the McLoughlins, Alan, Jake, and herself—could sit comfortably in the stern. Mr. and Mrs. McLoughlin sat next to Jake, facing Alan and Jennie, and Jennie glanced at them, concerned lest Alan's attentive gesture meet with disapproval. The McLoughlins smiled. But Jake had a set to his jaw that did nothing to hide his objection.

Avoiding Jake's eyes, she tried to forget he was there. Such a journey. How much longer before they got to the fort? She watched the passing shore gradually receding into the growing darkness, then looked back at the pleasant couple who would be hosting her visit. She wondered if Dr. McLoughlin had accomplished all he had set out to do in the weeks he'd been at the Falls. He'd gotten the town surveyed, but Pa said the accuracy was being questioned. Mr. Moss and Mr. Husspeth had done the job with a pocket compass and a rope—the rope being a rod long on dry days but shrinking on wet days.

Maybe the measurement wasn't accurate, but Jennie suspected most Americans refused to accept his survey, not because of inaccuracy, but because Dr. McLoughlin was British—just as they were refusing to accept the name he wanted, Oregon City. Such animosity! Jennie didn't understand it.

She observed Alan, then Jake once more. Clearly those two disliked each other. But why? Was it just politics that made them enemies? If it was politics, why did Jake seem friendly with Dr. McLoughlin even when many Americans weren't?

The McLoughlins chatted to each other in French, their voices low. The language sounded melodic to Jennie in the easy conversation between the two. The tenderness between them was a pleasure to see. Mrs. McLoughlin looked like a typical European woman with her cloth dress and cape wrapped around her ample figure, her silvered hair drawn back in a bun. Only a slight tawny complexion and high, flat cheekbones hinted of the Indian blood of her mother. And she wore moccasins.

Ice crashed against the bow of the boat, jarring the craft. Jennie grabbed onto her chair with one hand and Alan's arm with the other. She looked into the others' faces, but saw no fear in them.

"It's all right," Dr. McLoughlin said, smiling at her. "If it gets too bad, we'll head ashore, but our boatmen will know if that's necessary." The man's accent sounded a little different from Alan's, with a trace of French, she thought, maybe influenced by his wife's speech.

Chunks of white ice floated across the choppy surface of the great expanse of water, glistening even in the dim light of early evening. Much broader than the Willamette, the Columbia was also much rougher. Their small party had traveled the Willamette north from Willamette Falls until they reached the river's mouth where it flowed into the Columbia. Now they were proceeding upstream on the Columbia, by far the most difficult part of the journey. Only on the Columbia had they found ice. Jennie could hear it continually scraping against the sides. It made their progress rough and halting.

Lévêque spoke up. "Is slowing us too much, this ice."

"Indeed," Alan said. "At least the water's low, so you don't have too much current to fight."

"*Oui*, but with so many in the boat, is trouble enough this way." The wiry *voyageur* darted a quick look back at his passengers, his head low from the slouch of his shoulders, and Jennie caught a glimpse of his expression when he eyed Jake—an unveiled look of such hostility, it sent a shudder through her. Whether Jake noticed the bitter display, Jennie couldn't tell. She didn't think Jake's eyes had left her since Alan put his cape around her.

"Can we make it before dark, Lévêque?" Alan asked.

The *voyageur* lifted a hand, palm upward. The gesture appeared nonchalant, but his voice was taut. "I do not know, *M'sieu*."

Another chunk of ice hit. The boat shook again.

"*Sacrebleu!*" Lévêque held up the oar. "Is getting too dark to see them, *n'est-ce pas?*"

Watching the chunks of ice churn past, Jennie realized she could no longer see the banks of the broad river, as if the shores had dissolved into the river itself, the dark expanse of choppy water turning into a dark-gray blur a few feet away. She wondered how they would know if they passed the fort.

The boat slammed against a soft block of ice, shuddering to a near stop, and the ice rolled over the side of the boat, plopping onto Jennie's feet like a mound of snow. She gasped from the cold. Lifting her feet to get them on top of the mound, she still felt the icy cold through the soles of her holey boots. More of it piled in until the floor of the boat was buried in icy slush, as the craft lunged through the thickening flow.

Dr. McLoughlin's booming voice sounded above the steady scratch of ice. "Here! Let's get that out!"

He leaned forward and dipped huge handfuls of slush out of the boat. Jake dove into it too, and Mrs. McLoughlin and Alan. Glad for something to do, Jennie left her chair and joined them. The ice almost seemed to burn her hands, even through her gloves. They all shoveled with vigor, but more kept rolling in, piling up faster than they could scoop it out.

Lévêque's voice drew their attention. "Is the shore!" He pointed, his hand shaking.

Jennie tried to see what he was pointing at, but she couldn't see a thing. Darkness had come on so fast, it was night already. Was Lévêque imagining things?

Still, he insisted. "The shore! And the light, *mais oui?*"

"*Oui*," Marceau answered. "Is near the fort, *oui.*"

The two laughed and dipped the oars with new gusto. They chattered to each other in French and laughed again. Had they gone crazy? Maybe so, and they imagined they saw lights because they wanted to see lights. For a moment Jennie thought she detected the flicker of a light herself. But no. Maybe her own wish had inspired her to imagine it too.

A glob of ice sloshed onto her feet, the chill shocking her to action. Hands numb, she went back to shoveling. She wouldn't look anymore for lights that weren't there. She would shovel. A terrible crunch sounded. The boat shook, tilted. A startled cry escaped Jennie's lips before she could stop it. She took a step sideways to balance herself, and her foot came down on a slick spot. She landed hard in a mound of slush and slid across the boat deck. Scrambling for a handhold, she caught hold of a curl of rope to stop her slide, but the boat rocked. Would it go over? She couldn't see anything. The darkness closed in on her.

"Jennie! Miss Jennie!" Jake calling out to her.

Lévêque shouted. "Is the shore! We have make it! *Sacrebleu!* We have make it!"

The boat thudded to a stop. Jennie looked up. She could still feel the craft's gentle rocking. But she could see lights. A lot of them. Both Alan and Jake stood over her, each with a hand out to help her up. "Are you all right?" Alan asked.

"I just slid and lost my balance. I'm not hurt."

Observing first one, then the other of the two men, she caught the look of animosity that passed between them, and not knowing quite what to do, she put her left hand in Alan's and her right in Jake's. Quickly they helped her to her feet and out of the boat. She was so glad to be on solid ground she thought of little else.

Then she remembered her things. Her dress. "My bag. I left my bag in the boat. It has—"

"I have it," Jake said. He held the satchel in his other hand.

Aware she was still gripping both men's hands, she slipped free and took hold of the bag.

"Just a short walk to the wharf," Dr. McLoughlin told them. "Someone should be there with a wagon."

Jennie's skirts were wet and her boots so full of water they squished when she walked, but once she reached the wagon and got settled into it, her curiosity made her forget the penetrating chill. As the wagon rumbled along the roadway, she could make out the shape of the picketed fort ahead, a silhouette against the lights from inside. The fort itself was much larger than any of the forts she'd seen on the trail to Oregon. Scattered buildings lined the road outside the walls, their lights adding to the impression of the fort's massive size.

"What are these buildings?" she asked.

"The workmen's cabins," Alan said. "And that's the hospital over there." He pointed toward a larger structure.

"Do you live in one of these cabins?"

"Oh no. I live inside the fort. The gentlemen live inside."

"Oh." She puzzled over that. "How do you decide?"

"Decide?"

"Yes. How do you decide who's a gentleman?"

"Well, the officers and clerks are gentlemen, and the common workmen are not. It's simple enough."

Jennie's brows went up, but she focused on the fort again as they approached the picketed walls.

A sentry dressed in a Scottish kilt stood at the massive closed gate. He came to attention. "Dr. McLoughlin! Sir! Welcome home."

"Thank you, Murray."

Murray hurried to unbolt the large gate, lifting the giant latch, then swinging the double gates inward.

As the horses drew the wagon inside, Jennie looked around in amazement. "It's like a small city right here inside the walls."

Lights glittered around her now, twinkling from the many windows of the fort buildings—glass windows, *real* glass windows. And the buildings! There were real frame buildings. Not simple little crude log cabins like those at Willamette Falls. And those that were not frame buildings were tidily constructed with square logs. The frame house directly ahead of the front gate was magnificent. Larger even than the Haviland house in Utica. It had proper white weatherboarded walls, a proper shingled hip roof, shutters beside the tall glass windows, and a wide veranda that crossed the entire front, with a gracefully curved staircase forming a half circle from the veranda to the ground.

"A beautiful house," Jennie said under her breath.

Two smaller houses stood to one side of it, while a long one-story building stood at the other. Although the long building wasn't finely built like the house, it also had a shingled hip roof and real glass windows that looked out on the weary travelers with the friendliness of warm flickering firelight within.

"It is good to be home," Dr. McLoughlin said. "Good to be home." He turned toward Jennie. "I imagine you're ready to get inside and get warm and dry, young lady. Tut-tut, so wet and cold."

At his mention of the cold, Jennie shivered, but she remained intent on seeing everything. She tipped her head toward the magnificent structure ahead. "Is that your house, Dr. McLoughlin?"

"Yes, it is."

She beamed. *What a welcome change from cabin life!*

"Yes," the doctor said, "you'll stay there with us. Of course, only half the house is ours. We share it with James Douglas and his family."

"It looks like a lovely home."

Dr. McLoughlin nodded, then looked toward Jake as the wagon pulled to a stop by the curved staircase of the grand white house. "We'll be needing quarters for you, Mr. Johnston." McLoughlin stroked his chin. "I suppose we can get you a room in the Bachelor's Quarters."

"But, sir—" Alan began, his tone full of disapproval.

McLoughlin spoke with a ring of finality in his voice. "Yes, the Bachelor's Quarters."

Hearing Alan's heavy sigh beside her, Jennie looked up to see the bitter twist of his lips. But he didn't argue. The doctor was a warm and friendly person, but he had a stern way about him. Jennie didn't suppose she would argue with the man either. When McLoughlin directed Alan to see about arrangements for Jake, Alan stepped down from the wagon with only a hint of reluctance, and as soon as he helped Jennie down, he headed in the direction of the long building.

When Jake stepped down beside her, Jennie whispered to him. "What do you suppose is wrong?"

"With Radford? Well, it's only gentlemen who are allowed to stay inside the fort, and I don't think Radford considers me a gentleman." Jake grinned at her, and her brows rose. She wasn't sure Jake was a gentleman either, but she was surprised at the rigidity.

Motion back at the gate caught her eye, and she turned to see Lévêque and the other men who had rowed their bateau. Evidently they had followed the wagon on foot, definitely not being of the gentlemanly class. Lévêque's eyes locked on Jennie. A shudder swept through her. Then he dissolved into the shadows. The Scotsman in a kilt closed the big gates, ignoring Lévêque and the others as if they had never been there at all. Jennie shivered and again realized she was cold.

Chapter Eight

Fort Vancouver, December 25, 1942. Jake rubbed his hands over the fine wool of the black frock coat, and fingered the white ruffles of the shirt and the gilt buttons of the rich burgundy satin vest. Adjusting the bow in his black cravat, he bent forward to check it in the tiny mirror on the wall. He grinned at his reflection as he smoothed his dark-brown hair on each side, then in the back where a band held the longer hair in a tail neat as an otter's.

Alone in the small room, he spoke softly to himself. "Wonder if they'll know me. Maybe I should have asked for something a little less flashy."

But if he was going to do this, he might as well do it right. The outfit McLoughlin had loaned him was complete, from the fine coat down to the shiny black dancing shoes—even soft cotton hose. The tan trousers were similar to his buckskins in color and in the way they tapered to a close fit, but there the similarity ended. The trousers were soft and elegant—lacked the fringe, of course. Jake laughed. And they were clean.

He'd spent a pleasant day, mostly in the company of Dr. McLoughlin, following the man in his daily activities. Not even on Christmas Day did McLoughlin quit. He was a thinking man, and Jake had enjoyed discussing ideas with him—even about such touchy subjects as religion and politics, though steering clear of local politics. As for religion, it didn't matter to Jake whether a person was Protestant or Catholic, but he had a feeling

McLoughlin's Catholicism might be one thing alienating him from the American establishment.

Now Jake glanced around the stark little room a Company officer had been compelled to give up for him. Company gentlemen might dress well, but they didn't live so well. A small bed, a simple chest of drawers, a tiny table with a box for a chair, one trunk. That was it for furnishings. A few mementos hung on the walls—tomahawks, feathers, carvings, a couple of paintings.

Like most of the fort buildings, the Bachelor's Quarters were constructed in the Canadian post-on-sill fashion with sills of heavy, square-sawn timbers lying horizontally between upright grooved posts. Not a bit of paint on the unlined walls. But they did have glass windows.

He peered through the glass at the Big House where they were holding tonight's party. Obviously most of the construction money went toward that home built for the fort's top men—McLoughlin and his second-in-command.

Taking a deep breath, Jake glanced in the mirror once more and headed out. The noise of revelry billowed from the mansion as he approached it. The front door stood open, a crowd inside, milling about the long entryway. All were finely dressed—gentlemen in frock coats and ruffles, some with even more elegant cutaway coats, women in dresses of silk and velvet. If he hadn't known he was in the wilderness of Oregon, he could have easily thought himself at a party in one of the fine country manors or city houses in the States—with one exception: At this party, all the women had the dark hair and dusky skin of the tribal people. Jennie was probably the only white woman at the fort.

Maybe that was another cause for the American attitudes toward McLoughlin: his half-Cree wife. Jake had seen little tolerance for mixed marriages among the more pious American settlers. They certainly shunned Joe's Virginia and Doc Newell's Kitty.

He shook his head and edged past the crowd in the entry to make his way up the stairs toward the sound of music. He supposed he would find Jennie there. He hadn't seen her all day.

The whole upstairs was one large open room. Dancers filled the floor, moving in time to a waltz played by three men with violins in one corner.

Candles in several tall candelabras cast a soft light over the dancers, and it took Jake a minute to find Jennie.

A jolt of pleasure warmed him on sight of her. He'd never seen her done up so elegantly. Gold and red highlights glistened in her hair, which she'd drawn up at the back of her head with curls dangling onto her cheeks, accenting the fine lines of her face. For a moment he watched her. Then he became aware of the man in whose arms she was dancing.

Radford was impeccably dressed as usual, and he danced with the finesse of one accustomed to such occasions. But was it really necessary, or appropriate, for him to hold her so close? Or to look at her like a man hungry for cake? Jake tugged at the cravat that tightened around his throat.

When the music stopped, Jennie and Radford waited in the middle of the room, having moved a little farther apart, though Radford's hand lingered on her. Jake marched onto the floor and planted himself next to Jennie, bowing slightly. "May I have the next dance?"

She wheeled about to face him. Her eyes widened with mild surprise, complete lack of recognition, then shock. Her mouth fell open, and she gaped at him.

He allowed himself a quick smile and asked her again. "Would you dance with me, Miss Jennie?" He turned toward Radford and added in a tone he hoped sounded gentlemanly enough. "That is, if you don't mind."

Radford stepped back, slowly, face drawn taut, but Jake supposed the social graces allowed the man no choice.

Jennie finally responded, her tone filled with amazement. "Mr. Johnston! I didn't—well, you look so different, I—well, I didn't know you."

He grinned. The violins had started up again, and without waiting for her to say she would dance with him, he took her in his arms and began to lead her about the room in time to the music.

She looked up at him, brows high. "You—you know how to dance."

"That surprises you?"

"I—well—" Her gaze passed over him from his slicked-back hair to the fine dancing shoes.

He smiled. "The good doctor loaned me these clothes. I think I could almost pass for a gentleman in them, don't you?"

She didn't quite smile back, but almost. He dared draw her a little closer and let himself relax in the pleasure of her company, the rhythm of the music, the softness of the candlelight, the soft touch of her as she moved in unison with him.

"Enjoying your visit to the fort?" he asked.

"Yes, I went riding today with Mrs. McLoughlin—and Mr. Radford." She added Radford's name as if offering an apology, then brightened. "Did you know Mrs. McLoughlin rides gentleman fashion?"

"Astride the saddle, you mean? They all do, all the Indian women. It's easier—and safer in this rough country than riding sidesaddle the way white women do."

"The ones here at the party don't have sloped heads like the ones at the Falls, I see."

"Most of these aren't from around here. But I think some of the local Chinookan women have quit the practice—even if their own people may see them as slaves."

"Slaves?"

"Slavery's pretty common in the Chinookan tribes, and they tend to capture slaves from tribes outside the area with round heads."

She nodded, brow pinched. "I didn't know they kept slaves."

"Probably not as much as in the past. So many died from the diseases we whites brought them, their customs have been disrupted a little."

"Well, Mrs. McLoughlin seems nice. I can't talk to her very well because she doesn't speak English, but she doesn't seem at all—"

"Savage?"

Jennie looked up at him, then away, and sighed. "I don't mean to be intolerant. I—"

He tried to keep his tone gentle. "You just aren't familiar with them."

"I guess that's it."

He grinned, wanting to lighten the conversation. "Even mountain men are just people." Her sudden smile lit up her blue eyes, touching off a warmth in him, and he added, "You just have to get to know them."

"Mr. Johnston, I—"

"Don't, Miss Jennie. Don't try to explain. I understand. The better I get to know you, the better I understand." He raised his brows. "I have to admit I have a little trouble with intolerance."

She burst out with a lilting laugh. "Then, you're intolerant of intolerance."

He laughed with her. "I think you're beginning to understand me."

She sobered, a trace of defiance in her voice. "I suppose you think I'm intolerant, and therefore you have trouble tolerating me."

Grinning, he shook his head. "Not you. On the whole I find you very tolerable." Holding her in his arms, Jake was acutely aware of how tolerable Jennie Haviland was. She had some things to learn, but she meant well. "No, it's people that set themselves up as better than others—those are the ones I find hardest to tolerate. Some folks don't look too highly on us trappers, you know. They take one look and say, 'Yessir, he's a mountain man, so he's got a soul dark as a moonless night.'"

Her eyes widened, and he went on. "I recall when Joe and Doc and I came here to Oregon and passed by the Dalles, and it just happened to be Sunday. We asked for food, since we were half starved. And they informed us they couldn't help us—it being the Sabbath, mind you. Old Joe let it be known he didn't think it was much more agreeable to starve on the Sabbath than any other day."

Jennie tilted her head. "Maybe they didn't have anything to feed you."

"I don't know, but when we got to Fort Vancouver, I'll have to say even the British treated us better than our own people."

"You don't always seem very tolerant of the British."

"I'm here, aren't I, enjoying British hospitality? Look, I came because Dr. McLoughlin invited me, and I like him. He's generous, has a fine mind. I don't always agree with his views, or his decisions, but I respect his need to serve his company and his nation. He's probably risked the ire of his superiors already, doing as much as he has for us. So no. I'm not anti-British, just pro-American. I want the United States to enjoy what's rightfully ours, and I want a government in Oregon that will help hold the country for us—and give us protection. Is that anti-British?"

"It is if you fight the British over it."

"I'm not looking for a fight."

"But if the British go against this government idea of yours, you would fight, wouldn't you?"

"If I had to. Wouldn't you? I think your pa would."

The Shifting Winds

She studied the ruffles on his white shirt, a tightness around her lovely blue eyes, and he wanted to erase the pain in them. "Did I tell you how nice you look tonight, Miss Jennie?"

She shook her head a little and let out a soft laugh. "I don't think so."

"Well, I ought to be ashamed. I noticed right away. I should have told you sooner."

A smile smoothed the lines around her eyes, as he'd hoped. He wanted her to be happy, to enjoy the pleasant evening, especially this dance they were sharing. He dared draw her closer, and the music stopped. Though his feet stopped with it, he didn't let go of her.

Her hand on his shoulder slid down and pushed gently against his arm. "I think the dance is over."

"Appears to be." He let go of her waist, but kept her hand and caught the other. She looked at their locked hands, then up at him. He smiled. "It was a very nice dance."

A firm voice startled them both. "Beg your pardon. May I?" Radford. He was reaching for her, his words more a demand than a question.

With reluctance Jake released her, letting her delicate hands slide out of his and into the awaiting hand of Radford. "Thank you for the dance, Miss Jennie," Jake told her.

She gave him a slight nod, and was soon swept off into the crowd of dancers in Radford's arms, the music having started again. Jake stepped back from the swirl of dancing couples and, bumping a few, managed to reach the edge of the dance floor. It seemed less pleasant to him now, the music less mellow, the candlelight less soft, atmosphere less agreeable.

He wished he could take off his coat in the warm room. Maybe he should get some air. Downstairs, he strolled into the Mess Hall to see if anything interesting was happening there. Men sat in clusters playing cards, and Jake watched for a while. It was an impressive room with its lined walls of natural fir and all the fine furnishings. On the mahogany chest gracing one wall lay items of luxury such as he hadn't seen in years—delicate crystal decanters and goblets, gleaming silver. A long table sat against another wall, heaped with elegant dishes of food on a snowy-white cloth. He tasted a morsel of meat in a rich sauce, and an exquisite pastry, letting the flavors roll over his tongue. The British ate well, even out here.

Picking up another pastry from a delicate blue and white china plate, he recalled the tin plates the Havilands were using in their little cabin at the Falls. Quite a difference, but he supposed this type of service was more what they were accustomed to.

Still too warm, he wandered outside to the veranda. The air was cold and crisp, but it felt good to him. Wanting to escape all the confines, he left the house and made his way to the back gate of the fort. A garden lay just behind the gate, an orchard next to it. Strolling into the orchard, he looked up at the branches on the dormant trees reaching toward the sky like grotesque fingers pointing at the stars. He shivered. The frock coat wasn't warm enough for the cold winter evening.

But he felt something else—a familiar prickling at the back of his neck. Had he heard something? He didn't think so. But he sensed it. He turned to scan his surroundings. All he could see were trees and the black silhouette of the stockade against the light from inside. In the darkness of the orchard, he didn't know if he could distinguish a tree trunk from something else.

Standing still, he tried to make all his senses acutely aware. The smells of the fort wafted to him—smoke from the fires, baking bread, meat—and the nearer scents of crushed green grass and decaying leaves. The noise of revelry washed out any closer sounds. But he sensed a presence. Maybe his ears or his nose or even his skin told him. Something behind. He pivoted and saw a man jump out from behind a tree trunk. Smelled the rank odor of unwashed sweat.

Jake instinctively reached for a weapon. He always carried at least a pistol and knife, if not his rifle. But tonight, feeling safe in the congenial atmosphere of the fort—and not wanting the bulk added to the trim-fitting clothes—he'd left the weapons behind. Moonlight glinted on a knife blade in the attacker's hand. Jake dodged, but the man was quick, moving with the stealth of a cat. Lévêque.

The knife cut a slice in Jake's shoulder, like a deadly claw. A flash of memory reminded Jake of claws that had sliced that same shoulder. He grabbed Lévêque's right wrist to ward off another slash, and tried to get hold of the man's wiry frame with the other hand. Jake found nothing to grab onto. The man was all motion, too slippery to pin down. Then Lévêque caught Jake's right arm and locked it.

The man's strength surprised Jake. Though Jake was larger, Lévêque's arms had no give. Jake could hold him off, but couldn't escape the man's grasp or make him drop the knife. Jake leaned, trying to push the smaller man back, but couldn't do that either. Jake was about to go for Lévêque's legs to trip and throw him to the ground, when Lévêque's leg came out and tripped Jake before he could finish the attempt.

Jake landed hard on the ground. Still he held the knife off. Using the power of his size, he rolled the man over and gained the top, trying to reach Lévêque's throat with his right hand. But Lévêque slithered out from under him, never letting up on the firm grasp of Jake's wrist. They rolled again, never yielding each other's wrists. Lévêque kept pressing his knife toward Jake, while Jake kept trying to reach Lévêque's throat. Pain burned in Jake's cut shoulder, threatening to weaken him. Warmth spread from the wound.

The man drew a knee up, struck Jake in the groin. A new shock of pain seared through Jake's body, and he let out a cry, bending double as Lévêque scraped the knife across his other shoulder. Still clinging to Lévêque, Jake felt himself being raised and thrown back. His head hit something hard. Piercing lights flashed. And everything went dark.

With little attention to the dance steps, Jennie let Alan lead her about the floor. She couldn't see Jake anywhere and wondered where he'd gone. Still marveling at the change in him, she kept trying to align what she'd observed with what she'd assumed. Of course anyone could dress himself up and look better. But where had he learned to dance?

Alan leaned closer. "You're very quiet."

She smiled. "Just thinking."

He appeared to be studying her, and she returned his gaze. He did look fine tonight too. His dark-blue cutaway coat made a nice contrast with his immaculate blond hair, the azure blue of his cravat and vest bringing out the blue of his eyes. Those eyes, more intense than usual, focused on her, and she couldn't help being affected. The three violins twined in sweet harmony to heighten the glow inside her, until she thought she might just melt in his arms right there in the middle of the dance floor.

He spoke in her ear. "It is warm in here, eh? Would you like to go downstairs?"

They both stopped moving their feet, while others continued to circle around them. "I think I would," she said.

They worked their way through the crowd and downstairs, out to the veranda where the cold night air washed over them. He lifted a hand toward the curved front steps. "Perhaps you'd like to take a walk."

Invigorated by the chill air, she agreed. Stepping carefully across the rough ground in her dancing slippers, she kept a firm grip on Alan's arm. The fort's interior looked enchanting at night with the glitter of torches and lights through glass. Her voice resonated with her excitement. "I had no idea there was anything like this out here in the wilds of Oregon. What are all the buildings for?"

He chuckled under his breath. "Oh, we have living quarters, a blacksmith shop, storehouses, a chapel, dispensary, granary, fur store, trade store . . ."

"You have a regular town inside the fort walls."

"We're quite self-sufficient, to be sure." He pointed to a building in front of them. "That's the fort office where I live and work, along with another fellow."

She smiled. "Oh yes. You're a clerk, you said, and you do accounting."

He patted her hand tucked in his arm. "That's right. Would you like to see it? I think someone's in there."

It looked like a small house, probably less than half the size of the Big House. It was weatherboarded, like the big one, with a gable roof and glass windows, though painted dark brown in contrast to the Big House's white. Friendly candlelight glittered in the windows.

Alan drew her toward the building. "I've been wanting to show you my workplace."

"I'd love to see it, if that's all right."

"Certainly. Allow me." At the entrance he opened the door a crack and peeked in. "Oh, hello, Mr. Barnaby, Mr. Langley—ladies."

He smiled wide at Jennie and ushered her inside. Two other couples stood near the small fireplace opposite the door, glasses in hand. A red and white dog the color of Muffin scurried to meet them, nosing Alan first, then Jennie.

She smiled. "Is this—?"

He laughed. "Meet Cricket, Muffin's mama."

At a word from one of the men, Cricket trotted back to a blanket in the corner. Alan introduced Jennie to the gentlemen, and they introduced their elegantly clad lady companions. The ladies wore the kind of dresses Jennie had only seen in fashion pictures with their low-cut necklines showing off their dark, satiny shoulders. Maybe Ma should have cut the neckline lower on Jennie's, but she never would.

Jennie had a brief conversation with Mr. Barnaby about Muffin, letting him know how pleased her family was with their newest addition and thanking him for his kindness. Mr. Langley offered drinks, and Jennie accepted a glass half-filled with a golden beverage. One sip told her it was strong drink. Her parents didn't drink spirits, but she decided a small glass wouldn't hurt.

"So," Alan said with a sweeping gesture to embrace the room, "my quarters, my place of work, and the hub of business at Fort Vancouver. What do you think?"

Caught up in his enthusiasm, she laughed. "It looks very . . . businesslike."

Stark, but neat and orderly, the room had only two tall desks surrounded with several tall stools, the desks piled with books and ledgers and paper tidily stacked, ink bottles and rulers and pens beside them. The warm brown of wood lined the room from the smoothly planed wood floor to the wooden paneling on the walls to the paneled ceiling. Doors on the fireplace wall led to other rooms and a staircase to some kind of space above.

Alan took her arm and led her to one of the desks. Laying a hand on the desktop, he gave her a warm smile. "My desk. I spend a lot of time here." He lifted a large black book and handed it to her. "Journals. We have to keep daily journals of everything that happens around here—what the men are doing, what the weather is like, who comes and goes." He raised his brows, eyes alight. "You yourself will be in here, my dear."

She thumbed through the pages of neatly penned writing. "What do you do with it then?"

"We have to send a copy out to the superintendent every year along with information on the trade, the Indian situation—such as that." He took the journal from her and handed her another book. "Correspondence books. We have to make copies of letters—all the official correspondence." He gently slapped a hand on a pile of papers. "Right now I'm working on inventories. We have to weigh and measure and count every item in the district—not just here but in all the posts in the Columbia District. And believe me, the Hudson's Bay Company has a great lot to keep track of."

"Do you have to do all that yourself?"

"No, Mr. Barnaby and I both work on it. He's the other accountant."

She glanced at the foursome near the fireplace and nodded.

Alan riffled his slender fingers through the edges of the stacked papers. "I trust we can get these done in time."

"What's that?"

"The inventories. They have to be done by the time the eastbound express goes out to Canada in March. And the indents as well. You know, we almost have to see into the future here when we make our indents."

"What are indents?"

"Our requests for supplies. The whole process takes so long that—well, for instance, here it is the end of 1842, and the lists we make now are for the year 1846."

"Really? Why?"

His eyes smiled, and he swept one arm wide, his voice suddenly charged with drama. "It pleases me you want to hear of my travails, m'lady."

She laughed at his pretense and went along with it. "Kind sir, I want to know *everything* about you."

"Ooh. That's rich. Are you quite sure, m'lady, that you want to know it all?"

She lifted her own hand with a theatrical flair and placed it on the piled table. "Do tell me, sir. *All* of it."

He looked at her a moment, lips pursed, a twinkle in his eyes that looked a darker blue than before. She wondered how much of their exchange was jest and how much not. He laid his hand next to hers on the table and looked at the pile of papers. "They'll go overland to York Factory in Canada in the spring of 1843. Then late summer 1843 they go by ship to London. And given the time required for the Governor and committee to examine the lists, and to buy and pack the supplies, and a ship to travel from London, the articles we order with these lists won't reach Fort Vancouver until spring of 1845. Are you impressed, my fairest lady?"

"I am, sir. And you don't use them until 1846?"

"No, because we have to keep a full year's supply ahead in case of shipwreck or other loss. It gives you an idea how remote we are."

At his words, the isolation Jennie had felt since coming to Oregon struck her with new force. Only at Fort Vancouver had she seen anything in this vast western country that had any resemblance to a civilized community. Now even that seemed perilously remote. They were all so vulnerable.

Alan bent his head toward her and took her hand in his, leaving the jest behind. "You find it difficult too, being so remote, don't you?"

She sighed. "Are my sentiments so obvious?"

"I rather think so." His sudden tenderness touched a sweet chord in her. "My dear," he said, "enough of this. Shall we go?"

She looked at the drink in her hand. She'd only taken the one sip. She took another and couldn't stop a shudder. Alan reached for the glass. "You don't have to finish that unless you wish."

"Maybe I—" She let him take the drink and set it on the table. A slow warmth washed through her, like melting butter.

They told the others good-bye, and she held tight to Alan's arm as they left the building. Her legs felt heavy, her step uncertain. She thought he would lead her back to the Big House, but he turned the other way, circling the office and wandering toward the fort wall behind. A glorious moon shone above the picketed wall, a few skeletal branches rising from trees on the far side.

He spoke in a voice feather soft. "A beautiful night."

The place felt magical with the moon, the twinkling stars overhead, warm candlelight behind glittering glass on the many buildings. Alan stopped and turned toward her. With one hand on her shoulder, he raised the other to trace his fingertips over her cheek and into the hair at her temple. The caress sent that buttery warmth all the way to her toes, and she let out a soft gasp.

He whispered against her ear, his cheek close to hers. "I have wanted to ask you for such a very long time, my dear. Jennie Haviland, may I kiss you, please?"

His arms came around her, and she lifted her face. Her answer scarcely made a sound. "Oh, yes." His lips touched hers, a soft, gentle touch. She reached around to hold him close and his kiss turned powerful. She kissed him back, wanting that delicious warmth to grow.

He drew away, only a little, and his barely breathed words became a caress. "Jennie, Jennie, Jennie." Her own personal name coming from his lips. He kissed her ear, her neck, and her mouth again.

A footfall sounded behind her. She slipped out of Alan's arms and spun about, while strange currents jolted up and down her body. Someone was walking straight toward them, limping a little. A man. Large. She didn't recognize him in the shadows. But as he passed before a window, the light from inside illuminated him. Jake Johnston. Her first reaction was annoyance, then dismay at his appearance.

The fine clothes he'd worn so grandly were torn and rumpled, streaks of blood and dirt on the once-white ruffled shirt and on his face. Even in the dim light she could read the pain in his eyes, like the hurt she'd seen after his bout with the big cat. But there seemed to be something more this time as his gaze riveted on her.

When she spoke, her voice grated. "What happened, Jake—Mr. Johnston?"

His eyes never left her. "Ran into another varmint, this time in human form."

"Are—are you all right?"

His forehead creased. "I'm all right. And you?"

Jennie tried to look away from him and couldn't. He must have seen the kiss. And not another soul about.

"Maybe we should go back to the Big House," Jake said. "More people there."

"I—we were just—Mr. Radford was showing me the office where he works, and—"

Alan cleared his throat. "We'll be going back straightaway, but you'd better visit the dispensary. We can walk you there. Do you want to report someone for this attack?"

Jake shook his head. "Not until I learn a little more. And I'll go to the dispensary later. I'll walk to the Big House with you now."

Jennie rubbed her fingers over the soft nap on the green velvet skirt of her dress. She wanted to argue with him, but he sounded unyielding. Her protector. Even in his condition, he had to be her protector.

Jake motioned for them to go ahead, and she looked up at Alan. She couldn't read his face, but he clenched his jaw and offered his arm to lead her back around the office toward the Big House, Jake following close behind.

Chapter Nine

The Lower Willamette, January 1843. Muddy water swirled between shores of leafless trees, pale moss scantily covering their naked branches, roots clinging to the banks above the encroaching torrent. The colors dulled, as if in wintry suspension of the vibrance of life.

Jake glanced at the dimming sky as he dipped the paddle. Going against the current, they weren't making good headway. At least it wasn't raining now. He could even see a bit of open sky, but if that closed, dark would come fast. He called out to Radford, sitting in the middle of the canoe with Jennie and Mrs. Larson, the Indian woman who'd come along as chaperon. "I don't think we'll reach the Falls before dark. We should probably look for a place to go ashore and camp for the night."

Radford turned to face him, his brow creased. "I suppose we should. It won't be a comfortable night for the ladies, but we can't risk this in the dark." He looked ahead again and leaned toward Lévêque, who was paddling in the front. "Do you hear, Lévêque? Let's move toward shore."

The *voyageur* gave a sharp nod, never taking his eyes off the rushing water in front. Jake was glad for Lévêque's confirmation. And his skill. Jake had some experience with the paddle, but he was no match for the *voyageurs*. He'd offered to help on this leg of the trip so they could make it with only the one long canoe. Marceau, who'd helped bring the bateau down the Columbia, had returned to Fort Vancouver.

Water on the Willamette was high. It had been raining since Christmas, almost three weeks now, filling the river until the water had overflowed its banks. Logs torn from the shoreline swept past on a current much increased since their trip north. Despite Lévêque's strength and skill, the two struggled to make progress.

Jake observed the hunch of the man's back. If he'd ever doubted Lévêque's strength, he wouldn't now—not after their encounter at the fort. Jake hadn't seen Lévêque again in those three weeks at the fort, not until today in the presence of others. McLoughlin had been shocked, of course, when Jake returned the damaged clothing with sincere apologies, but Jake had passed it off as an accident. Radford seemed to think Jake had just had too much to drink and gotten into a brawl. That sort of thing happened on party nights. But Radford had suggested the accident story, since McLoughlin might want to investigate a brawl to exact punishment on the perpetrator. Jake went along with it because he wanted to deal with Lévêque himself.

Whether the attack was simple retaliation for Jake's interference with the beating Lévêque was giving that woman last fall, or something more, Jake didn't know. A warning? Something instigated by Radford? But if the man wanted to kill him, why hadn't he done it when he had the chance?

Whatever the case, Jake had Jennie's safety to think about. He would deal with Lévêque later. During the three weeks, he'd kept a pretty close watch on her, and she'd seemed more careful to keep in the company of others. He watched her now, sitting in the narrow canoe, stray gilt-brown hair escaping her bonnet to blow around her face, chin high, taking in every sight. If she felt any fear, he couldn't see it. She was tucked into the center of the canoe between Radford and Mrs. Larson, a little snug against Radford, in Jake's opinion.

A log loomed. Lévêque stabbed the water with the paddle to avoid it, and Jake worked to match the man's stroke. He didn't like this. It was getting too dark to see these logs. Again he spoke to Radford. "There's a cabin less than a mile ahead, I'd guess, if I know this bend of the river. It looks different with the high water, but I think I know where we are. A friend of mine lives on the east side there—Richard McCary. Maybe we ought to head for his place. He and his wife would be happy to put us up for the night. If it gets any darker, we won't be able to see the driftwood."

Radford leaned forward, a hand on Jennie's back. "Miss Haviland? Mrs. Larson? I think we should. If we can find this cabin, you'll be more comfortable than on the hard ground with rain pounding the little tent we brought."

"Yes, let's," Jennie said.

Mrs. Larson turned and smiled. "A good idea." She was the wife of one of the Englishmen living down in French Prairie, having spent the holidays visiting her sister at Fort Vancouver.

Jake was glad for the general agreement and watched the shore more carefully for the clearing where McCary accessed the river. The glitter of moonlight began to dance on the water, the reflection breaking into a myriad of pieces on the choppy surface. It became more difficult to distinguish between the rough water and the drift that floated on and just beneath the surface.

Lévêque's sharp voice cut through the din of rushing water. "*Allez à gauche!* Go left!"

Jake dipped the paddle hard on the right, seeing the log after the *voyageur*'s yell. Too close. Looking back at the moon, he saw thick heavy clouds moving across the sky, ready to swallow their meager light. "We'd better get ashore now and camp if we have to."

"Agreed," Radford said. "If there's a trail we might make it to your friend's cabin yet, but we need off this river. To the left, is it?"

"Yes."

"Lévêque! You hear?" Radford asked.

The *voyageur* nodded, and together he and Jake moved the craft toward the left-hand shore. With the current coming at them from the side, it took care to keep from upsetting the narrow craft, and again Jake was thankful for Lévêque's skill.

Jake wasn't sure he had his strength back after the injuries Lévêque wreaked on him. The cuts and bruises had healed pretty well, but Jake had spent too much time reading and recuperating at the fort. It took his full effort to keep up now.

Darkness dropped like a curtain. Jake could scarcely see the others in the canoe. He could see nothing around them—only the sky above, where a small cloud had covered the moon.

Jennie voice rose, a subtle hoarseness betraying her anxiety. "Can you see the shore?"

Jake locked his grip on the paddle and tried to sound reassuring. "It has to be there."

Moonlight illuminated her face once more, and Jake saw the shore, not far away. A brief glance at the sky showed the small cloud moving away, but a larger cloud, like a grotesque hand, edged toward the moon as if to grab their source of light and take it from them.

"Hurry," he said, "we won't have light much longer." He fought the current with his paddle, fought his fear, but his tension made his movements awkward. The craft rocked.

Lévêque yelled at him. "You'll turn us over, damn Boston."

Radford snapped at the man. "Lévêque."

Jake tried to match Lévêque's strong, even strokes. Yet no matter how hard they worked, the current defied them. Jake couldn't see the shore getting any closer. It almost seemed to move away from them. Then it disappeared. Their light—gone again. That cloud hand had clutched their light in its fist. Jake had no sense of direction to tell whether they were even headed ashore. Could Lévêque tell? The way the current churned, might it just turn them around so all their work carried them away from shore?

A jarring crash wiped out Jake's questions. A hideous ripping sound. A scream.

A log had hit them, something big. Blind in the dark, Jake felt the crazy sway of the canoe underneath, the water at his feet rapidly rising until he was sitting in it. A confusion of splashing and yelling and screaming echoed around him. He gripped the side of the canoe and ran his hand along the top edge until he felt a break. The front end wasn't there. His part of the canoe sank, and water engulfed him.

He fought to get his head up. Finding air, he yelled. "Jennie!"

He heard a cry, more splashing. While he treaded water to keep his head above the surface, he felt something, a piece of the canoe or floating drift, and grabbed onto it. He called again, gasping for breath. "Jennie." Water dashed over his face, and he kicked and scrambled higher on the drift.

He couldn't see anything. He wanted to tell her if she'd get hold of some drift she'd stand a better chance of staying afloat too. But water filled his face again, washing into his eyes and nose and mouth, and he sputtered and coughed.

Blinking away water, he realized he could see. The moon was back out. He scanned the water's surface. "Jennie, where are you?"

He could hear nothing but the rush of water. He saw something—a form of some kind bobbing on the current. He let go of the buoyant piece of drift with one hand and swam, fighting the torrent to reach the form. It was alive, moving independent of the current. An arm splashed, and with new hope he swam harder.

God, let it be Jennie.

Closer. Almost there. He felt long hair. Jennie's? Mrs. Larson's? Lévêque's? But no. He saw her face in the dim light of the moon.

Thank God, Jennie. It's you.

She coughed, fighting him as well as the water. She grabbed at his head and threatened to push him under. The piece of drift slipped away. He felt brutal, but he had to lock his arm around her throat to hold her defenseless against him. Still, she struggled to get free.

He managed to gasp out words. "Let me help you."

Water filled his mouth, and he choked for air. Near exhaustion already, he had to fight Jennie so he could save her. With nothing to hang onto to keep them afloat, he had to swim to shore with Jennie in tow. She pushed him under again, and he pulled free to get at her from a better angle. Approaching her from under the water, he took a firm hold with one arm around her waist, pinning her arms so they couldn't fight him. And with his free arm he swam with all his strength toward shore.

Darkness enclosed them again. He could only hope he was still going the right way. His muscles were spent, and he thought his lungs would burst. She twisted again, but his arm was clamped on her like a vise. He didn't think the arm had any more strength. It was just locked so tight it wouldn't move.

He saw the shore. The sky had turned light enough, or his eyes had adjusted enough. He could see it. Close. They would make it. He swam until his hand touched a branch. The trunk of a tree stood half submerged in the flooding river. Working his way through the tangle of brush at the river's edge, still in deep water, he held Jennie close to him so they could both cut through the same pathway. She wasn't fighting him anymore.

His feet touched ground—hard, firm ground—and taking great heaving gulps of air, he lifted her out of the water and climbed onto the bank where he could set her down. She lay there so limp, a charge of fear struck him. Was he too late?

His voice rasped. "Jennie."

He shook her, wanting her to move, react—something. He turned her limp body over and pounded on her back. She choked. Relief shuddered through him. She was alive. He pounded again, and she choked again, spitting up water. Then she lay there breathing long, deep, tremorous breaths.

Pain seized Jake's own lungs, and he began coughing up water, until he crumpled onto the hard ground beside her. Closing his eyes, he drifted on waves of fatigue, like the rise and fall of the river.

A soft voice stirred him. "Jake . . . Jake." He managed to lift his heavy eyelids. She was looking into his face, still lying next to him, propped on one elbow. "Are you all right?"

He let out a sigh. "Yeah. Just tired. How about you?"

"I'm all right. But it's cold." She was shivering.

He drew himself up and sat, rubbing his hands over his legs. He'd been too far gone to notice how wet he was, but at her mention of it he felt cold too.

"Where are the others?" she asked, sitting up beside him.

"I don't know. I only found you."

"But . . . do you think—what about Alan? And the others. And the canoe? It was gone, wasn't it? Broken up and gone. They'd have to swim. Do you think—?"

"I don't know."

"But, Jake—"

He put a hand on her shoulder, wishing he could reassure her. "They might have gotten out. After it happened, I didn't see anybody, and then I found you."

"Hadn't we better try to find them?"

He felt her violent shivering under his hand. "We need to get you dry and warm."

"But Alan—"

Jake felt a sudden unbidden resentment. So, it was *Alan* now, not *Mr. Radford*. But at least he was *Jake*. He shook his head. Silly conventions. "I'll take a look," he told her.

He slowly raised his body, which felt many times its normal weight, and headed out. The moon was shining at the moment, and he could see a little through the skeletal shadows cast by the leafless trees. He found the trail and walked downstream, stopping from time to time to call out for them.

Jennie was right behind him. "I don't hear anything, do you?"

"No, let's go on a ways."

"Maybe they're back the other direction."

"We'll check that in a minute. That's the way to the McCarys' cabin, and I think we'd better head for that pretty soon. Mrs. McCary will have something else for you to put on, and they'll have a fire."

As he tramped along the trail, he became increasingly aware of his own soggy, cold clothes. His buckskin breeches sagged and clung to his chilled skin. The wool coat hung heavily on his shoulders. How did that ever stay on him? Wind gusted along the trail, adding to the chill. He kept calling out, then stopped abruptly when Jennie fell against him.

"I'm sorry," she said. "I tripped on my skirt. It's soaked with water."

She sounded so dispirited, he wanted to take her in his arms and hold her. But he just turned and laid a gentle hand on her arm. "We'd better get you to the cabin."

"But the others—"

"I'll go down to the river and look around, but if I can't see anything on the water, we'll have to assume they're on shore or—" He shrugged. "Wait here and I'll be right back. You might try to wring out your clothes." He took off his coat to wring some water out of it, and was pleased to find it much lighter. She stood watching him, and he gave her a tender smile. "I'll give you a shout before I come back." He started to leave, then handed his coat to her. "You can wear this now that it's not so heavy."

She shook her head, but he turned away before she could protest. He plunged through the brush, down to where the water submerged the trunks of the trees, wading to the tree line for a good view of the river. The water came up to his waist, but by gripping trees he kept his balance against the current. He looked upstream and down. Was there something? He squinted to see better. No. Just a log. He called their names, but heard no answer.

He wasn't fond of either man. Yet somehow it seemed important, maybe more so because of his feelings, that he do all he could to find them. And he certainly didn't wish harm to Mrs. Larson. But he only saw the river rushing by in all its deadly power. If they were afloat, he supposed they'd be far downstream by now, unless they'd gotten hold of something to keep from being carried off with the current. Jake's body drooped, as if weights bore down on his shoulders. The wet chill seeped into his bones.

Clouds moved across the moon's face again and left him standing in darkness. He heard Jennie calling him.

He yelled back. "Stay there! I'll be there in a minute!" He felt his way through the snarl of branches, then stopped, unsure of his directions. "Jennie, where are you?"

"Right here."

Pushing on toward the sound of her voice, he paused again. "Jennie? Let me hear you so I know where you are."

"I'm here, Jake." She sounded closer.

He felt the edge of the water and stepped out of it, but he still couldn't see. "Jennie?"

"Right here." He could finally make out the dark form of her. "Jake?" Her voice quivered. "I was getting worried that you—"

He felt her hands reach out to him, and he didn't hesitate this time to take her in his arms. She seemed to welcome the gesture, pressing her face against his wet shirt and wrapping her arms securely about his waist.

"I'm right here," he said needlessly.

"You didn't see anything of the others?"

"No, nothing at all. I think we'd better go."

"It's so dark. How will we see the trail?"

"We'll be able to feel it. I can—with my feet."

"How?"

"Moccasins. I can feel the ground through them. Come on. We should go." He was reluctant to let her out of his arms, and she still held onto him.

Her voice went hoarse. "It was so awful."

Her body began to shake, as with silent sobs, and he held her tighter. His jaw brushed the tender skin of her forehead, and it was all he could do to keep from turning to kiss her soft face. "You're all right now. It—it'll be all right." He felt a raindrop. "It's starting to rain. Better move along before—"

"Before we get wet?" Her sobs turned into jolting laughter.

Glad for the relief of humor, Jake laughed with her, and took her by the hand to lead her down the trail.

It was slow going, feeling their way. Jake had a vague idea where they'd come ashore, but wasn't certain. Trying to smell the smoke of the McCary fire, he only picked up the scent of the dank musty woods and rotting leaves that made the path hard to follow. Branches and roots rose up to trip them, but they stumbled on. He kept peering ahead for a glimpse of firelight until his eyes watered, all the while keeping a firm grip on her hand.

"Are we almost there?" Her words quavered with exhaustion.

"It shouldn't be too much farther." But he began to wonder if he'd missed it. He could only see suggestions of shapes—a darkness on either side of the trail, a lightness overhead. Jennie was a dark form beside him. He couldn't see her face, or the trail, or his own feet.

We ought to be there by now. Did I take a wrong trail?

A soft snort sounded.

Jennie stopped and clutched his hand tighter. "What was that?"

The snort again.

"A horse," Jake said. "It must be—yes, it is!" The huge dark shape on their left was not more trees, but a cabin. "It's the McCarys' place. But there's no light." He frowned. "Is it that late? Even if they've gone to bed already, wouldn't the glow of their fire still show a little through the deerskin window?"

"Are you sure it's their cabin?"

"Pretty sure. Come on." He led her toward the dark shape that loomed larger as they neared it. The horse nickered, leaving no question of identity. Holding one hand forward, Jake felt the log wall of the cabin. He ran his fingers along one log and felt the door, then the latchstring—which was out. He knocked. No answer. Knocked harder, in case the McCarys were sound sleepers. Still no answer.

"Why would they have the latchstring out if they were inside sleeping?" he said under his breath. Deciding they must not be home, he lifted the string and pushed the door inward.

Jennie drew back on his hand. "Should we—is anybody there?"

Jake stuck his head inside. "Rich? Mrs. McCary? Anybody home?" He waited a moment. "Evidently not, but let's go in. It's wet and cold out here."

"Do you think we should?"

"Sure. They'll probably be home soon, and I know they'd want us to make ourselves at home until they get here."

It was as dark inside as out—maybe darker without the benefit of the sky's dim light. Still gripping Jennie's hand, Jake felt his way to where he remembered the fireplace to be. His fingertips brushed across it. Next to it he found fire tongs to stir the ashes. No sign of live coals. The McCarys had not been here for some time. He hoped they would come home tonight, but if they'd been gone awhile, they might not.

Not wanting to worry Jennie, he smiled in the dark to keep his voice casual. "I'd better start a fire. Looks like they let it die down here." He held up her hand, still tight in his, and patted it gently. "I'm afraid I'll need two hands for this."

"Oh!" She quickly drew her hand away.

Smiling again, he fumbled around his bullet pouch for his fire steel and a piece of flint, realizing with some surprise that the pouch had stayed around his neck through the whole ordeal. The punk he kept in there for tinder was soaking wet, so he felt around until he found the box where McCary kept his home supply. Jake's fingers came across kindling and logs, plenty of fuel for a nice fire, and all of it dry.

Laying kindling in the fireplace by feel rather than sight, he set the punk close and struck his flint with the fire steel a few times. A spark flashed. It took. Burst into light. Released them from the oppressive darkness. He blew on the punk and soon the kindling caught. Rivulets of flame rose from the thin strips of wood. Once that was going good, he placed a few logs over the top. As the light grew, it seemed to warm the room even before the fire began to heat. When he stood and smiled at Jennie, her face glowed in the firelight, adding its own warmth.

He nodded with satisfaction. "Well, I'd better close the door, and maybe we can find something to eat—and something for you to put on."

She lifted a hand, palm out, and shook her head. "Oh, I couldn't. This will dry soon. It's wool. I wouldn't want to use her clothes when she's not here."

"I'm sure she won't mind."

He pushed the door shut, and Jennie jumped at the sound. Did it bother her to be alone in the cabin with him? A brief picture crossed his mind—the night he found her alone with Radford in the family cabin in Willamette Falls, with only two young sleeping boys in the loft. And another picture of the two, almost as alone, kissing in the shadows of Fort Vancouver. A flash of anger rose, and passed as quickly.

Jake watched her standing by the fire, staring at him, wet hair hanging down in matted strings, wet clothes sagging and rumpled beneath his wool coat that hung like a tent over her. All he wanted to do was make her feel better.

"Are you hungry?" he asked, his tone soft, gentle.

She sounded listless. "I don't think so. I don't think I could eat anything. I—I'm just tired."

Jake glanced at the bed. Not much of a bed, but probably no worse than she'd become accustomed to. The cabin was similar to her family's, though this had an earthen floor and lacked some of the niceties like curtains at the windows and a coverlet for the bed to make it look like a sofa. This one just looked like a bed.

He motioned toward it. "Maybe—well, maybe you'd like to lie down."

Her eyes flared, and her mouth came open, but she didn't speak.

"Well, if you're tired, I'm sure they won't mind."

Getting no response, he went to her side, close to the growing warmth of the fire. She kept shivering, and he wished she would change out of the wet clothes or get under the covers or something to get warm. Maybe it was warmest here by the fire. He felt chilled himself. "Fire helps a little," he said.

She nodded, holding the coat tight across herself. "When do you think they'll come home?"

"I don't know."

"What if—what if they don't?"

"Well, if they don't, then—" He shrugged. "I don't know."

Her voice became flat. "We can't stay if they don't come."

Jake twisted his mouth to one side and let out a long breath. "No, I suppose not." He contemplated the unpleasant alternative of going five more miles to the Falls in the middle of a rainy night, and he damned the rigidity of convention. Sometimes these rules of propriety made no sense, but if she was intent on holding to them, what could he do? "I guess we could borrow the McCarys' horse—if we can see well enough to get to the Falls." There was still the Clackamas River to cross somehow, but he wasn't ready to contemplate that yet.

Her voice brightened. "Could we?"

"I suppose, but don't you want to stay long enough to get warm and dry? And maybe they'll come home and we won't have to go."

She smiled at him, apparently satisfied with the plan. "I do hope they come home. I'm so tired." She looked into the fire that had grown into a nice warming blaze, and he was struck by concern for her. More than tired, she was sad, beaten somehow. Her voice softened. "What do you think happened to them?"

"What's that?"

"Alan and the others. What do you suppose happened?"

"I really don't know."

She looked up at him, brow tight, eyes full of hurt and accusation. "You don't care either, do you?"

The remark cut him, and he looked into the flickering flame, then back at her. "I'm sorry, Jennie." Her focus was on the fire again. Tears welled and overflowed onto her cheeks. "Ah, Jennie." He drew her into his arms to hold her tight.

She didn't fight his embrace any more than she had out on the dark trail, and he took comfort in that. She wiped her eyes and pressed her cheek against his chest, watching the fire, her arms wrapped around him. Jake had no desire to move, but he began weaving from fatigue. "Jennie, are you sure you wouldn't like to rest on the bed?"

She glanced at him, and away, her voice firm. "No."

Unsure he could stand much longer, he took a breath. "Well, then, how about sitting down?"

A large log, some two feet in diameter and three feet long, lay on the earthen floor a couple of paces back from the fireplace. It appeared to serve as a bench for sitting in front of the fire. Jake motioned toward it, then got an idea. "Wait. We may as well be comfortable."

He pulled a couple of blankets from the bed and spread them over the log bench and down onto the floor in front. Bowing to Jennie, he gestured toward his improvisation with a broad sweep of one hand. "There. That should be comfortable—and close to the fire for warmth. Would you like to sit? You can sit on the floor and lean back against the log."

Her lilting laugh rewarded him for his efforts, and when she stepped forward to accept his outstretched hand, he nodded with satisfaction as he helped her to her seat.

She uttered a sigh of such deep weariness, Jake knew he'd done a good thing, and sitting next to her, he found his arrangement quite comfortable. It felt good to be off his feet, and he could see his exhaustion reflected in her drawn face.

She leaned her head back against the log and looked at him. "If those people don't—well, shouldn't we be going soon?"

"I suppose we should, but . . . in a minute."

She shivered, and he sat up. "You're still cold," he said. Except for their feet, they were farther from the fire now, and he was no longer hugging her. Reaching around her for the corner of one blanket, he drew it across her back, holding it there, then pulled her close to his own warmth. "We have to get rid of your chill somehow."

Her words slurred a little. "I'm just so tired."

Laying her head back on his arm to watch the fire, she slumped into the softness of the blankets, as if weights were drawing her down, until her head eased against his shoulder. His own chill began to leave, and his head, resting against the log, settled against hers. The homey smell of the hearth filled the room. Gazing dreamily into the flames, he was vaguely aware of the heaviness of his eyelids as he basked in the pleasure of Jennie's warm body next to his.

Jennie shivered. The dampness sent its chill into her, and she snuggled closer to the warmth, feeling comfort in the arms that drew her tighter. She wanted to see the face that went with the arms, but it was too dark. She saw the dance floor and all the people dancing around upstairs in the Big House. But she couldn't see the face of her partner.

If only they had a light. If they could just get the fire going. She couldn't bear the darkness. She stretched and moaned. She had to get her head above water—to breathe, to see. Someone was holding her, and she tried to look up so she could see his face. Her eyelids were weighted, but with tremendous effort she lifted them.

Jake.

He smiled at her, his voice soft. "Good morning."

She sat up, wide awake. And stared at him. She could see quite clearly because it was light in the cabin—from the light of day. Pushing away, she struggled to free herself from his arms and the blankets. "Morning! How can it be morning?"

She bolted to her feet and stumbled to the hearth, then turned and glared at him. He was still stretched out on the blanket, as she supposed he'd been all night. He was no longer smiling, but his brows were raised, his eyes unusually bright, the faintest suggestion of a smile playing about the edges of his eyes and mouth.

She flared at him, her voice rasping. "You said we would go . . . *in a minute.* Is this your idea of a minute?"

He lifted his hands, palms up. "I'm sorry, Jennie. I—well, we were pretty tired, and—"

"We've been here all night."

Glancing about the room, he nodded. "It appears that way." His slow, mellow drawl simply intensified Jennie's distress.

"How can you be so—? Those people. They never came home."

Again he looked about, this time resting his gaze for a moment on the bed. "Evidently not. Jennie—"

She put her hands on her hips. "And you shouldn't call me Jennie. You should call me . . . Miss Haviland."

He tipped his head. "Of course, Miss Haviland."

She shivered. The fire had gone down in the night, and now, out of the blankets and Jake's arms, she was cold. She moved closer to the feeble warmth from the few live coals.

Jake slowly lifted his lanky frame and stood, then picked up one of their blankets, carried it to her, and began wrapping it around her. "I'll get that fire built up, but you'd better take this to keep you warm until I can get that going. Unless your clothes dried faster than mine, you're still damp, and I don't want you getting cold."

She shook her head. "Don't worry about that." She threw down the blanket, knuckles back to her hips. "Jake—Mr. Johnston, we don't have time for a fire. We have to get out of here and get home."

His natural drawl stretched longer than usual. "Well, we've been here this long. I doubt if a few more minutes will make much difference. Besides, I'm hungry. Aren't you? Maybe we can find something to eat."

"I don't want anything to eat. I just want to leave."

He bent down to work on the fire as if she'd said nothing. He added kindling, piled up coals under them, and blew on the coals.

"Jake, didn't you hear me?"

He kept blowing, and a tiny flame burst from the kindling, then another, and he added a couple of logs. "There. I think we'll have a fire pretty soon now—and some warmth." He stood and hugged his arms across his chest.

She took a deep breath as the frustration rose. "Jake Johnston. I don't know why you're building that fire when I—Jake, I'm not staying here. I'm leaving." She started for the door.

"Whoa!" He grabbed her arm. "Not so fast. Do you know where you're going?"

"I'm going home."

"Do you know how to get there?"

THE SHIFTING WINDS

She looked into his calm, exasperating face. "I can follow the river."

He gave her a small, wry smile. "Can't we get something to eat first and then go?"

She laced her words with sarcasm. *"In a minute?"*

He chuckled, then sobered. "I'm sorry, Jennie—Miss Haviland. I really didn't mean to fall asleep."

The sincerity in his voice tugged at her unsettled emotions. Their ordeal on the river, the fatigue, the loss, now this compromising situation—all came over her with powerful force. Tears burned, and she didn't want to cry in front of Jake. She glanced at his hand holding her arm, and he opened it to release her. Moving away toward the door, he lifted the latch, drew the door inward, and the room filled with sunlight.

He peered at the sky. "Beautiful day out there. Looks like it'll stay that way awhile." He smiled at her. "We ought to have a nice ride on to the Falls, don't you think?"

She swallowed hard and blinked back the tears. Not trusting her voice, she nodded and looked away from him.

～※～

Jennie clung to the horse's mane and tried not to slide against Jake, but the old animal had a swayback, and without a saddle, both riders naturally slid to the middle.

She frowned at him. "Can you sit back a little?"

"I am trying, Miss Haviland . . . for my own salvation. But the slope and gravity are against me."

"You—well . . ."

"If you'd sit astraddle this old-timer, I think you'd be a lot a safer. I don't know if I can hold you on this way."

She patted the animal's scruffy brown neck. "I don't think he's going to throw us off."

Jake chuckled. "No, I suspect his bucking days are over, but I still wish you'd—look, we can get off and walk before we reach civilization. I am giving considerable thought to doing that now. But it's a long walk."

She pursed her lips. Every rocking step made her feel she was about to fall off. "The ladies at Fort Vancouver do ride gentleman fashion, don't they?"

"That they do. It only makes sense in this rough country."

"But the ladies at Willamette Falls don't."

He drew back on the reins and stopped the horse. "Are you ready to try?"

She looked into Jake's face. His brows were high, but he looked to be serious. "You won't mention it to anyone?"

"Never."

With his help lifting her, she managed to swing her right foot over the animal's neck and sit with her left leg on one side, her right on the other. The skirts of her dress wanted to slide up, but she tucked them around her, glad for the many yards of fabric.

"Better?" he asked.

She nodded. "I don't feel like I'm going to fall off now." He started to lift the reins, but she took them from his hands. "I can do the reins."

Riding was almost pleasant this way, though she wasn't entirely sure it was decent. And the animal's swayback still drew Jake close, his chest and legs pressed against her. They rode in silence through the pleasant sunlit morning. Was grief possible on such a day? She could not let herself believe Alan had been lost to the river. He had to be alive somewhere.

Jake's voice startled her out of her thoughts. "Well, Miss Jennie—may I at least call you that?—I suppose I really ought to marry you now—being's I've compromised your honor."

Jennie swerved so suddenly to look at him, she almost lost her balance, even riding gentleman fashion. Jake caught her and held her close to his chest. His face betrayed little more than the tone of his voice.

"You never compromised my honor," she said. Heat swelled inside her, sending sharp tingles across her flesh, and she went on with less certainty. "You—you didn't. Did you?"

He clamped his mouth tight, but his dark eyes glittered. She looked ahead and made herself busy attending the horse's reins. She wondered how she could tell.

He kept an arm around her waist and spoke softly in her ear. "Did you or did you not sleep the night in my arms, Jennie Haviland?"

She heaved a sigh and pushed his arm away from her, leaning forward to avoid the press of his chest, but his legs still slid close. She began to think her initial reservations about Jake Johnston were quite justified.

Hadn't Alan tried to warn her about these mountaineers? The thought didn't make her feel better about having spent the night in his arms—sound asleep.

He spoke in that exaggerated drawl again. "Well, if you don't want to marry me, we'll have to think of something to tell folks. Of course, if you'll marry me—"

She looked over her shoulder at him. "I wouldn't marry you, Jake Johnston, if you were the only man in this territory."

He frowned, but wrinkles at the corners of his mouth suggested a smile. "Then, I guess we'll have to come up with a story."

She brushed a stray hair off her forehead. "What can we say?"

"I suppose we could say the McCarys were home, and then we'd have to find them and ask them to tell the same story. They would, I'm sure."

"What if they're at Willamette Falls? Then everybody would know they weren't home."

"True. We could say the accident happened this morning, that our whole traveling party spent the night in the cabin together. But that would only work if—" He shrugged and looked away from her.

She clutched the reins tighter. How could he even contemplate a story that depended on such a terrible thing? She would not believe the others were lost. Was Jake really so unfeeling? A flash of memory crossed her mind—Jake bending over her brother Charlie and his bird. Whatever made her think of that?

"Rider ahead," Jake said, and she looked up the trail to see a man on a big white horse.

"I should get down lest he sees me riding this way." She drew the animal to a stop.

"No, wait. It's Joe. Joe Meek. You're fine. He won't mind at all."

"But *I* mind."

Jake reached forward to take the reins and nudged the old horse to speed up. His arms tightened around her, and she wanted to move away, but the horse's motion rocked her too much.

Joe's voice boomed out as he approached them, and he lifted his shaggy fur hat. "Well now, if'n it ain't Old Jake and—sakes alive!—Miss Jennie Haviland! What in tarnation?"

Jake called out to him. "Hello, Joe. What brings you out this way?"

"Jist huntin', that's all."

"Haven't seen McCary, have you?"

"Why, shore. He and the missus been over to Tuality a few days visitin' her sister, *they* have."

"Uh, when do they plan to go home? Do you know?"

Joe wrinkled his face in deep thought. "Well now, I figger they oughta be a-goin' home—lemme think now—yessir, today. Old Rich said they'd be a-leavin' next day after me, and I jist come over to the Falls yesterday. Why d'ye ask?"

Jake sighed heavily enough that Jennie could feel the rise and fall of his chest. "We stopped by their cabin and didn't find them at home." Joe's gaze sharpened on Jake first, then Jennie. She looked down at the horse's scruffy mane and wished Joe would continue on his way. "Had a little accident on the river," Jake said. "Log hit our canoe. Miss Jennie and I got out. Don't know about the others."

"What others?"

"Radford, his man Lévêque, and a Mrs. Larson from French Prairie. Maybe you know her."

Joe grunted. "Well now, no need to be a-frettin' less'n ye know there's cause. I reckon if you got out, they could too. When did it hit ye?"

"Last night."

Jennie glanced at Joe's face, and began carefully smoothing her skirts down to cover her legs. His brows rose, a sideways smile on his lips, and she had a feeling that behind those dark eyes a lot of thinking was going on. He finally spoke. "You folks make it to McCarys' cabin all right last night, did ye?"

"Yep."

"And nobody home."

When Jake shook his head, Joe nodded, then smiled sideways again. Jennie's face burned. It didn't help to have Jake sitting there all wrapped around her, and she wondered if it was necessary for him to hold her so tight.

"We have a small problem," Jake said.

Joe chuckled low in his throat. The sound set off unsettling vibrations in Jennie, and she stared at Jake. *Why did you have to tell him?*

She couldn't begin to read the expression in Jake's eyes when he looked back at her. She didn't see the brightness, but some kind of intensity. His voice sounded taut when he continued, looking at her as he spoke to Joe. "I think we could use some help with a story."

"Yessir," Joe said. "A feller cain't jist say he spent the night alone with a lady—even if'n it warn't rightly planned thataway. Well, if'n that ain't some fix, now, I wouldn't say so."

The sparkle returned to Jake's eyes. "Of course, if she'd marry me—" She stiffened, glaring at him, and he shrugged. "She doesn't seem inclined that way, so I guess we'd better say McCarys were home. Only trouble is, we need to find them to tell them they were home."

"Well now, if'n ye'd like this old coon to ride on to the cabin and wait, I shore'd be glad to, and I kin tell 'em jist as soon as they git tharselves home."

"Would you? I'll have to go back after I get Miss Jennie to the Falls so I can return this horse, but—you don't suppose they'd go to the Falls first, do you?"

"Reckon I don't know why they would. But if'n they do, I reckon you'll see 'em first, and if'n they don't, I will. Anyhow, I'll go on to the cabin now and wait. Do ye hear?"

"Thanks, old coon."

"Jist glad to help a friend—and a lady." A mirthful look came over Joe's broad, whiskered face. He gave Jennie a slight bow, turned his big white horse, and plopping his fur hat back on his head, galloped down the trail, the sound of his laughter drifting back.

Chapter Ten

January 1843. Leaning against a mossy tree trunk, Alan looked across the deadly churning water of the Willamette River to the small town of Oregon City where he could see the Haviland cabin. A tightness gripped his chest at the thought of the dreadful message he must carry. How could he tell them about Jennie?

"Sweet Jennie. I do wish I'd never taken you to Fort Vancouver. If only I could have found you."

He closed his eyes, wanting to escape the reality. But he kept seeing it in his mind. Everything had been such confusion in the terrible dark last night when the log hit and threw him into the water. He'd fought the current and the panic and the darkness, and he'd tried desperately to find Jennie. Somehow he'd gotten ashore and found Lévêque and Mrs. Larson, but no sign of Jennie or Johnston. The current had taken the three of them far downstream and kicked them out on the west bank. Throughout the long walk to the Falls this morning, they had continued the search for the other two.

Now the hopelessness bore down on him, the fatigue and loss. They'd seen no one except that couple they ran into this morning—the McCarys, Johnston's friends with the cabin. The McCarys were on their way home from Tualatin Plains and hadn't seen anything of Jennie or Johnston. It had occurred to Alan that the cabin wouldn't have been such a good stopping place last night after all, since the owners weren't home. Not that it mattered now.

"*M'sieu* Alan!" Lévêque, coming back from talking to some Indians living on this side of the river. "The Indians, they take us across in a canoe."

"Thank you, Lévêque." Alan drew away from the tree and tried to smooth his rumpled clothes. "I must be a sight," he said, more to himself than to Lévêque.

"Is all right. No need to impress these Bostons." Alan shot a hard look toward his attendant, but Lévêque continued, as if oblivious to Alan's displeasure. "I should have kill him. *Sacrebleu!* I don't know why I do not. But the river—she do it for me, *oui*?"

"What the devil are you talking about?"

"The *Américain*. Johnston. I beat him. For you." Lévêque grinned and gestured toward Alan, palm up, as if in offering. Then he shrugged with dramatic resignation. "But I do not finish, so the river—"

Alan pressed his hands to his head. "Lévêque! You? That's what happened to Johnston back at the fort?"

"*Oui*." Lévêque's tone didn't ring true. "He is trouble for you. I give him warning for you, *M'sieu* Alan, but the river, she see he give you no more trouble."

"You fool!" Alan grabbed Lévêque's shirt and began to tighten it at his throat.

Lévêque pulled Alan's hands away and whined. "I do this for you."

Alan stared at him with disbelief. The man averted his eyes, then gave Alan a wry smile. "I see how you don't like him and how he watch the *américaine* wench—*your américaine* wench." Lévêque's smile became a sneer. "I see his eyes on her. I know what he wants."

Alan pushed the man away from him. "You can't beat a man because he looks at a woman—or because I don't like him. Now Johnston probably thinks I—" Alan put a hand to his forehead, realizing Johnston probably wasn't around to think anything now. He frowned at Lévêque, wanting to penetrate the facade that hid the man's real purpose. Giving that up for the moment, Alan straightened and spoke with the authority of his rank. "Lévêque, if you want to fight with your friends, all right, but don't go after anyone else unless you clear it with me first. Do you understand?"

"*Oui.*" He rubbed a hand over the black stubble that darkened his chin and, with characteristic quick movements, turned toward the river. "Ah!" He showed not the least sign he'd just been reproached. "The Indians, they are ready. You see?"

Alan nodded as a couple of Indian men drew a canoe toward the water's edge, Mrs. Larson standing nearby.

The water remained high, but the Indians were skilled canoe men, and their canoe, made from a hollowed log, was sturdy. Once they got to the other side, Mrs. Larson excused herself, and Alan headed toward the Haviland cabin with a heavy step. He was a little surprised when Lévêque followed him, but didn't bother to send the man away. Company of any kind was welcome. As they approached the door, the little dog Muffin jumped up from the front stoop and barked, then, yipping with recognition, bounded straight to Alan.

A smile carved its way through Alan's frown, and he bent down to pet the animal. "Hello, Muffin." The dog wagged its whole body, licking Alan's cheek, and Alan scooped the soft warm creature into his arms and held it, wiping a stray tear on the soft fur. Alan had to snuff his nose before he could approach the door.

At his knock the crude wooden door swung inward. Then nothing moved. Mrs. Haviland stood in the doorway, her mouth open, face colorless, and, for one long moment, uncharacteristically silent. When she did speak, her voice was little louder than a whisper. "Why, Mr. Radford, you're alive. You are truly—oh, my." She stepped forward, hands outstretched. "I'm so glad to see you."

Alan grasped her hands, feeling some relief that he didn't have to be the one to break the news about her daughter. "Then, you've heard . . . about the accident. But from—who told you?"

"Why, it was . . ."

She turned her head toward the interior of the cabin, and Alan's mouth dropped open. Jennie appeared at the door beside her.

"Jennie!" The shock on her face must have mirrored his own. Letting go of her mother's hands, he reached out and embraced Jennie, so relieved to see her he gave no notice to anyone else as he held her tight. "Dear Jennie, I thought you were lost in the river. I thought—"

"I was afraid for you too. I couldn't believe, but—oh, Alan."

He heard Mrs. Haviland then. "Would you gentlemen like to come in?"

Gentlemen? Still holding Jennie, Alan looked up. Mrs. Haviland smiled, as if she wasn't unhappy to see him embracing her daughter. But he nevertheless let Jennie out of his arms, embarrassed now at his own impertinence. He wondered who else Mrs. Haviland had alluded to in her plural reference to gentlemen. He saw only Lévêque, standing just outside, and Mrs. Haviland with a hand on the door, smiling at the man. With black eyes darting about, taking in everything, the *voyageur* stepped inside.

Jennie took Alan's hand to lead him to the parents' bed and sat close to him without hesitance, her soft blue eyes full of concern. "What happened to you?"

He clasped her hand in both of his. "I tried to find you, but in the dark I could see nothing. I swam and finally landed on the riverbank. We kept looking for you, but—" He didn't want to say it.

"We looked for you too, and—Mrs. Larson—is she—?"

"She made it all right. You said *we*. Did—?"

Mrs. Haviland explained. "Mr. Johnston got her ashore, thank the good Lord."

Alan turned to Jennie's mother, having almost forgotten she was in the room. One of the older boys, the chubby one, hovered in a corner with the two little ones. Lévêque stood poised near the door, as if ready to spring at the first suggestion of danger.

Mrs. Haviland went on. "It certainly was fortunate Mr. Johnston found her in the dark. And fortunate they found their way to that cabin, so they didn't have to be out all night in the weather. What were their names, Jennie? The people with the cabin—the McClanes or McClarys?"

"McCarys," Jennie said softly, looking into her lap.

Her mother smiled. "Yes. She and Mr. Johnston spent the night with the McCarys so they were able to get warm and at least a little bit dry to keep from catching their deaths, and then they came on home this morning."

Alan stiffened as he watched Jennie. "Johnston and you—" Color rose in her cheeks, though she kept looking down. Her reaction did little to still his growing suspicion.

Mrs. Haviland answered for her daughter. "Yes. Mr. Johnston went back this afternoon to return the McCarys' horse."

Connections began to form in Alan's mind. He had met the McCarys earlier today. They were not at home last night. If the McCarys weren't home, Jennie and Johnston must have been in the cabin alone. Alan felt a nettling uneasiness imagining Jennie alone all night with a man like Johnston—and lying about it now.

Mrs. Haviland chattered on, as if nothing were amiss. "I do wish Mr. Haviland was home. He went to the Willamette Mission to do some legal work, and there was some talk down there about the animal problem. You know what trouble we've been having with wolves and panthers getting after the livestock. They sighted another panther near here the other day, you know. Why, it scares me to have the boys out hunting."

"Oh, Ma," Charlie said, his voice full of protest.

His mother paid no attention. "I let Eddie ride to the McCarys with Mr. Johnston, since he's been in so much lately."

Alan glanced at Charlie and little Robbie staring wide-eyed back at him. Turning his attention back to Jennie, Alan felt a strange constriction in his chest.

He spoke to her in his mind, words he could not say aloud. *Dearest Jennie. You, alone with that damned bastard. You're my girl, Jennie, the first girl I've met who could rid my memory of Marcella.*

Studying Jennie's face, he contemplated the differences. Though beautiful, Jennie lacked Marcella's perfect beauty, and yet with Marcella's perfection came a cold unreality. Jennie was not cold. She fairly glowed with warmth, freshness, innocence. The tightness clutched him so fiercely, he had trouble drawing breath. He wanted to say something, ask her all the troubling questions. He looked at Lévêque and could almost see the man's mind working. Lévêque had it figured out too. And Lévêque wanted to kill Johnston.

Alan clenched his fists. *I ought to kill Johnston. I should be the one.*

―✦―

Alan tossed a barrel into the corner with a strength he scarcely knew he had. The Company shack was a mess, and it made him angry. Everything made him angry—Patterson who stayed here to mind supplies, Lévêque with his knowing looks, the Americans—all of them. He wanted to beat on something. Someone.

Lévêque picked up a barrel and grinned at Alan. "So! The river, she does not take him after all, so Lévêque should kill him tonight, *oui*?"

"No! You keep your bloody hands off him."

"He sleeps with your *américaine* wench and you do not care?"

Alan lifted another barrel and raised it toward Lévêque. He was about to bring it down on the man's head but checked himself and tossed it in the corner with the others. "If anyone kills Johnston, I will." Sitting on a barrel, he pounded his palm with a fist. "If the bastard were a gentleman, I'd challenge him to a duel."

Lévêque's black eyes shone in the candlelight as his face twisted in a wicked grin. "Ah! Good idea."

Alan shook his head. "Obviously the man's no bloody gentleman."

"But I am happy to help."

Alan pointed a warning finger at the man. "You stay out of it."

A barking dog distracted them, and Lévêque peered outside. "Ah! Is the *Américain*. And the boy."

Alan leaped to his feet and pushed past Lévêque at the shack doorway to go meet Johnston. The man had drawn up his big black horse at the Haviland cabin, but when he saw Alan approaching he moved the animal in Alan's direction. "Radford! Good Lord! It *is* you. I'll be damned."

"You will indeed," Alan said, too low for Johnston to hear.

"And Lévêque. How about Mrs. Larson? Did she get out all right?"

Alan nodded. "She's all right. Johnston, I'd like to talk to you. Alone."

"Sure." Johnston turned his head to talk to the boy riding double behind him. "Eddie, do you want to take Old Blue over and tie him up?"

The boy grinned. "Yeah."

Alan watched Johnston, sizing the man up as he helped the boy off before climbing down from the tall horse himself. Johnston was larger than Alan by a little, not by much, and Lévêque had managed to get the better of him. Alan decided the fellow wouldn't be an impossible match.

As the Haviland boy led the black stallion away, Johnston called out to him. "I'll be over later, Eddie." He faced Alan. "Well?"

"Shall we go over to the shack?"

Making an about-face, Alan marched to the shack where Lévêque waited outside the doorway, Johnston keeping pace behind him. It was nearly dark outside, and Alan welcomed the candlelight in the shack. He wanted to get a good look at Johnston's face when he questioned him. Gesturing toward a barrel for Johnston to sit on, Alan took a seat on another where he could get a clear view of his opponent.

"I saw Miss Haviland," Alan began.

Johnston nodded, his face stoic. "It looks like we all made it."

Tensing, Alan went on, spitting out each word with distinct clarity. "I heard about your overnight visit with the McCarys." He saw no reaction in Johnston and tried to remain as stoic despite the anger burning inside him. "I happened to see the McCarys this morning. They were just then on their way home from Tualatin Plains. Indeed, they had not been home for several days."

A change of expression flashed across Johnston's face—surprise, perhaps alarm.

Alan knew he'd hit a mark, and his words turned icy. "Would you like to tell the real story now?"

Johnston answered in a flat voice. "I have nothing to tell you."

"Damn you."

Johnston's refusal to talk seemed to confirm his guilt. An unbidden picture loomed in Alan's mind of this brutish man with Jennie. Alan's anger flared. He jumped up and grabbed Johnston by the throat. "You dirty bastard."

Johnston's response was immediate, and Alan knew he'd gotten hold of something with strength that would take all his own to match. He felt Johnston's hands close on his own neck until he thought his breath would stop. Already fatigued from his bout with the river, Alan couldn't seem to muster all his strength, and his fingers on Johnston's throat began to lose their grip. He couldn't let the man get the better of him, but he had to get air, had to get the man's hands off his neck.

Letting go suddenly, Alan shoved both fists hard into Johnston's belly and heard the grunt that told him he'd made an impact. In that instant he felt some give in Johnston's locked hands. Twisting his body hard as he struck again, Alan slipped out of the man's clutches and gasped for air. But he saw the fist coming too late. It landed hard on his lower jaw.

The pain incited new rage, and Alan returned the blow, hitting Johnston hard on the chin with his left fist, then his right, then another left. But the man's arms came up to block him, and he couldn't get back at the face. He went for the belly again, slugging hard with his right fist while he tried to protect his face with the left. One of Johnston's fists found a way through, cutting the skin of Alan's jaw with a slicing blow. In a quick move Johnston tripped him and threw him to the floor, pinning him.

Alan could scarcely breathe, let alone move, but he summoned power to speak. "Dirty bastard. Ruin a girl like Jennie, will you?"

"What kind of girl do you think she is?" Johnston's breath sounded as uneven.

Alan let himself go limp. Then he gathered every bit of his strength and rolled, pinning Johnston. "No girl's reputation can afford a compromising situation like that."

Johnston rolled back to the top. "Her reputation won't be hurt unless you speak up, because you can be sure I won't."

Alan tensed beneath the man's weight. He had no intention of saying anything to hurt Jennie. But one like Johnston? Mountain men were notorious for bragging over such exploits, even stretching a story to build up their sordid reputations when nothing did happen. With sudden fury, Alan erupted, jabbing with his elbows, his knees, any part of him that could be used to hurt Johnston. Again the man's grasp broke. Alan scuttled around and threw himself atop Johnston, locking the man's arms to hold him down.

Johnston lay there without resisting. "Just what the hell are your intentions toward Jennie?"

"None of your bloody business."

"Do you plan to marry her, or are you just dallying with her?"

"I'm quite sure I don't owe an explanation to the likes of you."

Johnston's voice hardened. "If you won't tell me, I guess I'll have to assume you're dallying."

Alan felt himself raised, as if Johnston had exploded beneath him, and Johnston rolled him over and pinned him once more, a hand on his throat that threatened to stop his air.

Johnston's voice turned vicious. "Don't dally with her."

Tight in Johnston's grasp, Alan could barely speak. "I—I'm not."

"Then, you figure to marry her?"

"I—I—yes," Alan found himself saying.

"Have you asked her?"

"I . . . well . . . you can't . . . rush these things."

Johnston smiled, but with no humor in the expression. "Yeah? Looked like things were rushing fast as a flooding river there at the fort."

"You tend your own business, Johnston."

"I just made it my business. And talk about compromising. That wasn't very pretty the night I found you two alone in her family's cabin."

"The children were—"

"—damn young to be chaperons."

Johnston's inference grated on Alan, maybe more so because Alan was angry with himself about that evening. He well knew he shouldn't have stayed. But a man courting a lady could surely give her a kiss.

Johnston bent his face so close, Alan felt his hot breath. "You'd better have honorable intentions, man, and you'd better not harm her or her reputation in any way, or I'll kill you."

"You kill me? I should kill you. It's *you* that's compromised her."

Johnston spoke in a slow drawl as he looked down on Alan, hand still locked on Alan's throat. "Well, it doesn't appear you're in a position to do that just now, does it?"

Another voice cleaved the air. "Get off." Lévêque.

Alan looked past Johnston. The French Canadian held a handgun at Johnston's head.

"Off." Lévêque clicked the hammer of his pistol to assure Johnston of the imminence of danger.

Slowly Johnston backed off and stood, while Alan lay there drawing deep breaths.

Lévêque sneered. "Shall I kill him now?"

"No!" Alan scrambled to his feet.

"I guess you want to do it, *M'sieu* Alan? Is your wench he sleep with, *n'est-ce pas?*"

Johnston swung around to face Lévêque, but he stopped short when he confronted the gun pointing right between his eyes. Making a slow turn, so as not to incite Lévêque, Johnston glared at Alan. "Does anyone else know about the McCarys?"

Alan brushed his tousled hair back from his forehead. "Mrs. Larson. I'll talk to her. I trust she'll honor the need for silence—as I trust you will, and I—and Lévêque." He gave Lévêque a warning gaze. Lévêque just scowled, his gun aimed at Johnston's head. Alan blew out a sharp breath. "Let him go."

"Back to the wench?" Lévêque asked.

A spike of heat burned Alan's cheeks, and he witnessed the flash of anger in Johnston's eyes. Alan snarled at his attendant. "Lévêque!"

Lévêque's face went slack, as if the wind had left his sail, and he lowered the gun in a long, gradual drop. Johnston cast a dark look at the man, then at Alan, before slipping out the door.

Chapter Eleven

February 1843. Jake sat across from Joe at the Haviland table, the only sounds the steady rocking of Mrs. Haviland's chair and the occasional snap of a log on the fire. Little Robbie dozed in her lap, while Davie huddled over a couple of wood-carved soldiers on the floor. Jennie sat on a stump near the firelight, making fine stitches in a boy's shirt. The older boys sprawled on their parents' bed, backs against the cushions, Charlie checking his brother from time to time so he could maintain the same look of indifference.

Jake wanted to smile at the two, but the tension that gripped the family held him too. He and Joe had come over to talk to George Haviland about what he'd learned on his trip to French Prairie. But Mr. Haviland hadn't returned yet, and the daylight shining through the cabin's skin window had dimmed. They'd been expecting him for several days now, and another day was about to end as darkness moved in.

Jake absently stroked the soft sleeve of his new pale-blue hickory shirt. Kitty, Doc Newell's wife, had done a nice job on the shirt and black jean pants, the pants cut trim like his buckskins. She'd offered to make him new buckskins too. The old ones weren't worth keeping after the river. But he didn't know how he'd pay for her work, and he wasn't comfortable with that big a gift. As a compromise, she just whipped together a nice buckskin vest for warmth so he didn't have to wear that poor old wool coat all the time. He should have let the river have that one, but it still served him.

Muffin jumped up and went to the door, his tail wagging, and he began to whine. Everyone sat straighter. Jennie stood and laid her sewing on the stump. "Do you need to go out, Muffin?"

But before she could reach the door, the latch screeched and the door swung in. Mr. Haviland stood in the doorway. The rest jumped to their feet, Mrs. Haviland and children and dog gathering around him. Everyone chattered at once, and Mrs. Haviland hushed the children to tell him about Jennie's close escape from the river.

Mr. Haviland laid a hand on his wife's shoulder. "I heard about it." He turned to Jake. "I want to thank you. I understand you're responsible for my daughter's rescue, and I hope you know how much I appreciate it."

Jake nodded, not answering.

Amid the babble, Mrs. Haviland and Jennie put food on the table, and they all sat around him while he ate.

Mrs. Haviland bent close to her husband. "Whatever kept you so long?"

He furrowed his brow and focused on the plate of food he was devouring. Then he looked up, eyeing his sons. "Isn't it about bedtime for you boys?"

Moans rose. "Aw, Pa."

Joe chuckled. "Lookin' at yer pa stowin' away that food puts me in mind of a time we had us'n a feast on buffler—and the bars hangin' 'round."

Charlie faced Joe, eyes alight. "Would you tell us about it, Joe?" Mr. Haviland looked at his son with a mixed expression of amusement and sternness, and Charlie turned pleading eyes on him. "Just one story, Pa?"

Charlie's father pursed his lips and took a big breath. He leaned closer to the boy. "On one condition. You need to mind your manners and address Mr. Meek properly. He's not Joe to you, son. He's Mr. Meek. You need to respect your elders."

Eddie frowned. "But we don't have to call Jake Mr. Johnston, do we? He's not an elder." The boy lifted both hands. "Well, he's not old like you and Mr. Meek. He's like—well, a brother. And you wouldn't expect me to call Jennie Miss Hav-i-land." He stretched her name to exaggerate, and raised his nose at his sister.

Joe winced a little at Eddie calling him *old*, and Jake worked to keep a straight face as George Haviland turned to him. "I suppose that's up to Mr. Johnston," Haviland said.

Jake thought about that a minute. "Well, I don't want to interfere with the boys' proper rearing. Maybe when it's just the family it'll be all right."

Eddie's eyes lit up. "That'll be fine, Jake. Just fine." His brother grinned and nodded.

Jake had to laugh to himself. Joe was only eight years older than Jake, but in the boys' eyes, he supposed anything over thirty was pretty old.

"Now then," Mr. Haviland said. "If you boys will go on to bed afterward—with no argument—maybe we could have one short story—if Mr. Meek would like to tell you one."

They agreed readily, even the little ones, and Jennie's eyes shone.

Joe cocked his head. "Well now, I mind a time this old coon and a couple fellers I'm huntin' with have jist killed us'n a nice fat buffler cow. And after we feast on that'un, we still have meat aplenty. So that night what's left we split up, and each feller puts his meat under his head to sleep on. Now this coon's sleepin' fine, I kin tell ye, all wrapped up snug in a nice warm blanket, that meat under m'head. And then come daybreak, here I'm gittin' woke up by some powerful noise—somethin' big snuffin' 'round right close." Joe's brow twisted, eyes wide, and all four boys mirrored his expression. "And what d'ye think that'd be?" he asked, his voice low.

"A bear," Charlie whispered.

Joe nodded. "Grizzly, and a big'un. And I know my trouble right off. It's that buffler meat he's smellin'. Well now, you kin be shore this coon keeps mighty quiet whilst that old bar helps hisself to some o' my buffler. I jist crawls low in the blanket and holds right still. Do ye hear?"

Jake smiled at the boys' round eyes—and Jennie's.

Joe continued. "Well now, that old bar, he goes off a ways to eat it, *he* does, and then we fellers sit up to look, and doggone but that bar comes back. My heavens! Ye never did see men go flat so fast. We go plumb down and our heads under the blankets ag'in, and what d'ye know but

The Shifting Winds

that bar jist walks right over us. Yessir, he's a-walkin' on us, and what kin we do?"

Joe paused, but getting no answer, he went on. "Well now, this is a mighty uneasy situation, I kin tell ye, but afore long that ol' bar, he walks off ag'in, and then Mitchel wants to shoot.

"'No, no,' I tells him, 'hold on, or the brute will kill us, shore.'

"Well now, when the bar hears all that, he's right back and walkin' on our beds some more, *he* is. But that old bar, he can't quite make out our style and afore long he takes fright and runs away down the mount'in, *he* does. Yessir. And this coon is about wantin' revenge by this time. So I go after him, and I git a good shot, and down he goes. And then, do ye know what this hoss does?"

The boys shook their heads.

"Well now," Joe said, "I jist takes my turn at walkin' over him awhile. Yessir." Joe slapped his hand on the table and gave a firm nod. "I jist walk acrost him awhile, *I* do."

The boys grinned, and Joe spoke directly to them. "You fellers mind yer pa now and go to bed, but if'n ye feel somethin' walkin' acrost ye, don't move now, will ye?"

Everyone laughed, and the boys reluctantly got up with their mother and Jennie to head up the ladder to the loft.

Once the women and children were gone, Mr. Haviland's expression sobered, and he looked at Joe, then Jake. "I think you might be interested in the meeting I just attended—about predators."

Jake and Joe leaned forward, and Haviland went on, his voice low. "That was the stated purpose for the meeting."

Jake lifted a hand. "What was the real purpose?"

"I think it was Mr. Gray's idea—William Gray. You may know him."

Jake nodded. Gray was a former lay missionary who'd come through the mountains some years ago with Marcus Whitman and his party. A haughty fellow, not a favorite of the trappers, but Jake knew him to be a pro-government man.

"Anyway," Haviland said, "the idea came out when several of us were at Gray's house down at Chemeketa. As you well know, every time we try pushing through this idea of organizing a government, we meet opposition.

Men connected with the Hudson's Bay Company are opposed, and the French Canadians are content without government. They can depend on their patron Dr. McLoughlin—and their priests. They simply won't come out and support it. And for reasons I fail to comprehend, several of our own mission clergy are opposed."

Jake rubbed his chin. "Did you talk to Lee again?"

"I have talked to him on several occasions and have not been able to persuade him. He prefers we do nothing until the United States extends jurisdiction."

"That could be a long time coming," Jake said, "and we need help now."

Haviland pushed his plate aside and folded his hands on the table. "True, but in order to organize, we have to get the people to meet." His eyes took on a gleam. "So when we were talking at Gray's house a few of us decided, if we can't get folks together for a meeting on organization, we might get them together for a meeting about our problems with predators. You know how much trouble settlers are having with wolves and panthers."

"So you met?" Jake wished he could have been there.

"We did—on Thursday. But nothing really happened at that meeting. The few of us there just agreed to set up another meeting the sixth of March when hopefully we can get more people out."

"Where'bouts?" Joe asked.

"At Gervais's house. It's south of Champoeg, about halfway between Champoeg and the Willamette Mission at Chemeketa."

The stirrings of intrigue caught Jake. "And the purpose for that meeting—?"

Haviland leaned closer to the others, his voice dropping. "We don't want the word out to people who aren't pro-organization, but I'm sure of your sentiments. We'll try to get a good crowd—of our persuasion—and we'll talk about predators, all right. That is a problem we need to deal with, but then, unbeknownst to our opposition, we'll bring forward a proposal toward organizing the government."

Jake grinned. "A little subterfuge?"

"If that's what it takes."

"The Hudson's Bay Company people don't suspect?"

"I don't think so. We did have some Canadians at our meeting Thursday, but only those who don't seem to be against us."

Jake could hear the soft murmur of the women and children upstairs and kept his voice low. "What about Miss Jennie? Should she know? She's pretty thick with that Britisher Radford."

Haviland's brow tightened, a tiny pulse showing at his temples. "Better not say anything to her."

Jake looked at his own hands resting flat on the table, then glanced back at Haviland. "Just what are Radford's intentions toward her?"

Haviland snuffed up air. "He asked to court her last fall, but he hasn't said anything more." The man's whisper rasped. "Damn it, my whole inclination is to want to blow the man away, but I have no real reason—other than the fact that he's pursuing my daughter."

"What if he asks for her hand?"

"Then, I guess I have no reason to refuse. I'd rather she marry an American—what with the uncertainties between the United States and Britain. But Mrs. Haviland is fond of Radford, and Jennie seems to be. How do I refuse?" Haviland paused and let his shoulders drop. "I suppose, if we can avoid open hostilities between the two nations, maybe it'll work out."

Jake looked away from him into the crackling fire. "I'm not so sure there won't be war." The sound of footsteps on the ladder stopped him.

Joe made a soft grunting noise. "Well now, I'd say the crops oughta be mighty good this year, what with all this rain, and we kin use the wheat if'n thar's as many comin' overland from the States this next summer as folks are sayin'."

Jake held back a smile to put on a thoughtful face. "Ought to be."

"Yes," Haviland said, "it is good for the crops, all right."

French Prairie, Willamette Valley, March 6, 1843. Jake sat taller in the saddle when he came over the rise and saw the Gervais house nestled in the midst of the bright-green prairie. He tipped his wide-brimmed hat lower on his forehead to shade his eyes and glanced at George Haviland and Joe Meek, riding beside him. "Quite a place, isn't it?"

Haviland nodded. "Mr. Gervais looks to be pretty well established."

"He must be one of the first white settlers in this valley," Jake said. "I think he built his house in the early '30s, didn't he, Joe?"

"Reckon it'd be close to that."

The Gervais house was no crude log cabin, like those that housed most of the settlers in the Willamette country. Two stories high, it looked more like the buildings at Fort Vancouver with its post-on-sill construction of square-cut horizontal logs. But no glass windows. A large barn stood behind the house, built in the same fashion. Sheds and corrals surrounded the place. A small orchard showed signs of buds, almost ready to come into bloom.

"I was surprised they picked this as the meeting place," Haviland said, "Gervais being French Canadian, but of course we need some support from them or I don't see how we have enough votes to carry the day."

Jake nudged Old Blue to move down the gentle slope. "Gervais isn't your usual French Canadian. He did work for the Hudson's Bay Company, but he came into the country with the Astor people—back in 1811, wasn't it? Or 1812?"

"So he's American."

"No, he's Canadian. Astor got a lot of his men out of Canada, which I suppose was part of his problem, but when Astor sold out to the British, Gervais went to work for them. He's always been a freeman, though. He worked for the Company, but was never part of it."

Jake drew a long breath of the sweet spring air. They couldn't have asked for a nicer day. Blue sky, crisp warmth. A scent of honey mingled with new grass and flowers, a drift of smoke wafting through. Maybe the good weather would bring out the people. Quite a few horses stood outside the place already, tied to a long wooden fence.

"Looks like a good crowd," Haviland said, "considering some are probably coming by boat."

Jake chuckled. "I think I've gotten a lot more partial to horse travel myself."

The others laughed with him.

Haviland gestured with a broad sweep of his hand. "Aren't the French Canadians in this valley all linked with the Hudson's Bay Company somehow?"

"Yep," Joe said. "Former employees, most of 'em, I'd say."

"I think McLoughlin still keeps them on the Company books to keep it legal," Jake said.

Haviland lifted a brow. "How's that?"

"According to their rules they have to return their retirees back to where they enlisted—which for most means Canada. But some didn't want to go back. They have wives from the tribes around here, and kids. So McLoughlin loaned them seed and tools and kept them as employees so they could stay."

"Thus the name French Prairie."

"That's right."

Joe twisted his face. "Ye figger Gervais is fer us, then?"

Haviland shook his head. "I'm not sure, but he's on the committee that organized this meeting. I hope so. But whether he's aware of the meeting's true purpose, I don't know."

Once the three had tied their horses, they headed for the house. George Le Breton greeted them at the door, looking harried but businesslike as usual. "Glad to see you here. We're about to begin."

When Jake stepped into the spacious living room, he took off his hat and smiled to see the mass of people. Clusters of men stood around talking, some sitting on the furniture, others on the floor. A small fire sizzled in the great fireplace dominating one wall, a clay fireplace like most in the country, made of a clay and grass plaster spread over sticks. The smell of warm bodies and wool coats and buckskin clutched his nose.

Edging through the crowd, Jake studied the faces, some familiar, some not, then stopped when he caught sight of an all-too-familiar face. Radford. And beside him, Lévêque. Radford caught sight of Jake, and a sudden spark showed in the man's eyes, the Britisher's hostility poorly hidden. The *voyageur* didn't try to hide his. Looking away, not wanting them to know their presence affected him, Jake continued his observation of the packed room. Still, his thoughts stayed on those two. He wondered if they were aware of the primary purpose of today's meeting, and if so, what they might do to upset the plan.

A voice rose above the chatter. "Gentlemen, gentlemen, shall we begin the business we've come for?"

Haviland whispered to Jake. "I don't see any sign of the mission clergy."

Jake saw a few laymen, but none of the leaders. "They must not have been told. Radford's here, though."

"So I see."

The meeting was called to order, and Jake only half listened to the formal proceedings as he watched faces. He hoped it would be a peaceful meeting, unlike some of the lyceum sessions. The group chose James O'Neil as chairman, a fairly longtime resident, having come west in 1834 with Nathaniel Wyeth, when Wyeth attempted some American competition against the British—without much success.

Jake leaned toward Haviland. "Does O'Neil know?"

Haviland nodded.

Le Breton was selected secretary, and O'Neil asked for a report from the committee named at the last meeting.

William Willson, layman with the Methodist Mission, stood with a paper in hand. "Your committee beg leave to report as follows." He read, "'It being admitted by all that wolves, bears, panthers, et cetera are destructive to the useful animals owned by the settlers of this colony, your committee would respectfully submit the following resolutions . . .'"

Jake lost track of the words as he wondered how they would get the idea of organization out and what the reaction would be.

Willson kept reading. "Sixth, resolved, that a bounty of fifty cents be paid for the small wolf, three dollars for the large, a dollar fifty for the wildcat or lynx, two dollars for the bear, and five dollars for the panther."

Jake stroked a thumb over the rim of his hat. *Five dollars. Maybe I should go for that panther roaming near the Falls, though I'd as soon not fight him like I did his friend.*

"'. . . that no bounty be paid except the individual claiming a bounty give satisfactory evidence . . .'"

An undertone of discussion stirred. "Good," one man said. "I think we're finally going to have some means of protecting ourselves from these predators."

A loud voice boomed out. "Mr. Chairman."

Jake looked for the speaker. It was William Gray—pompous as usual, but Jake had a feeling Gray was to be the man of the moment. O'Neil recognized him, and Gray marched to O'Neil's side.

The man stood to his full height and lifted his chin to speak above the crowd. "No one would question that what we have done today is right. It is right that we should protect our property in animals which are liable to be destroyed by wolves, bears, and panthers. But how is it, fellow citizens, with you and me—and our children and wives? Have we any organization upon which we can rely for mutual protection?"

Jake glanced at Radford and saw a perceptible change in the man's expression. A sudden frown. Tight lips.

Gray continued. "Is there any power or influence in the country sufficient to protect us and all we hold dear on earth from the worse than wild beasts that threaten and occasionally destroy our cattle? Who in our midst is authorized at this moment to call us together to protect our own and the lives of our families?"

Jake wanted to smile. He couldn't actually like William Gray, but he couldn't fault the oratory.

"True, the alarm may be given," Gray said with a dramatic wave of both arms. "And we may run, who feel alarmed, and shoot off our guns, while our enemy may be robbing our property, ravishing our wives, and burning the houses over our defenseless families."

Jake allowed himself a slight smile. *Colorful, but possibly true enough.*

"Common sense, prudence, and justice to ourselves demand that we act consistent with the principles we have commenced," Gray said. "We have mutually and united agreed to defend and protect our cattle and domestic animals. Now, fellow citizens, I submit and move the adoption of the two following resolutions, that we may have protection for our persons and lives as well as our cattle and herds."

Jake eyed Radford again. The man's jaw clenched, which amused Jake and worried him too. What trouble might the man bring? Jake turned his attention back to Gray, who pulled a piece of paper from the inside of his coat and studied it, no doubt pausing for effect.

Finally Gray read, his voice more emphatic than before. "'Resolved, that a committee be appointed to take into consideration the propriety of taking measures for the civil and military protection of this colony.' And, 'Resolved, that said committee consist of twelve persons.'" With that, Gray stepped back and nodded toward the chairman.

"Mr. Gray has offered resolutions," Chairman O'Neil said.

The room began to buzz with talk, until Jake could scarcely hear the proceedings. Many in the room had known this would come up, but others showed surprise. Wide eyes, dropped jaws. Other faces beaming with excitement, hope. It was a step toward government.

Jake heard the call for a vote, and the room quieted as O'Neil reread the resolutions, then asked, "All in favor, say *aye*."

The *ayes* sounded loud and strong, and Jake added his to their number. Radford and Lévêque stood with mouths closed.

"Opposed, *nay*," O'Neil said.

Dead silence.

Jake watched Radford and Lévêque, expecting them to vote their opposition, but perhaps the overwhelming majority in favor proved inhibiting.

O'Neil called out names for the committee, and Jake was glad to see his host and mountain comrade Robert Newell among them. He wasn't so sure about some of the others, wondering if they might turn out to be dissenters. Babcock was a missionary, though a layman. Hubbard, O'Neil, and Gay were old-timers connected with the fur trade. Gervais and Lucier were French Canadians. A fair mix, and Jake supposed that was required for acceptance of the populace.

Haviland spoke up. "I move we adjourn."

Jake lifted a hand. "Second."

With O'Neil's announcement of adjournment, the press of excited people surged. Though men bumped him from all sides, Jake stretched to see Radford and caught sight of him just as the Britisher slipped out the front door. Lévêque, behind him, turned to cast a malevolent glare at Jake before slinking out of Jake's sight. A chill swept through Jake. The look was a threat, but he couldn't let it intimidate him. Pushing through the crowd, Jake managed to get outside, but he saw no sign of Radford or Lévêque.

He grumbled under his breath. "Well, no matter now. We'll meet another time, bastard. I've waited this long. My business with you will keep. I just have to be sure I find you next time before you find me."

Chapter Twelve

Oregon City, March 1843. Jennie wandered homeward from the store, her bonnet thrown back on her shoulders to let the warm spring sun touch her hair. Sweet life surged around her, sap rising, buds swelling, birds voicing their alluring melodies against the constant rush of the mighty falls and the tapping hammers on Dr. McLoughlin's mill. The sparkling scent of new growth filled her with such rich joy she wanted to dance on air.

The town of Oregon City looked rather promising with its tidy cabins numbering almost thirty now. And besides the second sawmill, they would soon have a gristmill. *Bread! Every day!* How fine it would be to say good-bye to boiled wheat.

She clutched the basket to her waist. Strange to buy things without money. Everything was barter here, goods bought with earned credit at the town's few stores. The supplies in her basket were purchased with credit her father had earned doing legal work.

With every step she noticed the unfamiliar feel of the moccasins, the only footgear she'd found that fit. Her boots were beyond repair. A wave of sadness struck. If only she hadn't lost her dress slippers to the river—and the exquisite dress of living green velvet.

She met a couple of Indian women going the other way, long blankets wrapped around their shoulders, baskets in hand. They nodded in passing, and she offered a flickering smile. None of the Indians lived right in

Oregon City, but they often visited, mostly from the nearby Clowewalla village, a band of the Clackamas tribe, and from another Clackamas village a few miles north. All the tribes around here were related to the Chinookans, like those who had guided her family over the mountains, and had the flattened heads.

A cluster of Clowewalla men sat by the riverbank now, the perpetual smoke drifting from their pipes as they played a game of chance, a favorite pastime for them. Hearing chatter behind, Jennie turned to see three dark-haired men striding toward the river. Kanakas. They were Hudson's Bay Company employees from the Sandwich Islands, hired to work on Dr. McLoughlin's sawmill. The doctor offered employment to Americans also. Sometimes Jennie wondered how the Americans could have made it in this country without the good doctor's help. Employment, loans, outright gifts of food and supplies. It pleased her that Alan had served to arrange all that.

Stepping around the corner of a neighbor's cabin, she nearly ran into two gentlemen in deep conversation, Mr. Shortess and Mr. Brown. They broke off their talk on sight of her, and Mr. Shortess stuffed a piece of paper inside his coat.

"Miss Haviland," Mr. Shortess said, tipping his hat without a smile. Mr. Brown gave a curt nod.

"Hello," she answered, ready to offer polite conversation. But the men turned and walked away.

Surprised at their lack of friendliness, she went to her own cabin and found her parents inside, sitting at the table with their heads together in serious discussion. They looked up when she entered and stopped talking. What was this? The two little boys, playing on the floor, greeted her with their usual delight, but her parents seemed distracted.

She set down the basket and placed her hands on her hips. "Pa, what's going on?"

"What do you mean?" He gave her an innocent smile.

Her exasperation sounded in her voice. "A minute ago I came upon Mr. Shortess and Mr. Brown talking as if they had a deep secret. Now I find you and Mother whispering together. What's going on? Oh, and the men had a piece of paper. Mr. Shortess put it away the moment he saw me—as if he didn't want me to notice. Do you know what it was?"

"It's a petition to Congress."

"The Congress of the United States?"

"Yes, they're looking for signatures."

She plopped onto the table bench beside her parents. "Well, they didn't have to be so unfriendly. I suppose since I'm a woman I can't sign, so it's none of my affair, but—"

Ma patted Jennie's hand, her tone gentle. "I don't think it's because you're a woman."

A disquieting warmth spread through Jennie. "Is it because of Alan? Am I to be ostracized because he's—"

Her mother squeezed her hand. "No, Jennie, I don't think it's that either."

Pa made a soft growly sound. "I refused to sign their petition, and they're not happy with me. No doubt since you're my daughter that passes to you."

"But why? What sort of petition?"

"It asks the United States to take jurisdiction over this country—which is fine."

"Then, why didn't you sign it?"

"Because it's so full of lies."

"Lies?"

"About Dr. McLoughlin. I can't sign something that falsely accuses a man like him."

Jennie bent toward her father, a hand at her throat. "Like what?"

"It accuses him of falsely claiming land here. They say he has no right to claim it and is seeking pay for what isn't his."

"Why wouldn't he have a right to claim it?"

Pa didn't answer. He seemed to be avoiding her eyes, and her disquieting warmth heightened. "Is it because he's British?" she asked.

Pa let out another growl. "He has as much right as the next man—British or no—as far as I can see. Of course, we have no government to substantiate anybody's claim yet. But it's a simple case of greed, I think. He happened to claim one of the most valuable pieces of ground in the country—here at the falls with all their potential for power. So they'll fight him by any means, fair or foul."

Jennie looked away from her pa and began stroking her fingers over the seam of her skirt. If people could be so mean to Dr. McLoughlin, how would they act toward Alan, and what would that mean for her?

"Oh, there's more," Pa said. "They accuse him of measuring wheat unfairly, and they say he can compete unfairly with his new mill because he has the Hudson's Bay Company behind him."

She looked up. "Is that true?"

"It may be cheaper for him to build and operate, but I see nothing unfair in the competition." He shook his head. "I'm not the only one who's refused to sign. Others know as well as I do that many of us would have struggled to survive without that man's help."

Jennie lifted her brows. "You didn't want his help when we first came."

"I admit that. I'd read about the Hudson's Bay Company in the New York papers and how they were taking over this Oregon country, reaping its wealth in furs, stories saying they'd effectively jumped our claim to what the country has to offer. But that was before I knew the Company's Chief Factor as a man. Sure, he's British and has to do his duty to his own nation, and as required by his position. But it's clear to me he never let his national loyalty interfere with his care for humanity."

Jennie sighed and rubbed the skirt seam again. She liked Dr. McLoughlin and didn't want to see him hurt. How could the Americans be so mean? She didn't want to see Alan hurt either. He'd stopped to see her on his way to the meeting at Gervais's place and again on the way home, when he'd seemed troubled and anxious to return to the fort. She wished she could talk to him now. She couldn't help thinking about the hostility between him and Jake. She hoped Jake wouldn't cause trouble.

Pa cleared his throat. "I'd like to see a government of all the people in Oregon, although if the British and Canadians refuse to join us I don't know what we can do about that. And if they choose to fight us, we'll have to fight them—but fairly."

Jennie looked squarely at her pa. "Do you think they will fight?"

He stood and began to pace. "I think the meeting at Champoeg in May will decide the issue. We'll have to get all our pro-government people out to that one. I don't want to fight anybody over it, but I think we need a government for protection of property rights and for protection against hostile Indians, and even some of the unruly Americans around here." Stopping, he gave Jennie a long, sober look. "I just hope it doesn't blow up into hostilities."

Ma let out a huff. "Well, there's another danger that worries me right now—the boys and their hunting. It's so dangerous for them, and they must try to behave like little mountain men. I don't think Jake Johnston is a good influence—or his friend Joe Meek and his stories." She lifted her hands, mouth twisted. "Have you noticed the way Eddie has taken on a drawl lately? He sounds just like Jake. And now, with bounty to be had for bigger game, they think they have to go for that. They could be hurt, and it's late now. They ought to be home."

Pa patted Ma's shoulder. "They're with Jake, aren't they? Whether you like him or not, he is an able hunter, and I wouldn't worry about their safety when they're out with him."

Jennie hopped up from the bench. "Ma, will you be needing me for a while? It's so nice out. I'd like to take a walk."

"Oh, that's fine, Jennie." She lowered her voice. "Do you want to take Davie and Robbie?"

Jennie sighed. She really didn't. She wanted to find Jake, but she didn't want to say that, and if she found Jake she could send Eddie and Charlie on home to relieve Ma's worries. It didn't seem like a good idea to mention that either, since Jake and the boys were probably up in the woods and the folks wouldn't like Jennie going up there alone.

Seeing Jennie's reluctance, her mother smiled. "That's all right. Go on ahead, but not far, now, will you?"

Delighting in the freedom and beauty of the day, Jennie walked rapidly through town. On the trail to the top of the bluff, her feet in the moccasins felt light and swift as they moved up the rocky incline. At the top she stood breathing hard, her face hot but spirits lifted as she gazed at the falls and the surrounding countryside. The scene never ceased to affect her. Though the place was only a little less wild than when first she saw it, she could look on it now without the despair. Perhaps she had grown to accept, if not yet to love it.

She turned from the view and continued up the trail into the woods, slower, deep in thought. She wondered how much her attitude had been changed by Alan's courtship. What would come of that? He hadn't asked for her hand. Would he? She did look forward to his visits, to spending time in his company, his kisses like stolen treasures—always brief now, nothing like the passion at the fort, but sweet as a taste of candy.

She pressed her fingers over her lips and closed her eyes, then heard a sharp bark. She ran toward the sound and stopped when she looked through the trees. Her heart jolted. Eddie and Charlie stood beneath a tall fir, staring up at the huge golden form of a panther on a limb above them, the creature's gaze riveted on them, while Muffin backed away slowly, hackles raised, teeth bared.

Eddie reached for the gun in Charlie's hand. "Give it to me."

Charlie shook his head and raised the gun to point it at the big cat.

Memories raced through Jennie's mind—Joe's words about panthers attacking children, the sight of Jake after one attacked him. She opened her mouth to yell at the boys, but before she could call out, the gun sounded, smoke belching from the tip of it. The cat yowled and fell. Or jumped. It lay on the ground without moving.

She started toward the boys, but hesitated when the panther stirred. It jerked, let out a terrible cry, and scrambled to its feet. Growling, snarling, showing its sharp teeth, it hissed at the boys, and they stepped back. Like a nightmare, everything moved slowly. Then the cat leaped, and the boys jumped as if on springs.

A wail rose from Jennie's throat. The cat's great paw lashed out at Charlie. He dropped the gun and fell onto his back. The cat, tossing its head, began to creep toward him. Eddie jumped into action. Screeching like a fierce cat himself, he leaped toward the panther, then snatched a stick off the ground and threw it at the animal. As if cued, Muffin barked, running in circles around them.

Eddie started toward his brother, but the panther turned toward him, blocking his way. "Get the gun, Charlie!" Eddie said, grabbing a handful of gravelly dirt and flinging it at the panther. "Quick! Get the gun and load it."

The cat, annoyed by the stinging barrage, hissed and crouched to spring at Eddie, but another fistful of dirt hit its face. It shook its head. Little Muffin, excited by the panther's bafflement, yelped louder, and the great beast turned to yowl in the dog's direction.

"Get the gun!" Eddie sounded breathless. "Get the gun while I keep him busy!"

Charlie just lay there, and Jennie ran to him. "Charlie? Are you—?"

Seeing her, the cat turned and hissed at her. Alarm surged through her. The cat moved toward her, but perturbed by another pelting from Eddie, it turned to snarl at him.

Jennie reached for the gun, but Charlie stirred and beat her to it. "I can do that," he said.

He had a powder horn slung over his shoulder, and with hands shaking, he managed to get the stopper out of it. He poured powder down the gun's muzzle, spilling it all over, but some went in. Jennie was going to offer to help, but the cat began moving toward Eddie. She couldn't let it hurt him.

She leaped toward it, yowling like a cat the way Eddie had done, as loud and fierce as she could. The startled panther slunk around to face her. Eddie threw another stick, and the cat swung back to him so fast, he fell over backward. Still, he scrambled to grab some dirt and throw it. Muffin yelped more furiously until the cat's attention turned to him, and constantly running in circles, the little dog added to the beast's confusion. Glancing at Charlie, Jennie saw him push a patched lead ball into the gun's barrel with the ramrod, shaking so hard she didn't see how he could do it.

Eddie threw a heavy branch that fell short. The panther jumped back and turned to face them all. Again it crouched to spring. The loud, deep-throated crack of a rifle sounded, and Jennie looked at Charlie. He was still ramming the ball in. Where had the shot come from? Checking the panther, she saw it lying flat on the ground. It wasn't moving. But who had killed it? She looked the other way and let out a long sigh.

"Jake."

He marched toward them with long strides.

Concerned for her young brothers, she turned back to them. Charlie had stopped in his efforts to load the gun, and she reached out to take him by the shoulders. "Are you all right?"

He nodded. His shirt was ripped all down the front, and she wondered if the cat's claws had reached his tender skin.

"Did it scratch you?" she asked.

He shook his head. "Just tore my shirt. I'm all right."

Jennie hugged him, but let go when she felt him stiffen. Charlie didn't take to her hugging these days, especially with someone like Jake around. Satisfied that Charlie was unhurt, she reached out to Eddie. "Are *you* all right?"

He was on his feet. His clothes were torn and dirty, and the bewildered look on his face made Jennie want to take him in her arms and hug him too.

"Oh, I'm all right," he said in a deep, mellow drawl that made Jennie think of Jake, and he backed off before she had a chance to get her hands on him.

It occurred to her that Jake was supposed to be with the boys. She faced him, anger rising in her voice. "Where have you been?"

He spread his arms out, the gun still in one hand, his eyes wide, as if her words had struck him. "I've been out hunting, south of here. Why?"

"I thought you were with the boys."

"I guess that's what your folks thought too. I just stopped by your place when I came home from hunting, and your folks were a touch surprised to see me and not the boys. I figured I ought to find them."

Jennie put her hands on her hips and glared at Eddie. "You were supposed to ask Mr. Johnston to go out hunting with you. You told Pa you would."

Eddie drew his shoulders high, the expression on his face pleading innocence. "We did go over to the Newells' house and asked for him, but he wasn't there."

"Then, you should have waited."

Eddie's voice became a whine, with no sign of the drawl. "But we wanted to go hunting."

"Yeah," Charlie said. "We been out alone before, and we wanted to get some bounty."

Jennie took a deep breath and let it out slowly. The boys looked so downcast, she decided maybe they'd had enough of a rebuke for the moment. "Eddie, it was a brave thing you did, trying to distract the cat that way."

"It was nothin' really," he said, drawling again. He turned toward Jake. "Guess the five-dollar bounty is yours, Jake. You're the one got him."

Jake glanced at the cat and shook his head. "You fellows put the first ball in him. I figure that makes him yours."

The boys' faces brightened until both wore broad smiles.

"So, what do you figure to do with him?" Jake asked.

Eddie cocked his head as he studied the beast from one end to the other. It looked awfully long, sprawled flat and lifeless on the ground. Little Muffin, at a fraction its size, peered at the thing, his little body rigid, ready to spring away in an instant if the big cat came to life again.

"Reckon we can cut the skin off his head and keep that along with the ears," Eddie said. "That's all we need to collect our bounty."

Charlie tugged at his brother's sleeve. "But we ought to take him home. He's got meat, lots of it, and we'll be needing meat."

Jake raised a brow and smiled at Charlie. "That's true. Maybe I could give you fellows a hand carrying him home. How would that be?"

Eddie shrugged, but Charlie grinned. "All right," Charlie said.

Jennie turned to Jake. "I was wanting to talk to you. Could we . . . talk?"

Jake's eyes widened with surprise, and she noticed an odd expression on Eddie's face. He glanced first at Jake, then at Jennie, his brows lifted, a funny little grin playing about his lips. "Charlie and me, we can go on ahead—and leave you two."

"All right," Jake answered. "I'll bring the cat later."

"Well, I'd stay so's I could help you, but I reckon you'd as soon I didn't, so—"

A little giggle erupted from Charlie, as he stood with his shoulders drawn up the way he did to make himself look taller. His round cheeks glowed pink, his eyes unusually bright.

Eddie motioned for his brother. "Come on, Charlie." Eddie's voice sounded businesslike, but he cast one more brief grin in Jennie's direction before he urged Charlie down the trail. Muffin followed without urging, trotting close on the boys' heels, glancing back a time or two at the big cat. Jennie stood beside Jake, watching her two meddlesome brothers and their small dog disappear at the turn of the trail through the woods, and she couldn't help feeling awkward.

"Well, Miss Jennie." Jake's tone showed no sign he'd noticed the boys' meaningful looks. "You said you wanted to talk."

She looked up into his dark-brown eyes and wondered if she didn't detect an extra brightness.

"Like to sit down?" he asked. "There's a rock over there." He nodded toward a big flat rock nestled among bright-green shrubbery, a shaft of sunlight touching its mossy surface.

Jennie went over and perched on one side of the rock, while Jake eased his frame down on the other side, setting his rifle against a nearby tree trunk. "Not much of a gun," he said, giving it a disparaging look, "but it's the best I could find here. Sure wish I hadn't lost my good rifle to the river. Best gun I ever had—a Hawken—favorite of the mountain man." His forehead pinched. "Funny thing. I think I regret losing McLoughlin's book almost more. I'd brought a book he loaned me. How can I ever replace that?"

Jennie studied the face of the man beside her. He was a puzzle to her. Somehow he didn't seem the type to place more value on a book than a gun. Shrugging that off, she decided to broach her subject. "I—uh—"

He inclined his head closer to give her a direct look.

She backed away a little and tried again. "I wanted to talk to you about the trouble here in Oregon over . . . government. There's a new conflict." She paused, not knowing quite how she wanted to express it. "Have you seen the petition?"

"The petition to Congress they're circulating?"

She nodded.

"Yeah, I've seen it." He looked away from her out into the thick woods.

"Did you . . . sign it?"

His head snapped back, and he frowned at her. "No, I didn't."

Her brows rose. Then she averted her eyes to study the moss on the rock between them, running her fingers over the softness. "Why not?"

"Do you know what's in it?"

"Some. Pa told me some things it said about Dr. McLoughlin."

"What makes you think I'd sign anything that sullies McLoughlin that way?"

"Because you're so—" She looked up at him.

"So *what?*"

"Well, you seem to . . . hate the British so much—well, not Dr. McLoughlin, but . . . Alan—Mr. Radford."

Jake snorted. "And that makes me anti-British? Like I've told you before, I'm not anti-British. I'm pro-American. I want a government here in Oregon—courts, law and order—and I intend to do what's necessary to help get that."

Jennie let out a long breath. "I just don't want trouble, and I'm afraid you—"

"You think I'm a troublemaker because I'm not fond of your Alan Radford."

Jennie scrunched her shoulders and bit her lips together. That *was* what she thought.

"It's true I'm not fond of Radford," Jake said, "and I don't trust his motives politically, but I wouldn't cause trouble just to get at him."

She observed Jake's face, the skin pulled taut, the throbbing in his temples, then concentrated her attention on the moss again.

He lowered his voice. "I'm not too sure about Radford's motives in regard to you either."

Her heart took an erratic beat, and she shot an indignant look at him.

Jake turned to look into the woods. "The man seems suspicious of our time together after the canoe accident."

Dread stirred in Jennie. "What did you tell him?"

"Oh, I think our little secret is safe, but I am concerned about you and Radford and what might happen if the Americans and British decide to fight over this country."

Struck by his verbalization of one of her greatest fears, she stared at him.

He faced her again. "If we do go to war, what then?"

"I . . . don't think we will. Do you?"

"I hope not, but if we do, where will your loyalties be?" His voice softened, his eyes gentle. "What do you treasure most? Your American heritage? Or this thing with Alan Radford?"

She grabbed a clump of moss and squeezed it, releasing its bittersweet scent, as she gazed into Jake's solemn brown eyes. "I'm an American. I treasure that, but . . . I treasure love too." She dropped the moss and held out her hands, her throat tight. "What does love know about boundaries and politics and national loyalties?" She leaned toward him. "If you fell in love with a British girl, would you deny that love just because she was British?"

He looked straight at her, locking her gaze with his. "I don't love a British girl."

For a long moment neither of them moved. A bird trilled nearby, and another, farther off, answered.

Jake spoke again, his voice so low she had to strain to hear. "Do you love him?"

A strange charge of warmth coursed through Jennie, and she couldn't break her eyes away from him. Finally she whispered, "I don't know."

Chapter Thirteen

Fort Vancouver, April 1843. Alan hurried through the soaking drizzle to keep up with Dr. McLoughlin as the old man charged across the fort grounds, shoulders hunched in an uncharacteristic stoop, cane gripped tight. The very air reflected the doctor's dark mood, all the colors streaked by the fine mist, as if the ashen wash of a paintbrush had swept across the lush new greens of spring, blurring and dimming them.

McLoughlin stopped short and wheeled about to face Alan. Every line in his brow and cheeks cut deep, but his gray-blue eyes showed more than anger. He looked like a man who'd been gutshot. He brushed one broad hand across his thick, unruly white hair, slicking the wet strands closer to his scalp, while the incessant drizzle added more fine droplets. He banged the tip of his cane so hard on the ground it stuck in the mire, then yanked it out.

His bellowing voice shook. "How can they say these things about me? When I've done so much—all I could—to help them?"

Alan felt inadequate before the man's tortured rage. *Bloody ingrates.* No man like Dr. McLoughlin should suffer such cruel indignation. The grand old fellow was too kind. What a shame to waste his generosity on those ungrateful wretches. Alan had feared that the same men McLoughlin was aiding would rise up against their benefactor and try to throw him out of the country. Wasn't that petition clear evidence?

McLoughlin slowly shook his head. "To lie about me. To their government." He slapped the cane against his palm, then jabbed the tip on the ground again to rest both hands on its golden head. Gravity tugged his features as he stood, mindless of the water dripping over him.

Alan reached out a hand, wishing he could somehow give comfort, but didn't quite touch the old man. "Sir, it's a bloody crime. Indeed, it shows what we're up against. I don't know what will come of that meeting in May."

McLoughlin lifted his chin and gazed upward. "I've not been too concerned until now. With all the people coming into the country, it seemed we might do well to adopt some plan to keep the peace. We have authority over the Canadians, but there's no authority over the Americans."

"But the government they propose would be against us, sir."

McLoughlin glanced at Alan, then looked beyond him to some distant place or thought. "I'm beginning to see that."

"Indeed, sir, if the Americans succeed in forming their government, they'll try to assume authority over everyone in the district—British as well as American."

The old man heaved a sigh. "And I suppose it will only strengthen the American position in the boundary issue."

Alan swiped at the rain on his face and bent forward to stress his words. "Sir, we've done so much in the country. We've had a foothold here for over twenty years, while the Americans have let it go until now. Our claims are quite valid."

McLoughlin rocked a little as he spoke. "That they are. That they are."

"What do you think now about war, sir? Will we have to fight for our rights, do you think?"

The man riveted his focus on Alan, and Alan straightened before the power in the old man's gaze. "I don't know," McLoughlin said. "It seems to me London's offers have been entirely fair. I don't know why we can't settle on a boundary without a war. The Columbia River seems a perfectly logical boundary, perfectly logical." He looked away, then back at Alan. "American interests are to the south, and we've kept our major investments to the north."

Alan nodded, and the old doctor continued. "I've told all our people who've settled to the south that they can expect territory south of the Columbia to become a part of the United States. They know."

As suddenly as McLoughlin had stopped, he picked up his cane, did a quick right-face, and walked again with long, brisk strides across the western courtyard toward the Sale Shop, his large feet kicking up rainwater as he went.

Alan hastened to keep pace. He wondered about his own plans to stake a claim in Oregon. He wanted to make a home for Jennie here so she could be near her parents, and the Willamette Valley offered beautiful country, rich ground. But how could he live among these ingrates who would do hurt to a man like McLoughlin?

Maybe he should take Jennie to London. She'd love the city and all its excitement—away from this remote territory that made her feel so lonely. He wanted her to be happy.

When he and McLoughlin passed the Indian Trade Store, he noticed the usual cluster of Indians milling about the building, waiting their turns to go inside to trade furs for supplies. None appeared to be laden with pelts.

Alan spoke low to direct his comments only to McLoughlin. "You know, sir, this influx of settlers isn't helping the fur trade any, and the Indians are getting more restless all the time."

"True enough, true enough." The doctor stopped at the open door to the Sale Shop. "There has been more Indian trouble of late—after being peaceful here for these many years."

"Well, I rather think they still respect you, sir—and your men as well. It's the Bostons they hate. And they're quite right. It's the damn Bostons who'll take their land and leave them with nothing."

McLoughlin looked straight into Alan's eyes. "About that meeting in May—what are the sentiments of our French Canadians down on the Willamette, would you say?"

Alan looked away from the piercing gray-blue eyes, then returned the old man's gaze. "The feeling's mixed, I think. There were several at the so-called 'Wolf Meeting' down at Gervais's place, and I didn't see much opposition then. However, I doubt they understood the hazards."

McLoughlin rubbed a hand over his broad chin. "Probably not. Most of them are simple souls." He straightened suddenly, tapped his cane on the ground, and clapped Alan on the shoulder. "My good man, I want you to go down there and talk to them. Mind you, it's only the uncertain ones you can hope to sway. A man that's set his mind is not likely to change it, but the uncertain ones can be swayed. Work on them. Yes, go to French Prairie, my good man, and work on them."

McLoughlin gave one sharp nod and pivoted on his heel to go into the Sale Shop, leaving Alan standing outside in the drizzle.

A little stunned, Alan called out to him. "Beg your pardon, sir, but when should I leave?"

McLoughlin called back. "Today. Now."

Alan watched the familiar shore and cast a quick frown at Lévêque in front, paddling with no apparent effort, hurtling the canoe southward. Removing the tall gray beaver hat, Alan raised his face to let the breeze ripple through his hair as he contemplated his task. He was thankful the rain had stopped, and if that lightness in the southern sky opened a little more, the clouds might break and let the sun through. His spirits lifted at the thought.

How would he sway the French Canadians? He'd best speak to their priest first, Father Blanchet. Alan stifled a smile as an idea struck. *Taxes. I'll talk to them about taxes. The bloody Americans will probably tax everything these poor folks own.*

Lévêque looked over his shoulder. "Do we stop at the Falls?"

"Not long. I'll need to hurry on to French Prairie."

The *voyageur* gave Alan a sneering grin. "You wish to visit the *américaine* wench?"

"Hold your tongue, Lévêque. She's not a wench." Alan gripped the side of the canoe, a sudden heaviness weighing on his chest. Whatever happened in that cabin with Johnston, Jennie was not the one to fault.

"These *Américains*," Lévêque said, "they are the enemy, *n'est-ce pas?*"

"Perhaps." Alan's voice softened. "But not Jennie Haviland."

Lévêque's gaze turned sharp. "An *Américain* is an *Américain*."

Alan returned the gaze, then broke it to watch the greening shore again. Lévêque was hitting on a real problem Alan didn't want to accept.

"How long at the Falls?" Lévêque asked. "An hour, you think?"

"Not more than that."

Lévêque nodded, his lips pursed. The man's expression sent a surge of uneasiness through Alan. Why did McLoughlin have to saddle Alan with this man? He wished Lévêque would go away and stay away. He glanced at Marceau in the rear. Alan could do with another Marceau, but he tried to shake off his concerns about Lévêque.

Jennie sat on the bank above the river, soaking in the sunshine and the beauty of the water, its deep-green calm below her dangling feet and its untamed fury in the falls to her left. Motion across the river caught her eye, people moving about the small village over there, and her body tightened.

There had been rumors for weeks about tribes rising up in the interior, but several days ago an incident happened a lot closer. A man from the Clackamas tribe only three miles away had stolen a white man's horse. Several men from Oregon City, including Pa and Jake, had gone to the village to arrest the man. When they got there, they found thirty or forty men all painted up with war paint and heavily armed with muskets, bows and arrows, tomahawks, and scalping knives. Though outnumbered, the white men rushed in, trying to capture the thief, but they met such resistance they had to retreat. Pa and Jake had talked into the wee hours that night about the danger—and the need for organized law to protect the settlers. The town was buzzing with it.

Jennie didn't think the village across the river had anything to do with it, but she still watched the place with new unease. Glancing upriver, she saw a canoe approaching. She shaded her eyes, squinting to identify the craft, her body drawn tight, ready to run if she had to. But a blond head in the canoe glistened in the sun. A rush of pleasure warmed her. She sprang up and ran toward the riverbank where they always came ashore.

Exhilarated by the wind in her hair and the wonderful ease of running in moccasins, she paused only a moment to wonder if it was ladylike to run to meet a man this way, then, laughing, decided she didn't care. She raced to the river's edge, reaching it just as the canoe pulled in.

Alan's face shone with delight. "Hello. Aren't you a welcome sight!" He leaped from the canoe and reached out to take her hand.

"I didn't know you were coming to the Falls. It's good to see you."

He did look wonderful, his face aglow from exposure to the crisp spring air, his voice as crisp. "Well then, how is it you're right here if you didn't know, eh?"

She laughed, gripping his hand tighter. "I saw you. I was sitting on the bank up there."

He grinned wide. "And came running, yet."

She tipped her head, embarrassed. "You saw me?"

"Your enthusiasm pleases me." He lifted her chin and touched his lips to hers, sending whispers of warmth through her. Then his expression became both frown and smile. "I have to go over to the storehouse to tend to some business, but I'll come see you when I'm done."

"Can you stay awhile this time?"

The frown deepened. "I'm afraid not. I have to get to French Prairie right away. I'm on assignment—Dr. McLoughlin's orders. And as you can probably guess, one doesn't argue with the good doctor's wishes."

She gave him a flickering smile. "How soon is right away?"

"An hour or so." He kissed her again, the faintest brush. "Where will I find you?"

"At the cabin, I guess."

With a quick good-bye he went on his way, striding toward the Hudson's Bay Company storehouse with quick, rhythmic steps. Ahead of him Lévêque darted toward the bluff where the trail rose up. She wondered why the *voyageur* was going up there. Then the man was out of her sight, and she tried to whisk him out of her mind.

───

Restless, Jennie sat on the front stoop and dug a stick in the soft moist earth of Ma's flower beds in front of the cabin. Time stretched long, and she wondered if Alan had forgotten her. The steady throb of her heart merged with another steady beat. Hard-soled boots coming quickly this way. She looked up to see Alan approaching, his handsome face set like stone. When their eyes met, he smiled, softening the lines about his mouth.

She dropped the stick and stood, wanting to rush into his arms, but he didn't open them, and she waited until he came within a forearm's length of her. They faced each other a moment, currents raging back and forth in that small space, tugging at her. His gaze reached somewhere deep inside her, the set of his face firm. His voice rasped. "Can you walk with me? We can visit while we walk. I haven't much time. The Indians are taking the canoe around the falls now, and as soon as we find Lévêque we'll be ready to go."

Her heart seemed to slump into her belly, but she turned and opened the door a crack to tell her mother she would be walking with Alan to his canoe at the river. Her mother agreed, not suggesting a chaperon this time. Maybe she thought one wasn't necessary in a busy town on a bright sunny day.

He held out his arm and she took it, strolling with him past the scattered cabins, her feet wanting to drag, as if that might delay his departure. "What takes you to French Prairie? And why the hurry?"

"Just business with some of the former Company men."

She waited for him to elaborate, and when he didn't she went on. "Nice day for your travels."

He gave her a quick smile. "Indeed. Hard to believe it was raining this morning at Fort Vancouver."

She stole glances at him as they walked, admiring the cut of his features, the golden hair glistening beneath the smart beaver hat, the large blue eyes and full lips. She remembered the passion in those lips, and longed to feel that again. "When will you be back?"

"A few weeks, I should say."

Weeks sounded dreadfully long. "Will you be going to the meeting?"

He shot a quick look at her, brows flickering upward. "Meeting?"

"The one at Champoeg everyone's talking about. It's going to be—" She clamped her lips together. Maybe she shouldn't be telling him about it. He was British, after all, and the meeting was organized by men who were quite pro-American, if not anti-British.

He shrugged. "Perhaps."

A weighty silence settled between them, the roar of the falls echoing in the void as they reached the portage trail. He let her go ahead on the trail, then put a hand on her back and drew her to a stop where they had a magnificent view of the mighty cascade. This was the place they'd stopped on their evening walk the day he began courting her. His voice barely cut through the crashing sound. "Beautiful on such a day."

She gave passing notice to the grandeur and turned her attention to the man at her side, wondering what had been happening in his life since last she saw him. "Have you finished with all your inventories and—what was it?—indents you had to get done last month? You were here such a short time in March I forgot to ask."

He nodded, watching the falls. "It was a poor time to be away from the office, but McLoughlin insisted."

"On account of the meeting at Mr. Gervais's house?"

He gave her another of those looks with the slight lift of his brows, but he didn't answer. Pa had said Alan was at the meeting on predators that began serious talk on organizing a government in Oregon. She wished Alan would talk to her about it, but he showed no inclination. The rumble of the falls coursed through her as she contemplated the hostilities that could break out over that issue.

Maybe he was troubled by another issue. He hadn't even hinted at his suspicions about the incident in the cabin. Given that he was a gentleman, he probably never would. She certainly couldn't say anything. But was that part of his tension?

With surprising suddenness, he turned to grasp her by the shoulders, his voice low but clear. "My dear." He took off his hat and wrapped her in his arms, pressing his cheek against hers. "It tears my heart to leave you so soon when I have so much to say to you."

What did he want to say? He hadn't been talkative at all. Why didn't he say it now? Hoping to draw him out, she looked into his eyes. A glitter shone in them. Tears? Her own heart wrenched, and she whispered, "Alan," forgetting she shouldn't address him so.

His lips came down on hers with all the passion of that other night, and more, and she answered his kiss with the fires of a longing she couldn't fully understand. She wanted to erase his tears, the distress she felt in him.

He drew back as quickly as he'd come upon her. "I must be going. They'll be waiting with the canoe."

She took his arm when he held it out to her again. He placed the hat on his head just so, and they proceeded up the trail, not trying to speak above the thundering water. Marceau and several Clowewalla men stood above the falls, two of them holding a canoe.

"Where's Lévêque?" Alan asked Marceau.

"I do not know, *M'sieu* Alan. He does not come."

Alan let out a huff. "If he doesn't come soon, we'll have to leave without him." He pulled a watch from a small pocket on his vest. His brow creased. "I do think we'd better go. I'll paddle myself."

Jennie squeezed his arm. "Will you be all right?"

"I can paddle a canoe, dear. I just don't usually have to." He leaned over to give her a quick kiss on the cheek. "Will you be all right walking home by yourself?"

"I come here by myself all the time. I'll be fine."

He kissed the other cheek and slipped away to the canoe, calling back over his shoulder. "I'll see you when I come back through."

The two men climbed into the narrow vessel, Marceau at the front, Alan in the rear. The rhythmic dipping of the paddles into the glassy green water moved the canoe out and away. Alan looked as if he'd been paddling all his life, the way he kept in perfect rhythm with Marceau. She watched until the craft grew small, then headed back down the trail.

Unsettling feelings stirred inside her, and when she reached the fork in the trail, she paused. One fork led into the town, the other toward the bluff. She felt much too restless to go back to the confines of the cabin. Maybe a brisk walk up the hill would ease her disquiet. She hurried up that familiar path, stopping at the top of the bluff to view the town and the falls. With a heavy sigh she proceeded into the woods.

She hugged her arms close, trying to recapture the wonder of his embrace, then touched the fingers of both hands to her lips.

Wind rustled the leaves, reminding her to be wary. There were dangers in these woods, which was why her parents had asked her not to walk here alone. Guilt warmed her cheeks. But she was no longer a child to be restricted by her elders. And the boys came up here all the time.

She watched for signs of anything that might harm her—panthers, bears, unsavory men. The story of those hostile Clackamas men flashed across her mind.

She peered through the trees. How would she see anything through the thick trunks and undergrowth? The pungence of greenery wrapped around her as it had on her first day here, the cloying scent of wild growth and ripe decay.

She took a sudden deep breath to fight her anxiety, and let the air out slowly. She was fine. If she didn't overcome her fears, she would always be a prisoner in this country—bound behind the closed doors of a tiny cabin. Shaking her head, she kept moving deeper into the woods, her mind returning to thoughts of Alan and fantasies of how life might be with him.

A sound kicked her out of the reverie. Behind her. She spun around to see. Nothing. "I'm imagining things." Still, she studied her surroundings in that direction. Taking another long, slow breath, she turned back to continue along the trail. And froze.

A man stood in the trail in front of her. From the Clackamas tribe, she thought. Chinookan of some kind, anyway. He had the flattened head and wore a tattered army jacket on top, only a breechclout below. Did she know him? He had swipes of red and black paint on his face, so she wasn't sure she would recognize him if she did. His eyes held hers, mesmerizing her. Where had he come from? Another stepped onto the trail beside him, also painted, chest bare, more paint spread across his naked skin. Terror seared through her.

Motion in her peripheral vision startled her, and she turned to see a third man next to her, on her right. She hadn't heard the slightest sound of his approach. He said something, but she couldn't understand him. She jumped at the sound of a man answering from the other side. The one with the army jacket. How did he move so quickly? He laughed, and the others laughed with him.

When she turned back to the one on her right, she realized he had moved closer. He spoke again, and she smelled the tobacco on his breath. She felt more than heard the army-jacket man move near. She sucked up air, and the bare chest loomed in front of her. They kept chattering and laughing. They were talking about her, laughing at her. She wanted to demand they stop, but all the black eyes focused upon her, paralyzing her.

One took hold of her left arm, another her right. Her body went rigid. She tried to will herself to move, to scream. But it was like a nightmare in which she could do neither. With tremendous effort she managed to open her mouth and force out sound. But so like a nightmare, it was the smallest, most inadequate utterance. A hand clamped over her mouth and stopped even that.

The horror of his touch roused her, and she found power to move. She jerked her head, trying to get free of the hand on her mouth, yanked her arms to break their grasps. She wrenched her whole body, jabbing her elbows and kicking her feet. And gained nothing.

The hand left her mouth, and she drew precious air, ready to scream, but a length of cloth came across her lips in place of the hand and closed tight. Someone was tying it, snagging threads of hair in the back so her eyes watered from the pain.

The men, still talking and laughing, began to drag her forward. She dug her toes into the packed earth, refusing to give in to them, but her efforts did little to slow their progress. She tried to look around, to see where they were going, but another cloth came across her eyes, blotting out sight. Again the tying, the pulled hair. She twisted and kicked again. Then one yanked her arms behind her back. A cord dug into her wrists and bound them together. Hands clutched her legs with little regard to where they touched her, and another bound her ankles. With a soft grunt one of the men lifted her and carried her close to his chest. She felt the rough fabric against her cheek. The army-jacket man.

Chapter Fourteen

Oregon City, April 1843. Mr. Carter leaned on the wall outside the Methodist store and stroked a hand over the stubble on his chin. "I jist don't quite know what we need with a gov'ment in Oregon. I cain't say as how I've missed gov'ment ner its taxes ner its politicians. Nossir. My missus and me, we're gittin' along jist fine without no gov'ment men tellin' us how we'd oughta live."

The man had come into Oregon City for supplies, and Jake had hoped to recruit another supporter for the cause. He was growing doubtful, though he tried to find points of persuasion. "Well, that's the thing about government, Mr. Carter. You don't miss it until you need it. Then it's pretty nice to find it there. What about that land you claim for your farm? How do you know you can keep it if there's no government to ensure your claim?"

The man lifted his rifle. "I figger this'll ensure it."

"Will that also protect you if the local tribes choose to attack?"

Carter just laughed. "You think these vermin-infested critters around here is goin' to pose a threat? Don't josh me, now, boys."

Jake kept hammering away. "Did you hear about Anderson's horse being stolen?"

Carter's tone turned contemptuous. "Them critters ain't got gumption enough to follow through on nothin'. Hell, half of 'em got the clap or some such. Better watch foolin' with their wimmen, boys. They'll give it to ye, sure. Now if there's danger amongst 'em, that's the danger." He chortled with glee.

Blowing a long breath, Jake looked at Joe.

"Well now," Joe said, "if'n we don't git law and order amongst us, then I reckon we kin scarce hope to save ourselves from any ruffians that come in off'n ships an' up from Californee."

Carter eyed the two trappers. "And over the Rockies?"

Jake looked at Joe again, and this time they both shrugged. Jake didn't understand the apathy when the need for organization seemed so vital to him. He threw one last remark at Carter. "Well, good luck with your farming. I hope you're a crack shot with that gun—in case somebody decides to relieve you of your property."

Carter laughed. "I am, boy. You bet I am."

Jake turned away, Joe following right behind, and they wandered slowly in the direction of the river. Joe grunted. "This coon's come acrost friendlier bars."

"Smarter ones, too, I'll wager. What do you say we go over to Havilands'? I'd like to chat with George Haviland awhile."

Joe raised his brows and grinned at Jake. "I reckon the company's good over thar."

Jake gave his friend a soft punch in the arm. "Don't be thinking so damned much, Joe."

Joe chuckled, but said no more.

When they got to the Haviland place, they found Mrs. Haviland in a high state of distress. "It's Jennie," she said. "I can't imagine what's happened. She's been gone all afternoon, and she only intended to be gone a few minutes."

"Gone? Where?" Jake asked.

"She went walking with Mr. Radford." Mrs. Haviland shook her head, a deep frown wrinkling her soft face. "She didn't expect to be gone long, because Mr. Radford had to be on his way to French Prairie."

A sudden warmth nettled Jake's flesh. He hadn't known Radford was in town. "She wouldn't have gone with him, would she?"

The lady's mouth widened, and her speech resonated with indignation. "I'm sure not. Jennie wouldn't. Mr. Radford wouldn't." Sighing heavily, she went on more calmly. "I sent the boys out looking. Some Indians up above the falls said Mr. Radford had gone on and that Jennie had headed back toward town. But that was a long time ago. What could have happened to her? Her father is gone—out somewhere to talk with folks about the government. I don't know what else to do."

Jake clenched his fists and took a deep breath. As much as he feared for Jennie, he didn't want to add to her mother's worry. "I'm sure she's all right," he said with more assurance than he felt. "She probably just went for a walk. Where are the boys now?"

"They checked above the bluff, but they didn't see her up there. They were going to look down by the river next. They should be back soon if you want to talk to them."

Jake didn't want to wait. "Let's take a look, Joe."

Joe tipped his head. "Ma'am, we'll find her, shore."

Quickly taking their leave, the two men headed out. "Let's go see those Indians," Jake said. "I don't know how well the boys communicate in the jargon."

"Good idea. And we'd better take hosses, I'm thinkin'."

Their horses were tied by the Methodist store where they'd stopped to talk to Carter, and in moments the two were mounted and on their way. They found a few men at the top of the portage trail from the local Clowewalla tribe, and Jake pulled his horse up to an old man with the typical flattened head, deep age lines cutting into his leathery pockmarked face.

"Did you see a girl up here?" Jake asked, speaking in the Chinook jargon. "A girl with a yellow-haired King George man?"

The old man remained expressionless, making Jake wonder if he'd understood. Jake was about to repeat the question when the man replied in the jargon, "A girl came here with a yellow-haired King George man."

"Did the girl leave with the King George man?"

Again the old Clowewalla was distressingly slow to speak. Finally, looking down at the ground, he shook his head.

Jake asked again, to be sure. "She did not go with the King George man?"

"No."

"Then, where did she go?"

The man turned with exasperating indifference and nodded toward town. "That way."

Jake looked at Joe, and they immediately turned their horses to gallop back down the portage trail. At the bottom of the trail they jumped to the ground to search for sign. It had been a busy thoroughfare, though, and it was impossible to find a single set of tracks in the confusion of footprints. Jake's uneasiness grew as troubling questions stirred in his mind.

"Well now," Joe said calmly, "if she headed this way and didn't go home, I reckon she might've gone up yonder on the bluff, it being the only other trail this way. Mind ye, I figger that's the next place to look. Do ye hear?"

Angry with himself for his loss of composure, Jake scowled at Joe and quickly led Old Blue past the man to hurry up the trail to the bluff top, dismounted so as to better see tracks. A close look might enable him to pick out Jennie's. He scanned with care. Nothing. The trail was hard, even in the woods, much of it covered by debris. Freshly broken twigs showed where someone had recently passed, but there was no way of identifying who.

Moving forward, he saw a little dog's tracks. That would be Muffin. Then moccasins. About the size of the boys' feet. Jake saw where the boys had given up and turned around, but he couldn't find any sign of Jennie's tracks. Not much traffic up here, but a little—enough to wipe out what few tracks she might have left in the littered trail. Still, he had to keep trying.

Jennie shifted her weight against the hard surface at her back. The men had set her here and left her, wrists still tied behind, ankles bound, the cloths still covering her eyes and mouth. She had no idea how far the one had carried her, but an eternity seemed to have passed without sight or voice.

She tried to draw a full breath through her nose, unable to open her mouth. The smell of smoke, a blend of campfire and tobacco, wafted to her. Sweat poured down her forehead and trickled between her breasts.

A presence loomed. Close. How could she not have heard him? She smelled the tobacco on his hot breath and felt him lean across the length of her. She shrank her body as tight as she could.

What is he going to do to me?

Tremulous sounds erupted in her throat, as she tried to stifle her cries. Hands closed over the back of her head, the warmth of his body wrapping around her. Tiny hairs pulled where the ties bound the cloth. The fabric dropped, and the backlight around his dark head invaded her eyes.

She clamped her eyelids shut, then looked up, desperate for sight. Her vision adjusted before her mind. What was she seeing? She gave her head a little shake. She was looking into the snapping black eyes of a *woman*. A stunning beauty.

The woman placed a forefinger over her full lips in a universal sign for silence. As Jennie began to breathe evenly again, the woman reached back and untied the other cloth, gathering both rags up and tossing them aside. Then she sat cross-legged on the ground a short distance away.

Jennie's words burst out despite the woman's signing. "Who are you? What are you doing to me?"

Again the forefinger. Jennie looked out the doorway. They were in some kind of rough enclosure made of a few angled boards and tree boughs. She saw the army-jacket man lying on the ground outside, propped up on his elbows, smoking a pipe as he gazed into a small campfire. One of the bare-chested ones lay opposite him.

"Where's the other one?" Jennie asked. "There were three."

The woman didn't answer.

Jennie studied her a moment. She didn't have the flattened head of the Clackamas tribe, but the men did. "Are you Clackamas? You don't look it."

A frown tightened the woman's smooth forehead, and she looked away from Jennie.

Again Jennie tried. "Do you speak any English?"

The woman glanced over her shoulder, then looked at Jennie again. "Two now."

The words sent a rush of relief through Jennie. "You speak English." It didn't matter what the words were. They were English words. "Can you tell me what—?"

The woman's sharp glare stopped her. The army-jacket man said something, and the woman answered him.

The Shifting Winds

Jennie lowered her voice. "Is this your village?"

The woman let out a barely audible huff. "We have strong houses. Not like this. They do not take you to the village. The chief would not like it. These men, they are—what you call?—rogues."

A dry sob shook Jennie, and she tried again. "Who are you? Why did you bring me here this way?"

"I am Clackamas."

"You don't look—"

"My mother goes with King George man. She does not do the boards in time."

The boards used to press their heads in that odd fashion, Jennie assumed. "So you're half English?"

Her lip curled, and she responded in a brusque whisper. "No. My father is Clackamas too. But when I come home my people think I am slave." She rounded her two hands above her head to illustrate. "I have the slave head. So I find my own King George man. He likes my head." She fixed her gaze on Jennie, then hunched forward, as if bent by a terrible weight.

Her pain touched Jennie despite her being Jennie's captor. Maybe the woman was a captive too, not bound by ropes, but caught in her own dilemma.

She had a distinctive scar on her cheek, like a flying bird, which only enhanced her appearance. She didn't slick her hair close to her head, like many of her people. Full and free, the glistening black strands seemed to defy any attempts to subdue them, the unfettered style giving her an intriguing flair. Her tawny legs showed beneath the skirt of cedar-bark strips commonly worn by women of the local tribes, beaded moccasins on her feet. The cedar bark rustled softly as she moved. Her tunic in a vivid cobalt blue hung loosely over her torso, the wide neckline showing off her shoulders. She'd tied it around the waist with a belt of braided leather and beads in bright reds and pale shimmery blue. A long necklace of shells and beads looped around her neck.

Jennie spoke again, wanting to draw her out. "What is your name?"

"My Englishman calls me Sally. He cannot say my Clackamas name."

"I—I'm . . . Jennie. What is your Clackamas name?"

She looked at Jennie for a moment, then shook her head. "You call me Sally. I have nice name. I do not like when I hear you Bostons scratch it up."

Sally's accent almost sounded French, like Dr. McLoughlin's. "Where's your Englishman?" Jennie asked.

Sally let out a whispered laugh of sarcasm. "He loses me in card game to *Lévêque*." The name burst out like a curse.

"Lévêque!"

The woman's black eyes flashed with lights as she stared at Jennie. "You know this Lévêque?"

"I—a little."

Sally's low voice became a growl. "Dirty bastard. Son of a bitch."

Jennie's eyes went wide. Sally had learned quite a bit of English, hadn't she?

The woman almost smiled. "You do not like my words."

Jennie didn't want to answer. She fought to keep the despair out of her voice. "Will you help me?"

"Lévêque would beat the hell out of me. This is Lévêque's work. He talks big, and these boys—they act the rogue for him. If the chief learns, is big trouble."

Jennie's brow tightened. "Lévêque beats you?"

The woman lifted her chin and pointed to a bruise below her jaw, then drew down the neckline of her tunic to show a scabby bruise above her breast. "It makes him feel like the big man. Dirty bastard." She huffed again. "Lévêque's gun—" She put her hands together, palms downward, and drew them quickly apart. "—no powder." Then she gave Jennie a subtle smile. "You understand, Boston?"

Jennie's cheeks burned, and she decided not to think on that too much. But she couldn't get over the thought of Lévêque beating this woman. "You should run away from him."

"He would find me. Then he will kill me, sure."

"You could go to the mission—down at Chemeketa. They'd help you."

The woman made a face. "With the Kalapuyas? No."

"The missionaries would keep you safe. Please. I'll help you."

Sally sat staring at Jennie for a long time. When the woman spoke, Jennie leaned forward to hear. "Lévêque is sure I do what he says."

Jennie had to move. Her wrists and ankles hurt from the rough cords that bound them. And her back ached. She heard snoring outside and looked up. Army Jacket's head had dropped onto his chest. He was sleeping. So was the other.

Sally saw it too. She looked at Jennie's feet. "You wear moccasins, Chennie. Good. You can run."

Jennie's heart began a slow acceleration, but she kept talking. "My boots wore out from the long walk across the plains. Sometimes we rode, but mostly we walked."

"Good. You are strong, Boston." Sally put her finger to her lips again. "I untie you, but you stay. Act like you are tied. Yes?"

Jennie nodded, tingles racing across her skin.

Sally stretched to look outside, and her face lit up. Evidently she saw something. "I go out. You stay. When I am outside, you scream, Chennie. Raise bloody hell. When the men come in, I hit from behind." She made a sharp striking motion with one hand.

Jennie gulped. "Will you kill them?"

"No, but better for them I do."

※

Jake kicked a stick out of the path. "Damn it. Why did she come out here by herself? She could be anywhere in these woods."

"Well now, old hoss, you gotta keep your head cool. No sense in lettin' yer anger bile up."

Jake thumbed the stock of his rifle, chin jutted forward. They'd found no sign since those two deep lines that cut along the trail, the kind of marks two dragging toes might make. After that, nothing. Lots of moccasins. Recent. But it was a busy trail. What were the Clackamas up to after that little fiasco with the stolen horse? How else might they take out their frustrations?

Joe leaned down from his horse and tapped Jake on the shoulder. "Don't be thinkin' too much, old coon. Worry won't help ye find her."

Jake's throat filled so he didn't want to talk now, and he climbed back on Old Blue.

※

The rustle of Sally's skirt sounded so loud, Jennie worried it would wake the men. Bending over Jennie's ankles, Sally untied the knot, then briskly rubbed Jennie's legs, stirring the blood under the bruised skin. Jennie bit her lips to keep from crying out, the pain so intense. But it gradually eased until she could move her legs freely.

"Better?" Sally asked.

Jennie nodded and leaned to one side so Sally could untie her arms. Once those were loosened she rubbed her own wrists, working past the initial pain to come close to normal feeling. At Sally's urging she put her arms behind again as if tied and let Sally tuck the bindings over her ankles.

Jennie's body tensed when Sally stood tall and tiptoed toward the doorway. The woman paused, looked back at Jennie, gave a firm nod, and disappeared. Jennie watched the two men, her heart pounding loud enough to hear. She drew a long breath and screamed. The sound reverberated through the tiny enclosure, shattering the quiet of the woods.

Both men bolted to their feet. Their painted faces became frightful masks as they gaped at her, eyes fierce. Jennie kept screaming, letting out all the horror she'd held inside. Army Jacket reached the hut doorway in a few long strides. A blur came down above his head—so fast Jennie could scarcely make it out. A large branch. The whack made her jump. The man folded, crumpled to the ground.

The stick swung again, straight at the face of the other man. But he'd seen what Sally did to the first, and he raised his arms to shield himself. The stick bounced off him, and he grabbed Sally by both wrists. She wrenched her body, grappling with him. Her stick flew from her hands and clattered against a tree trunk before sliding to the ground.

Sally yelled out. "Run, Chennie!"

But Jennie couldn't leave her. The man was too strong. Sally wouldn't be able to get away. Seeing the stick on the ground, Jennie darted for it. She snatched it up and made a wide swing at the man's broad back. The stick hit his shoulders so hard, the impact knocked it out of her hands. The branch thudded on the moist earth. The man didn't fall, but he appeared stunned. He let go of Sally and stood, hands out, not moving.

Using the moment, Sally leaped for the stick, raised it, and struck him on the head. He slumped to the ground, but he wasn't unconscious. He lay there moaning. Seeing some of the cords that dropped when Jennie came out of the enclosure, Sally scooped them up and began tying his wrists. Jennie looked for the others and, finding them, rushed to help. Sally took them from Jennie and tied his feet. He writhed, but the cords held.

Jennie looked at the other man heaped near the enclosure. "Is he dead?"

Sally shrugged and reached for her. "Run, Chennie. Run like hell."

The woman bounded forward and charged through the trees, and Jennie plunged after her. The giant trees all looked the same. Towering brush and ferns blocked their path. But swerving and jumping, they ran. Their moccasin-clad feet thudded softly on the thick debris of the forest floor. Echoed. A fire of fear raged through Jennie. Gave her strength.

Did she hear thudding behind? Snapping branches?

She raced faster. How far? How long could she run?

Her chest began to burn. She gasped for more air. A noise ahead. *What was that?* A snort.

Through the trees she saw motion. A black horse. And a white one not far behind. She let out a cry and found new energy.

Galloping hooves pounded the earth, resonated. She knew that black horse. It grew. Slowly. Closer. Larger. Debris rising from its hooves, drifting. Horse and rider emerging as one.

A few paces away Jake pulled the animal to a sudden stop and leaped to the ground. He ran straight to her, and she flung herself toward him. They met in a sudden embrace and clasped each other tight.

She couldn't stop the tears, the sobs, and didn't try. She was safe. He held her, pressed against him, and stroked her hair, his cheek against her temple. She felt his head turn, ever so slightly, and the brush of his lips on the side of her brow, so soft she wasn't sure she'd felt it. She looked into his face, startled, and he bent closer. She thought he was going to kiss her, but he didn't move, just looked at her. His eyes glistened with tears.

When finally he spoke, his voice barely sounded above the whisper of breezes in the trees. "Are you all right?"

Another sob caught her breath, and she nodded a little. "I am."

He hugged her tight again, and she nestled her face against his soft hickory shirt.

Joe cleared his throat, his words uncharacteristically tender, yet firm. "You ladies runnin' from somethin' we oughta be knowin' about?"

Jennie drew back a little, but Jake didn't let go of her.

Sally answered. "I think they do not give much trouble now."

"What happened?" Jake asked.

Jennie told him how the Clackamas men had abducted her and how Sally came to her rescue. She motioned toward her friend. "This is Sally. She's Lévêque's . . . wife."

Jake gave Sally a nod. "I'm mighty grateful to you, ma'am. I think I've seen you before."

She smiled at him. "You save me that beating. I owe you the favor, but I am surprised I give you one now."

"How many men?"

"Only two," Sally said. "They have not much fight anymore."

Jake looked up at Joe. "Maybe you and Sally should go after those two. She can show you where they are, and I'll take Jennie home."

Jennie took his arm. "No, Sally needs to go with us. We need to take her to the mission to keep her safe, so Lévêque doesn't hurt her."

Sally spat on the ground. "I am done with that bastard. I get word to the chief. He can take care of those two Chennie and I left behind."

Jake stepped away from Jennie, hands clenching. "Was Lévêque involved in this?"

Sally gave him a long look before she spoke, her words soft, as if the trees might hear. "Is Lévêque's work."

"Why?"

"You ask him."

Jake's voice sent a chill through Jennie. "I'll do that, right before I kill him. Where is he?"

"Probably halfway to the fort now."

Jake took Jennie's arm and led her to Old Blue. "You want in the saddle? You can ride astride the way you did that other time—until we get close to town. No one here will mind."

She shook her head. "I can sit sideways on a man's saddle. I've done it before."

"Not as steady."

"I'll be fine."

He pursed his lips and nodded, then lifted her into the saddle with both her feet to one side, and scrambled on behind. She carefully hooked one leg over the saddle horn and tried to reach the stirrup with the other. She couldn't reach.

Jake closed his arms around her. "Do you want me to raise that stirrup?"

"I can manage. I'd rather just go."

Joe started to make room for Sally on his saddle, but she leaped up and straddled the big white horse behind him, latching her arms around his waist.

They rode side by side where the trees allowed. Jennie looked back at Jake, who had an arm on either side of her and one hand on the reins. "You don't have to hold on so tight, and I can do the reins."

He didn't let go. "Old Blue can get frisky sometimes."

Sally laughed. Jennie looked over to see the woman pointing at her, but the woman faced Jake when she spoke. "You watch out for this one. She swings good stick."

Jake's eyebrows shot up, and Jennie tried to explain. "That man was going to hurt Sally, and I couldn't let him."

Sally kept watching them, and her eyes took on a sudden glitter. "You have good man, Chennie."

Jennie waved a dismissive hand. "Oh, Jake—Mr. Johnston isn't—"

Sally lifted one side of her lips. "Chake Mister Chohnston has plenty powder, I betcha."

Heat flared in Jennie's cheeks and spread like ripples on the river. She was keenly aware of Jake's arms around her, but she wasn't quite ready for him to let go either. Her emotions were as unsteady as her position in this saddle in the aftermath of that terrible ordeal.

"Well now," Joe said. "Mind ye, this makes me think o' the time the Crows made off with my Mount'in Lamb. My first woman." He smiled at Jennie. "And a fine one too."

He gazed into the trees before them with a faraway look, as if seeing that other time and place, and Jennie felt herself moving there with him, wanting to be carried away from her troubles on his gift of story.

"Yessir," he said. "We'd been out on Powder River huntin' buffler, some of us fellers with our women along, and jist afore we come back into camp we see that Mount'in Lamb is missin'. Well now, soon as we see that, we take off right smart on our best buffler hosses to find her."

He faced Jennie. "Ye know what we find?"

Jennie gave him a wavering smile, her subtle reaction encouraging him to go on.

"Thar's my Mount'in Lamb, captured by this bunch o' Crows. They's a tribe o' Injuns in the mount'ins. Pesky fellers sometimes—not so bad as the Blackfeet, but not to be trusted anyhow. Well now, we find them Crows jist happy as kin be, surroundin' my purty Mount'in Lamb, feastin' thar eyes on her fine feathers and ready to pluck the bird to take her trinkets fer thar own. A dozen o' them Crows thar is and only six o' us. Now, if'n that ain't some fix, I wouldn't say so. And seein' 'em thar 'round my woman, I'm a mite edgy, I kin tell ye, so I moves out my hoss to git closer afore I decides jist what to do."

Joe nodded, the intensity of his voice increasing with the pace of his story. "Well now, that hoss o' mine happens to be a right spirited critter, mind ye, and he gits a mite skittery about all my hasty maneuvers. And takin' fright, he jist runs like a bar is chasin' him right smack-dab in the middle o' them Crows." Joe slapped the saddle and shook his head with exaggerated gravity. "That startles 'em some, I kin tell ye, and I reckon they must've figgered this coon is some fearless warrior with mighty great medicine. And bein's it's too late fer this child to be prudent, I jist starts the battle with yellin' and firin' and makin' shore my shot counts."

He paused and shook his head again. "Yessir, and then my comrades, not to be outdone, they comes right along and jumps into the fight too, and Mount'in Lamb gits away and another Crow bites the dust." He gestured with one finger, as if to make a point. "They go fer odds, and by numbers they had it this time, shore, but when things go bad fer 'em, they'll cache ever' time. And these pesky Crows cached, *they* did."

A slow smile moved over Joe's face, his eyes brightening. "Well now, ye kin figger this coon's plenty happy then. I have my Mount'in Lamb back, and we ride back to camp with mighty big hearts. And the other fellers, they's a-bein' mighty free with the compliments, tellin' Old Joe what a brave and gallant soul he is, attackin' the Crows single-handed thataway."

Joe chuckled and turned toward Jennie with a wry smile. "I took their compliments quite natural—nor did I think it worthwhile to explain to 'em . . . that I couldn't hold my hoss."

Jennie let out a giggle, then burst into laughter, releasing the terrible tension with it. Caught by the infectious sound, the others broke into hearty laughter with her, their convulsive outbursts echoing through the thick green forest.

Champoeg, May 2, 1843. Jake breathed deep of the fine spring air, inhaling the sweet fragrance of nature's rising, as he and George Haviland strolled from their camping spot toward the small Hudson's Bay Company storehouse where the meeting would be held. Rolling prairie surrounded the town. Firs cloaked the hills on the horizon and scattered in clusters across the prairie. Everything bursting forth with life. A band of deciduous trees lined the nearby Willamette River, blocking his view of the water. The storehouse lay at the edge of the low rise above the riverbank.

"Rich country around Champoeg," Haviland said. "I see why it's attracted so many farmers."

Jake nodded. "The Kalapuyas have always maintained this prairie with fire. It's a special place to them. They get together here for council and food gathering, where there's easy access along the river."

"*Champoeg*—that's an Indian word, isn't it?"

"It is, though probably a little garbled by our inability to make the sounds they do. Comes from a Kalapuya word for a root that grows around here."

"Camas?"

"No, but similar, I think."

Kalapuyas were wandering around the area now, no doubt curious to find out what these white men were up to with their meeting today. The woods had been full of campfires last night on the eve of the meeting.

Haviland bent toward Jake as they approached the small vertical-log storehouse. "Looks like a real crowd."

Jake scanned the mass of people, trying to estimate. "A hundred, you think?"

"And more coming. We could have half the population here."

Jake stroked his chin. "I suppose there must be a couple hundred white men in Oregon south of the Columbia."

He smiled, seeing Joe under a tall fir tree talking hard to a French Canadian. Colorful today, Joe had chosen a bright-red flannel shirt to go with his ragged buckskin breeches, a soft-cloth toque on his head. Over his shoulder he carried the ever-present powder horn and bullet pouch on their elaborately fringed buckskin strap, his rifle in hand.

Doc Newell stood nearby. Of course he'd be here, having served on the committee that drew up the report for today. Calm in manner and innately wise, if not highly educated, Newell was a strong force for organization in Oregon. Jake was glad to see other mountain men in the crowd too—Doughty, Ebbert, Russell, Gale, Wilkins—talking together by the storehouse.

Le Breton was here, bustling as usual, speaking briefly to one man, then scurrying off to another. And Gray, strutting around with a serious face. And the Canadians. Jake knew some of them, and he couldn't help wondering what effect they would have on the meeting's outcome. Certainly if their Hudson's Bay Company benefactors retained any influence, they would be opposed.

Moving into the crowd, Jake picked up snatches of conversation. "They'll tax us to heaven," one French Canadian said. "Even our windows, *n'est-ce pas?*"

Jake frowned and kept moving.

Another grumbling voice. "I don't think they should even be here." A Mr. Judson, who worked down at the Methodist Mission. "This should be a meeting of Americans. We're the ones who want a government, and we should have it."

"But, Mr. Judson," another said, "if we're to have a government here, it must govern all the people in the area—French Canadians as well as ourselves."

Jake glanced toward Haviland, still by his side. "A few differences of opinion." As they moved closer to the storehouse, an angry shout rose behind them. Looking back, Jake saw several men clustered about Judson, pushing and shoving, their voices raised in an unintelligible clamor.

Le Breton's feeble voice quavered beside him. "Gentlemen! Gentlemen!" The little man rushed to the scene of uproar, calling out to them, though his words were soon drowned out.

With only a moment's hesitation, Jake headed after Le Breton and shouted, "Men! We came here to have a meeting, not to fight."

Others joined in to call for peace, and gradually the furor died down.

Le Breton yelled at the top of his small voice. "It's time the meeting came to order. Let's get inside as best we can."

The crowd began to converge on the Hudson's Bay Company storehouse like a slow mudslide. By the time Jake got to the building, he could only squeeze inside the doorway. Many others waited outside. Observing the crowd inside and out, he could see there were too many for the size of the room, but maybe those outside could hear if they pressed close to the open doorway. And press they did. The formalities began with the selection of a chairman and secretaries, but Jake's attention focused on the crowd.

That attention narrowed. Outside, among the men clustered at the door, he saw Radford. Jake locked his hand tighter on his rifle and searched for Lévêque. Marceau stood near Radford, but Jake saw no sign of Lévêque.

"Mind ye, Old Jake, we got business to attend to now."

Jake swerved, startled to see Joe had come up beside him—and that he'd accurately read Jake's expression. Haviland was watching Jake too, but he looked puzzled. The man didn't know about Jennie's capture by the Clackamas. Jake and Joe had honored her wishes not to say anything about it. They'd given an abbreviated explanation for Sally's presence, and everyone seemed to accept it. Jake hoped the missionaries could protect Sally. In any case, he couldn't explain any of this to George Haviland, and even if he did see Lévêque, he couldn't do anything to settle accounts now. Joe was right. This wasn't the time.

Rubbing a thumb over the cold rifle barrel, Jake turned his attention to the meeting. Dr. Ira Babcock stood on a box in front, having been selected chairman. He named secretaries and called for a report from the committee.

Mr. O'Neil stepped onto the box and, with paper in hand, began to read. "'Resolved, first, that a supreme judge with probate powers be chosen to officiate in this community;

"'Second, that a clerk of the court, or recorder, be chosen;

"'Third, that a sheriff be chosen;

"'Fourth, that three magistrates be chosen;

"'Fifth, that three constables be chosen;

"'Sixth, that a committee of nine persons be chosen for the purpose of drafting a code of laws for the government of this community to be presented to a public meeting to be hereafter called by said committee, and to be held at Champoeg, on the fifth day of July, 1843;

"'Seventh, that a treasurer be chosen;

"'Eighth, that a major and three captains be chosen.'"

Lowering the piece of paper, O'Neil looked toward the chairman and nodded. Babcock acknowledged him and asked for a motion. A response rang out, clear and full. "I move that the report of the committee be accepted."

The motion was seconded, and Babcock called for discussion. Discussion arose, not organized discussion, but a general murmur among the crowd. One man's voice broke through the murmur. "Does this mean we'd be a-havin' a United States gov'ment?"

"It means organization," another said, "and providing ourselves with protection through the enforcement of law and order."

"But is it a gov'ment fer Americans?" the first asked.

The other answered, "It's a government for the people of this colony—all the people."

"Will it cost us? Will it mean taxes for us?"

"Not if we don't vote in taxes."

Babcock spoke out over the murmuring crowd. "Gentlemen. Order, please. Would you please address the chair?"

"Mr. Chairman!" a man said.

Babcock recognized him, but Jake didn't hear the man's words. He was studying the crowd. Quite a few French Canadians. Without actually counting them, he guessed they could well be in the majority. If they chose to fight this, the thing could well lose. Where were all the

Americans? There were many like Carter who opposed government, and others who didn't care if the country had law and order. Jake heard a call for the question.

Babcock's voice gradually stilled the undercurrents of talk. "It has been moved and seconded that the report of the committee be accepted. All in favor, say *aye*."

Jake joined many others. "Aye."

"Opposed, *nay*." The *nays* sounded loud. Too loud.

Babcock looked perturbed. "Gentlemen, I am unable to decide. Those favoring the motion to organize will please say *aye*." Again the *ayes*.

"Those opposed, *nay*." The *nays* came out loud and strong once more. Babcock appeared baffled, then lifted his hands in a show of defeat. "Motion lost."

The room erupted in confusion—voices clamoring, men pressing against each other. Some in the rear backed out of the building, shaking their heads. Jake stood there, stunned, unable to believe what he'd just witnessed.

Lost. As much as we need this?

He pounded a fist against the roughhewn doorframe and let the flow of bodies push him outside into the bright May sun. He found no pleasure in the glorious spring day now. Dark clouds seemed to have blocked out all rays of hope. Then, through the haze of his disappointment, he realized the sunshine *had* dimmed. A shadow lay across the gathering from a big gray cloud that covered the sun. Looking up, he noticed Radford a short distance from him, looking smug and satisfied. Jake didn't like losing, especially to that man.

"Damn," he said under his breath. "I need to talk to that bastard anyway."

He started toward the man, then heard someone beside him.

It was Babcock, sounding distressed. "The meeting's not adjourned."

Jake stopped to listen, while he kept an eye on Radford.

The high-pitched voice of Le Breton barely sounded over the babble. "I think we should call for a divide."

"What's that?" Newell.

"A divide," Le Breton said, "a vote by separation into two groups."

"Can we do that?"

"With a new motion we can. It's the only thing I can see that will save the day for us. And we can risk it. We have the votes. I'm sure of it."

"I believe you're right." Gray spoke now. "We've canvassed every man here, directly or indirectly, and I know the sentiments of most. I believe you're right."

Jake turned to the speakers. They stood a couple of paces from him, clustered near a tall fir in front of the storehouse, lines of tension on their brows. Glancing at the crowd, Jake didn't see anyone leaving. They seemed confused, some upset, some pleased, but whatever the attitudes, an electricity permeated the atmosphere, like a mountaintop during a lightning storm.

"Mr. Chairman," Le Breton said, though Jake doubted he could be heard by anyone more than two paces away.

Babcock acknowledged the man.

Those near Jake gave attention to the meeting's leaders, but the buzz outside their close circle continued. Haviland stood close by, and Joe, both as intent as Jake on what these leaders were doing.

Le Breton stretched as tall as he could, raised his chest, and blurted the words. "I move that the meeting divide and be counted—those in favor of the objects of this meeting taking the right, and those of the contrary mind, the left."

Gray lifted a hand. "I second the motion."

The murmurings among the crowd in the outer ring did not cease. The tight pack of men loosened up as those on the edges began to drift away. "They can't hear," Jake said. "Babcock doesn't have their attention. Why doesn't he call them to order?"

Joe laid a hand on Jake's shoulder. "Well now, I don't rightly know, but I reckon they need a stronger voice here." Joe straightened and marched boldly toward the meeting's leaders. There before them he raised his rifle in one hand and cupped his other hand at his mouth. His great voice boomed out. "Who's fer a divide?"

A hush fell over the crowd.

Joe drew a line in the dirt with the heel of his moccasin. And with the fearlessness he might have shown venturing into a bear's den, he strode off to the right, planted his tall, powerful frame out in the open between the trees, and yelled once more. "All fer the report of the committee and an organization, follow me!"

As if the sun had chosen to applaud him, it slipped from behind the shadowing cloud and shone down on the brave mountaineer.

Grinning, Jake marched to Joe's side and found others taking their places in line. Without a leader, the bulk of the French Canadians roved as if rudderless, but their line gradually took form over on the left. Men moved one way and another, bumping into each other. Angry voices rose. One swore near Jake. "Let me through, damn you." The man took hold of someone in front of him to push the fellow aside.

The response was immediate. The other fellow swung around with jabbing elbows. "Watch who you're pushin'!"

A brief scuffle arose as two more struggled to make their way past each other and through the crowd to their respective places.

Jake shook his head. Over a hundred men, he guessed, and it wasn't an easy matter for them to create order out of the confusion and form into lines. He saw Gervais heading toward the right.

"He *is* our man," Jake told Joe, "even if he is a Canadian."

"Well now," Joe said, "I reckon that's good, because I figger we'll be a-needin' him."

Another French Canadian came to the right—Laderoute, then Bellique and Bernier and Donpierre. There were Englishmen too—not connected with the Hudson's Bay Company, but Englishmen nonetheless.

Jake felt a surge of hope. "Hell, we've got it sure with all this extra support. How did they manage to sound so loud with their *nays*?"

"It'll be close yet." Haviland was keeping a tally while the men continued to fall into their desired places.

Finally, though the lines were far from military straight, the crowd looked pretty well divided.

"Mr. Le Breton," Babcock said, "will you take a count?"

Le Breton nodded. Adjusting his spectacles, he stepped to the head of the line on the right, and as he walked along counting, Haviland kept scratching figures on a small piece of paper in his hand. He looked up, his expression bleak. "Damn. I count fifty for us, fifty-two for them."

Jake stared at him. "Are you sure? Even with all the extra French Canadians on this side?"

"There aren't enough French Canadians over here to do it. What happened to our Americans? We don't have half our population here. Where the hell are they?"

"Hell, I don't know." Jake's shoulders slumped, as if someone had laid a heavy pack on them. He thought about leaving now, but stayed in line.

Haviland kept grumbling. "It was probably a mistake to hold the meeting here in the heart of the French-Canadian settlement. Made it too easy for them to come."

Jake bitterly eyed the opposing line. Radford was there, of course, and his man Marceau. Still no sign of Lévêque. He must not have come.

Jake noticed a heated argument going on at the end of the opposing line. A French Canadian by the name of Matthieu was talking to old Lucier. Although a Canadian, Matthieu had worked as a trapper for the American Fur Company in the Rocky Mountains. The man had been staying at French Prairie with old Lucier since coming to the Willamette with the immigration last fall.

"You know Matthieu?" Jake asked Haviland. "Came west with you, didn't he?"

"Yes, he did. I know him, but not well."

"Wonder what he's saying to old Lucier there. He's sure talking hard."

Like Gervais, Lucier was an old-timer in the valley. Also like Gervais, he was a former Astor man who'd always remained a freeman even while he worked for the Hudson's Bay Company. Although both Gervais and Lucier had served on the committee that put together the report for today, Lucier had joined the dissenters.

At the end of Joe's line, Le Breton announced in his high voice, "Fifty on the right—*for*." Then he hurried to the other side and began counting there.

Jake watched Le Breton move down the opposing line on the left, and glanced at the two French Canadians at the end of that line, their voices rising with an occasional word or phrase in French, hands flying to punctuate each heated outburst. Sounds blurred. Jake took a deep breath and let it out hard. The suspense was gone for him—and for others who'd counted already. Faces to the right looked glum, while those on the left looked hopeful, on the verge of victory, though they waited for the official count. Bees buzzed. The sun's growing heat intensified the scent of new foliage and warm bodies. Le Breton was taking a long time to count. It wasn't like Le Breton to do anything slowly, but perhaps it only seemed slow to Jake. He wished the man would get it over with so they could all go home.

The secretary finally approached the end of the line, where Matthieu and Lucier still chattered, both gesturing, as if they might lack the power of speech without their hands.

A breath of wind stirred the nearby branches, giving voice to the trees, and a small dust devil lifted a circle of fir needles.

Old Lucier gave a firm nod, and just as Le Breton was about to finish the count, Matthieu stepped out of line. Sudden quiet resonated. Lucier moved out with him. The two men marched to the line on the right and stood, tall and proud. Even the short, stocky Lucier looked like a big man at that moment.

Le Breton looked confused. Brushing a hand over his head, he looked up to study the line once more, then deliberately marked something down on the paper. "Now then," he said, in command again, "that's fifty-*two* on the right—*for*. Fifty on the left—*against*."

The crowd remained motionless. Then a vibrant energy stirred beside Jake. Old Joe bellowed, "Three cheers fer our side!"

The energy caught and exploded. The crowd came to life. Jake yelled for joy, his voice drowned out by the cheers of his mountain comrades and others in the right-hand line. They'd won. Victory was theirs, and it was sweet.

"Whoo-ee!" Joe said, grabbing Jake by the arm. They both jumped into the air, grins of sheer glee spread over their faces. "Old Jake, this country will be the United States yit."

A pounding noise rose, barely audible over the cheerful cries. Babcock was whacking a tree trunk with a stick, trying to gain their attention. The yelling subsided only a little, but Jake heard Babcock's announcement.

The chairman shouted. "Motion carried!"

His words met with a new uproar, and Jake, whooping and hollering like the rest, slapped friends on the shoulders and danced around, lifting his feet high. The pounding noise came through once more, and Jake brought his elation under check enough to hear what else Babcock had to say.

"Will the meeting please come to order!"

Jake became aware of a general flow of movement where the opposing line had been. The dissenters were slinking away, withdrawing in defeat. In their midst he saw Radford and Marceau. Jake glanced toward the chairman and felt a pang of guilt over the chairman's distress at the breakup of his meeting. But Jake had that score to settle. He didn't want Radford to get away before he had a chance to confront him.

"I'll be back later," he said to Haviland and followed the retreating men.

He caught up with Radford in the trees by the river where a line of canoes waited. Radford turned and looked at him, jaw set tight. The man gave Jake a curt nod and waited, saying nothing.

Jake lifted his gun slightly, vertical in his hand, then propped it on the ground. "I need to talk to you."

"Yes?"

"Where's Lévêque?"

Radford's brow creased. "He went north, up near Fort Thompson in the northern Columbia Department, to see his wife. What do you want with him?"

"Fort Thompson! Why now?" Jake let out a soft, mirthless laugh. "Of course."

Radford looked away toward the river that glistened with diamonds of light. "His wife's ill." He turned back to Jake, a tilt to his mouth. "One of them. Why are you asking?"

Jake clutched the rifle tighter. "Do you know where Lévêque went the day you last came through Willamette Falls and left Miss Haviland up above the falls?"

The man directed a sharp gaze at Jake. "Lévêque didn't show up, and Jen—Miss Haviland told me she walks up there alone regularly. I didn't go off and abandon her as you seem to imply."

Jake snuffed up air. "Maybe not, but she could have used an escort home." He went on to tell Radford in considerable detail the events of that day and Lévêque's apparent role in it. As the story unfolded, Radford's face went white. Then his cheeks flushed red.

When Radford spoke, his voice carried a hissing edge. "I'll kill the bastard."

"No. I will. Is he coming back? Or do I have to go to Fort Thompson to find him?"

Radford pressed a hand to his forehead. "He'll come back." Running his fingers through the hair on his scalp, he pounded his fist in his palm and gave Jake another direct look. "He won't expect us to be talking to each other."

"No, I don't suppose he would. He wouldn't expect Sally to talk either, and he was careful not to be seen."

"Where's Sally now?"

"Safe."

"We might need her testimony, but she'd *better* be safe. He could do her serious harm. I guess you aren't going to tell me where she is."

Jake picked up his rifle and held it horizontal across his waist, finger stroking the trigger. "I have all the testimony I need to blow that son of a bitch away. Will you work with me on this? Let me know when he shows up?"

Radford looked into Jake's eyes for a long while, a sharp energy passing between the two men. Finally he nodded. "I'll see the bastard never hurts Jennie again."

The familiarity in her name on Radford's lips sent a twinge through Jake. He gave a brusque nod in return, slanted his gun to point at the sky again, and spun on his heel to stride away with long steps.

Chapter Fifteen

Champoeg, July 5, 1843. The perfume of lush foliage rose off the profusion of trees and brambles lining the Willamette shore, enriched by the heat of the July sun. Jennie wandered closer to the water's edge, and the river added its own scent of life, savory as spice.

She breathed deep of the heady bouquet as she strolled along the trail bordering the Willamette River below the Champoeg clearing. Now that the opening formalities were over, she wanted to be away from the crowd to enjoy the tranquil beauty. Sounds of revelry reached her, even here, though muffled by the high bank that blocked her view of the gathering.

Folks were no doubt eating again and chattering about the new government. She paused, hearing music. Maybe there would be more dancing. She smiled, debating, then decided it was too pleasant by the river.

She was glad her whole family had come to Champoeg for this get-together. They'd had a lovely Fourth of July celebration yesterday. People had come from all over the area to put on a fine picnic. And Reverend Hines had given a rousing speech in honor of the day that marked America's independence from Great Britain—and in honor of the decision for government in Oregon. A grand day for Americans, if not for the British. Today they would have the meeting to make the new government official.

She let out a sigh, thinking of Alan. She wished he could be as happy as Pa and Jake and all their American friends who'd worked so hard for organization. The thing appeared to be moving forward peacefully, and she was thankful for that. Still, she knew Alan had worked to prevent it. She hoped he would come to Champoeg for the meeting. She'd seen so little of him in the last few months, and every visit he'd been rushed and distracted.

Drawn by the shimmery water, she stepped off the trail toward it. At the edge she wrapped an arm about the trunk of a leaning tree to watch the drifting ripples.

She started at a nearby sound and jumped back from the tree. Jake stood below the trail only a couple of paces away. His low, mellow voice blended with the rush of water. "Hello. Beggin' your pardon. I didn't mean to startle you."

She clapped a hand over her heart. "You walk so quietly."

"Force of habit, I guess." He chuckled a little.

She let her eyes pass over him, from the thick brown hair glistening even in the shaded light, the blue-striped hickory shirt, sleeves rolled up, the new buckskin breeches with their long fringes running along the outer seams, the moccasins that let him walk so quietly.

He lifted his face to gaze at the great river, his hair tied back, revealing a certain elegance in his profile. "Beautiful, isn't it?" he said. "Wild, free."

She focused on that profile, the vibrance in his expression. "It is."

He glanced her way, little lights dancing in his dark eyes. A resonance filled his voice. "I do love this land, Miss Jennie. It's going to be American land one day, and Oregon will be a state. I'm sure of it. We have the makings of a government now with law and order and courts." A wry grin lifted one side of his mouth. "And believe it or not, this old coon is going to be a lawyer."

Caught by his enthusiasm, she gave him a warm smile.

"I'm practically a magistrate already," he said. "Think of it. This old mountain man a magistrate, and my old mountain buddy Joe Meek, the sheriff. What do you think of that?"

She laughed. "I think it's fine. I'm very pleased for you—and you're not really old."

Crinkles formed around his eyes. "It's just a saying."

"I know."

Their appointments had surprised her, but what the two lacked in education and background, they certainly made up for in dedication and enthusiasm. "The laws sound good," she said, "for the most part."

"You've seen them?"

"Pa showed them to me. He was on the legislative committee, you know."

Jake put a hand to his chin and gave her a direct look. "What part don't you like?"

She shrugged and studied the ground between them. "Well, the land provision that prevents claims on town and water power sites."

"The anti-British faction got that one in." He shook a finger toward her. "I wasn't for that, I want you to know, and your father wasn't either."

"It's obviously an attempt to block Dr. McLoughlin's claim at the falls, isn't it?"

Jake nodded, then looked toward the river again, face taut. A sudden smile relaxed the tension in his cheeks. "They had some fiery sessions over setting up some kind of executive. People out here are real skittish about power figures. No kings for us, I'd say. I suppose the three-man executive committee will be all right."

Her voice lightened. "At least we won't have taxes. Some folks thought we'd be taxed on everything—including the air we breathe."

Taking a deep breath of the soft summer air, she laughed and felt a pleasant rush of warmth at Jake's responding chuckle. It surprised her how comfortable she felt talking to him. He seemed relaxed, easygoing. Maybe some of the underlying tension over this government controversy had vanished with this agreement.

"Are you really going to be a lawyer?" she asked.

"Looks that way." He let out a short laugh. "Maybe I should get me a fancy new frock coat and fine trousers—maybe a satin vest—or do you suppose I can be a lawyer in hickory and buckskin?"

She reached out to place a hand on his arm. "I think you can be a lawyer in whatever you want to wear."

"I don't suppose a lawyer needs to be too awfully literate, does he?" A sober frown creased his face, though Jennie detected a spark in his eye. "Of course, the Rocky Mountain College was an excellent school."

Jennie didn't know what to think. She was sure he was teasing, but she knew so little about his past. He was obviously intelligent. Could he possibly have been illiterate before going into the mountains? It suddenly occurred to her she didn't care. What mattered was now. They lived in Oregon now, where no one had any real status. They were all poor, all struggling. And the past didn't matter.

He watched her as if trying to read her thoughts, his eyes warm, smile tentative. He reached out to brush a stray hair off her cheek, his fingers sending a streak of fire down her neck.

"Miss Jennie," he whispered.

A fierce tug drew her, and without realizing she had moved, she was in his arms. When she lifted her face to him, he leaned toward her. He was going to kiss her. She knew it, and at the same moment she knew she wouldn't turn away. She met his lips with hers, touching them softly, and slipped her arms around his neck to hold him to her. He pressed down harder, caressing her lips with sudden power. Warm feelings burned with the sweetest fire she could have imagined.

When he stopped, he stared into her face, his eyes glistening, mouth open in shock. Her breath caught. He closed his eyes and raised his chin, then pulled her to him again, his cheek to hers. He kissed her ear, her brow, her cheek, and found her lips again, closing his mouth over them with the hunger of days and months of fierce longing. She answered him with her own hunger, not realizing she'd felt it before, but knowing now.

Those warm feelings wrapped around her heart and held it fast.

When he released her lips, he backed away and brought his hands from around her waist to take hold of her shoulders. His brows rose, eyes still bright, and he shook his head slightly.

She wanted to tell him she knew. She loved him. She didn't know how that fact had escaped her before, but she had no doubt now. Still, she didn't see how she could say it just yet.

He smiled finally. "Maybe we ought to get back to the party. There—uh—there should be dancing."

She took his hand to walk with him, and as they followed the river trail, she recalled another time they had walked along the river together—the night of the canoe accident, the night she spent in his arms. Had she loved him then?

Once, he'd helped her up the dirt bank that led to the prairie, he let go of her hand. But as they made their way through the clusters of chattering people, he stayed close by her side. Folks were getting ready for a new dance. A form dance, a reel. She wondered if he would know the steps. Without hesitation, he gave her his arm and led her out to find a place among the dancers.

It was a motley group. Everyone's clothes showed signs of wear and much mending. Many wore moccasins on their feet, like Jennie. No sign of poverty's oppression showed on their faces, though. Everyone jubilant, smiles wide, eyes sparkling.

The music began, and Jake surprised her one more time with the absolute precision of his steps. Grinning at her, he lifted his brows, as if enjoying the surprise on her face.

She shook her head. "Someday, Jake Johnston, you really must tell me where you learned to dance."

He laughed, and she had to laugh with him, until she got all mixed up in the dance steps.

She had just gotten back into the proper routine when George Le Breton came up behind Jake, speaking to him in a voice too low for Jennie to hear. Jake nodded to the man and turned to Jennie. "I'm afraid I have some business to attend to. Would you excuse me, Miss Jennie?"

When he left, she felt very much alone in the midst of the frolicking dancers. The sun's heat bore down on her, and she wandered back toward the shady riverbank.

She'd been swept up in the euphoria of Jake's kisses, but without Jake there, reality began to press in on her. Alan. What about Alan? She remembered his nice kisses, and his fine smile, and his intense eyes that could take her breath away. Glancing back at the crowd, she wondered if he might still come for the meeting. Other men of the Company were here. And he'd always been a sort of leader to them. What would she say to him? And how could she let him go?

At the steep embankment, she scrambled down the slope to the river trail, and she had to run. She stretched her legs and raced along the soft dirt path, wanting to escape the dilemma that tore her heart in two pieces. She ran until she was gasping for breath, then turned and made her way to the river's edge. How would she tell him? She couldn't bear to see his pain. She dropped to her knees and began to rock. Tears rolled down her cheeks, sobs welling from deep inside.

How did I fall in love with two men? But I have done just that.

If she could be like one of those men in the Bible and have two—only the other way around with the woman having the two. But Jake and Alan disliked each other so much she'd have no peace at all.

Oh, Jennie, what a silly thought.

Hiccups of laughter chased through her sobs.

Alan strode along the river path, looking for her. Someone had seen her go this way. Surely she hadn't gone too far.

A familiar voice called from behind, and he turned. Marceau was hurrying toward him, a piece of paper in hand. And someone else was walking through the nearby trees, a mountaineer. Joe Meek.

Clenching his teeth, Alan watched Marceau approach.

The *voyageur* stopped a pace away and stood breathing heavily. "I have look for you. All over I have look for you."

"I thought you were at the fort."

"*Oui*, but the good *docteur* sends me here, and since a letter comes for you, I bring it to you. Is from Montreal, from your woman, I see."

A jolt struck Alan. His *woman*? Marcella? But what would this *voyageur* know about her? Alan glanced in Meek's direction. The mountaineer had stopped walking and was standing beside a tree, watching Alan with eyebrows raised, no doubt having heard Marceau.

"I see is from your woman," Marceau repeated unnecessarily. "I don't look." He gestured with his hands, his tone full of reassurance. "But the seal, she is broken and I see. You are surprised to hear from your woman, I think? But happy, *oui?*"

Alan glared at the short, stocky French Canadian, good, dependable Marceau, then checked to see what Meek was up to. The mountaineer didn't say anything, but a slight twist of his mouth suggested a smile.

With a quick nod he turned and walked away. Alan supposed word would get back to Johnston and then to Jennie. He drew in a sharp breath, and let the air hiss out between his teeth.

Marceau's forehead pinched, head tilted, as he continued holding the letter toward Alan. Finally Alan took it, deciding he could do nothing about Meek. The piece of paper flopped open, unsealed as Marceau had said, and Alan was surprised at his reaction. His hand shook so he couldn't focus on the words. Looking up, he realized he was alone again. Marceau had slipped away, no one else in sight.

Seeing a log close by, he went over and sat. He expected to struggle with her French, but was surprised to see the fine script in English.

My dearest Mr. Radford,

I thought you would return to Montreal by now, and I have waited to talk with you about this matter which would better be discussed face to face. But now after so long I decide to write you, because I must tell you this. I know we quarreled and you thought I cared for Mr. Boucher because he asked for my hand in marriage. But don't you know, my father gave me the choice and I did not accept Mr. Boucher's offer. Will you return soon so we may have these words together?

You see I am writing in English. I have tried to learn much English since you are gone. And please forgive me. I show this personal letter to my English teacher to make sure I write it correctly, but do not worry. She is very discreet. . . .

Alan rumpled the letter in his hands and pressed it into a ball. Standing, he faced the river and started to throw it, but shoved it in his pocket instead. He didn't need any more people reading his mail. His messenger *would* have to be Marceau, who could read English. He hoped the *voyageur* would be as discreet as Marcella's teacher. That book in his life was finished and closed. He would not reopen it.

He stepped out on the path with new purpose. He needed to talk to Jennie. Then he needed to talk to her father, a daunting prospect. And he needed to talk to Johnston. Lévêque was back in the country.

Alan had found a piece of property in the valley here and wanted to stake a claim on it. Maybe this new government he'd fought so hard would turn out to help him after all. He would live among Company retirees, away from the Americans, but close enough for Jennie to visit her parents occasionally. And maybe with the conflict behind them, the Americans would even become more agreeable. Many had greeted him this afternoon. He'd missed the dancing, but there would probably be more this evening. Jennie would enjoy that.

He caught sight of motion on the riverbank ahead. A bit of pale blue. A dress. Red and gold highlights glinting off long, brown hair. His heart warmed. She drew him like a magnet drew iron, and he was helpless to resist. He smiled, picking up his pace. When he came near, he paused, body tightening. Something didn't look right—the way she was sitting, her shoulders bent over her lap, shaking.

He plunged forward. "Jennie, what is it? What's wrong?"

When she glanced up and saw his face, she let out a wavering cry. "Oh, Alan. Mr. Radford." She jumped to her feet and ran to him. He opened his arms to her, but she stopped and took his hands instead, looking up at him while tears streaked her cheeks.

He drew her hands together and lifted them to his lips, kissing her soft knuckles. "What is it, my dear?"

"I can't marry you, Alan." She looked away from him. "Oh, I shouldn't be saying that. You haven't even asked for my hand. But I thought you must be about to. Oh, I'm saying this all so badly."

"No, my dear, you're not. Of course, I was—I was going to—I planned to—" He let out a sudden breath.

She straightened, swallowing hard, and spoke with terrible clarity. "You can't pay court to me any longer, Mr. Radford. I love someone else. I didn't know before, but I do now."

His throat nearly closed. "Who?"

She looked at the ground between them, then up, almost meeting his eyes. "Jake."

He blurted with disbelief. "*Johnston?* Not Jake Johnston. How can you—?"

"Yes, I do love Jake Johnston." The words raked across Alan's flesh.

A twig snapped, off to his left, and Alan swerved his head to see what it was. Joe Meek. Back to eavesdrop again?

Alan snarled at him. "Why don't you go away and tend your own business, Meek?"

"I'm goin' right this minute, Mr. Radford, sir. Jist checkin' on my constit-u-ents. As sheriff o' this Oregon country I have m'self a job to do."

"Well, do it somewhere else, why don't you? We're quite all right here."

Meek pursed his lips and sauntered off without another word.

Alan turned back to Jennie. She was watching him with dreadful tenderness. "Oh, Alan," she whispered. "I love you too."

He took her in his arms and held her close to his heart. "And I love you, Jennie. I always will."

She drew her head back to look into his face. "How is it possible to love two people at the same time?"

Wiping an annoying wetness from his cheek, he reached into his pocket for his handkerchief. His fingers brushed against the wadded paper, and his breath caught. "I think it is quite possible."

She leaned her forehead against his chest. "I'm sorry."

Nuzzling her hair, he forced an even tone. "I want you to be happy, Jennie." She looked up again, her face serene now, lovely. His voice grated. "May I kiss you one last time, my dear?"

She stroked her fingertips across his lower lip. He kissed them, then drew her hand aside and touched his lips to hers. She didn't draw away, and when he pressed harder, she returned the caress, not so much with passion, but with the tenderness that only made him love her more.

Jake stopped dead in his tracks, unable to believe what he was seeing. Jennie! Kissing Alan Radford?

Jake spun about and stomped away so he didn't have to see it. Nearly blinded by a rush of fury, he stormed back along the trail. A pang clutched his chest as if a rope had cinched him tight enough to stop his heart, and he walked faster, expanding his chest with deep breaths to shake off the sensation. He felt like a fool. He'd been so sure, minutes ago, sure he was the one she cared for when she kissed him—just the way she was kissing Radford now.

Well! Had that all wrong, didn't I?

He'd come across Joe looking smug and bright-eyed. Jake couldn't quite figure that out, since it was Joe who told him where he could find Jennie. He ran his fingers through his hair and ripped away the band holding it back. Nothing made sense.

Leaping up the bank to head for the prairie, he muttered under his breath. "Time I got back to the doings. I worked hard for this day. I ought to be able to enjoy this. Damn it."

He'd been looking forward to good times—a new government, him with a position as magistrate. And soon George Haviland hoped to have something worked out so Jake could qualify as a lawyer. Then, on top of it all, he'd thought he had found someone he wanted to spend the rest of his life with. How could he have been so wrong? "Well, if she likes Radford's style, let her have him."

Pausing on the rise of ground that overlooked the prairie, he scowled down on the scene. The beauty that had touched him before did not impress him now. Nor did the excitement rippling among the crowd. Oregon was beginning to seem a little small to hold him and Radford too. Maybe he should give up his position as magistrate and head for California.

Something was happening below. Le Breton stood on a stump talking, but Jake couldn't hear him. The more he thought about it, the more he thought he should leave Oregon. He'd never been to California, and folks said there was fine country down that way. Maybe he'd stay for the rest of the day's activities. Maybe not. He would leave sometime today anyway. No need to go back to Oregon City. He had his horse and bedroll at Champoeg with him.

I don't need attachments either. Got along fine this far without them.

Glancing toward the river, he wondered if Jennie would show up soon, then scoffed at himself.

As Le Breton droned on, Jake scanned the faces. He saw the boys, Eddie and Charlie, and felt a twinge. He'd miss them. And their pa. And Doc and Kitty. His lips made a smile, but it didn't catch on with the rest of him. Joe. He would miss Joe. Was there another man in the world quite like Joe?

He heard a voice in the trees. It sounded like his name. But not quite. Turning, he saw a woman. "Sally." He strode toward her, and she looked up at him, her black eyes big.

"Chake." She sounded scared.

"What's going on? Are you here with Reverend Lee and the others from Chemeketa?"

She kept her voice low. "Lévêque is back. Looking for me. Help me, Chake." She gave him a flickering smile. "I am leaving this country. Please. Do not let him stop me. You want to get him for Chennie. I know. Please get him for me too, Chake."

"Where is he?"

"On his way from Chemeketa. The boys tell me."

Jake laid a hand on her arm. "I'll find him. Stay with the others. Don't be alone."

Jennie sat watching the lazy flow of the river. She felt a strange and surprising peace after talking with Alan. He would be all right. He was a good man. If it weren't for Jake she'd have happily married Alan Radford. She smiled. But there *was* Jake. Her heart warmed, thinking of him. She wondered how long he would stay at the meeting. He was probably enjoying all that.

A rustle in the trees alerted her, and she looked up. Her mouth dropped open, and she jumped to her feet. "Sally."

The woman walked to her with long strides, a wide smile on her beautiful face, her cedar-bark skirt whisking with each step, the beads and shells chattering over her bold-red tunic. "Chennie. Hello."

Jennie reached out and clasped her hands. "How are you? How are things at the mission?"

Sally laughed, eyes alight. "I try to watch my language, but I burn their ears too much."

Jennie bit her lips but couldn't stop a giggle. "Do you like it there?"

Sally waved a hand. "They are—what you say?—stuffy. That the word. Yes?" She leaned forward, vibrating with excitement. "But I do not stay. I go to the States. On a big boat. Big as a house. Maybe I can meet a nice man in the States. Wear fancy clothes like at the fort, but better. Maybe so."

"Are you really going?"

"Yes. Reverend Lee—he makes arrangements." She gave a short laugh. "He has to get me out of here before his ears burn right up."

They laughed together. "I'm glad for you, Sally. You'll feel safer there. I hope you're very happy and find a wonderful man."

"You have good man. Chake."

"Yes."

Sally's brows went up. "Oh. You do not argue now." She turned serious. "He helps me. Lévêque is back. Chake will get him. For you. For me."

A sliver of ice pierced Jennie to her core. "He went after Lévêque?"

Sally put her hands on Jennie's shoulders. "Do not worry. I go now with Reverend Lee. Be happy, Chennie."

"You too." Jennie reached out, unsure she should, and embraced Sally. Her friend's arms came around her, and they held each other. "Be safe," Jennie whispered.

Sally drew back, clutched Jennie's hands, then turned and ran away through the trees. Jennie watched her go, feeling competing tugs of hope and fear.

Motion at the edge of the prairie caught Jake's eye, a rider on a gray horse. The animal was agitated, and the rider was making an ineffectual effort at calming it. The horse swung around so Jake could see the rider's face. Lévêque. *Here at the gathering already.*

Damn bastard. I've got a score to settle with you. Several scores.

Moving with stealth, so as not to attract attention, Jake headed in Lévêque's direction. Blue was tied to a tree not far from Lévêque. Jake needed to get Blue before he lost sight of the man. That gray horse, fine though it might be, would never outrun Blue.

Jake was ready for revenge, and he'd found something on which to vent his rage. Keeping behind groups of people to screen himself until he got to the cover of the trees, he edged toward his big black horse. If Lévêque continued facing the other way, maybe Jake could reach

Blue unnoticed. Blue looked nervous, though. Seeing his master creeping through the trees, the big stallion skittered around. His movement spooked the gray horse, and it spun about.

Lévêque's black eyes met Jake's. A charge ran through Jake, as if the man had touched him with a bolt of lightning, stopping him on the spot. Lévêque also appeared to be struck dumb. The world froze.

The gray horse snorted and danced backward. Lévêque reacted. He came to life with the animal, and the gray lunged through the woods. Jake moved too, as if released. A few long bounds brought him to Blue's side. The stallion was only haltered. No saddle. But without hesitation, Jake untied him and leaped on the bare back.

Seeing a flash of gray through the trees, Jake turned the big stallion toward it. Blue exploded into action, welcoming the chase. He loved to run, and sensing the urgency in his rider, he responded with rippling power. The old racer homed in on the gray. That was the horse ahead of him in this race, and that was the one he had to overtake. Instinct and training. Blue had both. The gap narrowed. Lévêque's mount wasn't slow, but he wasn't Kentucky Blue.

Trees closed in, and Jake lost sight of the gray. But Blue thundered on, as if crazed by the madness of the chase. Would he race senselessly? Even if he lost track of the opposition? Jake saw them again. Blue was still gaining ground.

"Go, Blue. We'll get 'em now."

Lévêque looked back, fire in his dark eyes, but if he hoped to slow Jake with the menacing look, he was bound to be disappointed. There was no slowing Blue. Then it was not the look but the glint of dark metal that gave Jake reason to pause. Lévêque had a gun, a handgun, and he had it out, pointing at Jake.

A hard yank on Blue's rope told Jake what he'd already suspected. This halter wasn't made for riding. Without a bridle's bit, Jake had little to no control. Like Joe, when the man tore into the Crow camp after Mountain Lamb because he couldn't hold his horse, Jake rode full tilt into the range of that handgun because he couldn't hold his horse. Blue was in a race and wouldn't slow until he finished it.

Electrified by the thrill of danger, Jake leaned low on the animal's back to become a small target while he pulled out his own pistol, never once taking his eyes off the target ahead. Clearly Lévêque was no rider. The expert boatman was out of his element on a horse's back, bouncing and moving out of rhythm with his mount. Jake was in his own element this time. He might not be in control right now, but he rode as if he were part of the horse.

Blue's speed began to draw Jake too close to the end of Lévêque's gun, and he wished he could stay back out of range until the man took a shot. After that, Jake could move up while the man held an empty gun—provided it wasn't one of the new multiple-shot pistols. It didn't look big enough or unwieldy enough to be one of those. Lévêque was having trouble, though. He bounced so much he had trouble aiming. Jake hoped he would hurry it up because Blue was closing fast.

Jake heard the explosive charge and the whistling ball over his shoulder in almost the same instant. A puff of smoke clouded the end of Lévêque's gun. Watching to see if the man might have another shot, Jake breathed easier when Lévêque stuck the pistol back in his belt and whipped the gray horse for greater speed. It was a one-shot gun, and Lévêque wasn't going to try reloading on the run.

Jake clutched his own handgun, wishing he had his rifle. But with sudden conviction, he decided he wouldn't use a gun anyway. Killing Lévêque with a gun would be too easy. Jake shoved his own still-loaded pistol into his belt and concentrated on his timing. Blue's long legs and endurance let them gain quickly. The gray was no match for him. Lévêque kicked and whipped his animal, turning every so often to give Jake a threatening scowl, but something about the look of him suggested a man in panic.

Jake tensed for action. Blue moved alongside the gray horse without hesitation, the pounding of his hooves rumbling with the hoofbeats of the other animal. The scent of horse sweat and rich dust filled Jake's nose. And the acrid odor of Lévêque's fear. The man went for his knife. Giving him no time to reach it, Jake sprang onto the man, threw him off the gray horse, and crashed with him onto the hard ground.

The jolt left Jake shaken, but it had to be harder on Lévêque, taking the brunt of the fall with Jake's weight on top of him. The wiry *voyageur* lay flat on his back under Jake, stunned. Quickly recovering, Jake took advantage of Lévêque's momentary passiveness to lift him and twist his arms behind his back. Jake knew the strength of those arms, and he wanted them immobilized, especially the knife arm. He didn't want to give the man a chance to get hold of the knife that was still in its sheath. With one hand gripping Lévêque's arms in a contortion he hoped would hold them, Jake threw the greater weight of his own body against the man's skeletal frame to pin him flat while locking the other hand on the man's scrawny throat. Taut, ready, Jake only vaguely heard hoofbeats retreating, growing gradually softer in the distance.

Lévêque shook. He still had fight in him, and it took considerable effort for Jake to hold him down. Carefully avoiding the man's knees, which had taken him in the groin last winter, Jake twisted Lévêque's arms harder until the man quit moving. Jake was determined to put an end to the man's struggles once and for all, but first he had some questions he wanted answered.

His words came out in a hiss. "Tell me, Lévêque, what the hell did you have in mind when you sicced those Clackamas on Jennie Haviland?"

Lévêque lay there glaring up at Jake. If the man was afraid, he hid it well now. Jake guessed he'd have to get rougher if he wanted answers. He pressed down on Lévêque's throat until the man uttered a sound of protest.

Jake's voice rose. "Tell me."

"I—I only want to scare her." The words rasped. "I didn't mean nothing."

"Why? Why did you want to scare her?"

"*M'sieu* Alan—" Lévêque had trouble speaking, his words breaking off into a croaking gasp.

Jake let up a little pressure on the man's throat. "Go on."

"*M'sieu* Alan—he should stay away from the *américaine* wench. You know she sleep with you when she belong to *M'sieu* Alan. I just pay her some for that. And you."

Jake's slow-burning rage flared, and he squeezed the man's throat harder, then released it to pull out his own knife, spitting his words out like weapons as he raised the knife over his target. "Son of a bitch. She's no wench. And your quarrel with me has nothing to do with her. You're done abusing women, bastard. Done."

The Shifting Winds

The fear in Lévêque's eyes showed plainly now, and Jake took vengeful pleasure in it. He wanted the man to suffer. Lévêque squirmed, but Jake had a good grip on him. Confident in his superior position, Jake let the man writhe like a worm in a futile attempt to escape the inevitable hook. Then he placed the knife blade against the man's throat.

At the touch of it, Lévêque stopped moving, his black eyes wide. "No. Do not do it, *M'sieu*." His voice became a mere whisper, his lips scarcely moving, the slightest fluctuation of his throat vibrating against the blade. "I will go away. I will never bother her again. Or you. Or anybody. Is a promise. Never. Please do not do it."

Jake pressed down on the knife. "Save it, Lévêque. You're a dead man."

"Hold it right thar!" Joe's voice.

Startled, Jake almost softened his grip on Lévêque. How had Joe Meek turned up so suddenly without a sound? Jake knew the man was capable of a stealthy approach, but it took powerful concentration to keep from reacting to this total surprise.

"I have a job to do here," Jake said, maintaining the pressure of the knife. "Don't be slowing me down, Joe."

"Jist back off easy-like, Jake, m'friend, and let Old Joe have him now." Joe's voice sounded gentle but unyielding.

Still holding Lévêque tight, Jake looked up. Joe stood with a rifle pointed straight at him. Jake gaped at his friend. "What the hell? What're you trying to do, Joe?"

"I'm a-tryin' to git ye off'n that critter afore ye kill him."

"But why? There's no one in this whole Oregon country that deserves killing more, and nobody to care if I do."

Joe nodded, but he kept the gun leveled at Jake's chest.

"You don't figure to do it yourself?" Jake asked, suspicious. "This one ought to be mine. I owe him."

"I don't figger to kill him."

"Then, why stop me?"

"Well now, Old Joe Meek would be more'n glad to see this bastard git his throat slit, but the *sheriff* cain't let ye do that, Old Jake. It ain't rightly lawful."

"And if I don't stop?" Jake's tone turned bitter. "Would you shoot me for performing this kind of justice?"

Joe inclined his head, raising one brow, but he didn't move the gun. Jake could see the hammer pulled back, the weapon ready for firing. He couldn't believe Joe would do it, but he couldn't be sure he wouldn't either.

"Jake," the man said, "thar's laws in this country now, law and order, and if'n Frenchie here has broke the laws the courts will decide."

Jake stared at his comrade of the mountains. He'd never known Joe Meek to back down from a good fight. Meek might be the man's name, but *meek* he wasn't.

"Hand him over to me, Jake," Joe ordered. "It's my bounden duty as sheriff o' this here Oregon country to take him in."

Jake shook his head. "Have they sworn you in already?"

"They will afore this day is done. I figger that's plenty good, and I don't figger to start this job with a murder on m'hands."

Jake looked down at Lévêque. The beady black eyes showed a trace of hope mixed with cowering fear. The look was irritating. The man had slithered away from Jake before, and now he had him. How could Joe do this?

Jake glared at Joe's rifle. "You'd kill me to save this one?"

"I ain't aimin' fer yer vitals, Jake, but if'n ye ever had a rifle ball in ye, I reckon ye'll know it ain't right smart to argue with one."

Once Joe mentioned it, Jake could see the rifle was aimed higher than his heart. It would hit his shoulder. At this range Joe could place the ball with certain precision, but could he limit the damage? Jake had been hit once, back in the mountains. He knew the pain—and danger—in case the wound didn't heal right. Debating whether the pleasure of killing Lévêque was worth the hazard of a rifle ball in the shoulder, Jake fingered the knife handle and maintained his hold on the man despite a growing stiffness from keeping so long in one position.

"Ye wouldn't want to be a-defyin' the law now, would ye, Mr. Magistrate?" Joe asked.

Jake snorted. "You play dirty, Joe. You know that."

"I play to win. Tell me, now, will ye, what crime do ye figger to charge this critter with?"

Jake let out a tight laugh at the irony. He'd worked so hard to get law and order in this country, and that very law and order was thwarting him in the revenge he sought. "A legal charge? What could I charge this scum with, this insect who's barely a cut above the vermin crawling through his greasy scalp?" Jake mulled it over awhile, and the fever that had brought him here began to cool. Joe's way was best. Jake knew it.

Looking toward his friend, Jake finally answered. "How about a charge of inciting Indians to malicious mischief?"

Joe nodded. "I figger that sounds right official-like. Now, will ye git off'n my prisoner so's I kin take the feller in?"

Jake got up slowly, every muscle crying out, and moved away from the squirming little man on the ground.

"Git up, Frenchie!" Joe pointed the gun at Lévêque now.

The man scrambled to his feet and stood, quite humbled before Sheriff Meek.

Jake heard the sound of hoofbeats and turned to see Blue loping toward him. No sign of the gray horse. "Well, Blue, I suppose you won the race, huh?"

Blue nickered.

"This feller got a hoss?" Joe asked.

Jake shrugged. "Not anymore, I guess."

"Well then, I reckon I walk to Champoeg. Got my hoss ground-tied back in the trees. We'll jist tie this varmint up and throw him over m'hoss. My first prisoner won't be gittin' away."

Jake nodded. "I'll walk as far as your horse with you, and then I think I'll go on ahead and get my saddle and bedroll."

Joe's brows went up, and he gave Jake a quick look before he turned his attention back on the prisoner. Blue trotted up to Jake and nuzzled him in the chest, and Jake took the rope to lead the animal as the three men set out, Lévêque trudging along in front, just ahead of the point of Joe's rifle.

They'd been walking a short while when Joe spoke up. "Ye figger to be goin' someplace?"

"Yeah. California."

"Californee!"

"Why not?"

"Well now—when?"

"Today. Soon as I get my things."

"Today! Well, if'n this ain't some. I don't figger it, Jake. Ye're a magistrate here in Oregon. What ye doin' runnin' off to Californee?"

"I'll have to decline my position, but I figure I've done my duty helping Oregon get a provisional government, and now I want to go to California."

"But ye've always been right taken with this Oregon country, Jake. Ye figgered to settle here, I'm thinkin'."

"Well, I've changed my mind."

Joe nodded toward Lévêque and frowned. "Ye wouldn't be a-goin' on account o' this, would ye?"

"No, I'd already made up my mind. It was an exciting challenge to get the government started, and now that it's started, the excitement's over."

"But thar's plenty to be done yit. Do ye hear, now? Why, until Oregon is a part of the United States, we jist cain't be restin' easy. This provisional gov'ment—it's jist a temporary fix. They'll be a-needin' a heap more help from men like you if'n it's gonna last."

"Oh, I'm sure you and Doc and men like George Haviland will be able to handle it."

"Speakin' o' Haviland," Joe said, a meaningful resonance in his voice, "what about Miss *Jennie* Haviland?"

"Don't ask *me* about Jennie Haviland." Jake didn't do much to disguise his bitterness. "Ask Radford. She's his girl."

The surprise on Joe's face was plain, but he didn't say anything.

"Anyway," Jake said, "I'm going to California, and I'm going today. It's just something I feel I have to do."

Stepping up to Joe's horse, they stopped, and Joe turned toward Jake with a look of resignation on his broad face. "Well then, if'n ye must, I reckon ye must."

Chapter Sixteen

Champoeg, July 5, 1843. The moon's scattered reflection rippled on the river's gentle flow, and Jennie watched it, hoping to soothe the tension constricting her shoulders. The sky held a little gray, but was almost dark. Where was Jake? She rubbed the back of her neck. Her muscles were so tight, little needles prickled across her flesh.

She'd long ago helped Ma put away the remains of supper at their campsite in the Champoeg woods. Now she had time and had returned to the spot where Jake had kissed her and she'd known beyond doubt that she loved him.

But the haunting image of that terrible man Lévêque kept sweeping back to her.

Oh, Jake, please be safe.

She sensed a presence, the slightest sound, scarcely louder than the steady beat of her heart. Her breath caught. The footfall of one who could walk with the quietness moccasins allowed. She turned in expectation, ready to reach for him, then dropped her arms to her side. Joe Meek.

He tipped his head. "Well now, if'n it ain't Miss Jennie. How d'ye do?"

She tried to keep the disappointment out of her voice. "Hello, Mr. Meek."

He stepped up beside her to share her view of the moonlight on the water. "Mighty purty river, ain't it?"

She looked up at him. "Mr. Meek, do you know where Jake—Mr. Johnston is? Do you know if he's all right? He was going after Lévêque, and he's not back yet."

Joe gave her a quick smile. "Don't ye be worryin' about that varmint. I have him in confinement, *I* do. But it's Jake that caught the critter."

She let out a quavering sigh of the deepest relief. "Then, Jake's all right?"

Joe twisted his mouth. "A little bruised mebbe. Nothin' worse I could see with my eyes."

"Where is he?"

A long silence let her hear the rush of water and muffled voices of exuberant campers in the distance. Joe appeared to be chewing on something. She was about to ask again when he spoke. "Miss Jennie, might this old coon be so bold as to ask ye jist what thar is betwixt you and that Radford feller?"

Startled, she turned to stare at him. "Alan? Mr. Radford?"

He nodded and returned her gaze.

Surprised by his question, she looked back at the moon's reflection, her words soft. "He's no longer courting me."

"Ye ain't his girl, then?"

"No. No, I'm not."

"Not at all?"

She frowned at the man beside her. Was he dense? "No, I am not Mr. Radford's girl. He—he *was* courting me. You knew that, but not anymore."

"And why not?"

"Well, because I told him I couldn't marry him."

"Oh." Meek responded with a brevity Jennie hoped would conclude the questions. But he went on. "Well. Mebbe he'll be a-goin' back to his woman in Montreal, then."

"Woman! What do you mean?" She gaped at Joe.

He lifted his hand in a casual gesture. "Ye didn't know about her?"

"What are you talking about?"

Joe stroked his whiskers. "Well now, he does have hisself a woman in Montreal. This coon heard it right plain when the feller got a letter from her jist this afternoon. There'd be no mistakin' that. But there could be some mistakin' the meaning of *woman*." Joe leaned toward her, his voice low and gentle, as if to soothe. "It ain't rightly uncommon fer a man to have a woman back home and one in the wilderness too, though I reckon most often it'll be an Injun woman out here. But *woman* wouldn't necessarily be meanin' the same as *wife*."

"But he—"

"Mebbe she's a fee-an-say."

"A what? Oh, a fiancée."

"That's right, and mebbe he had a little change o' heart after meetin' you. If ye're feelin' poor used, Miss Jennie, I can tell ye I'm a fair judge o' men, and I figger Mr. Radford was a gentleman. I never saw sign to think otherwise. But if'n he ain't a-courtin' you now, I reckon mebbe it don't rightly matter."

Jennie hugged her arms across her waist. But she did care for Alan, and he'd said he was going to ask her to marry him. She didn't believe he would say that if he had a wife. A fiancée maybe. Was that why he knew a person could love more than one?

Another thought struck, and she spun about to face Joe again. "What about Jake? He doesn't have a . . . *woman* somewhere, does he?"

Joe tilted his head. "Jake? My old friend Jake Johnston?"

"Yes."

The man's face was unreadable in the dim light, but he finally gave her an offhand answer, as if the matter was of no real consequence. "No, Miss Jennie, Old Jake doesn't have hisself a wife. Or a fee-an-say. Never did set up a tent with one, to my knowin', and this coon met him first thing when he come out to the mount'ins. He's barely dry behind the ears at the time."

She took a quick breath and let it out slowly.

Joe tugged at his beard. "Might I ask what thar is betwixt you an' Old Jake?"

She hesitated, but she thought about Jake and the dancing sparkle in his eyes, the easy smile, the sweet mellow drawl, the warmth of his strong arms. Her words spilled out, soft but full of the emotion she felt. "I love him."

Joe nodded. "I had a mind that's what I heard."

"What?"

He bent down to look straight in her eyes. "Have ye made that fact plain to Old Jake?"

"Well, I haven't exactly *told* him, not in words, but—"

"Ye've given the feller some sign."

She frowned at Joe, wondering what he meant by that. "I—I let him kiss me."

Joe nodded, a smile playing about his lips. "Well now, I reckon Old Jake is a mite soft on you too, Miss Jennie, but somethin' must've happened to make him think you ain't returnin' those sentiments."

"Why do you say that?"

"Because he's plumb left fer Californee."

She gasped, reaching out to take hold of a nearby tree. "No! But why? When? I don't understand." Then it came over her like a crushing weight. "He doesn't love me. It was just a kiss to him, and I thought—" Her voice choked up, tears making the moonlight on the river blur before her.

"Miss Jennie." Joe put a gentle hand on her shoulder. "Don't ye be a-cryin' now, ma'am. Did ye talk to Jake this afternoon? I recollect him a-lookin' fer ye—oh it'd be the middle of the afternoon, I'm thinkin'."

She shook her head. "I saw him, but it was early afternoon—when folks were dancing."

"Oh, I figger this'd be shortly after the dancin', ma'am."

She tried to think back. She had left the dancing and run along the river trail, upset about Alan. If Jake had been looking for her, how did he fail to find her? Alan had found her. A niggling anxiety stirred.

"Miss Jennie, I reckon Old Jake jist don't understand that ye take to him over that Radford feller—if'n ye ain't made it right plain to him. I reckon he loves you."

Fighting the tears, Jennie grasped onto Joe's words. "Do you . . . think he does?"

"I reckon."

"Has he said anything to you?"

"Well now, Old Jake never jist comes out and says, but a man kin tell about these things in a feller he knows right well." Joe looked over her head, tugging his beard again. Then he grabbed her by both arms, moving his face close to hers. "Miss Jennie, do ye love that young feller or not? Jake, I mean."

Caught by surprise, she didn't answer.

"Do ye?"

"Well, yes, of course."

"Well then, are ye goin' to jist let him ride away without tellin' him?"

"But you said he'd already left."

"Well now, he cain't be too far yit. Come along, girl. Ain't no use a-frettin' if'n thar's somethin' ye kin do."

Without waiting for a response, he took her by the hand and marched off, towing her behind with such long strides she had to run to keep up. They scrambled up the bank and made their way through the trees at the edge of the prairie until she heard a nicker and saw his big white horse. The mountaineer didn't hesitate when he got to the animal's side, just grasped her at the waist and lifted her right off the ground.

"Mr. Meek!"

With the ease of a man hoisting a child, he plopped her astride the saddle.

Heart racing, she started to get off. "What are you doing? I can't ride like this." She tried to find the stirrup to get off in the most graceful way possible when Joe jumped on behind the saddle.

"Let's go, boy," he told the horse. With his arms at either side of her, he reined the animal around, and it broke into a gallop.

Jennie could only hang on. She couldn't get off at a run, but she had to protest. "Mr. Meek. What are you doing? Let me off."

He didn't answer, and he didn't slow down.

"Mr. Meek, please. You can't just abduct me this way. It isn't—"

"Ma'am," he said, his tone defensive, "this is the sheriff ye're a-talkin' to. Would the sheriff abduct a lady, now? Or jist see justice done?"

"But I can't ride this way."

"Cain't ride what way?"

"This way—across the saddle—like a man."

"Well now, it seems I saw you ridin' this way with Old Jake afore." Joe huffed. "I don't figger thar's much of any other way when ye got some hard ridin' to do. Jist hang on, little lady, and Old Joe will git ye thar."

"Where?"

"Well now, I figger he'll be down the trail here a ways. Do ye want that feller or don't ye?"

Clinging to the saddle with one hand, she tried to keep her skirts down with the other, while she bounced more against the horse's rhythm than with it. "I—of course I do. But could we go a little bit slower?"

"Slower?" He sounded surprised. "Well now, I reckon we could. I jist figgered ye'd be anxious." He pulled back on the reins and spoke to his horse. "Whoa, boy. Slow it down, big feller. This young lady is a-slappin' leather a mite too much, I reckon."

As the big white horse slowed to a gentle rocking lope, Jennie managed to match the rhythm of its movement. The gentler gait became rather soothing, and she thought she could actually enjoy riding this way. After all, Mrs. McLoughlin rode gentleman fashion. And Sally. Jennie supposed Joe's wife did too.

"Is Sally all right?" Jennie asked. "Lévêque didn't—?"

"She is. We locked that varmint away afore he ever came close to her."

Jennie heaved a sigh. "I do hope Jake isn't far."

"Yes'm. What d'ye figger ye'd be a-wantin' most? To see that feller? Or to git off'n this hoss?" Joe chortled, and she laughed with him. "Ye know," he went on, turning serious, "I reckon ye made a right good choice, young lady. You won't be findin' a finer man in the country than Old Jake."

She smiled. "No, he may have had humble beginnings, but he's a fine person, and here in Oregon—"

Joe gave a sharp hoot. "Humble beginnings? Where ye gittin' sich an idea?"

Jennie glanced back. The moon on Joe's whiskered face showed a clear expression of surprise.

"Well," she told him, "from Jake, I guess. From what he said, I—"

"Miss Jennie, yer Old Jake—he may be poor now since the beaver played out in the mount'ins. But his pa and ma—they jist happen to live in one o' them highfalutin mansions in the heart o' the purtiest Kentucky hoss country ye ever did see. Do ye hear? And his pa raises the finest racing stock money kin buy—money the feller ain't rightly short of."

"Jake's father? You mean Jake didn't grow up poor and without schooling?"

Joe laughed. "Miss Jennie, Jake never saw poor afore he went into the mount'ins. Never short o' money and never short o' learnin'. His pa even sent him to one o' those fancy schools back East where sons of the bigwigs go, and he took hisself a summer in Paris. That's in France, I s'pose ye know."

She shook her head. "I don't understand. Why did he let on like he was illiterate before he came west?" She thought back, recalling certain indications—his dancing, the way he'd worn the fine clothes, his ability to act as a gentleman. But why the deception?

"I reckon he had a touch o' rebellion. Ye know, folks looked down on us Rocky Mountain trappers when we come into this country, and Old Jake—he didn't take kindly to that. Made him a heap put out to see how a feller got judged on his pedigree afore his true worth."

"Why did he leave such a fine home?"

"Well now, a man needs more'n a silver spoon in his mouth, I reckon. Jake's a man as needed to see the world, do fer hisself. He had a fondness fer racin' and he done a mite of it fer his pa—trainin' and ridin' in the races, till he got a mite too big fer it and went off to that fancy school. That hoss he rides—Old Blue—he's one o' the best racers—Kentucky Blue would be his fancy name. Jake's pa gave that'un to him when he left for the mount'ins. As to why he left, though, I figger he jist wanted to have some excitement mebbe."

Jennie tried to swallow a laugh, and it came out with an odd sound. She struggled to take in what Joe was telling her. Jake, the son of a wealthy man who raised fine race horses? Eastern schools? Summers in Paris? "But why didn't he tell me?"

"Well now, I reckon he wanted ye to take him fer hisself, not fer what he had."

The steady hoofbeats of the big white horse nearly drowned out her words. "I guess he got his wish. I fell in love with him, just him, not knowing any of it."

"I reckon that's the way it oughta be."

She was almost angry with Jake at the same time that she admired him. "He shouldn't have lied to me."

"Well, my heavens! Did he lie or jist fail to mention a thing or two? 'Course, I recollect a time . . ." Joe's voice took on a lilt, becoming the voice of the storyteller that had captured Jennie from the beginning. "One day some fellers from the Crow tribe got ahold o' me, and if'n I hadn't done some purty smart lyin', well now, I reckon I wouldn't have my scalp today. Why, this coon lied so good, those Crows had to take a bow to me, *they* did. When they learned the truth—after I'm safe, mind ye—they said I'm sich a right smart liar I could out-lie the Crows."

He began to chortle, then broke off. "Campfire ahead. That'll be him, I reckon."

Joe urged the horse to move faster, and not wanting to protest the animal's speed now, Jennie grabbed the saddle horn with both hands and hung on tight. Jake sat stretched out by the fire, leaning on a log. A fierce warm ache clutched her heart. She knew she loved him too much ever to let him ride away from her without trying to stop him.

He leaped to his feet, rifle poised.

Joe called out. "Hold yer fire! It's jist Old Joe here."

Jake lowered the gun at the sound of Joe's voice, and Jennie kept a tight grip on the saddle as Joe charged into Jake's camp and drew the animal to a jolting stop.

"And a friend o' yers," Joe added.

Jennie felt the man's hands at her waist, and before she could say anything, he lifted her off the saddle and set her on the ground.

Joe gave a little grunt. "I reckon I've done my part fer you young'uns. Now I figger it's up to you."

At the sound of stomping hooves, Jennie swung around to see Joe turn his horse away. He was in the saddle now, leaning forward, and the horse broke into a gallop, running off into the darkness. She bit her lips together and turned toward Jake. The sight of him made her take a step back. She didn't see the least sign of welcome in his expression. His brow clenched with a terrible scowl, not a speck of light in his dark eyes.

His voice sounded like a surly stranger's, grating, harsh. "What are you doing here?"

"I—well, Mr. Meek brought me. He just . . . brought me."

Jake's expression didn't change. "Why the hell would he do that?"

Jennie stared at the man she loved, and she thought her heart was breaking, it hurt so much in there. Tears welled in her eyes, and she longed to run into his arms and have him hold her as he had before. Clearly he was not inviting her to do so. Her answer barely rose above the murmur of his campfire. "I didn't want you to leave."

Jake's brows shot up. He flexed his jaw, voice flat. "You know, I thought something had changed between you and me, but I see it hasn't. You're right back to kissing Radford like you did before. And that's fine. If that's what you want, I want you to be happy. But I don't need to stay around and watch it." He was trying to sound strong, but pain wove through his words.

"Oh, Jake, you saw him kiss me after—"

He let out a short laugh. "I don't know who was kissing who. You didn't appear to be just standing by."

Her throat tightened, giving a tinny sound to her response. "Jake, he'll never again kiss me. I had just told him I couldn't marry him, and he was sad, and I was sad for him. He isn't a terrible person, Jake, even though he was your rival."

"I didn't say he was. I—what did you just say? About marrying him?"

"I told him I couldn't because—" How could she tell Jake the rest, with him staring at her that way, so cold and unfriendly? She wanted to tell him when he was holding her, warm and loving. Something seemed to grip her heart, the pain making her eyes water.

"Because—?" His voice rasped with his own pain, and she couldn't bear it.

She pressed a hand over her mouth to stop a sob, but it came out anyway and the tears began to flow. "I told him I couldn't marry him because I love *you*."

Jake took a sudden sharp breath, and she blinked at her tears so she could see his face. He still didn't sound like himself. "You told him *what?*"

She wiped her cheeks. "I told him I love you, so I can't marry him."

A tumult of emotions flickered across his face. "And how long have you felt that way?"

She shrugged. "I don't really know. I realized it today when you kissed me, but I'm sure I've loved you for a while." A single tear spilled onto her cheek, and this time Jake stepped forward and wiped it away with his fingertips.

"Jennie." He sounded tortured. "Jennie, I'm sorry. I—"

He reached out and pulled her into his arms, and she wrapped her own around him, knowing as before that she belonged right here, that she always would. The dreadful ache in her heart turned rich with warmth, and she raised her face to his. He brought his lips over hers and held them there, caressing, sending sweet fire down through her. Then he just held her, his cheek pressed against hers.

When he spoke, a subtle brightness lightened his soft voice. "So, what now? Were you planning to take off to California with me?"

She gave a short laugh. "Well, no. I couldn't." She leaned back and faced him. "Jake, I'd go anywhere with you. If you want to go to California, I'll go." She looked down into his chest. "Well, you know, after everything is—" What could she say? He hadn't asked her to marry him. She glanced into his face again. "Do you really want to go to California? I thought you loved Oregon."

He shrugged and smiled. "Well, I was thinking Oregon wasn't big enough for both Radford and me, but maybe that doesn't matter now."

"Mr. Meek is of the opinion he may go back to Montreal."

"How would Joe know Radford's plans?"

"Joe seems to gather lots of information." She smiled. "Even some about you."

"Me? Oh-oh." He gave her a wry grin. "What's Joe telling now?"

She heaved such a sigh, he turned solicitous. "Would you like to sit down? I think I'm ready to get off my feet."

She took his hand and let him lead her to the log where he'd been sitting when she and Joe first approached. Blankets lay across the log and down in front of it—a familiar arrangement. Bowing slightly, he gestured toward the blankets, and when they sat next to each other, he wrapped his arms around her, not unlike he'd done at the McCary cabin.

"Cold?" he asked.

"Not this time." Glancing at him, she saw a brief glimmer in his eyes as he caught her subtle reference. She nestled against him, relishing the familiarity.

He touched his lips to her forehead and bent down to look into her eyes. "About that information Joe is gathering. And spreading."

She watched Jake's face. "He told me about your family, the mansion you grew up in, the fine horses, the elite eastern school, summers in Paris."

"Just one summer."

"Sorry."

The dancing lights of the campfire reflected in his dark eyes, the sparkle brightening as a small sheepish grin lifted the corner of his mouth. "So you've found me out." He gave her a sudden direct look. "When did you learn about this?"

"Tonight, while we were riding here."

His shoulders relaxed, as if he was satisfied with her answer, and he leaned his head against the log to gaze into the fire. "Then, you found out about it after you'd made up your mind—about how you feel."

She brushed a hand over the back of his fingers. "I decided it didn't matter what your background might be because I love you anyway."

He caught her hand and leaned over to touch his lips to hers. Then he grinned. "You know, Old Joe's like a leaky sieve with a secret, but I'm glad you know."

Jennie recalled another secret in Joe's keeping, but she cast off the thought as she puzzled over Jake. "Why did you pretend?"

"It started when I came out to Oregon and saw the attitude toward us mountain men. I sort of enjoyed shocking some of those pious folks rather than trying to impress them."

"I have noticed you like to shock people."

He reared back, feigning hurt feelings. "Have I shocked you, darlin'?"

"Well, you do like to tease."

He chuckled low in his throat.

She tried to maintain the lightness in their conversation, but couldn't quite bring it off. "Jake, you didn't—well, compromise me in that cabin. Did you?"

He let out a sudden laugh, then tried to sober. "Jennie, would I compromise the girl I love?"

"But you didn't love me then."

His eyes were still bright with his tease, but his voice turned warm. "Didn't I? Jennie, I think I've loved you since the first time I ran into you—or you into me—quite literally. I didn't know that at the time, but on some matters I am pretty illiterate—things like love."

She studied his warm eyes and whispered, "Then, you do love me."

"Ah, Jennie. I love you more than I have any idea how to say."

He wrapped his arms around her and kissed her with a fire that said as much as all the words she knew, and she answered him with her own kiss.

When he drew back, small wrinkles formed at the edges of his eyes. "Miss Jennie, we are going to have to get married if you're going to persist in sharing my bedroll with me."

"Jake!" She gave the blankets a dubious look. She hadn't thought of them as his bedroll.

He laughed and hugged her to him again. "You will, won't you?"

"Will *what?*"

He faced her. "Marry me. I know I have to ask your pa, but I'd like to hear your thoughts on it first."

"Oh!" Her breath caught. "Oh!"

Jake bent closer, head tipped down, eyes raised to her. "Well?"

She skimmed her fingertips over the sides of his face. "Of course I will, but—"

"But what?"

"Not because you're compromising me."

Those little creases edged his eyes again. "I may have to keep teasing you, darlin'. I don't know as I can help myself."

"Well, I guess it's one of the things I love about you." She traced her fingers on down to his shirt and tilted her head. "I suppose you speak French."

"With a drawl."

She let out a soft giggle. "So, your drawl is real."

"Oh, honey, I come from Kentucky. That is not going away. It's quite natural, and I got a fair amount of teasing about it from my classmates back East."

"Well, I rather love that about you too."

For a moment she admired his strong face, a fierce tug around her heart. "I am glad you're an American, though it's not why I love you. It's just that I love our country as much as you do, and this Oregon country—I want it to be ours. We will stay in Oregon, won't we?"

"If that's your choice."

She answered without doubt. "It is."

They lay back, mesmerized by the flicker of flame in the campfire. Bright coals flared in the depths of their little hearth. She snuggled close to him, at home in his warm arms. His soft lips brushed her cheek, her neck, sending tantalizing tremors through her.

His voice turned hoarse. "I expect I ought to be getting you back to camp before somebody decides I've carried you off."

Jennie didn't want to go anywhere. She sighed. "In a minute."

He turned and grinned at her. Memory struck. Those same words at another time, another place, on another bedroll of blankets. She burst out laughing, and he tossed his head back to laugh with her.

"Are you sure you want to risk that again?" he asked.

"Maybe not, but I think I can trust you."

He glanced over his shoulder. "If you look back yonder you'll see a white horse in those trees. I don't think the good sheriff has let you out of his sight."

Following Jake's gaze, she saw the moonlit horse. "Mr. Meek does take his job seriously, doesn't he?"

"And he may not trust me quite as much as you do." Jake chuckled. "Good Old Joe. He'd trust my intentions, but beyond that, I couldn't say."

Jake's eyes shone with a warm reflective glow, and she closed her arms around him for one more kiss.

Epilogue

Eastern Nebraska, May 2, 1870. Jennie looked out the window of the train at the green countryside whisking by. Six days it had taken them to cross the plains that took her family months to cross on the Oregon Trail west. And here they were just sitting in comfortable seats. The new railroad, finished only last year, let a person travel clear across this broad continent, opening such wonderful possibilities. Folks from Oregon had to take a short sail to San Francisco, but then a swift-running train could carry them the rest of the way.

She glanced at Jake, his head back, eyes closed, the slightest smile on his lips. The constant thrum of wheels on the tracks blended with the murmur of voices of the other passengers. Smoke drifted in the open cracks of the windows, overlaying the scent of fresh new grass and flowers.

Excitement stirred her heart. She was going to New York City to meet Elizabeth Cady Stanton, who'd been working tirelessly for women's rights, even the right to vote. All those years and they didn't have the vote yet. But the fight was far from over. The territories of Wyoming and Utah had given their women the vote. More would come.

Women needed advocates in so many ways. Divorce laws. Keeping families small. Jake had served a couple of terms in the state legislature where he tried to promote women's concerns, among other causes. And through the courts he'd used new laws to help women free themselves from hurtful marriages. He'd always supported Jennie's work in helping other women.

When she and Jake were married and she discovered where his kisses led, she knew something had to be done or they would have babies trailing out the door. They paid a visit to Joe Meek's Virginia, who knew exactly what to do. Why didn't more white women know these things? Virginia knew about the few days between monthlies when a couple needed to wait, but if they couldn't bear to wait, there were ways, and if those didn't work she had herbs to ensure the next monthly. She didn't promise all this as a perfect solution, but it helped Jennie and Jake enjoy those sweet fires on a quite regular basis without the worry. And it tended to work for them. They had their first baby three years after marriage, and two more about three years apart, only the last one being a surprise.

But other women needed to know. Jennie spoke with friends and others her friends sent to her, always approaching the subject with care, and she found many willing to accept packets of herbs from her. An old preacher got wind of it and spewed fire and brimstone down on Jennie, but Jake and her pa put the fear of God in that one until he moved on to California.

Jake reached over now and clasped her hand. "You're thinking rather loudly, Mrs. Johnston. I can almost make out the words."

She turned to see the bright sparkle in his dark eyes. That look never failed to touch her. He just seemed to grow more handsome with time. A little gray at his temples only enhanced the depth she knew in him. "I love it when you call me that, Mr. Johnston. I'm glad you came with me."

"I didn't want to miss seeing New York City. Haven't been there in years. And with Gabe in the firm now, I have more time." Gabriel, their eldest son, had become a lawyer like his pa. Anna, their daughter, was married now, and young Caleb would be going off to college in the fall. Jake stroked his chin. "Maybe next year we could go to Paris. Just for the fun of it."

She put a hand over her heart and smiled at him. "I'd like that. Oh, I would."

"Then, let's."

She raised her brows. "Do you remember how to speak French?"

He squeezed her hand, eyes brightening again. "I think I can manage—as long as they're patient with my drawl."

She laughed and enjoyed the warm ripples of his laughter joining hers.

Afterword

The Provisional Government of Oregon initiated on May 2, 1843, was a beginning. While a number of problems remained to be worked out, organized government was continuous in Oregon from that year forward.

In 1844 the land provision that unfairly restricted Dr. John McLoughlin was modified. And in 1845 the new oath of office provided that participation in this provisional government would not affect national loyalties of US citizens or British subjects. McLoughlin and other Hudson's Bay Company people were formally invited to affiliate with the organization that year, and the invitation was accepted.

Still, the controversy over McLoughlin's land claim at Willamette Falls lasted for several years. Caught between anti-British Americans and his own countrymen who questioned his loyalty to Great Britain because of his aid to Americans, the benevolent McLoughlin seemingly could not satisfy anyone. When his superiors diminished his authority in the Company by creating a board of managers instead of one Chief Factor over the Columbia District, McLoughlin resigned and moved to Oregon City, settling on a part of his claim. There he built a fine house—which has been moved to another part of the city and restored so it stands yet today—and soon afterward he became a citizen of the United States. Still, not all men of his day appreciated or trusted him. The question over his land claim remained in litigation until some years after his death, when the legislature passed most of it on to his heirs for the consideration of one thousand dollars.

The boundary issue in Oregon was not settled until 1846. Murmurs of possible war between the countries continued until then. Why Great Britain backed down and gave up land north of the Columbia River—land now constituting much of the State of Washington—is not altogether clear. Apparently Londoners didn't think this small patch of distant ground was worth a war. As soon as they felt they could gracefully back off to the 49th parallel, they did.

The May 2 meeting at Champoeg depicted in the story is generally accepted by historians as significant. There is some debate on how much the boundary issue was affected by it. Certainly American settlement was a factor that helped win the area for the United States. From that first organized immigration of 1842, shown in the story through the Havilands, the flow of US settlers traveling overland to Oregon continued. The annual influx soon numbered in the thousands. The organization that effectively began on the second day of May 1843 may well have helped establish American political dominance among the people there, encouraging this growing westward migration.

Oregon received territorial status in 1848, and in 1850 land laws backed by the power of the US government went into effect with the Donation Land Law of 1850, which at the outset offered 640 acres of free land to married settlers with the wife's portion in her name, and only 320 acres to singles. Later settlers received half as much, but wives still received their portion. Women had finally found some measure of recognition. Oregon gained statehood in 1859.

Historical details presented in the story are reasonably accurate. Minutes of the various meetings are extant, and where the minutes fail to present a well-rounded picture, contemporary accounts by persons attending the meetings are available. These accounts do not always agree. Nevertheless, certain events, especially of the May 2 meeting, have virtually become tradition in the state—the close vote (although contemporary writers disagree on exact figures), the crossover of Matthieu and Lucier, and Joe Meek's role. A large mural in the Oregon State Capitol building depicts Joe Meek and his immortal "Who's fer a divide?" which may well have saved the day for the Americans in the confusion that followed the first vote of the meeting.

Thanks are also due Joe for his bravery and diligence as sheriff. In 1847 an Indian uprising resulted in the Whitman Massacre and the death of missionaries Marcus and Narcissa Whitman. Joe's own daughter, a student at the mission, was captured during the massacre and died of measles while in captivity. Joe rode to Washington, DC, to press for territorial status. There he stayed as a guest of President Polk, whose wife was a niece of Joe's mother. After Oregon became a territory in 1848, Joe was appointed territorial marshal by President Polk, serving for five years. Photos show that the mountaineer finally traded his buckskins for fine cloth dress suits and, for a time, an elaborately decorated marshal's uniform with fox fur hat, complete with tail.

Like Jake, Joe Meek came from a wealthy background, his father a Kentucky plantation owner and slaveholder. Joe went through boyhood with little supervision and found more delight in fishing with his father's slave boys than learning in school. During the run-up to the Civil War, Joe became a staunch Union man and helped organize the antislavery Republican Party in Oregon. One of Joe's deepest griefs was seeing his Indian wife and half-Indian children ostracized by many in Oregon whom he'd worked so hard to help.

The characterization of Joe in the story is fairly accurate. The tales he told are true—that is, Joe actually told them. They are as true as Joe chose to make them when he relayed them to Mrs. Frances Fuller Victor for her book *The River of the West*, an account of Joe's life in the mountains and in Oregon, published in 1870.

Many other historical personages are presented in the story. Except for the Havilands, Jake, Alan, Lévêque, and Sally, most of the book's named characters were real and in most instances performed somewhat as shown in the book. William Gray's speech at the "Wolf Meeting" is almost verbatim from the account he wrote in his *History of Oregon*, published several years after the event. Excerpts of the reports given at the meeting came out of the minutes.

The altercation between the men of Oregon City and the nearby Clackamas tribe after the horse theft actually happened.

On a side note, the experiences of Elizabeth Cady Stanton and Lucretia Mott at the 1840 antislavery meeting in London led to the historic convention at Seneca Falls, New York, in 1848, which initiated the fight for women's suffrage. And while women did not get the vote for many years, the first successes were in the West.

The central British-American conflict as presented through the story's lead fictional characters was a real conflict of contested territory in that day. Historians may debate the significance of the May 2 Champoeg meeting, but one cannot discount the energy that can build from such a heroic moment of hope. Like a spark from the old fire steel, that hope may have sparked a fire that helped America win the heart of a place called Oregon.

About the Author

Janet Fisher's love of history and storytelling developed early when she heard tales of her pioneer ancestors who came west over the Oregon Trail. Her first book, *A Place of Her Own*, tells of her great-great-grandmother who followed that trail and dared purchase a farm on the Oregon frontier in 1868 after her husband died. Janet grew up on that farm, which she now owns and operates. After earning a master's in journalism with honors from the University of Oregon, Janet taught college writing, wrote freelance for newspapers, and began writing novels about Oregon's pioneers. Her work today focuses on following strong women through history.

For more information see janetfishernovels.com.

PHOTO BY ROBIN LOZNAK